D0903662

EX
LIBRIS

#18

Romance
Treasury

Romance Treasury

THE ROMANCE TREASURY
ASSOCIATION

NEW YORK · TORONTO · LONDON

These stories were originally published as follows:

THE GUARDED GATES
Copyright © 1973 by Katrina Britt
First published by Mills & Boon Limited in 1973

PAY ME TOMORROW
Copyright © 1974 by Mary Burchell
First published by Mills & Boon Limited in 1974

THE DARLING PIRATE
Copyright © 1974 by Belinda Dell
First published by Mills & Boon Limited in 1974

ROMANCE TREASURY is published by
The Romance Treasury Association, Stratford, Ontario, Canada.

Editorial Board: A. W. Boon, Judith Burgess, Alice E. Johnson and Ilene Burgess.

Dust Jacket Art by Gerry Sevier
Story Illustrations by Muriel Hughes
Book design by Charles Kadin
Printed by Alger Press, Oshawa, Ontario and
bound by T. H. Best Printing Co. Ltd., Don Mills, Ontario

ISBN 0-373-04033-4

Printed in Canada   A033

CONTENTS

THE GUARDED GATES

The Guarded Gates
Katrina Britt

Dionis didn't entirely believe her sister's engagement would last any longer than her previous broken ones. But when Angela asked her to redecorate the villa in Spain where she expected to live, Dionis regarded it as a boost to her career. And it fitted in with her own holiday plans.

Unfortunately, no one had informed the villa's owner of the proposed changes. Darkly handsome Don Juan Vicente de Velez y Stebelo made his disapproval clear — not only of the alterations, but Dionis.

"It's hardly a woman's vocation," he told her arrogantly. "I understood interior decorating was a man's job." Yet strangely enough he let her finish the job. Dionis couldn't help wondering why

CHAPTER ONE

"Why, of course I'll do it," Dionis said rather forcibly, adding a little ruefully, "I wish you hadn't sprung it on me so precipitately, though."

"You have a week to adjust yourself to a change of plan," replied her sister coolly, taking a cigarette from a gold case by her plate at the table. With slow deliberate movements, she flicked a matching lighter taken from her purse and blew out a line of smoke. "Fortunately, you already have your passport to go to Spain. I know you're keen to see that furnishing exhibition in Madrid. You can still do so—the villa isn't far from Barcelona. I have a picture of it somewhere." She rummaged in her purse to bring forth a postcard which she handed across the table. "Here it is—the Villa Acacia."

"What a lovely place!" Dionis exclaimed. The golden glints in her long hazel eyes toning with the lights in her chestnut hair became more pronounced as she stared entranced. "So deliciously Spanish, with the ornamental balconies and all that gorgeous bougainvillea. If the grounds are anything to go by the interior must be lovely too." Steadily, she looked across the table into her sister's cool blue eyes. "You did say Antonio rents it from a distant relative?"

"I did." Angela met the sober gaze. "The villa is already furnished. Period stuff," she added contemptuously. "I want it modernized. All this elegant antique furniture is nice to look at, but not to live with. Not for me, anyway. I like all the modern conveniences."

Dionis looked thoughtfully at her sister's beautifully smooth round face. The dark blue eyes and really flaxen hair were all the more attractive because of the model figure they were attached to. Her body, long-legged and supple, had rounded curves, which she knew how to show to their best advantage. The suit she wore accentuated every curve seductively. An approaching waiter was now bringing their coffee after an excellent meal in a new restaurant recently opened in the West End of London. His gaze barely lingered on the hard blue eyes, finding them rather jaded in comparison to the natural freshness of her companion. In his opinion the long hazel eyes of Dionis were definitely more eloquent, more alluring. Her eyelashes, darker than her hair, curled upward toward neat brows in a small piquant face made for laughter. She thanked him for the coffee with a smile he returned.

A fascinating creature, he thought, with the most attractive smile he had seen for a long time and a mouth that no man could look upon without wanting to kiss. Definitely the disturbing type; that fragile, small-boned look made him instantly aware of his own masculinity. Sadly, he walked away, wishing he were twenty years younger.

Unaware of his interest, Dionis stirred her coffee thoughtfully as she spoke.

"This furniture in the Villa Acacia, does it belong to Antonio or the landlord? Most people are rather touchy about their belongings and I dare say the Spanish are no different in that respect from anyone else. It will be moved?"

Angela's laugh grated. "My dear Di, you're far too sentimental." Dionis's concern for the feelings of other people, including those she had never met, amused Angela. "The furniture belongs to the owner, Don Juan Vicente de Velez y Stebelo. Tony is having it stored in the attic," she said flippantly. "Personally, I couldn't care less what's done with it as long as the villa is modernized."

Dionis drank part of her coffee, appalled as usual by Angela's hard determination to get her own way. With mixed feelings, she watched the beautifully manicured pink-tipped fingers tap a tube of ash from her cigarette into the ashtray. Then Angela picked up her coffee to the jangle of a lucky charm bracelet on her wrist. As she did so the stream of sunlight blazed on the sapphire engagement ring on her finger. It reminded Dionis that Angela had been engaged four times in as many years since she was twenty-one. Now, at twenty-five, and obviously willing to settle down, providing it was worth her while, she was marrying a Spaniard she had met six months ago while on holiday in Spain.

Angela, a fashion buyer for an exclusive West End salon, traveled extensively in her job. Dionis often found herself wishing, without rancor, that she had some of her sister's poise and self-confidence. But not at the moment. The callous disregard Angela was showing for other people's belongings filled her sister with a primitive and passionate desire to shake some feeling into her.

"Wouldn't it be more satisfactory to have the approval of all concerned? I mean, I've no desire to be a party to upsetting anyone. This relative of Tony's, for instance. Will he mind his furniture being stored?"

Her voice was even enough as she spoke, but Dionis tried in vain to prevent the warm flush rising beneath her clear skin, a fact her sister was quick to notice. Angela controlled herself with an effort. It was really infuriating the way Dionis reminded her that she had a conscience. It was a sensation she particularly disliked, and she hastily tried to be perfectly charming in order to disarm her completely.

"You're worrying unnecessarily, my pet," she said soothingly. "Everything has been taken care of—Tony saw to that before he left for Bermuda. As you know, I'm flying there tonight to join him. So you see you'll have a free hand with no interference from anyone. You can take your time going over the villa and noting the essentials. Everything you require will be shipped from London in a private container." She drew on her cigarette confidently. "As for the distant relative who owns the villa, he has so much property, one villa more or less isn't going to worry him. He leads a busy life, dividing his time between his residence at Cadiz and another at Castellon. He also has a villa not far from the Villa Acacia, but he rarely uses it. So you won't be bothered with him."

Dionis sighed. It sounded simple, too simple. "I wish you weren't going away so soon. We really should discuss it more fully. It's not as though Bermuda was near enough for us to get in touch quickly in case of emergency," she said, wishing she felt more enthusiastic about the job. Vaguely apprehensive, she could not prevent an odd sensation of foreboding rippling along her nerves despite her sister's cool reassurance. If Angela's fiancé had money why did he not build a villa to suit their requirements? Could it be that the distant relative from whom he rented the villa objected to anything modern clashing with the Spanish achitecture of the surrounding countryside?

Angela was saying, "I'm leaving everything to you. You have excellent taste. Who knows? Modernizing the villa might well make you famous in that particular part of Spain. Quite a number of English people are settling there for the sun. When we're married, Tony and I will entertain a great deal. Consequently, the villa will be seen frequently by our guests and you could have orders galore."

The dark blue eyes were suddenly calculating, leaving Dionis in no way deceived by her sister's smooth tongue. She knew Angela was not offering her the job to help to further her career. As usual, she was doing it for her own ends. Angela had a knack of making every advantage to herself appear as a gift from the gods to anyone whose help she enlisted in that direction.

With doubts strangely tangible, Dionis said levelly, "You do intend to marry Tony?"

"Of course I do." Angela blew a practised line of smoke into the air. "Actually, Tony wanted us to get married and go to Bermuda, combining a honeymoon with a business trip. However, I told him that was definitely off. When I marry I want a grand affair with all the trimmings and a honeymoon completely divorced from business of any kind." She admired the sapphire ring on her left hand with some satisfaction. "Why do you ask?"

"Because it would be tragic if you had the Villa Acacia furnished to your own requirements and then broke off the engagement. After all, the villa isn't in London; it's in Spain. If you did decide not to marry Tony he could end by marrying a Spanish girl who would possibly prefer the villa in its original state. Have you thought of that?"

Angela flashed the ring impatiently. "I wear his ring."

"Which I seem to recall is the fifth engagement ring you've worn to date," Dionis commented dryly. "You were equally enthusiastic over your other engagements. Remember Ralph Waldron? You were all set for marriage and a long honeymoon on his yacht when his business wobbled. Then there was Charles Frayne who owned the chain stores. He was too bossy. Clifford Brennan was exciting until—"

Angela cut in frigidly. "Please, spare me the post-mortem! At least I didn't marry the first man who asked me. I am endeavoring to get the best out of life."

Dionis shook her head. Her look was tender and sweet. "Angela darling, the only way I know of to get the best out of life is by giving of your best. Please give me your promise to marry the man."

"Don't you preach to me!" Angela was furious. Dionis was relieved that she kept her voice down low enough to blend in with the buzz of conversation going on around them at the other tables. "Look, it would be only too easy for me to put someone else on the job."

"Good luck to them," Dionis answered, in no way perturbed. She was too familiar with her sister's outbursts to be intimidated by them.

The rasping breath coming from Angela's lips was like an engine blowing off steam. She followed it by a deadly calm. Apparently it was essential for her not to alter her plans, for she smiled, a sharp-edged smile suggesting claws well hidden. Thoughtfully she tapped the ash from her cigarette again. Her voice was low, cajolingly so.

"Let's not quarrel. You know I'd rather you did the job, Di. Besides, this engagement is different from the others. There's something about Spaniards that I find strangely exciting. They're so fervently masculine and courteous. There's an underlying passion in them, making you constantly aware of being a woman."

Dionis said firmly, "That's exactly what's worrying me. Your Spaniard isn't likely to take the brush-off calmly—at least not as calmly as the average Englishman. Besides, I'd hate to see the man left with a constant reminder of you in the modernized Villa Acacia. I know you regard my consideration for other people's feelings as sentimental, but that's the way I am."

Angela stubbed out her cigarette with unnecessary force and finished her coffee. "I'm well aware of that," she said, putting down her cup sharply. "However, you'll just have to take my word for it." She glanced impatiently at her watch and picked up her handbag and gloves. "I have an appointment for a facial and hairdo at two with André."

Dionis held out the postcard. "Your picture," she said.

Already there was a faraway look in Angela's eyes as though she was well ahead with future plans. "Keep it. Remember, everything is taken care of. You'll hear from Tony in due course. And stop worrying." Slowly she rose to her feet to smile down at her sister's anxious gaze. "I know you won't let me down. Take care of yourself."

"You, too."

Dionis swallowed a rough obstruction in her throat and looked dazedly at a small packet Angela had pushed across the table toward her. Then she was watching her sister walk gracefully across the dining room to the pay desk, the cynosure of male eyes. Dionis returned her wave as she left and opened the small packet to see a bottle of exclusive French perfume. *How typical of Angela*, she thought despairingly, *so ruthless and so generous*.

Was it only that morning that Angela had arrived jubilantly from a trip to Paris, her last trip for her firm before checking out as Tony's fiancée? Putting the perfume in her bag, Dionis lingered over the last of her coffee, endeavoring to keep pace with the events almost sweeping her off her feet. The assignment to modernize the Villa Acacia had come out of the blue. While she had recognized it as a heaven-sent opportunity to prove her ability in foreign fields, Dionis wished she could feel more enthusiastic about it. Glancing around the spacious dining room, she appraised the modern décor of bold colors, the clever murals and cunningly placed lights. What an exciting world interior decorating opened up! She knew she was a natural at it. The endless thrill of matching exclusive designs and shades, creating beauty from drabness and squalor and seeing it all come to life gave one a deep, satisfying feeling of achievement. Yet while she loved the unlimited scope of color and the bold designs of modern trends, she retained a deep respect for elegant antique furniture and works of art.

Putting down her cup, Dionis looked again at the picture of the Villa Acacia, exuding a whiff of Angela's favorite perfume. Did Angela's fiancé share her preference for a modern villa? Dionis knew none of its history, tragic or happy. She attributed to it all the sadness of far-off things, hallowed by the gentle fingers of time. The garden was beautiful and spelled romance to her quick imaginative brain. She hoped the furniture had been stored away when she arrived. She was not at all enthusiastic about stripping the place of all its character to fill it with alien furnishings. Maybe she was being too sensitive about it. Angela could be right—life was much simpler when viewed from a practical angle. Placing the postcard of the villa in her purse, she drew out her wallet, intent upon leaving a generous tip. It was not as much as she had intended, but she gave all the coins she had in her purse, searching for a five-pound note as she did so. It was not there, although she had had it the previous evening. Then she recalled Angela borrowing it from her that very morning until she went to the bank. Paying for the lunch had been Angela's way of returning it. Oh, to be like Angela!

The last week Dionis was at home simply flew by. She

shopped for bright sandals, beach wear and day and evening dresses, drawing recklessly on her savings. Slacks and a pretty top were her usual working attire. However, she was going to a foreign country not so advanced as go-ahead London. Besides, the Villa Acacia might be in a place where conventions were a religion, so she would prepare for any eventuality. Looking back, she could still not quite believe that she was working for herself. The decision had followed several successful jobs she had undertaken, two of which had been furnishing and decorating a children's home and a home for the elderly.

With absolute confidence in her ability to carry them out, her employer had given both assignments to her. Cesare Delusi, a versatile Italian, was a genius in his job as an interior decorator of modernistic design. Well past the early stage of delicate experimenting, he now juggled brilliant variations and themes confidently, each one sculptured, each dynamically successful. It was he who had encouraged her to branch out on her own, giving her his blessing plus an offer to help her out of any difficulty. Delusi was a household name, and anyone who had been employed by him was invariably assured of a successful future. For her first lone assignment, Dionis had decorated a luxury penthouse for a wealthy pop singer, who had been delighted with the result. When orders began to pour in, Dionis had completed those demanding her immediate attention. The others she had left in abeyance while she planned a short holiday abroad, to include the Modern Furnishing Exhibition in Madrid. Decorating the Villa Acacia would change her little jaunt into a kind of busman's holiday, and she set off full of youthful enthusiasm.

The journey to Spain proved to be uneventful. Arriving in Barcelona, Dionis saw Gaudi's famous church, a bullring of Moorish design, and was driven across an impressive modern bridge with four stone eagles on stone pillars set high above it. Soon the industrial suburbs were left behind for flat uninteresting country. Her traveling companions were a mixed bag of tourists and housewives who were returning to outlying farms after shopping. The older women were proud and dignified in their black clothes. The younger ones were more talkative and decidedly pretty. Everyone was happy and no one except Dionis appeared to be in the least put out by the erratic way the bus was being driven. Dionis sat gripping her seat as they skidded around blind corners at a terrifying speed, missing pannier-laden donkeys by a hair's breadth. Dionis was surprised on looking back to see the gentle creatures still on their feet plodding on.

Fields scarlet with poppies and green with vines flashed by with the bus gradually slackening speed. They were now passing scattered farms, and presently the driver pulled up with a shrieking of brakes to allow passengers off. Then away they went again at the same terrifying speed along white roads where the early evening sun shed a rosy glow over vineyards, irrigated fields and distant hills. Wearily, now, Dionis began to look for landmarks. According to the instructions sent to her in a letter from Angela's fiancé, she should now be nearing the inn where he had booked her a room for the length of her stay in Spain. Yes—still clutching the back of the seat ahead, she could see the hill of three windmills, a definite landmark since she believed the inn was a little farther on.

"The *senorita* from Inglaterra!"

The driver's raucous voice startled her as much as the violent jerk of the bus as he hastily jammed on the brakes. Fortunately for Dionis, she was still hanging onto the seat or she would certainly have been shot down the gangway and through the windshield. Shaken, she rose to her feet and reached for her small case from the bus rack. The rest of her luggage was in the trunk of the bus. With surprising agility for his great bulk, the driver was out of his seat and heaving her cases from the trunk. To her surprise he carried them across the white dusty road into the courtyard of the inn, where she rewarded him with a generous number of pesetas.

The soft glow of evening filtered through the lemon trees enclosing the courtyard. Dionis gazed upon small tables and chairs set out in shade before looking toward the patio. Through the open door of the inn the shining brass and white walls appeared cool and inviting after the heat of the bus. The air was filled with the perfume of flowers: scarlet bougainvillea bloomed against outside walls, climbing roses, jasmine and orange blossom abounded. She breathed it in deeply, loving the warmth, the color.

"Senorita Ward?"

The alien tones softly spoken in English roused her and she turned to see a plump little woman shapely in a black dress. Large dark eyes regarded her kindly.

"*Si*. Senora Lopez?" Dionis proceeded to air a little of her elementary knowledge of Spanish.

The *senora* smiled, inclining her head. "*Si, senorita*. You are expected. Please to come this way."

Senora Lopez led the way indoors to a small reception desk where Dionis signed the visitors' book and filled in a registration card. On their way upstairs the *senora* informed Dionis that she was the only guest. Alterations were being carried out at the back of the inn and no more visitors were being accepted until the work was finished. Don Antonio had booked the *senorita*'s rooms some time ago, and Senora Lopez understood that Dionis would be out all day except for meals. Lunch would be at two-thirty, tea at six and dinner at ten.

Dionis wondered if the *senora* knew the nature of her visit and decided it was not important. The conversation had taken them to a room where a four-poster bed with a colorful woven bedspread gave a gay air to somber furniture. Hot and sticky and a trifle weary, Dionis eased off her white sun hat, pushed pearl-tipped fingers through the heavy waves of hair and looked at windows shuttered against the heat.

"The Villa Acacia, is it far away?" she asked, perhaps foolishly, for Tony would naturally book her into the nearest inn.

"No, Miss Ward. The Quinta Acacia is only a little way up the road from here." Senora Lopez walked gracefully to the window facing them and opened the shutters. "See, there it is through the trees."

Dionis saw a pretty red roof in a panoramic view of vast blue sky etched by trees and bounded by distant hills. Maybe it was because she had already seen a picture of the villa that the scene confronting her appeared more familiar than strange. Indeed it seemed that the hot sun, the perfumed air and clearly defined beauty of the landscape were all combined in a welcome so warm that she immediately had the feeling of belonging. Senora Lopez had put her at her ease and Dionis thanked her warmly as the woman withdrew. With the best part of two hours before dinner was served at ten, she made her way to the bathroom where she discovered a newly installed shower beside the rather antiquated bath.

Under the shower she washed away the stickiness of travel, used the soft fluffy towels and creamed the dryness from her skin brought on by the heat and dust. The cleanliness and homely atmosphere banished her weariness and she hummed softly when she returned to her room and her cases had been brought up. The second window of her room overlooked the courtyard where a sudden cackle made her open the shutters to look down. A goose was waddling over the cobblestones of the courtyard below. So that was where the inn got its name—El Ganso. The Goose. It seemed that the Spanish, like the Romans, regarded geese as watchdogs.

Dionis emptied her cases, filling cupboards and drawers smelling sweetly of potpourri, debating as she did so whether a life free from ties was not the best kind after all. Her thoughts dwelling on her father, she visualized a laughing, daring man who as a successful racing driver had traveled the most dangerous circuits in the world only to meet his death on a quiet English country road one fateful Sunday afternoon. Her mother had met him at the airport after a successful Grand Prix and they had been driving back to their home in Surbiton when a stolen car driven by two youths had crashed into them head on. Death had been instantaneous for them both.

Dionis had been eight and Angela eleven at the time. They had been brought up by their paternal grandparents, who had seen both girls launched in their respective careers before emigrating to Canada to join their other son. Dionis loved her grandparents dearly and had clung to her grandfather on the quay where she and Angela had gone to see them off.

Her grandfather had said, "I'm not so upset at leaving Angela as you, my poppet." His deep-set eyes beneath shaggy brows had been directed toward her sister who, perfectly composed, was talking to her grandmother. "Granted, she's only three years older than you, but she's always been able to look after number one. Whereas she allows her head to rule her heart, you're inclined to do the opposite. However," he had counseled wisely, "keep your illusions, providing you keep your rose-colored spectacles well polished in order to be able to see beyond them if the occasion arises."

Did she have rose-colored spectacles, Dionis wondered. She only knew that the tender care of grandparents had resulted in her growing up happily uncomplicated. And so far Spain had lived up to her expectations—the warmth and courteousness were there. When she had put away her empty cases Dionis saw there was time for a quick visit to the Villa Acacia. Eager to see it at close quarters, she draped a white wooly jacket over her blue suit and went quietly downstairs. An appetizing aroma of food came from the kitchen and she could hear the sounds of activity. Should she ask particulars about the villa, whether she would need a key or if there were caretakers there? Reluctant to trespass on the *senora*'s domain, especially since she was busy preparing dinner, Dionis decided to stroll along to see what the situation was. Silently she passed through the courtyard, empty except for a purring white cat who came to rub against her leg.

"Aren't you lovely?" she said, bending to stroke the soft thick fur before going on her way. Strolling along the white dusty road in the warm summer evening, she was instantly aware of the brilliantly clear air and the intoxicating vividness of her surroundings. There was not the fresh green of her beloved England but the clarity of light, light so powerful that everything, trees, hills and villas, was outlined in a vividness stirring to the senses. It was like some powerful drug giving her the palpably keen power to observe everything around her. The vast area of sky burnt to gold by the sun, the red gold distances where the faint tinkle of goat bells drew her gaze to a goatherd sharply outlined in the oblique light, filled her with wonder. He stood with his cloak thrown carelessly over one shoulder giving a dramatic air to a scene that could have belonged to an old Spanish painting. Gradually Dionis felt the power and languor wrapping her in a pleasant cocoon of warmth that numbed her senses.

Then she saw the Villa Acacia, looking just like the photograph except that now it bore a neglected air. It was a long white building with a belfry, a pillared patio and a porch topped by a trellis of vines casting lacy shadows in the late evening sun. A profusion of scarlet flowers spilled from behind iron blaconies set against windows scenting the air with their fragrance. The silence was tangible as she walked through the garden overgrown with weeds and creepers to the ornate bell at the side of the front door. There was no reply to the hollow sound reverberating through the villa and she stepped back to look up at closed shutters.

Then making her way to the back of the house, she strolled, wandering in a trance as she stared at tangled thorns, creepers and dead branches. At length she sat down on a marble seat half hidden by creepers and trailing roses cascading down from the high stone wall behind her and endeavored to take stock.

Looking around, Dionis could see that in this rich sunsoaked land everything grew with mercurial swiftness. Obviously the villa had not been empty long. That being so, the task of putting the garden to rights was not too formidable. A good man could do it in a couple of weeks. She would ask Senora Lopez if she knew of such a man. Apart from making the place look more inviting it was essential to have it done as soon as possible before it grew worse.

The villa was enchanting and she could visualize the

grounds when they were immaculate once more, forming a perfect frame for the modern interior. Closing her eyes, Dionis felt the charm of the place washing over her in fragrant waves. What utter bliss it would be to spend a summer here! She could fit so easily into this life in the sun with its brilliant contrasts of color, its sense of time-lessness in a majesty of landscape that filled her with awe. The casual stroll back to the inn was extremely pleasant and she found herself looking forward to her late meal.

The courtyard of the inn looked cool and inviting with the gay little tables spotlighted by beams from an orange sun filtering through the foliage of the lemon trees over-head. An olive-skinned girl in a black dress and swinging gypsy earrings hummed softly to herself as she set one of the tables. Vital and alive, she lifted dark eyes remark-ably like those of the *senora* when Dionis appeared.

"*Buenas noches, senorita,*" she said, resorting to English with a flashing smile. "I am Tercia, the daughter of Senora Lopez. I am to tell you that everything is ready when you are."

Dionis smiled in return, warming to her fresh young look. "*Gracias,* Tercia. I shall be down immediately."

When she returned, Tercia was touching the pretty flower arrangement in the center of the table. She straightened on seeing Dionis and drew out her chair with an inviting gesture. Seconds later she whisked away in a manner so sparkling, so effervescent, as to leave Dionis feeling nondescript and negligible. She felt like some pale ghost escaped from another planet, tempted by the loveli-ness of this Eden set in a foreign country. This young sultry creature, although younger than her own twenty-two years bubbled with life. Belonging to a race whose blood ran more swiftly through their veins, she was capable of intense emotion, of violent likes and dislikes. It stemmed from the hot sun, the vastness of the skies and was reflected in smoldering dark eyes through which powerful unspoken communications were transmitted at a glance. Dionis, taking stock of her own placid existence, realized that while she had not scaled any great heights, she had not reached any great depths either. Her sense of isolation was muted by a drowsy warmth of goodwill and a tranquillity she had not known for a long time.

The meal was simple by Spanish standards, cooked perfectly over a charcoal fire, which Tercia assured her was responsible for its excellent flavor. Dionis enjoyed the iced soup, a stimulating aperitif for the omelette and chicken cooked with tarragon that followed. She sensed Tercia's friendly curiosity as she brought each course; the girl probably found her as alien as she found herself. She was nearing the end of her meal when she saw Tercia leaving the courtyard preceded by the short stocky figure of a man.

"Tercia has gone with her father to the house of her *novio*." Senora Lopez was there with freshly brewed coffee. "She is engaged. In two or three years perhaps she will marry. Tercia is now but seventeen."

"So long?" Dionis asked wonderingly, watching the graceful movements of the *senora*'s hands pouring out the coffee.

"*Si.* Tercia and her *novio* have known each other's ways less than six months. Before that they communicated through Miguel's brother. It is the custom," said the *senora* tranquilly.

"Their marriage was arranged, of course."

Senora Lopez smiled. "Both families hoped for the match. Miguel fell in love with Tercia when she was fifteen. He was nineteen. Tercia adores him. But it is well that they should reach a more discerning age before they marry."

The *senora* gathered the used dishes together and departed, leaving Dionis to enjoy her coffee. With her eyes fixed dreamily upon the shadows through which Tercia and her father had disappeared, Dionis visualized the girl's future. It would be poles apart from that of an English girl. Not for Tercia the modern conveniences the average Englishwoman claimed as her right. A charcoal fire and braziers to keep out the winter's bite would be Tercia's only luxuries.

The light was fading now, filling the courtyard with shadows. The cloistered courtyard with its mixed fragrance of charcoal and lavender and the excellent meal were having their effect. Dionis felt drowsy, but it was a drowsiness underlaid with a strange restlessness. The night was far too beautiful for her to leave it and go to bed. She was contemplating taking a walk when a thought inhibited her. In Spain young women did not go out alone at night. It simply was not done, not even by Englishwomen, unless they wished to make themselves conspicuous. She had already defied the conventions by going alone to the Villa Acacia. It seemed she had no choice. Rising reluctantly, Dionis was about to walk to her room when the glow of a brazier in the small covered patio to the right of the porch caught her eye. Senora Lopez stood on a stool lighting the brass hanging lamp attached to the patio ceiling.

"*Gracias* for a wonderful meal, Senora Lopez. I enjoyed it very much," Dionis assured her sincerely.

The *senora* stepped from the stool and set it in a corner. "I am happy that you are satisfied, Miss Ward. Pray do not go to your room. Come, sit for a while on the patio.

The night is young and we in Spain do not retire early. For most of us the day is just beginning."

She gestured to a cushioned seat running the length of the pillared patio by the wall. A glowing brazier filled the air warmly, keeping at bay the slow drop in temperature that the night invariably brings. They sat side by side facing the glow. Beneath the soft light of the hanging lamp the *senora*'s hair shone like the blue black plumage of a bird. For all her plumpness she was decorous, with her tiny hands and feet, fine ankles and expressive eyes. It occurred to Dionis how much more feminine a woman appeared when she was modest and well versed in the arts of being a woman. Englishwomen had lost some of the art of sitting decorously since they chose to wear trousers.

The *senora*'s dark eyes suddenly met her own. "I have the key to the Villa Acacia, Miss Ward. You will be going there tomorrow?"

"Yes." Dionis did not enlighten her about her recent visit. She decided not to mention it until she knew how much the *senora* knew of her reason for being there. At an inn there was always a considerable amount of gossip going on. Fortunately, she was the only guest at the moment, which was just as well.

"Did Don Antonio have a housekeeper?" she asked casually.

"*Si*. A woman from the village came each day to cook and clean. Since Don Antonio left, Paco the gardener has been in charge. Unfortunately, he strained his knee and has been away. He lives with his sister in the village." She shrugged philosophically. "Do not expect to see him at work when you arrive there tomorrow. He has promised to return to work this week. It is possible he will put in an appearance before lunch. After lunch is the siesta, so he might return after four in the afternoon. Then, Miss

Ward, Paco will work like two horses until quite late.''
She lifted her head and Dionis, following her gaze, saw a
short broad-set elderly man entering the courtyard.
"*Buenas noches*, Don Fernando," she exclaimed
welcoming the newcomer with a smile. "Miss Ward, may
I present Don Fernando de Peralto, a very old friend and
the plague of my life."

"*Buenas noches*." He bowed courteously over Dionis's
hand. His clothes were of an expensive cut although worn
to his figure. His face had the sallowness of middle age,
but his dark eyes were young and glowing. It was left to
the small beard, precision-cut, to give his face the
strength of character which Dionis found so arresting.

He had been followed into the courtyard by several
men who made their way inside the inn to take wine.
Dionis was about to make her own excuses and go to her
room when the *senora* went to serve the men. After all,
Don Fernando was a perfect stranger and she might find
it difficult to make conversation with him. Yet she
hesitated, feeling his courteousness and air of understanding like a gentle restraining hand upon her shoulder
bidding her to stay. He had taken the stool the *senora* had
used when she lit the lamp and now she was back carrying
a tray containing two glasses of wine and a box of cigars.
Don Fernando leaned forward to help himself to a cigar
and the *senora* flicked a lighter.

"I don't know what you would do without your glass of
wine and cigar, Don Fernando," she said teasingly,
placing a glass of wine on a low table near him and
offering Dionis the other. "This is on the house. I think
you will like it—it is a local brew, but a good one. Now, if
you will excuse me I will return to attend to my
customers."

Dionis graciously accepted the wine, although she

wondered if she had room for it after the very satisfying dinner. Feeling Don Fernando's eyes upon her, she drank a little.

"Good?" he asked in English.

"Very," she replied, as indeed it was. "Do you speak English, *senor*?"

"*Si*. I have conversed with many of your countrymen over the years on this very spot and have enjoyed every moment of it."

Dionis warmed to his air of gentleness and pleasing dignity suggesting great wisdom and tolerance. His whole bearing showed him to be a man of breeding and intelligence. He smoked his cigar while Dionis sat content to savor the beauty of the evening in the company of a man she felt instinctively that she could trust. She fell to thinking of her reason for being there and wished she could have been there earlier in order to see her sister and Antonio together. Witnessing Angela's reaction to her fiancé might have convinced her of her sister's sincerity. Past experience had made Dionis wary where Angela's love life was concerned. To most women, a man, a home and children were the ultimate aims in life. While her sister might not be capable of a deep and abiding love for any one man, Dionis doubted whether she would be content with the affection of a husband and family. There would have to be the added excitement of all that wealth could bring. How could Antonio be wealthy when he rented a villa from a distant relative? The fact that Angela had fallen in love with the country could strengthen her resolve to marry her Tony and settle down at the villa. Dionis fervently hoped so.

"Did you have a good journey?" Don Fernando asked. "You will soon settle and become one of us."

Dionis smiled and nodded. The wine had imparted an

inner glow. If the lovely evenings on the patio were to be the end of each working day then she was certainly looking forward to them. The warmth of her welcome had been most reassuring, Don Fernando's company enchanting. He was studying her now with a keen shrewd gaze.

"Forgive me, Miss Ward, for using the old approach of suggesting that you and I could have met before. Apart from the fact of your name being familiar the shape of your face, the faint charming slant to those lovely long eyes and a certain cadence in your voice all strike a chord in my memory."

A small pleat deepened between her neat eyebrows. She smiled comprehendingly.

"My sister Angela was here a short while ago. It is possible that you met her. But she is nothing like me. She is blonde and beautiful."

"And are you not beautiful, Miss Ward? Beauty is in the eye of the beholder." His smile was a wise one. "I remember your sister—the *novia* of Don Antonio." He stroked his small beard reflectively. "*Si*, you both have that family likeness. You also bear the same name of a very dear friend of mine who passed away some years ago in tragic circumstances."

"Ward is a fairly common name in England, *senor*," Dionis assured him.

There was sadness in the dark eyes and a faraway look. "My friend was English also. He had two small daughters and a wife whom he adored. It is all of fourteen years since he died. Yet I can see him as though it was only yesterday sitting in the very place you now occupy." He shook his head sadly. "He was so much in love with life and eager for the thrills it offered. So sad that after touring all the most dangerous racing circuits in the world he should meet his end on one of your quiet country roads."

Dionis was experiencing a tide of emotion coupled with a strange excitement.

"Fourteen years ago, *senor*, I was eight years old. My father died that year in similar circumstances. He was also a well-known racing driver. Your friend's name? Was it. . . ." But Dionis was unable to say more. Her lips were too unsteady to form the words.

"His name was Alexander John Ward."

"He was my father, *senor*."

"But this is wonderful, Miss Ward! It is indeed a small world. I am greatly honored to make your acquaintance. I had a younger brother also a racing driver. Alas, he was killed on the track. Your father stopped his own car during that fateful race in order to try to pull my young brother clear of the blazing car. But it was too late."

"I'm sorry, *senor*."

Don Fernando nodded his head. His eyes were shadowed with unhappy memories.

"Senor Ward tried to take his place by calling to see us as often as he could. He helped us a great deal in the first difficult months of bereavement. Your father was a remarkable person."

"I was so young when he died. My memories of him are neither very clear nor are they many. Please tell me how you met him and all about him," Dionis implored.

"What can I say except that he was one of those clean-limbed young Englishmen it has always been a pleasure to meet. You are very much like him."

Dionis's eyes were wide with surprise. "Really? My father was fair-haired and blue-eyed, more like Angela."

"In coloring, perhaps, but his true character and personality live again in you, *nina*. You have inherited all that made him great—his ideals, integrity and tolerance and his zest for life. All are mirrored in those long dark eyes of yours which are as eloquent as once his were."

Dionis flushed with pleasure. "How sweet of you to say that, because now I feel as if he had never left me." She smiled demurely. "I don't think I'm as courageous as he was, but it's nice of you to say so."

"You are brave enough to strive to do the right thing, and you like people." His glance flickered over her, kindly and analytical. Dionis looked startled.

"But how can you tell? We've only just met," she cried.

"Intuition and the experience of an old man."

"I can't believe it!" she breathed with stars in her eyes. "To think that my father actually sat here and talked to you as I am now. You have no idea what it means to me to know that." She laughed, an enchanting laugh of pure happiness. "I can never feel strange here again after what you have told me."

Don Fernando, cigar in hand, studied the ash as he spoke. "Your first impressions of us will account for everything appearing alien to you. Yet, like you, we belong to an ancient race of people who have clung to our ideals. We still cling to the old traditions, more violently perhaps because we live nearer to the soil. But our fundamental desires remain the same."

They talked for a long time, and Don Fernando answered her eager questions with courtesy and charm. Dionis felt she would always remember her first evening in Spain with the patio bathed in a golden glow from the gilt hanging lamp and the softly burning brazier. Don Fernando's cigar mingled with the nocturnal scents of exotic blooms set against white walls and rich dark shadows. She thought of her father with a little thrill of pride. Because of him the inn had become an enchanted place.

CHAPTER TWO

Dionis awoke to the cackle of geese and the tinkle of goat bells. For bewildered sleepy moments her eyes roved around the strange room. The cool beauty of tiled floors covered by delicately colored rugs complementing the cheerful counterpanes, old Spanish furniture against white walls—all formed a neat classic study coming to life beneath the gentle fingers of sun pushing through the shutters. Instinctively, her eyes were drawn to the dressing table on which lay the keys to the Villa Acacia given to her the previous evening by Senora Lopez. While she was eager to start work again she was also aware of a strange foreboding.

This strange reluctant feeling at the start of a new assignment was as unfamiliar as it was unsettling. Somehow the thought of her father being held in such high esteem by the local people added to her uneasiness. She wanted nothing to happen to spoil that image. Padding to her window, she opened the shutters to breathe in the perfume of climbing roses. Tercia was crossing the courtyard below carrying a pitcher of milk. Her full-skirted dress swung from swaying hips and the sun glinted on the Spanish gypsy earrings. She was singing, but stopped as soon as her mother whispered for her to be quiet. Then the *senora* was stepping back to look up at Dionis's window before following her cheerful daughter indoors. Dionis waved.

She had showered and put on a wrap when Tercia appeared with her breakfast—fruit juice, fresh rolls, homemade cherry jam and honey. The coffee was delicious. Well fortified inwardly for work on the Villa Acacia, Dionis put on a suit in navy sailcloth trimmed with white, stepped into white sandals, armed herself with a pad and pencil and, picking up her bag, went out to do battle. Downstairs she exchanged greetings with Senora Lopez, who was pleased to hear that she had slept well.

"You will be in to lunch, Miss Ward, at two-thirty?" she queried.

"*Si, senora*, unless you would prefer me to take a picnic lunch," Dionis replied thoughtfully.

"No, no. You will come back to the inn for lunch, then upstairs to your siesta. You will work much better when you return to the villa later," the *senora* said firmly.

Dionis capitulated nicely, although, in her opinion, the siesta was a bore, making a big break in her working day and one she had not foreseen. She opened the gate to the Villa Acacia, once more shuttered and secret, and walked through the overgrown garden, taking deep breaths of the perfumed air. The *senora* had been right about Paco the gardener. He had not arrived. In the silence, Dionis found it easy to regard it all as a dream. Externally, the Villa Acacia was beautiful, a joy to look at. The baroque-paneled front door sheltered by a classical porch was enriched by ornamental brackets. She appreciated the entrance being placed more to one side of the façade instead of dead center, thus ensuring that there was no drafty throughway to the back of the villa. When she opened the door, she stood for several moments feeling excited and strangely breathless.

As she had hoped, the furniture had been removed, and the interior was sweet and clean. In the hall the exquisite Moorish tiled floor was dominated by a graceful staircase which curved upward to the first floor. The motifs in the wrought-iron balustrade were charming, as were the arched doorways. The one to the left led to the dining room, kitchen, larder and back door. To the right were the study, lounge, library, cloakrooms and nursery. Dionis loved the nursery, picturing a dimpled, chuckling baby blowing bubbles to the sun outside on the patio overlooking the kitchen garden. With dreams in her eyes, she gazed at the open fireplace, the lovely ceiling from which polished brass lamps hung gleaming softly in the muted sunlight streaming through the shutters.

It was evident from the immaculate condition of the walls and ceilings that the whole interior had been decorated throughout not long before. The planning of the ground floor had accomplished a convenient distribution of rooms with their easy access from one to another. The plan was repeated all through the villa, giving a feeling of spaciousness. There were three bedrooms, dressing rooms and bathrooms. All were high-ceilinged and roomy. Looking up at magnificent alabaster carving and cornices, Dionis pictured a deep contrasting color against paler walls. The bedroom furniture in built-in units would be ideal, but not against the outer walls where they would be open to damp and condensation when the temperature rose or fell. They could be fixed to the inner walls where they would strengthen the partitions between rooms. The charm of the place filled her with delight as she measured up the rooms and jotted down details in her notebook. She discovered that the master bedroom had a degree of privacy with each of its attendant rooms opening out onto the landing instead of leading into each other like the rest. Already she was visualizing a white wool covering on the walls enhanced by rich cream transparent drapes fully gathered and reaching to the floor. The heavy draw curtains would be cream laced with cinnamon with a matching bedspread in a chunkier fabric. Generously built-in furniture would mean that the rest of the room would only need the minimum of furniture. Two petal-shaped chairs in white cane to match the built-in units would be ideal.

It was heartening to have a free hand with no one butting in to stem her flow of ideas. And it was a great help to have the rooms cleared of furniture. Curious as to where it had been stored, Dionis made her way up to the top floors built in the rafters and gingerly opened a door. The furniture was there. Rather guiltily she glimpsed a charming lacquer cabinet, really lovely tapestry-upholstered chairs and several intriguing little footstools before she gently closed the door. She hoped nothing would deteriorate with storage. While the villa appeared to be in excellent condition any defect in the roof could allow rain to come in and ruin the furniture beyond repair. She might be worrying over nothing. Anyway, it was no business of hers, she concluded as she descended the stairs.

It was suffocatingly hot in the midday sun when Dionis went to the porched entrance to hear the scuffed sound of rope-soled espadrilles on the garden path. And suddenly there was Paco. A thick-set figure of medium height wearing neat and patched clothes, he came forward shyly, hat in hand, his small eyes shiny as black olives.

"*Buenos dias, senorita,*" he said, continuing in halting English, "I must apologize for the state of the gardens, but I have hurt my knee." He gestured to his left leg where a neat patch on his trousers covered the offending limb. "I have almost recovered. The pain now is only irritating to me because I have never been ill. I am as strong as an ox—anyone in the village will tell you." He straightened proudly and smiled, showing rather yellow strong teeth. His sallow face had a melancholy look, but Dionis took to him on sight. He could be around fifty, but he obviously was rather sweet and naïve as he added shyly, "I am Paco."

"You're not to worry about the garden, Paco. Accidents will happen. You must be sure the knee is quite well before you start to use it," Dionis said with a gentle smile.

"I am sure, *senorita*. Senor Juan Vicente de Velez y Stebelo would be angry to see the garden so. I will start immediately to put it to rights," he said with a quaint dignity.

Suddenly Dionis was looking overhead where a great bird had appeared to hover ominously. In that split second it swooped into the branches of a tree nearby and emerging silently with its prey, it swooped away into the blue distance. So sudden, so unerringly direct was it that Dionis stared in a fascinated horror. She shivered in the heat to meet Paco's sympathetic gaze.

"*Mas vale que fuerza, senorita*," he quoted. "Skill is better than strength."

For a long moment they looked at each other, while Dionis experienced an emotion more disturbing than anything she had ever known. Was it the bird of prey showing her the cruelty of nature here as anywhere else? Or was it the mention of Don Juan? So he would be angry over the state of the garden. She only hoped he had given permission for the conversion of the villa.

Putting the incident behind her rather sadly, she said, "I'm sure it won't take long to put it to rights. But whatever you do you must not tire the knee. I want your promise on that, Paco."

"*Gracias, senoria*. You have my word." He had brightened at her obvious concern. "I have relatives, all craftsmen, who would gladly assist the *senorita* in her work in the villa. You have only to say the word."

"*Gracias,* Paco. I shall certainly need them when my materials arrive. I will let you know."

Dionis watched him amble to the garden shed for his tools. He really was a pet, she decided, returning to the villa to make a final check before she left for lunch. Paco had gone when she finally emerged from the villa. The sun blazed down on her uncovered head and she arrived back at the inn hot and thirsty. She ate her lunch at one of the small tables under the lemon trees in the court-yard—gazpacho soup, ice-cold, both an aperitif and a delicious thirst quencher. Ham, meat, cheese, fruit and crisp rolls with fresh butter followed. There was a rosé wine and mineral water. Dionis chose the latter.

After lunch, she went to her cool shuttered room for the siesta. Lying on her bed, she tried to relax, but her thoughts were too occupied with her job. Her brain was afire with plans inspired by the blue distances, the velvet illusions of light and shade, the shimmering radiance of exotic colors, the sudden richness of black and white. She was impatient to start and found herself hoping that her work would meet with Antonio's approval and Don Juan Stebelo's also. Now why on earth should she think of Don Juan, a man she had never met and was not likely to meet.

After a quarter of an hour lying on her back Dionis had had enough. She had a wash and brushup and was again on her way out. Silence greeted her as she went quietly downstairs. The inn was shuttered and silent. No sound came from the kitchens or any part of the house. The cat stretched out beneath the lemon trees did not bother to lift its head when she walked across the courtyard. The white dusty road unwound slowly before her in a fra-grant aura of lavender and wild thyme, and when the sudden clip-clop of a horse's hooves drew nearer behind her, Dionis drew in at the side of the road.

"Buenas tardes, Miss Ward," came the familiar voice, and she stopped as a horse-drawn carriage drew up beside her. Don Fernando's face beneath his straw hat beamed as he offered a hand with Spanish gallantry to help her up beside him. "Are you not enjoying the siesta?" he asked on a surprised note.

"I'm eager to get on with the job," she admitted frankly, sitting beside him all smiles. "Besides, it's cool inside the villa. You do know I'm decorating it in the modern style, *senor*?"

"*Si*. I was at the inn the night Don Antonio came to book rooms for you. So it makes two of us abroad in the sun when we ought to be taking our siesta. I am not doing it by choice. I am on my way to pick up Inez, my wife. She is visiting a sick friend and wanted to be home for the siesta. Unfortunately, the horse cast a shoe and I am well over an hour late at calling for Inez."

"She'll be wondering what's keeping you. Isn't this lovely?" Dionis watched the bright blue and white tassels swinging on the harness as the horse trotted proudly along.

"You do not find it tame after your fast cars?"

"Not at all. It is most relaxing, and quite the perfect way of seeing the countryside." She was smiling at him when a tornado in the shape of a long silver car shot past, leaving them in a cloud of white dust. "My goodness," she gasped, "it seems you have your road hogs here too, *senor*!"

He shrugged resignedly. "All part of the mechanical age which is creeping into every country these days. Fortunately, we don't see many cars on these byways where donkeys are invariably used."

When he dropped her off at the Villa Acacia, his eyes rested upon her uncovered head. "You did say you were working indoors?"

"I did." She smiled somewhat ruefully. "I know I should be wearing a hat and it's very remiss of me. I forgot sunglasses too."

He shook his head in mild reproof. "That is one thing you will learn while you are here—to take your time. The true Spaniard takes his time and savors life to the full."

"I'll remember that—and please call me Dionis."

"With pleasure, Dionis. I am Fernando to all my friends."

"*Adios*, Don Fernando. *Gracias* for the lift. It was lovely."

Walking through the garden of the villa, Dionis knew Paco would not be back until after the siesta, and not then if his knee troubled him. Siesta could mean any time up to four, which was the hour when the shops opened again. He had cleared away quite a quantity of dead leaves, weeds and branches and piled them into a compost heap in a corner of the garden. She could hardly wait to see it restored to all its former glory. There, for instance, by the solid thick stone wall was a pretty bird table. It was almost entirely hidden with trailing vines which she pulled in an effort to tear them away. They were stubborn and strong, defying all her efforts to dislodge them. Warming to her task, she found secateurs in the garden shed and set to work in earnest. What treasures she uncovered— oleanders, myrtles, nasturtiums and camellias nestling in their beds of cool damp earth beneath the tangles of weeds.

She had cleared the bird table when she saw the garden seat. Intrigued, she started to clear this too, discovering to her delight that it was pure marble exquisitely tiled in garden scenes. The scrolled effect of the arms and the back of the seat formed a perfect frame for the pretty scenes depicted in really lovely pastel colors. It was hard work dislodging all the thick growth choking it. A man would have accomplished it in half the time and the sun was really far too hot for such demanding work, but Dionis kept doggedly on until her back began to ache and her head throb from the heat of the sun.

Her clothes clung moistly to her skin and she was exhausted by the time the seat was finally cleared. She forgot her discomfort as she gazed in admiration at the work of art depicted by the tiles. Then suddenly the seat was blotted out by a red glow beneath her eyelids and accompanied by a giddy feeling of nausea. Blinking furiously to dispel it, she turned. The car moved smoothly, making scarcely a sound, and drew up not many yards from where she stood.

Dionis seemed scarcely able to breathe. She watched the car arrive and the man who got out of it with a feeling of never having met anyone so repellently remote, so . . . so perfectly high-bred and regal. He was of medium height, lean and spare with the suggestion of hidden strength in the wide shoulders. His ears were set closely against a well-shaped head which he carried proudly, almost haughtily. His olive features were lean and handsome. From the high noble forehead, long nose with slightly flaring nostrils down to the mobile mouth and well-defined jaw, he exuded power and authority. He was immaculately dressed in light tan suiting sharply tailored to fit his athletic form like a glove. His dark eyes beneath level brows narrowed at her between black lashes. There was a quality of strength and vitality about his alien look, a kind of censure that annoyed even while it intrigued, and she addressed him frigidly.

"*Buenas tardes, senor.* Can I help you?" she said slowly in a mixture of English and Spanish. The man looked well educated and her Spanish was restricted. She was not giving him the opportunity of curling his lip and looking down that long aristocratic nose at her mistakes.

"*Buenas tardes, senorita,*" he replied suavely. He spoke in deep cultured tones, taking his time as he looked at her flushed face, tumbled hair and over bright eyes. "I would say you are the one in need of help. May I ask what you are doing here?"

His English was as faultless as she knew it would be. It was also well chilled as he stood striking an open palm with driving gloves which he clasped in his other hand.

She lifted a small chin defiantly, goaded by his cold regard, his hauteur.

"I might ask the same of you, *senor.* Will you please state your business? I'm busy."

He raised a dark brow maddeningly. "So I observe. Doing men's work, *senorita*? Where is Paco, and why is the garden in a state of neglect?" He looked around him, frowning heavily, his dark eyes eventually taking in the bird table and marble seat, the theme of her labors. Finally, his lips thinned as he looked down on the secateurs on the garden seat. "What exactly is going on here?"

Once more his eyes were on her face. His jaw came into prominence and her heart filled with misgiving.

But she collected herself to ask firmly, "What authority have you to ask that question?"

"Allow me to introduce myself," he said coldly. "I am Juan Vicente de Velez y Stebelo. I own the Villa Acacia."

Phew! Gingerly, Dionis wiped a trickle of perspiration from the side of her nose with a shaking finger. So much for Angela's assurance that this Spanish autocrat and herself would never meet. What a name! What a man! They matched perfectly.

"I beg your pardon," she said. "I understood you were

away." The pain in her temples was now acute and she longed to lift her hand to shield her eyes from the hurtful glare. Apparently it did not affect him in the least. He was accustomed to it. His deep tan had been painlessly acquired. He continued to flick the palm of his hand with his gloves, allowing his eyes to flicker over her again probingly.

"I came to see Senor Antonio Alba Terino to whom I let this villa. He also acts as one of my agents, and as I have not heard from him for some time, I am here to find out why. You are a guest here?"

"No. I am here at the *senor*'s request to modernize this villa."

He looked startled, so startled that he stopped flicking his gloves to grip them with both hands.

"Please define modernize," he demanded in icy tones.

"I'm an interior decorator," Dionis replied laconically.

His regard was nothing short of contemptuous. "I understood interior decorating to be a man's job. It is hardly a woman's vocation."

Dionis had the feeling of being relegated to the status of a Russian serf. Again she lifted her head, wishing that it would not throb so painfully. The red streaks inside her lids flashed again frighteningly.

"It's a perfectly respectable career for a woman, I assure you. I do the planning and carry out the light jobs myself. I engage workmen to do the heavier ones."

"You surprise me. You have the delicate look of one needing protection. You are certainly not fitted for this type of work. But this is beside the point. If you have been inside the villa you will be aware that it has only recently been decorated throughout."

"It did occur to me," she said inadequately.

He waved his gloves contemptuously to take in the garden. "I presume this is also your province."

Dionis moved uncomfortably. It was growing apparent with each embarrassing moment that this Spanish nobleman or whatever he was had no idea of Antonio's intention. Perspiration oozed from her afresh as she endeavored to explain.

"No, it is not. As a matter of fact, Paco has been incapacitated by an injured knee. He started work again only this morning and will be returning after his siesta."

He made a gesture of distaste. "Then will you kindly explain, *senorita,* why you are doing his job?"

"The explanation is perfectly simple and Paco is in no way to blame. I was enchanted by a glimpse of this delightful garden seat and the bird table and I couldn't wait to see what they were really like beneath the tangled undergrowth."

She gave a brief smile in an effort to lighten the oppressive atmosphere. When he ignored it, she flashed him a hostile look from beneath her lashes, thinking that too was unlikely to penetrate his formidable front. Angela's fiancé was lucky not to be within range of those long sinewy brown hands, which looked to be as capable of gripping his throat as they now gripped the driving gloves. She quivered inwardly, thinking of all the furniture stored aloft and hoped to keep him from seeing it until she was sure none of it was damaged. Help was at hand, although it was to cost her dearly. There was a sudden singing noise in her ears, the sun became a guided missile making straight for her face and she stifled a moan as blackness engulfed her.

Everywhere was bathed in a reddish glow when life flowed again in her limbs. Her eyelids weighed a ton, or so it seemed as she lifted them. She was half sitting, half lying in the circle of strong arms. A cool hand was on her burning forehead and she was feeling so sick and ill she was glad of his support.

"How do you feel, *senorita*?" he asked, one hand, remarkably gentle, pushing the damp tendrils of hair from her damp forehead.

But Dionis did not answer. She had never felt so ill in her life. The blackness was coming back again with a deepening of the red glow behind her eyelids.

Gently, he lowered her back against the seat and withdrew his arm.

"Keep still," he said quietly. "I'm going to open the car door."

He was back almost immediately to lift her gently in his arms and she knew no more.

CHAPTER THREE

Dionis opened her eyes to a strange room. The pain in her head dulled her faculties. But she could see there was beauty in the room, the cool beauty of delicately lovely furniture and colors. A lacquer dressing table handsomely inlaid matched a small writing bureau. Nearby were two pretty chairs elegantly shaped and beautifully upholstered, a tall vase of flowers, a silver bowl of fruit on the bedside table. Dionis glimpsed these things through a maze of pain as a nurse moved silently toward her. She bent over her in concern.

"How are you? Rotten, I know. Sunstroke can be decidedly painful even in a mild form," she said, English in her speech and in her appearance. She wore a neat little frilled cap on her nut brown hair and was short, rather thickset but shapely in her uniform. She had brown eyes, a rather snub nose and a generous mouth. Before Dionis could answer she was pouring out something into a glass from a bottle on the bedside table. Then, very capably, she lifted Dionis gently on her pillows and tipped the contents of the glass down her parched throat.

It was a relief to lie back again on her pillows. Sunstroke, the nurse had said.

Dionis had never known such pain. Waves of color advanced and retreated beneath her eyelids. There was a brief confusion of wandering in dark places before everything was mercifully blotted out. The last thing she remembered was something cool being placed on her hot forehead.

She opened her eyes again to the murmur of voices. A man stood at the side of her bed smiling down upon her benignly. Around forty, he had bushy eyebrows and a wise look.

"How are you feeling, *senorita*?" he asked, standing broad and comforting in the soft light. "I am Doctor Horatio de Quexeri at your service."

"Much better, *gracias*, doctor," she answered, as indeed she was. Her eyes still ached, but the pain in her head had dulled and was bearable. She glanced around the room, aware of the artificial light. "Is it evening?"

"It is ten o'clock," he replied with a smile as he proceeded to lift her wrist in order to take her pulse.

"Oh dear!" Dionis exclaimed. "Senora Lopez will wonder what's happened to me!" It was then that she realized she was wearing a pair of her own pajamas. Someone must have fetched them from the inn.

"Do not distress yourself, *senorita*. The *senora* has been informed. A day or so in bed will put you right again. And you will be well looked after here at the Villa Jacaranda." The doctor laid down her hand to address someone behind him. "A different kind of quest for you, Don Juan—an English rose among exotic blooms."

Don Juan came forward. His smile had a spontaneous and irresistible charm. Then he was looking analytically at Dionis, his dark eyes full of a curious light.

"You are fortunate that your attack is but a slight one, otherwise you could have been very ill. I trust you will not linger too long in the sun without a hat in the future, Miss Ward."

And let this be a lesson to you, Dionis thought hollowly, for his manner could not have said so more plainly. She quivered at the male element in his voice with its alien intonation. How she resented him, resented his power to rouse an exciting response in her, no more than a vibration at the moment, but it was there—she could not deny it. He was the kind of man who would make his presence felt in any room, dominating it with his air of distinction and arrogant charm. The evening dress he wore was immaculate with no trace of exaggeration anywhere. But she was in his house and some sort of apology was called for.

"I apologize for my thoughtlessness, *senor*," she said. "You have obviously been put to a lot of trouble on my behalf. I'm probably keeping you from your guests at this very moment."

"It is not important," came the cool reply. "What is important is that you will soon be well again."

And from under your well-shod feet, she thought dryly.

Aloud she said, "I'm grateful for that, since there's no reason why I shouldn't now go back to the inn, where I can take things easy until I've fully recovered."

For a moment the room was still and quiet, full of flowers and soft shaded lights and the cozy atmosphere of rich furnishings. Don Juan lifted his head and looked strangely feudal.

"I am afraid you will have to reconcile yourself to staying here for the time being. The building alterations at the inn and the noise are not exactly conducive to your recovery. Do you not agree, doctor?"

The doctor smiled down at her kindly. "Of course." He patted her hand as it lay on the counterpane. "Enjoy your convalescence, *senorita*. You will be the envy of *senoritas* for miles around. A pity you do not know any of them. You would have much enjoyment over a cup of chocolate giving an account of your stay beneath the roof of one of our most eligible bachelors."

His words were teasing, his manner easy enough for Dionis to give a light reply. And, although the thought of staying beneath Don Juan's roof filled her with dismay, she managed to say airily, "I shall be able to tell my friends about it when I return home."

She liked the doctor in the well-worn dark suit that proclaimed his calling as quietly and unobtrusively as the impression he gave of confidence and kindness.

"And make some young Englishman jealous?" he scoffed.

"Perhaps," she answered, aware of the dark still figure by the doctor's side.

"You will have your little joke, *amigo*," Don Juan said. "You will be calling again tomorrow?"

"I will be here, although your little English nurse seems fully competent." He picked up his small bag. "*Adios, senorita*. Sleep well with no more pain. Delighted to have met you."

Don Juan, his shoulders square and erect, walked with the doctor to the door with the easy grace of an athlete. He could not be more than thirty, Dionis mused as the door closed behind them. He might even be in his twenties and matured beyond his years by his experience and education. She fell to wondering how he had known she was staying at the inn and how she came to be wearing her own pajamas. She could only surmise that Paco had arrived at the Villa Acacia as Don Juan was driving away in his car, and he had made a few hurried inquiries. Probably Paco had been dispatched to the inn to tell Senora Lopez what had happened and to bring the pajamas back with him to the Villa Jacaranda. He had not taken her to the inn because he thought the *senora* had enough to do with the alterations there. How sickening that this should have happened and all through her own carelessness. Dionis lay back with closed eyes.

"May I come in?"

The sweet-accented voice in English fell pleasantly

upon her ears. Lifting her head from the pillow, Dionis saw a lovely Spanish young woman hovering in the doorway.

She said, "Please do."

The newcomer entered. She was small, dark and about twenty years old. Her black evening dress had bands of velvet around the full skirt and the only note of color was in the scarlet scarf encircling her slender throat. Long diamond earrings matched the jeweled scarf pin winking in the light with every movement and a ring flashed on her hand as she lifted a finger to red lips. Dionis smiled conspiratorially. It was an effort, for she could not have felt less like receiving visitors. Her head was too fuzzy and it was far too much trouble to concentrate. But this lovely creature with her tiny feet, trim ankles and lovely expressive hands was really bewitching. Her skin bloomed like a ripe peach and her small laugh like tinkling bells brought dimples into play as she walked gracefully across the room as though to music.

"Welcome to the Villa Jacaranda, Miss Dionis Ward," she said in a delighted whisper. "I am Rosalba Maria de Velez y Stebelo, Juan's sister. My brother tells me you have come from Inglaterra and I am dying to meet you. But you are ill, and I am sorry."

"And so you should be. It was for precisely that reason that I forbade you to come to this room, Rosalba. Please go."

Rosalba swung around as Don Juan entered the room. Her lovely mouth pouted mutinously as she met his stern gaze.

"But I only wanted to see the English *senorita* . . . ."

"You have seen her. Now go!" he commanded.

For a moment it seemed that Rosalba hesitated. Then the proud dark head inclined graciously toward Dionis.

"*Buenas noches, senorita.* I trust that you will enjoy a good night and that you will soon recover."

She drifted from the room like a lovely ghost. Dionis, gazing tenderly after her, met her brother's dark eyes.

"I apologize for my sister's curiosity and lack of good manners," he said formally. "She is a minx." The thin mobile mouth lifted at the corners, but only for a moment. Then he was across the room to look down on her pale face and shadowed eyes. "The doctor says it is possible that you have slept off most of your attack, although the aftereffects could linger for a day or so. Nurse is bringing you some refreshment and then you will be left alone to rest. The nurse will stay within call during the night in case you need her."

His voice was kind, but his manner was impersonal. Dionis tried to infuse warmth into the pale smile she gave him, finding his steady regard too unsettling for words.

"You're very kind," she said. "If I've slept most of the trouble away you can't object to my returning to the inn in the morning."

He digested this with a slight smile which she fancied was tinged with mockery.

"I think not," he replied after a pause. "I would have to put the Villa Acacia out of bounds for a while if you did in order to protect you from your own impulsive actions." He turned as nurse entered with a covered tray. "Ah, here you are. *Buenas noches*, Miss Ward. Sleep well after your refreshment."

The dark eyes fastened on her own with a glitter that compelled her to capitulate against her will. He had a few words with the nurse in a low voice, then closed the door silently behind him. Dionis had soup, which was the only thing she felt inclined to swallow, and it was not long before she was asleep. She awoke to the glow of morning light filtering through the closed shutters. She had slept all through the night, a dreamless sleep that had refreshed her surprisingly. No pain lurked in her temples and her eyes when she blinked them felt clear and bright. She had a yearning to dip her face into cool water and revel in the pleasure of bending a head free from pain. All was quiet when she left her bed to go beneath the shower. She had combed her hair and was back in bed feeling ready for anyone who appeared when the nurse arrived with her breakfast tray.

"You're awake, I see," was her greeting as she carried the tray to the bed. "How are you this morning? Feeling like breakfast, I hope?" She placed the tray across Dionis's knees and smiled at her cheerfully. "You look much brighter."

"I feel it—in fact there's no reason why I should stay. It's so uncalled-for to have you here when you could be nursing someone who is really ill," Dionis replied firmly, warming to the nurse's friendly smile.

"But, my dear, you're not keeping me from nursing someone else. I just happened to be available when you needed me." She glanced meaningly at the chair beside the bed. "Mind if I stay while you eat? I've already breakfasted."

"Take a seat," Dionis said affably.

The nurse sat down, taking knitting from her apron pocket, a tiny white shape on short knitting needles. "Bootee," she said laconically. "I'm here on a visit to my sister Doris. She and her husband, Felipe Alpurro, are housekeepers here in the Villa Jacaranda. Felipe's family have been in the service of Senor de Velez y Stebelo's family for generations. Don Juan had no idea how ill you were yesterday when he carried you in from his car. You might have been toiling all day in the hot sun and then, of course, the sunstroke would have been very severe. So he asked me to look after you. I suppose he thought my being English would help you better than someone Spanish whom you couldn't understand. I'd do anything for him. I absolutely adore him."

Dionis bit into a fresh buttered roll and watched the knitting needles fly.

"I understood Don Juan spent most of his time at his other residences in Cadiz and Castellon," she said curiously.

"He does. It's quite unusual for him to stay here long, much less have visitors at this time of the year unless he has business with his agents. If his other residences are as nice as this, he's a very lucky man. Each time I come here the Villa steals a little more of my heart. I simply adore Spain—the leisurely long days, the smiling sunlit faces, the music and song and the underlying passion which an Englishman would scoff at but which really exists all the same." She sighed as she counted her stitches.

"Take Don Juan, for instance. He has everything, a body like an Adonis, charm and magnetism, and he's a real man and a gentleman to boot. He's also an Olympic yachtsman, holds a Karate black belt, flies his own plane and is perfectly splendid on horseback. He's the answer to every woman's dream and makes me weak just to think about him. What wouldn't I give to be young and beautiful!"

Dionis laughed. "You speak like someone with one toe in the grave."

The nurse looked surprised. "Do I? I don't feel ancient, especially when I see Don Juan's dark smoldering eyes. I've never known what it is to be beautiful with enough magnetism and charm to attract the opposite sex. The Stebelos have everything, including good breeding and wealth."

"Wealth isn't everything," Dionis drank her coffee.

"I agree. But it has a lot of influence. For instance, I'm here on an extended leave, thanks to Don Juan's influence. Doris, my sister, is expecting her first baby. It's overdue and she's very nervous about it. She wants me here when it happens. When Don Juan heard about it he contacted the matron at the hospital in London where I'm a nurse. The result was that she agreed to extend my leave. I'm thrilled to be able to be here when the baby arrives. I'll have nostalgic moments, though, wishing the baby were mine."

"You can marry and have babies of your own."

The nurse lowered the knitting into her lap and stared down at it. "I'll not be as fortunate as my sister. She's lovely, and like you, she can manage to look interesting, even when she's ill." She cast an appraising eye over the delicate texture of Dionis's skin, admiring the long lovely eyes. "Those violet shadows beneath your eyes add to your appeal. If I had them I'd look perfectly ghastly. I used to look awful after a spell of night duty at the hospital." She sighed and picked up her knitting and Dionis looked at her averted profile, the brown hair scraped back into a tight bun to accommodate the nurse's cap, the rather snub nose and deep chin. As though conscious of her scrutiny, the nurse looked up to meet her gaze, surprising Dionis by the beauty of her brown eyes between thick stubby lashes.

"You're well on the way to being good-looking," Dionis said cheerfully. "It only needs a bit of effort. As most men notice a woman's eyes and legs you'd do well to concentrate on those. Your eyes are lovely." She put her head on one side, picturing the nurse's face softened by an aura of hair. "Have your hair styled and use a brightening rinse. Change your flat-heeled shoes for pumps with a medium heel. They would be just as comfortable and ten times as smart as those flat shoes you wear. Your legs, like your eyes, are one of your best features."

The nurse lifted a slim leg to survey her feet ruefully. "I take size eights and wear low heels for comfort. I'm dead on my feet most days at the hospital."

"You're not at the hospital now," Dionis said firmly. "Your feet might be long, but they're slim and would look more elegant in pumps. Besides, you have a high instep, so you do really need a moderately high heel to give some support."

The nurse appeared to be looking at her feet with new eyes. "You know, you have something there," she said brightly. "Thanks, Miss Ward. I'll see what I can do about it."

"My name is Dionis."

"And mine is Joan—Joan Ford." Nurse Ford grimaced ruefully. "Not a very romantic name, like Rosalba de Velez y Stebelo."

"Don Juan's sister?"

"Yes. She's dark, luscious and lovely. They're a beautiful family." She wrinkled her snub nose. "I don't like that friend of hers, Dolores de Liscondo. She won't be pleased to hear of Don Juan carrying you up to this room from his car. She's certainly got her sights set on him as a husband."

Dionis used her table napkin. "I'm surprised the man is still single. They still arrange marriages in Spain."

"Don Juan was betrothed to a younger sister of Dolores years ago. The marriage was to have taken place when Don Juan reached the age of twenty-five, but a series of incidents prevented it from happening. In the end Don Juan's *novia* decided he was not for her and went to live with a wealthy aunt in Madrid. She has since married a diplomat there."

"What kind of mishaps prevented the marriage?" Dionis asked curiously. "Don Juan doesn't strike me as a man who would let anything get in his way."

"To begin with, Don Juan lost his parents. They were killed when the horse taking them in their carriage to church bolted. Then Don Juan's *novia*'s father died."

"So his fiancée went away to leave the coast clear for her elder sister Dolores. Is she beautiful, too?"

"Most Spanish women are," Joan Ford said without rancor. "They're so essentially feminine, which is all to their advantage since most of them tend to run to obesity later in life. Mind you, I think a beautiful Englishwoman is hard to beat." She gave Dionis an appraising look. "You, for instance, are everything I wanted to be, with those red lights in your luxurious hair, your slim build, pretty legs and wide-set, lovely eyes—the exact opposite to me."

Dionis smiled. "Stop belittling yourself! Men usually prefer women with personality and sex appeal as a partner. You have both."

Joan Ford beamed. "You've made my day! Now I'll have to do something about myself." She cast an experienced eye over the breakfast tray. "Can't you eat any more?"

"I've enjoyed what I've eaten. What time do you think the doctor will arrive?"

Joan Ford pocketed her knitting and lifted up the tray. "Probably before the morning surgery." Her head turned toward the door as someone knocked. "I wouldn't be surprised if that isn't him now."

It was. He came in, took Dionis's temperature, asked the same questions as he had done the previous evening and clasped her hand in parting. He had listened, a line of perplexity between the thick brows, when she had asked for permission to go back to the inn.

"Certainly, if that is what you want. Senora Lopez is a good provider and I can see you are aching to leave this bed. I have dined at the inn on various occasions. Go by all means, but you must rest for several days and keep out of the sun. *Adios, senorita*. We shall meet again."

"He's a nice man," Joan Ford said, when the doctor had gone. "Doctor Horatio de Quexeri. I love these Spanish names. They're so romantic."

Dionis said impishly. "Do you fancy being called Senora Quexeri?"

Joan Ford colored furiously and laughed as she again made for the door with the tray. "Get away with you!" she exclaimed. "First you try to glamorize me, then you set about getting me a husband. What about yourself? Don Juan is still a bachelor."

"Thanks. But I wouldn't have Don Juan Vicente de Velez y Stebelo for all his wealth. I like Doctor Quexeri. He's less complicated and a perfect pet. So get cracking with that glamor before it's too late," Dionis chuckled.

"The doctor appears to be in great demand."

The deep mocking voice with its alien intonation struck Dionis's heart like a gong. Don Juan was standing in the doorway surveying them both with a narrowed gaze. Dionis flushed to the roots of her hair, wondering how much he had heard of their conversation. His manner gave nothing away. To her instantly alert senses, his lazy air belied the ironic smile hovering on his lips, making her disturbingly aware of him. He really was a very attractive and disturbing personality. She could have hugged

Nurse Ford for her blithe acceptance of his presence. Her blush was for the man himself, for his magnetism and charm she had admitted he had in abundance. His imperious rap on the door had gone unnoticed in their laughter.

Nurse Ford reached the door with her tray. "*Buenos dias*, Don Juan," she said. "The doctor has just left."

"*Buenos dias*, nurse. I have seen him," was the smooth reply. He stood aside for her to pass through the doorway and Dionis longed to call her back for moral support.

"*Buenos dias*, Miss Ward." He strode across the room to the foot of the bed. "I believe you are feeling much better." There was an odd little smile on his lips and she felt a strange undercurrent of actual dislike flowing between them.

She gathered scattered wits. "Yes, I am. I'm very grateful for your hospitality. You've been more than kind."

"Yet you cannot wait to get away." He continued to look at her steadily and to her annoyance she found herself blushing as vividly as Nurse Ford. But not for the same reason. She did not like the man. He was far too superior and discerning. While he would be as relieved as she was to know she was leaving, it was the manner of her going he disapproved of. Having a guest so eager to leave his villa was a new experience for Don Juan de Velez y Stebelo, and one he did not care for.

"There's no point in my staying," she argued. "I've recovered sufficiently not to need the care of a nurse and there's no reason why I shouldn't return to the inn."

His face had hardened and his expression chilled her. "You are far too independent, Miss Ward. A day or so here at the villa would have acclimatized you gently to the heat and you could have returned to resume work on the Villa Acacia with renewed vigor. However," the wide shoulders lifted arrogantly, "since you prefer to leave now there is nothing more to be said. While I appreciate your eagerness to get back to work I am sure you can find the time to look over the Villa Jacaranda with me before you leave. We will take it gently." An odd little gleam came into his dark eyes, tinged with mockery. "Who knows? You might possibly find inspiration in our antiquated décor."

The gesture was so unexpected, Dionis was startled, and looked it. She hardly liked the crack about the décor, but she could hardly blame him. She would have felt the same in his position.

Her smile was very demure. "I'm always willing to learn. If you will give me ten minutes, I shall be very happy to see around the villa."

He was waiting for her at the foot of the fine staircase. Dionis looked down on the tanned rather austere features, saw the momentary gleam of white teeth and felt her face again grow hot. She was as bad as Nurse Ford at blushing at the man, she told herself irritably. The blush receded as he conducted her around.

It was, he explained, a seventeenth-century villa built in the Catalan style. The rooms, high-ceilinged and superbly designed, were ostentatiously beautiful. Dionis looked around with lively interest, noticing how the lacelike alabaster molding and intriguing mosaics of the ceilings contrasted against the plain walls.

"The Moorish influence accounts for that," he said when she commented on it. "Whenever they reclined, the Moors always lifted their eyes to the heavens. So their artistic talents were concentrated upon the ceilings."

Gazing upward, Dionis pictured virile, handsome, swarthy Moors lying on their backs admiring the décor of the ceiling as they would a beautiful woman. It occurred to her as she looked that the Moorish influence was still predominant in the Spanish people. Don Juan with his expressive dark eyes and mobile sensitive nostrils would have looked the part when dressed in the flowing robes and fabulous earrings of his ancestors. Was he as cruel as they had been? Or had his breeding toned down that streak in him? He was a Spaniard, nevertheless.

Beauty was the theme throughout the villa—a cool gracious beauty of priceless cabinets gleaming with objets d'art, elegant furniture unique in shape and design, exquisitely upholstered in delicately lovely colors. Floor vases and pedestals held flower arrangements. Here and there were rich rugs, handmade and priceless—all these delights Dionis saw as she walked enthralled beside her host.

With wide enchanted eyes, she looked upon treasures handed down from generation to generation, mellowed but still perfect, untouched by the gentle fingers of time. Through wide-flung doors leading out onto the patio came strange aromatic scents from the garden.

"It's enchanting!" she breathed, standing motionless on the threshold looking out. Her hair, catching red glints in the sun, framed a vital small face to which only her eyes gave color. When she had started the tour of the villa, Dionis had felt a trifle embarrassed at the thought of competing with such loveliness with her modern décor. But the uncomfortable sensation had vanished in a genuine wave of admiration at all she saw. Scenes like Goya paintings enchanted and now she was gazing on the beauty outdoors. She smiled and her lips parted to show small pearly teeth. "Everything is so beautiful, and now this!" she exclaimed, gazing at the morning light spreading itself over deep awnings and jalousies protecting windows and patios from the heat of the sun. In the sleepy silence trees stood out starkly against the blue sky and purple creepers cascaded down the white walls of the villa.

"You like it?" he asked her.

She turned sparkling eyes to see him leaning negligently against the door, hands in pockets, level dark brows lifted query-wise, watching her.

"It's fabulous! Earlier you implied that the *décor* might provide me with a few ideas for the Villa Acacia. You were right." She gestured toward the grounds with a slim expressive hand. "The contrast of violent and exciting color will be my theme for the Villa Acacia."

"And will your designs live and breathe like the Villa Acacia's former décor?"

"In a way. They'll certainly harmonize with the surroundings!"

He said no more but led her outside to the patio. "I trust you have no designs on the grounds of the villa," he said with a hint of satire.

Against the texture of his white cuff, his hand was brown and firm on her elbow as he turned her along the length of the villa. The faint aroma of a freshly groomed fragrance came to her as he walked beside her with an aloof but attentive impartiality. The walled courtyard with its enchanting fountain, the delicately lovely tiles, the flowering trees and shrubs seemed now to be ironically beautiful.

She thought of the smaller courtyard of the Villa Acacia and the enchanting garden. Then she looked up to find him looking down at her speculatively. She did not like it. The man was making her lose her sense of humor.

"As I said before, I'm an interior decorator. Even if I were an experienced landscape gardener I could never improve upon all the beauty surrounding us. It's a miracle how all this loveliness withstands the test of time."

"One theory could be that the architecture is so much part of the land that it has taken root and is therefore part of it. I like it. The Moors might have been noted for their cruelty, but they left behind them a heritage of beauty which is unsurpassed. It is good that we Spaniards have inherited the appreciation of beautiful things."

"You are pure Spanish, *senor*?"

Dionis looked up at the well-shaped head outlined against the white walls of the villa as they walked. His smile was utterly charming. He gave the impression of being entirely self-sufficient, untouched by lesser important lives such as her own.

"Not entirely," he answered. "I had a great-grand-mother who was English. Incidentally, her name was Victoria and she came from Sussex."

She longed to ask him more. But something held her back, a kind of restraint combined with a wish not to become involved with relationships that could only be temporary and, in his case, only superficial. He would remain untouched by it. They were poles apart and it was better for them to remain so. How tragic it would be to fall in love with him! The color rushed to her pale cheeks at the thought. She avoided his downward listening look to say inconsequently, "It doesn't show. You look decidedly Spanish."

"Does that dismay you?"

The dark eyes flickered over her. He was handsome and virile in the sharp sunlight, erect and sure of himself.

"Why should it?" she answered flippantly, needled by his look of sardonic amusement. "I find the Spanish women delightfully lovely and essentially feminine."

"And the men?"

"Very foreign," she said. The next moment she was uttering a cry of delight at the sight of a tall urn set in a corner of the courtyard overflowing with flowers. Her laughter bubbled up at him like a spring. "Forget-me-nots! My favorite flower. May I?" She ran forward and with a beautiful graceful gesture cupped the falling sprays to inhale their fragrance.

He joined her, amused at her rapture. "Allow me."

She straightened and he gathered the delicate flowers into a neat little posy. Dionis gave him a swift look of surprise, then held out her hands like a child when he gave her the flowers.

"Would you not have preferred roses?" There was a teasing quality in his voice which affected her strangely.

"No, thanks." She looked down at them tenderly.

"Are you always so easily pleased, Miss Ward?"

"But they're my favorite flowers." Her eyes met his levelly. "Surely it's the simple gifts in life that give the most pleasure?"

"You have a garden at home?"

"No. My sister and I share a flat."

They had walked to the end of the villa where a wrought-iron gate was set in a high stone wall leading around to the back gardens. Through the iron tracing, Dionis could see immaculately laid out grounds beyond where a fountain played in the sun.

An old man was trundling a barrow of compost away from them toward the orchards beyond and the air was thick with the perfume of flowering shrubs and trees. Don Juan opened the gate for Dionis to go through, but she was so intent on the beauty of the gardens that she failed to see the step. She stumbled and would have pitched headlong had not his arms whipped out to haul her back against him. The unexpected contact with his lean strong body startled her more than the actual tumble. Excitement raced through her veins like a consuming fire and her heartbeats threatened to choke her. *Now, now*, she upbraided herself, *it's only the reaction at being saved from a bad fall.*

"Sorry," she murmured on regained breath, aware that he could feel the deep throbbing of her heart as he held her against him. "I ought to have looked where I was going. Thanks, *senor*."

"No harm done," he said equably, retaining his hold to give her time to recover.

Dionis wished she could agree with him. It was true as far as he was concerned. Holding her in his arms meant nothing to him. She could feel those years of experience in the strength of him. He was a past master at the game of love, whereas she was only a novice. When he released her Dionis knew he had succeeded in awakening a response in her hitherto unknown in the carefree relationships she had enjoyed with men friends. They walked past the fountain spraying a rainbow of colors in the sun to a shady seat beneath an archway of climbing roses, and because he seemed to expect it, she sat down.

"How is the head? You are feeling well enough to go?" he asked quietly, intent on her bowed head.

"I'm quite recovered, thanks, *senor*," she replied, surprised she was still clutching the posy of forget-me-nots in her hand despite her tumble.

"I still say those forget-me-nots should have been roses," he murmured, reaching up to the arch above her head. The next moment he was offering her a flower, his eyes filled with a curious light.

"Thank you, *senor*," she said, looking at the crimson velvet petals of a half-opened rose.

Her heart gave a curious lurch at the touch of the lean

fingers brushing against her own and her eyes fell from his. She was very conscious of herself and of him, the more so because of the silence that followed as he sat down nonchalantly beside her in the opposite corner of the marble seat. He disturbed her; she could feel his presence even when she was not looking at him.

His next remark startled her profoundly. "What exactly are your plans for the Villa Acacia?"

Dionis hid her discomfiture well. The last thing she had expected or wanted was to have to explain her intentions to the owner of the villa. Normally, she could have done so quite easily, but Don Juan's voice was redolent of disapproval before she began. Dionis had taken it for granted that her sister's and Antonio's ideas coincided with each other's. Don Juan was different. His ideas would only coincide with one other, his own.

"I have a letter from Don Antonio stating that he gives me a free hand in redecorating the villa," she told him. "It's to be done throughout in modern décor. My sister Angela prefers it to be modernized before they marry."

"This idea of Don Antonio having a *novia* is extremely puzzling to me. I have never known him go so far in his affairs before, especially when he is not free."

"What . . . do you mean?" she stammered.

The stilted question came from her lips, but Dionis felt someone else had spoken them. He was frowning now as if there was really something he did not understand.

"Simply that the man is not free to choose a second *novia*. He is already betrothed to a young Spanish woman in Barcelona."

Dionis went paler than ever. Eyes lowered, she said flatly, "I don't believe it. Antonio is engaged to my sister Angela. She has gone to join him in Bermuda, and they plan to marry."

Her fiery glance saw dark eyebrows lifted enlightening like a careful insult and she longed to slap his face. "It's not what you think," she said cuttingly. "My sister is a decent young woman and is not in any way promiscuous. They will be in separate rooms."

"Spare me the details," he said icily. "I have no confirmation of this engagement, nor have I been consulted about these alterations to the Villa Acacia."

Dionis tried to assume a cool indifference, a herculean feat beneath the smoldering gaze of his dark eyes. "Antonio could have written to you. I believe you flit about from one residence to another, so the letter could easily have gone astray."

"Have you met Don Antonio?"

"No, I have not."

"Then you will have no idea what kind of a man he is."

She lifted a chin militantly. "On the contrary. My sister assures me he's a good-hearted young man, and I take her word for it. She's far too clever and discerning to be taken in by a rogue."

"Exactly." The deep voice vibrated on a thread of steel.

"What do you mean, *senor*?" Dionis flashed as anger mounted.

"I believe your sister paid a brief visit here a short while ago." His mouth lifted cynically. "What I heard of that visit was not favorable."

Dionis felt the hot blood rush beneath her skin, lending a sparkle to the long hazel eyes. Her small nostrils dilated. The strain of the last week had pushed her control beyond the limit.

With a burning sense of injustice and a hurt which brought the threat of tears, she blazed, "How dare you judge a person you have never even seen?"

He returned her fiery gaze unperturbed. "I am merely

doing what you have done. You have not met Don Antonio; yet you take your sister's word that he is a good-hearted man. I have done the same regarding your sister."

Dionis was trembling. Her head began to ache and she felt sick and fed up with the whole venture. But if Angela had deceived her, she was still her sister, and no one was going to get away with insulting her. His face was set in a bronze mask. He looked so formidable, so sure of himself that her heart quivered.

"I demand to know what you have been told about Angela," she said shakenly.

He answered laconically as she knew he would. "What I have heard convinces me that they deserve each other."

It was hopeless, she thought, looking at him appalled. It was like trying to get through a brick wall. The intensity of feeling made speech for the moment impossible and she could only stare at him like a bewildered child. She looked down at the flowers in her hand as he leaned back in his seat surveying her coolly. It was evident that he looked on Angela as some kind of an adventuress and probably looked on herself as such too. What he thought about herself was irrelevant. But she was going to put him right about Angela. No one was going to belittle any member of her family unjustly and get away with it!

"I think I can give you a much truer picture of my sister Angela than any casual acquaintance," she began in a strange detached voice hardly recognizable as her own. "To begin with, she's a decent hardworking young woman who is merely rather foolish in her love affairs. She's a buyer in a fashionable West End store in London where she is held in high esteem. I can assure you she's no adventuress. She has been engaged to no less than two millionaires and broken off the engagements herself."

Outwardly he appeared to be in no way impressed. Sitting negligently in his corner, he drummed flexible fingers on the arm of the seat and surveyed her calmly.

"Don Antonio is a long way from being a millionaire, or even a man of means," he said dryly.

"I know nothing about that. The only thing which concerns me is that my sister might be in love with him." Dionis raised eyes from which the sparkle had gone. "I have to take that chance."

By now her head was throbbing and the urge to get away was almost unbearable. Her face was rigid, a pale mask in which her eyes burned beneath leveled brows.

"I am sorry, but I do not share your optimism over this affair," he said at last. "I am inclined to be rather cynical regarding this true love business." His eyes narrowed at her exhausted look. "However, I suggest you go back to the inn and rest. I trust you will be sensible and take the full siesta each day."

Instantly, Dionis was on her feet to walk beside him to the courtyard where the sun shone on the long body of the car. He opened the door and helped her into the front seat, saying, "Your night clothes will be laundered and sent to the inn."

Dionis made no reply. Against such callous indifference, there was nothing she wanted to say. The journey was made in silence and eventually the big car swung into the courtyard of the inn. It was her intention to slip out of her seat before he could come around to her door. In her anxiety to be gone, she fumbled with the lever and the door remained closed despite her efforts.

He said curtly, "Before you go, Miss Ward, I would like the keys to the Villa Acacia, please."

Dionis gave him a wide-eyed incredulous gaze. "I beg your pardon," she said.

He held out a lean hand. "The keys, please," he

repeated. "Do not look so upset. I only wish to make sure that you rest and are fully recovered before you commence work there. We can discuss your work there when you are more fit."

She was shattered. She had expected opposition from him, but nothing so high-handed as this. The urge to throw in her hand and steer clear of the whole business was strong until she thought of Angela. She had to be loyal, and in antagonizing Don Juan, she was doing her sister a great wrong. After all, he had the last word about the villa, and Angela's fiancé was also a distant relative. The sense of conflict between them had to be swept aside. If Don Juan's tenants could find the lighter side to his nature, then he must have one. She would never find it by being openly aggressive. Opening her handbag, she took out the keys and dropped them in his hand.

"*Gracias,*" he said, dropping them into the pocket of his jacket. Then he was leaning over her to release the catch on the door. In her haste to be away she caught the hand holding the flowers against the side of the doorway and scattered them in all directions. Simultaneously, they bent to pick them up. Whether by accident or design, Don Juan's foot obliterated the rose and squashed it flat. He looked at her swiftly, but she kept her eyes on the flowers now intact in her hand. Her voice was barely a whisper when she thanked him and went swiftly indoors.

Senora Lopez greeted her as she entered, eyeing her pale face and worn look anxiously. "How are you, Miss Ward? Better, I hope. We were so sorry to hear about your collapse, but happy to know you were in good hands."

"I'm quite recovered except for a tiresome headache." Dionis smiled wanly. "I never have headaches as a rule. I'll probably feel better tomorrow."

While she spoke, Dionis was on the alert for the sound

of Don Juan's car. It came as she finished speaking and with relief she heard him leave. She had never disliked anyone so much in her life.

"We must take more care of you," the *senora* was saying.

Dionis said firmly, "Please don't think any more about it. I'll be all right. I appreciate you having me here at all when you have to deal with workmen on the premises. You already have enough on your hands without extra work."

"The workmen are not coming for a day or so. Don Juan's orders until you are quite well again. The alterations are temporarily postponed. I also have to make sure you do not go out into the sun for the next two days."

Dionis stared in dismay. "But it isn't necessary for Don Juan to be so high-handed. I can keep out of the sun, but to stop the workmen . . . it's ridiculous!"

The *senora* shrugged. "It is entirely Don Juan's concern, since we rent the inn from him. The alterations are being carried out under his directions. He's a clever and astute man with an eye on the future when there will be more and more tourists coming this way. Don Juan is a very kind and considerate man and we all love him. Now, if you're going upstairs to rest, I will bring you a cool drink."

So the *senora*, like the inhabitants of the surrounding farms, was under the jurisdiction of Don Juan, Dionis mused, going slowly and thoughtfully upstairs. She recalled the short journey to the inn with the big car slowing down when it neared farm entrances where a farmer's wife and sometimes the farmer working with his men acknowledged him courteously. Their dark-complexioned faces had eased into smiles of genuine warmth and affection when Don Juan had driven by, lifting a hand accompanied by his charming smile. Dionis entered her room, closed the door and stood for several thoughtful minutes to review the situation as it stood. Her faculties were suddenly numbed by the immensity of her task. Hitherto the course she had taken had been utterly unknown to her. Undisputedly, she had taken the job of her own accord, but she did not feel that the choice had been wholly hers. It seemed that from now on she also would be under the supervision of Don Juan, who heartily disapproved of her to begin with. Dionis put the small posy of forget-me-nots he had given her into a small glass vase of water and wondered about the rose. Had he stepped on it deliberately, regretting his action in giving it to her? He evidently looked upon Angela and herself as a couple of adventuresses, out for what they could get. She pushed slim fingers through hair that felt too heavy for her head. Her temples ached and she hoped fiercely that she was not going to be ill again. Only by keeping fit and on her toes could she be a match for the exasperating, arrogant Don Juan Vicente de Velez y Stebelo.

CHAPTER FOUR

Dionis was up the next morning and downstairs to breakfast before Senora Lopez could send up a tray. She took her place at the little table beneath the lemon trees. The pleasing aroma of freshly baked rolls and coffee wafted through from the kitchen quarters. Tercia, swinging gracefully across the courtyard with the pitcher of milk, was surprised to see her there. After making the most solicitous inquiries regarding Dionis's attack of sunstroke, she expressed her delight at her recovery. She herself would not have been in such a hurry to leave the Villa Jacaranda and the exciting Don Juan. He was so *simpatico*, so attractive. Did not Dionis agree? When Dionis just smiled she went on enthusiastically.

"Everyone is so happy for him to be here. We see so little of him. Soon we expect to hear that he and Senorita Dolores de Liscondo are affianced."

Tercia, standing poised with the pitcher of milk on her shapely hip, bubbling with the joy of living, made an enchanting picture. Her gypsy earrings and dark liquid eyes along with her soft feminine curves and peach-bloom look gave the impression of her having been brought up barefoot in a happy, sunlit land. Her behavior had been disciplined by loving parents to prepare her for the sweet satisfying role of wife and mother. Lucky Tercia!

"Tercia, do not gossip about *el senor*. I am waiting for the milk."

Senora Lopez appeared in the doorway to shrug apologetically at Dionis before following her daughter indoors. Dionis had to smile. Here like everywhere else in the world over the chief topic of conversation in the feminine community was men. So Don Juan was on the brink of being engaged to a sultry beauty with the delicious name of Dolores de Liscondo. Well, good luck to her! She would certainly need it.

Dionis spent the morning in her room writing letters and catching up with her correspondence. Senora Lopez brought her refreshment mid-morning, inquired how she was feeling and said Don Juan had inquired in a similar vein. Dionis was happy to inform her that she was feeling quite well again and hoped to stay that way. She had apparently slept away her headache of the previous day and was more than thankful. When she went down to lunch there was a letter beside her plate at the small table beneath the lemon trees. The beautiful script was not familiar, so she slipped it into the pocket of her linen dress to read later.

Four German students, who had stopped by for lunch, sat at the next table and spoke to her in perfect English. There were the usual polite exchanges about the weather and the young men talked of their journey through Spain with haversacks on their backs. Between Calpi and Tarragona they had stopped to pick large ripe juicy oranges from the trees by the roadside—it was a recognized custom for passersby to be allowed to pick them and quench their thirst. Looking Dionis over appraisingly, they inquired politely if she was on holiday. Reveling in their excellent English, she replied diplomatically and said she was there at the invitation of a relative.

The young students, big and blond in their shorts, took their leave after lunch. Dionis imagined them taking their siesta by some cool mountain stream before continuing on their way and promptly forgot all about them. Going to her room, she opened the letter. The heading on the

notepaper was in gold lettering, an invitation to dine at
the Villa Inez on the occasion of the silver wedding of
Don Fernando and his wife Inez. A warm feeling of pleasure brought a smile to her lips at the thought. It would be
nice to go out after spending all day at the inn.

Dionis slept through the siesta and awoke feeling
refreshed. Opening the shutters of her windows, she
breathed in the perfumed fragrance of country air. The
shimmering heat of the day had given way to a dry
brilliance where trees stood sharply outlined against the
blue sky with the distant tinkle of goat bells like fairy
music to her ears attuned to city sounds.

At a little after six she had tea in the courtyard, where
she nibbled delicious little pastries and drank hot chocolate. She had become used to life at the inn, the comings
and goings amid shadows, music, laughter and a life rich
in its utter simplicity. This evening, the air seemed to be
full of music. Tercia was singing in the kitchen, a sentimental love song in Spanish, and very faintly Dionis
could hear the soft twang of a guitar. The cat came to rub
gently against her legs, then scampered suddenly to the
kitchen in response to the *senora*'s gentle call. Dionis
refused to think at all of Don Juan or Angela and was
determined to enjoy her little break away from their
demands. She would study her Spanish after tea until it
was time to dress to dine with Don Fernando and his wife.

At nine-thirty Don Fernando's little horse and carriage
arrived, and with the delicate pink chiffon skirt of her
evening dress held high above her silver slippers, Dionis
ran downstairs. Agustin, a large thickset man, who did
odd jobs for Don Fernando, helped her up beside him and
they set off into a night of breathtaking beauty.

Agustin was the type one usually met in a
village—carefree, indifferent to monetary gains, invari-

ably polite and helpful. His natural aptitude for singing on all occasions gave one the opinion that he was a little soft in the head. But to Dionis he was part of this strange and wonderful country. For a while there was no sound save the clip-clop of horses' feet as they sped along beneath a sky alive with stars. Dionis was content to enjoy the beauty of the night, the mysterious shadows broken occasionally by the lights in the houses and the nocturnal scents rising on the cooler air. When Agustin's voice lingered softly on a flamenco, Dionis felt it was the perfect touch, bringing a throbbing ecstasy and delight to the beauty of the night. He sang with feeling in Spanish.

"*Gracias*, Agustin. That was lovely," she said when he helped her down at her destination.

The Villa Inez, Don Fernando's home, was a white belfried building overlooking a valley. From the open door in the brazier-lit patio came the amiable chattering of guests. Dionis was giving the horse the two lumps of sugar she had remembered to bring when Don Fernando came out to greet her.

"*Buenas noches*, Dionis," he said, greeting her warmly. "I trust you have recovered from your illness."

When she assured him that she had, he stood aside for her to enter the house where she was greeted by his wife.

Dona Inez was petite and gentle in her beautiful high-necked lace blouse and flowing skirt. The fine black lace covering her gray hair framed a face full of character and charm. She greeted Dionis kindly when Don Fernando introduced her. As she held out a small white hand her eyes scanned the slender figure in the pink and silver gown, noting the fair skin and long hazel eyes with satisfaction.

"The pain of too much sun has gone, *nina*?" she asked, nodding her head wisely. "You will get used to it, although your lovely fair skin is more enchanting without the tan. I am sure the *senoritas* will look upon it with envy—and I can see you breaking some male Spanish hearts too!" Dona Inez gave an impish smile. "Fortunately, Fernando's heart is long past the breaking stage. Come, I will introduce you to our guests." Her accented English was as delightful as the daintiness of her small hands and tiny narrow feet. Dionis felt the spontaneous warmth of her welcome wrapping around her like a cloak. The beautiful room, cool and spacious with its air of faded elegance, held a calm and dignity that beckoned her in. Dona Inez drew her to the first couple who stood chatting together glass in hand. "You are already acquainted with Doctor Horatio, I believe."

Dionis answered politely, acknowledging the doctor, who congratulated her on her swift recovery. Then Dona Inez was speaking again, introducing his companion, a young Spanish woman who could have been in her late twenties. She would have been good-looking but for the small sloping chin which gave her a birdlike appearance. Her hands were bare of rings, but she had a magnificent diamond brooch at the neck of her high-collared black dress.

Dona Inez said, "My husband's sister, Dona Peralto. Miss Dionis Ward from London."

Dionis looked into dark rather sad eyes. If the woman's manner was reserved, Dionis felt a shy warmth in her greeting. Her black hair, coiled into the nape of her neck, was beautifully smooth and neat and her slightly hooded eyes were made interesting by the thick black lashes. Her nose was short and hooked very slightly. Pity about the sloping chin Dionis thought. It seemed rather out of place with the rest of her face. Dionis wondered if the woman was interested in the doctor. The soft flush on her face might have been heightened by his presence.

Dionis was introduced to the rest of the guests, who included her host's son and his wife. A servant supplied her with a glass of wine and she found Don Fernando at her side. As they drank their wine, he told Dionis that his son Ruiz had been married a year. He and his wife were expecting their first child. Naturally, he and Dona Inez were delighted. Dionis looked toward the daughter-in-law, a plump, glowing young woman who had the appearance of being fed entirely on peaches and grapes. Her young husband was looking at her very tenderly while they drank as though to each other.

Time passed with Dionis mingling with the guests along with Don Fernando. Mechanically counting the guests, she discovered she was odd man out. The fact made her slightly curious, and when Don Fernando escorted her back to his wife, Dionis had a feeling of anti-climax.

Feeling rather strange, she saw Dona Inez turn and followed her eyes toward the door. Someone had just entered, striding in with his usual exciting male vitality. Dionis stood rooted to the spot as Don Juan Stebelo, in top form both physically and mentally, made straight for his hosts. His unexpected appearance was like a hand imprisoning her heart. But she did not pause to wonder why this man entering the room like a cool mountain breeze should have the power to ruin her evening. She only obeyed the sudden urge to move away until the quivering of her nerves had subsided. The chance came when she moved to a table near the door to put down her empty glass on a tray. It was then that the guests moved of one accord toward the dining room.

"*Buenas noches*, Miss Ward. How is the head?"

The cool voice held a smile and Dionis realized with dismay that Don Juan was to escort her in to dinner.

"I'm quite well again, thanks," she replied, adding

meaningly, "I hate having to mark time before starting to work again."

"A pity this zest for work has to find an outlet doing someone else's job," he said cynically.

"One learns by experience," she answered, gathering courage with every word. "I am ready any time to discuss the alternations at the Villa Acacia, *senor*."

"In other words you want the keys?" he commented whimsically.

"If you have no objections."

"Rather late in the day for that, wouldn't you say?"

They had reached their places at the table and he seated her before taking the chair to her left. Dionis made no reply. As she picked up her table napkin with shaking fingers it suddenly became imperative for her to do the job. Returning home without tackling it would leave her forever wondering just how versatile she could be on foreign soil. Apart from letting Angela down, there was a stubborn streak in her, a burning desire to show Don Juan that a woman could be as good as a man in interior decorating.

Doctor Horatio, taking the seat to her right with Dona Pilar beside him, claimed her attention for the moment. When she glanced again at Don Juan he was immersed in conversation with a man on his left. An immaculately dressed cousin of Don Fernando's from Madrid, he appeared to be well informed on world affairs.

Ever conscious of Don Juan's nearness, Dionis gave all her attention to Pilar Peralto and the doctor on her right. Pilar Peralto had an exceptionally high color and her nervousness in the doctor's presence was obvious to Dionis, who did her best to draw her out. Inexperienced though she was, instinct told Dionis that poor Pilar was in love with the big kind man by her side and he could not have been less aware of it. All that was feminine in Dionis longed to shake him into that awareness, and by the end of the meal she had the satisfaction of seeing Pilar's color return to normal.

After dinner, the women went onto the lantern-lit patio where Dionis sat with Dona Inez, her daughter-in-law and Pilar Peralto until the men joined them.

It was then that Dionis escaped into the lantern-lit grounds. She took with her the memory of Pilar looking very attractive with a deep glow of happiness lighting her features when the doctor took Dionis's place beside her. So much for Joan Ford, the little nurse, and their joke about changing her name to that of the doctor. How nice it would be if he did marry Pilar. Unlike Joan Ford, the Spanish woman had little opportunity for meeting suitable males in her inhibited existence. And it would be better for her to marry one of her own kind. There was a difference between the two races of temperament—the English with their cool Saxon strain and the Spanish with their *furia espanola* or Spanish fury. Again she fell to wondering about on Juan. How much of that *furia espanola* was she to encounter in him before her task was done? She had a notion that that icy reserve of his hid volcanic eruptions underneath. A slight movement in the trees reminded her of the huge bird swooping for its prey and Paco's words, skill is better than strength. Quelling a shiver, she thought that Don Juan had both.

The beauty of the garden was something she would not have missed for worlds. Away in the dark blue distance, the hills rose majestically beneath a blue veil of light, deepening to black velvety darkness where it was pricked by the lights of scattered villas or farms. It was like a garden of Eden, for though nothing seemed real, nothing also seemed impossible. Behind her on the patio conversation was laced with laughter, subdued and foreign to her ears. Perhaps she had sensed her own isolation and had escaped of her own accord. But not for long. Someone else was strolling through the garden behind her, someone who was making his presence felt, affecting her physically and mentally in a disturbing fashion.

At last she turned to see Don Juan. The scent of his cigar had alerted her to his male presence. A lean hand, brown against the white texture of his cuff, lifted to remove the cheroot from his mouth. His deep voice when he spoke vibrated quietly on the still evening air.

"Don Fernando and his guests are gathered on the patio, Miss Ward. They wait to hear the song of the nightingales in the garden. The birds will not sing if anyone is wandering about to disturb them. Will you join us?"

Dionis felt her face go hot. Why did he always have her at a disadvantage? Walking beside him, she was aware of everything about him, his erect nonchalant walk, the faint emanation of his masculine fragrance and his powerful and predominant personality. As they approached the warmly lit patio, the guests looked an alien crowd and Dionis felt their dark gaze upon them both as she left Don Juan's side to take a seat beside Don Fernando.

"Did you enjoy the garden?" he asked politely.

"Very much. The loveliness lured me out," she replied, instantly at ease. "I had no idea of the nightingales singing."

Don Fernando studied the tip of his glowing cigar. "I doubt if you disturbed them. From here you looked like an enchanting moonbeam flitting about in the dark places."

The soft buzz of conversation was flowing again as

before, no louder than the muted strumming of a guitar in the far corner of the patio. Gradually conversation dwindled into silence with the guitar being twanged very softly. Then gradually another sound swelled in the silence, the pure trill of liquid notes from feathered throats. The guitar ceased and the nighingales combined their efforts until the beauty of their song mounted to a crescendo of loveliness. The guests sat or stood silently, lost in their spell. When it was over the warm response still lingered in Dionis's eyes. With soft lips gently parted, she lifted her head to gaze out into the garden, seeking a glimpse of the nightingales, but she looked no farther than the brass hanging lamp suspended from the ceiling of the patio as her eyes met the dark glittering ones of Don Juan. For brief electric moments he held her gaze captive before she lowered her eyes. Charmed into forgetting his presence by the liquid notes of the feathered songsters, Dionis was again vitally aware of him. Like several other male guests, he had remained standing to smoke a cigar and was leaning against one of the marble pillars supporting the patio. He had joined in the general conversation, but had not spoken directly to her. Now someone was twanging the guitar again and a pleasing voice sang flamenco softly.

Others followed, all in Spanish, until Don Fernando, moving about among his guests, spoke in the musician's ear. The result was a flamenco song in English for Dionis, who caught Don Juan's mocking smile when it had finished. The party broke up in the small hours with Don Juan keeping himself aloof from Dionis until he was actually taking his leave. Then, to her dismay, he offered her a lift. Her acceptance, coming from a wary heart, was stilted. Don Fernando kissed her hand and she slid into the spacious interior of Don Juan's car, the last guest to depart.

While she had enjoyed the evening and the nightingales, a strange restlessness had invaded her usual calm. Dionis could not define it, but she knew with a quiver that the man sitting so silent beside her accounted for it. As a guest along with him at the Villa Inez, she had felt a sense of equality. There they had been a man and woman meeting on equal terms. Now his silence gave her the feeling of reaching out for something that could never be hers. There was no place for her among these people whose lives had flowed along on tranquil lines long before she arrived and would continue to do so long after she had gone. The young woman from Inglaterra's invasion into their midst would soon be forgotten, except by Don Fernando who had known her father.

Don Juan seemed intent on returning her to the inn as swiftly as possible. In no time at all they were turning into the lantern-lit courtyard.

"Tired, Miss Ward?" he asked, opening her door and looking down into her eyes with the intent way he had, and his smile brightened the gloom. "You will become accustomed to keeping late hours and taking the siesta." He paused, his hand on her arm. "You are fully recovered from your illness? No head pains or dizziness?"

"Quite recovered, thanks. And thanks for bringing me home."

"It is a pleasure." He helped her from the car and because he seemed to expect it she held out her hand. He took it, gave a half bow, and said, "*Buenas noches*, Miss Ward—sleep well."

Dionis was quite unprepared for the cold metal coming in contact with her hand. Foolishly, she stared down at the keys to the Villa Acacia. He had gone before she could thank him.

Dionis awoke the following morning free from the frustration of the last few days. Her heart leapt with joy at the thought of being able to concentrate on her job at last. Leaving her bed, she took a peep at the forget-me-nots in the vase of water to see if any roots had sprouted on the end of the stalks. Silly of her to expect them yet, but everything seemed possible this morning. She must remember to tell Tercia not to throw them away as she wanted to plant them in a small pot and take them back home with her when the time came for her to go.

When Tercia brought her breakfast at the little table in the courtyard she mentioned the flowers.

"But we have forget-me-nots in the garden at the back of the inn. You can have some with roots to plant in a little pot now if you wish," she exclaimed.

"They wouldn't be the same, Tercia. These were a gift, not something I have asked for."

"Ah!" Tercia waggled a finger knowingly. The gypsy earrings gleamed no less bright than her dancing eyes. "It is an admirer who has given them to you!"

Dionis felt the blush steal up from her neck, but was saved the embarrassment of a reply by the sudden appearance of a middle-aged man of medium height whose form was vaguely familiar. Then she remembered him accompanying Tercía that first evening on her visit to her *novio*. He was her father.

"Tercia," he said on a note of command, "you are not to question the *senorita*." When Tercia had fled back to the kitchen, Senor Lopez gave Dionis an apologetic smile. "Tercia is young and full of romance. You must allow for her inquisitiveness."

Dionis smiled. "I am young and romantic too, Senor Lopez, and I find Tercia is adorable. Already I love her."

He nodded understandingly. "It is good to see you do not take offense. Some Englishwomen visitors I have found cold and austere." His smile made him appear boyish and there was a twinkle in his eyes. "However, we live in hopes that our warm sun will melt them into being human before they leave. Enjoy your breakfast, *senorita*, and your day."

At the Villa Acacia, Paco had obviously been busy while she had been away. Disfiguring weeds had been cleared away, revealing pretty pink and white oleander, bright red jasmine and blue plumbago. Bees were humming their appreciation of a tidy hunting ground among flowers tied back neatly against white walls and terraces. Indoors, Dionis decided that the lovely designed ceilings would look impressive in deep tones of color against paler walls. A long curved chaise longue in the lounge would look well with leather and chrome chairs, a really thick carpet in a neutral shade and colorful cushions.

The dining room would be more austere. For instance, a long oval table and matching chairs covered in melamine in a pastel blue would accommodate the maximum number of guests with comparative ease. The ceiling would be in a warm apricot with charming brass hanging lamps to reflect colorfully on the plain white walls.

At twelve o'clock, pleased with her morning's work, Dionis went outdoors to see a perspiring Paco mopping his brow. He was sitting on the garden seat in the shade of the trees. Beside him was a picnic basket.

"*Buenos dias*, Senorita Ward," he said. "Come, sit down in the shade, for when the sun moves around this seat will be too hot to sit on." He smiled as she obeyed and sat beside him. "You are better, *senorita*? Don Juan was angry that I had not let him know about my knee. He said he could have put someone else on the job while I was indisposed." He gave her a sheepish look. "He blamed me, *senorita*, for your collapse."

"Oh dear, Paco! I'm so sorry, and it was all my fault. I told Don Juan so."

She watched him open a flask from the basket and fill two thick mugs with sparkling liquid.

"Lemonade, *senorita*. My wife makes the finest lemonade in Spain." He handed her one of the mugs.

"*Gracias*, Paco." Dionis drank thirstily, reveling in the cold sharpness in her dry throat. "Hmm, it's very good indeed," she said, lowering her mug to look around the tidy grounds. "You've made a very good job of the garden, Paco, and I appreciate it very much."

Paco drew a hand across his mouth after taking a satisfying drink and looked around unimpressed. "There is still much to be done."

Dionis emptied the mug and gave it back to him. "*Gracias*, Paco. That was lovely." She put on the floppy-brimmed hat she had taken off inside the villa. "I'm going back to the inn now and will leave you to it. I'd hate Don Juan to come and find me here at the hottest hour of the day. I'll be back after the siesta." She stood up. "Don't work too hard. And take care of the knee. How is it today?"

"Like a discontented wife, always complaining." He grimaced as though with remembered pain. "I ignore it, and soon it will become tired of having no attention and settle down to work without bothering me."

"Like a discontented wife?" she teased and laughed. Paco laughed too.

The sudden change from grave to gay for which the

Spanish people were gifted amused Dionis. She was still smiling when she arrived back at the inn to be met with a delicious aroma from the kitchen quarters as she went up to her room.

"This is good, *senorita*," Tercia said, arriving as soon as Dionis sat down at the small table in the courtyard for lunch. "There is chicken with rice and peppers cooked only in the best oil and not too heavily spiced for the English palate."

Dionis sniffed appreciatively as Tercia set down an appetizing dish.

"Smells wonderful," she said lightly, turning her head as a young man entered the courtyard carrying a large square box in his arms.

Tercia drifted toward him, lifted the box lid and peered inside. What she saw inside evidently satisfied her, for she nodded her head and gestured toward the kitchen. The young man obeyed, but not before he had flashed his dark eyes at Dionis and whispered something swiftly to Tercia in Spanish. Tercia laughingly shook her head and Dionis saw his cheeky grin before he disappeared into the inn.

Tercia came back to the table to pick up the now empty tray to stand with it on her hip in a typical feminine pose. Her eyes sparkled with fun. "You have an admirer, *senorita*." She shrugged as though in no way surprised. "He is only one of many who have paid you compliments. I refer to the workmen on the alterations at the back of the inn."

"But I've never seen the workmen," exclaimed Dionis in some surprise. "I've only heard them."

"They see you on your way to the Villa Acacia from the roof at the back of the inn where they are working."

"Really?" Dionis tried the paella and found it delicious. So even a quiet country inn had eyes! She gazed upward to the roof of the inn when Tercia had disappeared inside, expecting to see the flashing of teeth and dark eyes. But all was quiet except for a tiny bird peering down at her inquisitively with tiny bright eyes.

CHAPTER FIVE

Dionis dutifully had her siesta and was back again at the villa before Paco had returned. On her way there, she had wondered what treasures were stored amid the furniture at the top of the house. One or two items like floor vases, pretty footstools, or screens would blend beautifully with the décor she had in mind. On her way up to the top of the villa where the furniture was stored, Dionis paused to reflect whether Don Juan would care to loan his furniture to the modern décor. Anyway, she argued, she could ask, and using it was much better than having it in storage. Opening the door of the store room, she saw a miscellany of furniture and heavy gilt-framed oil paintings. Then her eager gaze alighted upon two floor vases, incredibly lovely in shape and design. How fabulous they would look filled with trumpet jasmine in the lounge! Her enthusiasm dampened a little when she saw they were beneath a rather precarious pile of chairs topped by an exquisite lady's writing desk. The small writing table did not look too secure, but she dared not disturb it in case the whole lot collapsed. However, she was slim enough to crawl in beneath the structure and gently ease out the vases.

Cautiously, she crawled forward on all fours, reached out tentatively for the rim of the nearest vase and eased it gently toward her. Within minutes it was free and she placed it down by the door. The second vase was wedged behind a solid table leg and she had to crawl in still farther to reach it. At last, after a great deal of breathless maneuvering the vase was out. In her delight, Dionis forgot caution and on moving out dislodged the chairs hanging precariously above her head. The pile of furniture swayed ominously and before she could put the vase down there was a crash. For pulsating seconds, Dionis stood holding her prize. It was some time before she put the rescued vase down beside the other to look at the collapsed furniture.

The beautiful little lady's writing table had slipped down between the fallen chairs. Gingerly, she moved forward and her hand flew to her mouth in horror. One of the delicately curved legs was buckled grotesquely, snapped off just below where it joined the table top. With a rasping breath of dismay, Dionis straightened to push back her hair with a trembling hand. This was awful, far worse than anything she had dreamed could happen. What was she to do now? As she leaned back miserably against the closed door, she wished she had never entered the room. What an intolerable situation to be in! Anyone with the scantiest knowledge of antiques could see that the thing was valuable, and her own innate honesty would not allow her to keep silent about it.

Why had she had to be so eager? Then as though one catastrophe was not enough, the sound of voices came from the garden. Oh no, it could not be! But there was no mistaking that deep baritone voice. Holding her breath, Dionis listened.

Don Juan sounded lighthearted. "I will find the *senorita*, Paco. *Gracias*."

With her heart threatening to knock a hole in her ribs, Dionis listened to the light firm footsteps as he searched in the downstairs rooms. Those few precious moments gave her time to pull herself together. Leaving the room, she closed the door quietly behind her and went downstairs. She caught him between rooms, hatless and faultlessly attired in a dark suit.

His sudden smile was one of extraordinary charm. His white teeth gleamed.

"Forgive this intrusion," he said politely. "I was passing with my sister and a friend when they expressed the desire to see the Villa Acacia—and you."

He had walked to within feet of where she stood at the foot of the staircase and was immediately frowning at Dionis, who stood petrified, unable to answer. He followed the frown up quickly as was his way and asked with concern, "Are you all right, Miss Ward? You look pale and upset."

Dionis pulled herself together with an effort. His perceptiveness was amazing. She gave a wavering smile. "Yes, thanks, *senor*. My delicate look is deceptive. I'm healthy and quite well."

The pleat between the dark eyes deepened. She had the feeling that he was not altogether satisfied. "Even so," he commented slowly, "I am of the opinion that you have chosen the wrong profession. Something less strenuous, less demanding would have been better in your case."

"But I love my work. I've made a success of it too."

He gave a shrug of distaste. "I would not care for a sister of mine to do such work." His mouth thinned and Dionis caught a glimpse of his virile Moorish ancestors in the cruel set of his mouth as he paused to look around the empty hall. "I see the furniture has been removed; otherwise I am sure you would not have hesitated in tackling part of the job of moving it yourself." He regarded her broodingly. Miserably, it occurred to her that to tell him now of the wrecked writing table would be disastrous. It would only serve to prove his belief that the job was too much for her.

Dionis wrenched her thoughts away from the incident

of the writing table to dwell upon Don Juan's sister and her friend waiting outside the villa. And suddenly there they were.

"Ah, Juan! We wondered what was keeping you."

The words were uttered lightly, seductively in Spanish by a vision of loveliness, one of two young women who appeared in the entrance to the hall. The most dominating of the two, like her companion, was dressed expensively in a model dress of Spanish lace. Her glossy black hair, parted in the center, framed her pretty face with a disciplined smoothness and was knotted in the nape of her rather long neck. Dark eyes beneath strongly marked brows stared curiously at Dionis and her beautifully shaped mouth drooped a little at the corners at the sight of her figure so slender and sweet, her fair skin in strong contrast to her own olive one showing no flaws in the sunlit empty room.

Don Juan said smoothly, "You have already met my sister Rosalba, Miss Ward."

Dionis smiled as Rosalba came forward with dancing dark eyes. Apart from their dark rich coloring, brother and sister were not very much alike, for Don Juan was so essentially masculine and Rosalba so feminine. They were alike in their mannerisms, Dionis thought. Both had that nonchalant well-bred look, the same way of assessing a person with that faint amused smile, so enchanting in Rosalba, so disturbing in Don Juan.

"I trust you have fully recovered from your illness, Miss Ward," Rosalba said in English.

Dionis replied politely in the affirmative and Don Juan introduced Dolores de Liscondo. He was smiling at the slightly taller woman who came forward in a haughty, withdrawn manner. Dionis, looking at the calm impassive features, felt a strange wariness inside her. After Rosalba's warm greeting, Dolores was as chilly as an east wind.

Dolores followed Don Juan's lead and spoke in educated English. "You must pardon our curiosity, Miss Ward, but when Juan told us about you decorating the Villa Acacia we were frankly curious. I wanted to see the English Amazon who dares to take up a man's profession." The long lashes came down in an attempt at demureness, veiling the surreptitious glance at the slim trousered legs.

Dionis had put on her working attire this afternoon, primrose pants with a matching sleeveless top. She met the derisive curl of the *senorita's* red lips with a friendly smile. "It's a woman's profession too," she said without rancor.

"But not as yet in Spain, Miss Ward. We Spanish women prefer to leave the more masculine jobs to the men, who like their women to be absolutely feminine."

"But, Dolores, women in Spain are following professions hitherto dominated by men. We already have two very successful women lawyers practising in Madrid. As for being feminine, I find Miss Ward delightfully so," Rosalba said teasingly and dimpled enchantingly at her brother. "Do you not agree, Juan?"

Don Juan took his time at looking Dionis over. "Miss Ward is certainly no Amazon, although she is determined to prove herself one," he replied at last, his regard openly mocking.

Dolores smiled disdainfully. "I believe practically every Englishwoman smokes and that the majority wear trouser suits like the men."

Dionis lifted her chin. She was not averse to criticism, but the supercilious remarks of the haughty Dolores irritated like an open wound. "There is nothing new in women wearing trousers," she said quietly. "Eastern women have worn the equivalent for thousands of years and Frenchwomen are said to look even more seductive in them." She borrowed Rosalba's impish smile. "I prefer them myself for working in. Not only are they more comfortable, one can bend or climb in them freely without embarrassment."

But Dolores was not to be outdone. "Naturally, when one is doing a man's job," she murmured, "dressing like one is essential."

Here Rosalba came to the rescue and Dionis could have hugged her. "I am sure neither you nor I would look half as attractive in them as Miss Ward does. She is small-boned and very chic in her boyish slimness. My curves, like yours, Dolores, would be rather too obvious."

Dolores pursed her lips primly. "I do not know about you, Rosalba. I would hate to look like a boy."

"I am pleased you are not a boy, Dolores."

Don Juan's eyes twinkled his approval of her feminine charms. No secret here of his admiration for his sister's friend, Dionis thought. His comment partly appeased the Spanish woman, who was now looking around the empty hall. But her target still appeared to be Dionis.

With a look which was openly challenging, she said, "I love this villa and I am sure no improvement could possibly be made on the original furnishings. Would it be presumptuous to ask what exactly you plan to do, Miss Ward?"

Dionis hesitated, hating the idea of disclosing her plans beneath two pairs of critical eyes. Rosalba was sweet and was no malicious meddler. Dionis liked her and knew she would understand. Dionis had a good knowledge of her work and was confident in her ability to make a success of the job in hand. But it was the thought of wandering through the rooms outlining her plans and drawing nearer to where the wrecked writing table was stored that sickened her. Hoping for the best but expecting the worst, she said, "Not at all. Shall we begin with the kitchen?"

She led the way through the downstairs rooms, outlining her plans as she went. Don Juan asked questions with that quick brain of his always one jump ahead of everything she outlined. Behind her façade of coolness, her thoughts chased each other like demented hornets. However, she did manage to draw the line about going upstairs. Returning to the hall after a tour of the downstairs rooms, Dionis stood and gave brief details of the built-in whitewood furniture she had in mind for the bedrooms and the colorful decorations for each bathroom. When she had finished her face was flushed with the awareness of letting her tongue run away with her. It was something she was apt to do when she warmed up to her favorite subject, her work.

Don Juan said dryly, "Thanks for telling us your plans, Miss Ward. It has been most interesting. As far as I can see there is not much you can do until your materials arrive." He glanced at his wristwatch. "Therefore I suggest you accompany us for a run in the car and return later to the Villa Jacaranda for tea."

To Dionis the invitation after the last grueling hour was a bit much. Her smile was quite an effort. "I'm sorry. As I feel rather disheveled I would prefer to return to the inn. Thanks all the same."

"Then you must allow us to offer you a lift." The dark eyebrows lifted in the direction of her floppy-brimmed hat and handbag which she had plunked on the pedestaled rail at the foot of the staircase when she had arrived.

Meekly, Dionis put on the hat and they all walked

outside to the long car glittering in the sunshine. Rosalba and Dolores climbed into the back seat and Dionis was put in front with Don Juan, who slipped in behind the wheel. Paco was hard at work near the gates, his hard-muscled arms stripped to the elbows as he yanked out weeds. Dionis waved and he gave them all a courteous bow. The drive back to the inn was accomplished in silence, with Dionis feeling relegated to the position of being given a lift. She was very conscious of her soiled hands from handling the furniture, her disheveled appearance and shiny nose against the cool fastidiousness of the two young women behind her. Somehow she felt too worn to care.

She still had not told Don Juan about the writing table. Feeling a far different being from the happy young woman who had set off to work so optimistically that morning, she waited until the car purred to a halt in the courtyard of the inn. Then she was out swiftly, thanking Don Juan for the lift and smiling farewell to his sister and her friend.

That evening Dionis wrote down all the materials she would need for the Villa Acacia and wrote a letter to Angela telling her that Don Juan knew nothing of her fiancé's intention to modernize the villa. She made no mention of the dreadful accident to the small writing table—Angela would probably be amused by it. Dionis could imagine her basking on the hot beaches looking fabulous in the briefest of bikinis. To Angela the Villa Acacia was as far away as the moon.

It was a long time before Dionis went to sleep that night. As she tossed and turned in the bed she wondered how her former employer, Cesare Delusi, would have reacted to the incident of the wrecked writing table. She could imagine him offering his sincere apologies and replacing it with something equally expensive. She could not do that. She had not that kind of money. Her mouth curved sweetly when she thought of Cesare. What fun he had been to work for, so enthusiastic over every job be it large or small. Congenitally honest and painstaking in his work, he gave of his best unstintingly. His success had been richly deserved and had in no way spoiled him. He sent checks home to his family in Italy regularly, for he adored his momma and pappa and the six brothers and sisters of which he was the eldest. Thinking of Cesare sent her to sleep with a smile on her lips.

After breakfast the next morning Dionis caught the bus to the village. Her errand was mainly to mail her letters and to buy stamps. The sooner the list of the materials she needed was sent to London the sooner she would receive them. This morning she was not so downcast. How could she be in the brilliantly warm morning of another perfect day? Her piquant face in the frame of chestnut hair showed a lively interest in everything going on around her. Eagerly scanning the view from the bus window, she glimpsed the narrow winding street of the village shops as the bus rounded a bend to draw up in the little market place. Dionis stepped out to a sleepy silence. Deep awnings and closed jalousies protected shop windows from the heat and dazzle of the sun. Walking past a small gift shop displaying pottery and a garage, she reached the post office and was immediately surrounded by children. They clustered around her, staring at her solemnly with large round dark eyes. Dionis smiled down at them, fondled a black curly head and went into the post office. It amused her to see several of the children sidle into the post office to see what she was buying. She bought stamps and handed over her letters, using her halting Spanish to the postmistress who came to ask her requirements.

The woman was delighted that she spoke Spanish. Her plump face beamed.

"You speak Spanish and understand what I say, and you love children. That I can see."

Dionis laughed, saying her Spanish was very limited. But the woman insisted that she spoke it beautifully. The children smiled their approval and suddenly Dionis found the shop full of customers. The arrival of a young woman from Inglaterra was an event—anything was an event that caused a stir in the charmed air pervading the solitude of a country village. And this woman was young, vivacious and full of life with dancing eyes. They treated Dionis as a friend, asked how long she had been in Spain and if she liked it. Warmed by their friendly reception, Dionis talked with them, slipping in a nod or a smile when she met language difficulties. She bought sweets for the children and left the shop charmed and won over completely by the spontaneous welcome of complete strangers.

In the small gift shop, she lingered and bought mementoes, then wandered down to the spotlessly clean little café where gay tables meandered out onto the pavement. There, Dionis agreed with the proprietor that it was indeed a good morning and ordered coffee and cakes. Savoring each blissful moment of the blue and gold morning, she nibbled a delicious pastry leisurely and drank her coffee. The sun was really hot when she gathered her purchases together to make her way to the bus terminus.

Tercia wanted to gossip when she waited upon Dionis at lunch time. She had seen her arrive at the inn the previous afternoon in Don Juan's car. So Don Juan had given the *senorita* a lift. What was it like to ride in such an expensive car? Don Juan was so handsome, so exciting. His sister was so beautiful. Tercia did not care for Dolores de Liscondo.

"She has been angling after Don Juan for years." Tercia wrinkled a small nose in a grimace of dislike. "She gives herself airs, that one. I do not believe any of Don Juan's friends would wish him to marry her. The *senorita* is much too self-centered to make him happy."

"She might love him very much," Dionis suggested.

Tercia shrugged. "Not she. She loves his wealth and social position." Setting the last of the dishes on the table, she stood posing gracefully with the empty tray on her hip. Her eyes held a dreamy look. "Always I have longed for a ride in Don Juan's car." She sighed deeply. "I do not think I ever will."

"I don't see why not." Dionis picked up her soup spoon and gave Tercia a fond smile. "One of these days he will stop to give you a lift. You will see."

But Tercia shook her head. "*El senor* is so seldom around these parts as a rule. At the moment, he is here to see how the alterations to the inn are progressing. Everyone adores him. When he needs workmen, he has only to lift a finger and the men are there. For *el senor*, they will do anything. For anyone else, they would come and go as they pleased."

When Tercia returned to the kitchen, Dionis discovered that her appetite for the well-prepared lunch was nil. The mention of Don Juan had brought back only too vividly the accident to the small writing table. If he was so prompt at getting things done then he would certainly lose no time in having the furniture removed from the Villa Acacia. He was not the kind of man to leave it in storage to deteriorate. She had to see him as soon as possible to explain about the damage to what might well be a family treasure. But how? A letter would take too long. He could act in the meantime. She would have to call and see him personally. The Villa Jacaranda was some distance away, and Spanish women did not go out alone at night, unless accompanied by a duenna. There was this afternoon after the siesta, which left little time before tea.

She was still pondering over how to get there when Tercia returned, aghast to see she had eaten so little.

"Was it not to your taste, *senorita?*" she asked anxiously, removing the practically untouched dishes.

"I'm sorry, Tercia. The lunch as usual is delicious, but I'm not hungry. I think I'm in need of a siesta."

"Are you not well?"

"Yes, of course." Dionis wished she could have confided in Tercia. But it was out of the question. The matter was much too personal. The dark eyes raked her face wonderingly.

"We are going to a *corrida* this evening, *senorita*, a special one for funds to supply the old people with extra food and fuel for the winter. Do you think you will be well enough to come with us? There is a party of us going by bus."

Dionis quelled a sudden shiver. Bullfighting was not in her line and nothing would persuade her to go. Then an idea occurred to her. Watching Tercia fill the tray with the last of the dishes, she asked thoughtfully, "Will it be a private trip? What I mean is, will the coach be calling to pick you up from the inn?"

"*Si, senorita.* The coach will also bring us back to the inn where we shall all have supper. You will come?"

Dionis shook her head. "I'm awfully sorry, I can't go

to the bullfight. But I would appreciate a lift as far as the Villa Jacaranda. My fare could go to the proceeds. Could it be arranged?"

If Tercia thought the request a strange one, she did not comment on it. Instead, she replied with all the airiness of youth, "I do not see why not. I will have a word with the driver of the coach. You will be ready to leave at six o'clock this evening."

There were a few elderly women accompanying the two dozen or so young people in the coach when Dionis clambered aboard that evening. Greetings were exchanged and she took the seat nearest the door in order to slip out when she reached her distination. Tercia sat behind her with her *novio*, a likable young man who strummed a guitar and accompanied it in a good baritone voice. Tercia, a bright peony threaded through her black hair, looked sparkling in a full-skirted dress and open sandals.

Dionis thoroughly enjoyed the ride to the villa; the guitar, the singing amid ripples of laughter brightened an otherwise unenviable journey. She had not the least idea what she was going to say to Don Juan to excuse her carelessness in causing damage to the writing table. Whatever approach she decided upon would disintegrate beneath the steady gaze of a man who was not to be trifled with. On reaching her stop, she alighted and waved the bus out of sight around a bend, realizing with deep, heavy heartbeats that the Villa Jacaranda was but five minutes' walk away. She went forward almost with dragging feet, through the elaborately carved gateway leading to the drive. The place lay in a sleepy silence broken by the soft cheep of birds and the slight rustle of feathery palms. Dionis approached the mammoth residence crowned with graceful eaves still and silent amid the shade of trees and exotic plants. There was no sign of life and instinctively she held her breath, fully prepared to walk on tiptoe in case her footsteps would be heard on the gravel path.

She had reached the magnificent courtyard when the sudden sound of voices on the clear evening air sent her swiftly behind the nearest tree. Three figures appeared without warning in the wide entrance porch—Rosalba, Dolores and Don Juan. Dionis stifled a moan of dismay to see his car standing nearby. They were obviously on their way out for the evening. With a pull at her heartstrings she watched him walk proud and erect with his long easy stride to the car. He looked dangerously attractive in well-cut evening dress as quietly and unobtrusively he opened the car door and assisted his companions inside. Watching him walk around the car to take his place behind the wheel, Dionis knew a wild urge to dash out and stop him before he could set the car in motion. But the idea of explaining her unwarranted intrusion beneath three pairs of startled eyes took more than her kind of courage.

Helplessly, she watched the big car swerve around and sweep along the gravel road until it went from sight. Of course, they could be going to the bullfight if it was for a charitable cause. What bad luck! A few minutes sooner and she might have seen Don Juan before he left. Useless to think of that now. She could not call at the villa and leave a note, for her visit would be sure to raise comment. She could wait for his return and catch him as he was going in. Why not? It was a perfect evening and warm enough to spend outdoors.

With rising spirits Dionis looked around for a suitable

spot away from prying eyes at the villa. She found it in a vast old tree branching out into two thick separate trunks a few feet from the ground forming an obliging curve in which she could recline. Sinking gracefully into the hollow, she found it as accommodating as a hammock.

Closing her eyes with the scents of wild thyme, jasmine and wild roses filling her nostrils deliciously, Dionis felt a calmness of spirit washing over her and she slept. She awoke to a sudden chill in all her limbs, feeling the inadequacy of the little woollen jacket she had unthinkingly slipped on to combat the night chills. Hugging herself for warmth, she sat hunched up, wondering if she had by any chance missed the return of Don Juan to the villa. The Villa Jacaranda still looked silent and deserted with no sign of the car in the courtyard. The rosy glow of early evening had now faded, casting a dark blue curtain over the sky where stars winked at the newly risen moon. Chilled though she was, Dionis allowed her romantic thoughts full rein. What a wonderful place this was for lovers' meeting—a tryst by this beautiful old tree. How many couples had it seen through the years transported to heights of bliss by the welcoming gleam in each other's eyes?

But such dreams did not keep her warm. She was suddenly aware of chattering teeth and it seemed an age before the arc of a car's headlights lit the sky. As it sped along the road hidden from her view, she prayed that it would not pass the turning to the villa. The sigh of relief she gave when the torchlike beams turned in her direction was audible on the night air. Dazedly and numbed with cold, she watched the long body of the car slide past and whisper to a halt in the courtyard. Don Juan sliding from his seat to open the door for his companions was the cue for Dionis to leave her hiding place. She did so painfully, sure that all her joints were frozen solid. Infusing life into stiff limbs, she fled after him as he followed the two women indoors.

Against the muted lights of the villa, Dionis was like a transparent, graceful ghost. Her hair, a cloudy halo, framed a face in which her long eyes gleamed darkly, anxiously. She seemed scarcely to breathe as she reached out silently to touch his arm. He was startled, to say the least, but he took in the situation and rapidly assumed his usual calm. As for Dionis, she stood palpitating and breathless, one hand lifted to put a finger against shaking lips, acutely aware of the man confronting her with a narrowing gaze.

She heard his intake of breath. "*Madre mia!*" he exclaimed. "What has happened? Are you in trouble of some kind?" He removed the hand resting restrainingly on his arm to clasp it in his warm ones. "Why, your hand is frozen! Why are you so cold, and what are you doing here all alone? You are alone, are you not?"

Dionis nodded. She was trembling with cold and another strange emotion she was in no fit state to define. "I must talk to you," she whispered urgently. "I won't keep you long."

He led her indoors to a warm, rather austere room of studded leather furniture. There he seated her in a comfortable chair and strode to a cabinet.

"Drink this. It will warm you," he said, returning with a glass of golden liquid. "Take it slowly." He placed the glass in her cold hands, curling her fingers around it with his warm ones.

Her teeth chattered against the glass and she tried to push it away after a few sips. But his hands were around hers like a vice, forcing her to drink every drop. Then, ordering her to stay put, he strode from the room. He was back in minutes with a wine-colored quilted masculine robe which he helped her into, tucking it around her warmly when she sat down again.

"Now," he said grimly, "you will tell me what has happened." He had perched on the arm of a chair a few feet away from where she sat, his eyes raking her pale face and pinched look. Snug and warm in the dressing robe with the brandy already sending the heat through her body, Dionis was beginning to feel decidedly light-headed. But her brain remained clear as she told him falteringly about the accident to the small writing table. He listened with set features when she described crawling in beneath the furniture to reach the floor vases.

"I took such care not to disturb anything, and I could have died when the pile of furniture suddenly swayed and crashed. The leg of the writing table is beyond repair, I'm afraid. I'm awfully sorry—I would have done anything to prevent it happening." She lifted a face into which the color was gradually returning. "It's a lovely piece of furniture. I suppose it's valuable."

"It was," he corrected her dryly. "However, I accept the fact that accidents will happen." And suddenly he was leaning forward menacingly, angrily. "What I find so hard to accept are these foolish impulsive actions of yours that are continually landing you into trouble. Namely, clearing the garden seat that day in the heat of the sun, struggling beneath furniture that could have trapped and even maimed you, and now this visit to the Villa Acacia alone and at night."

Dionis stared at him wide-eyed and miserable. "I had to come before you had the furniture removed. Don't you see? I couldn't have had the removal men blamed for something I'd done."

"I doubt if they would have been," he argued uncompromisingly. "Who brought you here tonight?"

There was a short uncomfortable silence, one of those silences holding a warning of unpleasantness to follow. Wondering how she could play down the hours of waiting, Dionis knew with despair that she had to tell him the truth. Winding the silk cord of the dressing gown around her fingers as though to gain courage from it, she told him of her journey there in the coach.

His eyes narrowed shrewdly. "At what time did you have this lift?" he asked quietly.

"A little after six. I arrived to see you leaving in the car, and decided to wait for your return."

He looked incredulous and consulted his watch. "*Dios!* All of five hours. Where did you wait?"

"Sitting in a tree."

"You sat in a tree? I cannot believe it. Why did you not call and leave a message for me?"

Dionis moved uncomfortably, for he was looking at her as though she had taken leave of her senses. "I . . . I thought it might arouse comment."

"And this sitting in a tree like a frightened squirrel—that would not have aroused comment? No?" Don Juan frowned. He looked almost savage. His dark eyes gleamed with a fierce intensity.

"No one saw me. I was well hidden among the trees. I had no idea you would be returning so late," she said in a low voice.

"Late?" he echoed exasperatedly. "Eleven-thirty is not late. The night is only just beginning." Dionis felt his gaze on her bowed head. "What if I had not returned until dawn? You would still have waited?"

She made no answer.

"Well?" he demanded firmly.

He did not raise his voice, but there was something in it that made her quiver. She looked up at him then in swift distress. "No, of course not. If only you knew how terribly sorry I am to have caused you all this upset! And now I'm keeping you from your guest. I must go." She sat up as if to rise, but he stayed her with a restraining hand. Dionis felt choked, unlike herself, curiously passive.

"You must have missed supper," he said, and although his look was grim, his voice was free from harshness. "I will get you something."

His words aroused her as nothing else would have done. "No, please, I beg of you. I couldn't eat a thing. I'm not hungry and have never felt less like eating."

Don Juan had risen to his feet. Pushing his hands into his pockets, he stood regarding her silently, and it seemed to Dionis that neither of them breathed.

At last he spoke slowly and forcefully. "I have a mind to forbid you to continue with this work on the Villa Acacia. What do you say to my giving you a check to cover expenses and the time involved? You could spend a holiday here and see everything before going home."

She stared at him aghast. "You mean give it all up when I've already ordered most of the materials? You can't do this to me!"

"Allow me to correct you. I can do as I wish with my own property."

Dionis bit her lip to stop it shaking. His offer had shaken her to the roots. He was right. Wondering how it was all going to end and knowing that this particular job had been doomed from the start, she stared up at him, appalled. With a curious ache in her heart, she realized that in their way of life they were poles apart. Better to have the fact rammed into her now before further complications arose. Sick with disappointment, she freed herself of the robe and stood up, feeling small and defenseless beneath his dark brooding gaze.

"I wonder if you would mind me using your phone to call a taxi from the village?" she asked with a quiet dignity. "I'm sorry I've brought you all this trouble."

He was studying her intently as he would a mathematical problem. To her surprise, when he spoke again his voice was quietly gentle.

"You do not have to apologize for having spent an uncomfortable evening. I will take you back to the inn."

Dionis went with him out to the car. They met no one on the way. All was silent. He helped her into the spacious front seat, tucked a car rug around her warmly and slid in behind the wheel. The car heater was on and she settled back in her seat feeling hollow and spent. Don Juan thrust the long nose of the car forward and soon they were purring along with the headlights lighting up the silent countryside. An owl hooting dismally somewhere above them in the trees found an answering note in her heart. Her visit to the Villa Jacaranda had availed her nothing. Yet she was not sorry. She felt terrible about the wrecked writing table. Somehow it dwarfed all her other problems, this breaking of something valuable that could not be replaced. She would have felt the same in his place, and upon reflection did not blame him in the least for his decision not to allow her to continue at the Villa Acacia. After all, he was not at all happy that his villa should be altered in such a fashion.

Don Juan sat beside her, his profile clear-cut and somehow tight. Dionis tried to assume an air of indifference, found it utterly out of keeping with her sensitive nature and said impulsively, "I really am sorry about your dear little writing table. I'll do anything to put it right."

"You are living dangerously," he answered without taking his eyes from the road ahead. "That impulsive remark can cover quite a few possibilities." He accelerated and the car beams illuminated trees flanking the road. "Forget it and be thankful it was not your leg that was broken."

"I think I would rather have done that than caused all this trouble," she said ruefully.

"I will not have you wishing harm upon yourself. This thing had to be. However, I shall be happier if you have manual help at hand in future to prevent any further incidents. You say you have sent for the materials?"

"Yes."

"Immediately they arrive, you are to let me know. I will see that you have assistance. You will require painters, decorators, carpenters and a carpet-laying expert. Am I right?"

"Something like that," she said, her spirits rising as she realized he was going to let her go ahead with her plans. But she had not forgotten Paco's offer of sending along his relatives. It was pushing her luck to tell Don Juan this. However, a promise was a promise.

"Paco has relatives in the trade and I more or less promised I would hire them," she said, glancing hopefully at his profile.

"Paco's relatives are no doubt experienced. There is a building boom going on in Spain at the moment and most skilled men are working at full pressure. The men I have in mind are excellent in their work and will stay until the work is finished. I cannot say the same for Paco's relatives, who will probably come when it suits them, a few evenings a week or weekends."

Don Juan spoke with narrowed gaze on the road ahead. It was right what he said, of course. Most skilled men were apt to go after big contracts, fitting in the smaller jobs in between when it suited them. Dionis did not blame them in the least, though it did prove both frustrating and trying when one was given a limited time to finish a job.

"You are very kind," she said warmly. "I fully appreciate your offer and accept it gratefully."

He tossed her a jaded smile. "Do not worry too much about Paco. Some of his relatives are included among the men I shall send to you. In a rural community such as this most of the inhabitants are related to each other." He paused, then said, "I would be pleased if you would accept the loan of one of my cars during your stay. I have several at the Villa Jacaranda, also an excellent driver on whom you can depend. Carlos is out at this moment taking my sister and her guest to call upon friends."

"That is very kind of you, *senor*, and if the Villa Acacia was very far away from the inn, I would accept with pleasure. As it's only a short pleasant walk away I can manage nicely without a car. Thanks all the same."

His voice was decidedly cooler. "I was thinking of tonight. Had you gone to the Villa Jacaranda and asked Carlos to run you back to the inn when I had left he would have done so gladly. He could then have informed me when I returned of your visit and I would have come to the inn at the earliest opportunity to discuss things with you over a glass of wine."

Dionis caught a hint of censure in his voice. He was no doubt regretting the curtailment of a pleasant evening in the company of his sister's friend through her own unexpected appearance.

"Yes, I'm sorry about that. Your guest perhaps will not take kindly to your absence tonight."

He said suavely, "Spanish women are not so independent and usually accept the absence of their hosts or menfolk without question."

She shot him a swift glance. "I find it hard to believe that your women are so lacking in spirit."

"They have spirit. They can love or hate passionately, but they are rather more subtle about their possessiveness."

"An ideal wife from a man's point of view," Dionis murmured. "I'm surprised you've remained a bachelor for so long."

The moment she had spoken she would have given anything to recall her words.

He digested this with extraordinary calm. Indeed, Dionis was beginning to wonder whether he had heard her when he answered in dry cynical tones.

"I am twenty-nine. Do you consider that past the marrying age?"

"Good gracious, no! As a matter of fact I'm of the opinion that no man is mature enough to marry until he's at least twenty-five."

He favored her with a mocking glance. "Then there is hope for me, would you not say, Miss Ward? Tell me this—at what age would you say a woman is right for marriage?"

"Twenty-one," Dionis answered promptly. "Women usually mature quicker than men."

He said with a hint of satire, "This is all very interesting. Do your powers go as far as giving advice on the kind of partner one should choose?"

Dionis laughed lightheartedly, though she knew no reason why she should feel so happy apart from knowing she could carry on with her job. Her laugh was an enchanting sound, low and husky.

"No. I was only airing my views on the subject," she said demurely.

Something glittered in his dark eyes, a mixture of lively interest and amusement. "How old are you, Miss Ward?"

"Twenty-one."

"Ah, the important age?"

"The age of independence which you so strongly disapprove of in a woman."

"And the ideal age to marry. You have a *novio* in London?"

"A *novio*," Dionis laughed at her stupidity. "A *fiancé*? No, I haven't. My work is my only love."

"Speaking of your work," he said, swinging the big car around to enter the courtyard of the inn, "Senora Direnso, a seamstress of some repute who lives in the village, is very clever with her needle. She would only be too delighted to help you with your soft furnishings."

"Why, thanks, *senor*. I'll remember that."

He switched off the engine and turned in his seat to look at her thoughtfully.

"You are warmer now? No shivers after spending your evening in a tree?"

Dionis had to smile. His answering one rocked her heart. "I feel fine, thanks," she answered.

He slid from the car and Dionis had time to unwrap the car rug from around her legs and step out before he came to help her.

"I have asked Senora Lopez to serve you with hot soup and a little refreshment in your room. But first you must take a hot bath to prevent a likely chill." The dark eyes suddenly gleamed maliciously. "You must not risk a chill which might put you back a few days from this work that you love. *Adios*, Miss Ward. Sleep well."

CHAPTER SIX

Brushing her hair before her mirror the next morning, Dionis found herself recapping the events of the previous evening with the thought of Don Juan awakening a strange, excited emotion inside her. Something had happened to her during that short journey with his wide shoulder touching her own as the car swerved around hazardous bends. Instinctively, she found herself longing, yet dreading, to meet him again. The powerful emotion his presence invariably awoke in her was not love. It was more like a mixture of fear and dismay. There was no doubt that he disapproved of her wholeheartedly. He was only enduring her presence until her job at the Villa Acacia was completed. His suggestion to employ men he could guarantee as being trustworthy had been prompted with the idea of getting the job done in the minimum of time. He was a man who did everything with a purpose—it was to send her packing before she could cause him any more trouble. Besides, she constituted a threat of demoralizing his sister and her woman friend with her ideas of Women's Lib. His sister Rosalba had been reared on graciousness, disciplined by noble gestures and protected from vices by curtailed freedom, and more than likely an arranged marriage was to be her fate. Don Juan would naturally choose a wife like his sister, with soft curves, smooth olive cheeks and eloquent dark eyes that would look reproachfully at him when they had words. He, of course, would have the last one. Yet he would make a wonderful lover, Dionis was sure. She had felt the tenderness in his hands when he had tucked the dressing robe about her and again when he had wrapped her in the car rug to take her back to the inn.

Dionis could understand Angela falling for Antonio if he was as attractive as Juan. Well, she would be leaving Spain with no complications. And she would never come back. If Angela finally settled in Spain she would be sure to make fleeting visits to London to do her shopping. They would see each other, thus saving Dionis the necessity of going to Spain. Soberly, Dionis went down to breakfast, where Tercia was full of the events of the bullfight the previous evening. Dionis listened, but did not encourage her to talk. The last thing she wanted to hear was a description of the bullfight. The very thought of it made her squirm with pity, not only for the poor wretched bull but also for the unfortunate horses. Though well padded, they would feel the fiendish thrust of the bull's horns when it constantly charged.

"It was wonderful, and the matador was so handsome and brave," Tercia said enthusiastically. "You must go to see one before you leave, *senorita*. Everyone goes to see a bullfight when they come to Spain."

Dionis smiled and was silent. To Tercia, bullfighting was the national sport, something to be proud of. Dionis shivered. In her opinion the whole thing was barbarous and did not bear thinking about.

She was in her room after breakfast getting ready to go to the Villa Acacia when a knock came on her door. To her surprise she opened it to see Dolores de Liscondo looking as luscious as a peach. The dark eyes and vivid red mouth, however, held a hint of insolence that immediately put Dionis on her mettle.

"*Buenos dias, senorita*. Did you want to see me? Do come in."

Dionis gestured to the one comfortable chair in the room and closed the door.

Dolores entered, declined to sit and rummaged in her handbag to take out a lace-edged handkerchief. Holding it up by one corner, she dangled it meaningfully.

"I found this handkerchief on a chair in Juan's study this morning. I presumed it was yours, since it bears your initials. I saw you using a similar one when we visited you at the Villa Acacia."

Aware that this was no friendly visit, Dionis reached out a hand. "Thank you. I am sorry you made a special journey to return it. It was not that important."

"I did not make a special journey, Miss Ward. Carlos is driving Rosalba and myself to visit friends. I slipped in to return your handkerchief, leaving Rosalba in the car." The lovely eyes hardened. "I saw you last evening getting into Juan's car. I was standing at my window when you left the villa."

Dionis looked at her with no more than a polite interest, although the hot color crept up beneath her clear skin.

"Really, *senorita*? I had business with Don Juan which does not concern you in the least."

Dolores moved purposefully across the room to lean back against the dressing table to face Dionis. "Anything that concerns Juan concerns me also. You must know we are practically affianced."

Dionis said evenly, "You are both mere acquaintances of mine, therefore I know nothing about your private affairs. Why take the trouble to inform me of them?"

Dolores paled, the small nostrils of her perfect nose distended with hate.

"Because it is essential for you to know that Juan is not as eligible as you appear to believe. He belongs to me."

Dionis looked at the dark smoldering eyes, the set features as Dolores tried to control her emotions, and found she was having to control her own, too. The reason for it could only be the Spanish woman's obvious hatred of herself. It had nothing to do with what she had said. Why should it? What did she care if Don Juan was practically engaged to the woman? She spoke with a quiet dignity.

"I still fail to see what it has to do with me."

"Miss Ward." Dolores was now calm and watchful. Her look was one of having underrated her opponent. "You came alone late last evening to see Juan at the Villa Jacaranda. In Spain women of good breeding do not go abroad at night alone, especially to visit a man. Such an action would be totally misconstrued. Juan would not enlighten you about ignoring the proprieties. It is left to you to behave with decorum while you are here."

Dionis controlled her temper with effort. "*Senorita*," she said coldly, "your action in coming here using the handkerchief as an excuse to see me leaves me a little confused as to the truth of what you say. If there is an understanding between you and Don Juan then it is not necessary to call to see me at all."

The dark eyes flashed. "I wanted to warn you."

"Warn me?" Dionis echoed, staring at the proud haughty face. "You mean to keep away from Don Juan? Can it be a case of what you cannot have yourself no one else shall?"

Dolores drew herself up indignantly. "How dare you?" she cried.

But Dionis was equal to her anger. "And how dare you come here on such an errand? Too bad you didn't know that your precious Juan doesn't like me nor I him. If you ask him he'll tell you so."

116

"Why should I ask him? You attach too much importance to yourself, Miss Ward," Dolores said with hauteur.

"On the contrary, you are attaching too much importance to my presence in Spain. You evidently assume that I'm important enough to constitute a threat to your hopes of marrying Don Juan or you wouldn't have come." Dionis, her face pinched and white, moved to the door. "Frankly, *senorita*, I find this conversation extremely distasteful. I would be obliged if you would leave at once."

She opened the door and, to her relief, her visitor swept from the room on a wave of expensive perfume. Closing the door, Dionis walked to the chair and sank into it, conscious of how insidiously the trend of events was pushing her toward greater intimacy with Juan. Had Dolores not come to see her she would have carried on blithely with her job, allowing it to dominate every thought. Now his image was pushing itself back into her mind and from now on she would never be entirely comfortable until they had seen each other for the last time.

Steady, she told herself. Was this the sensible Dionis Ward, the eager interior decorator with a yen to rise in the design world? A woman who until now had never been really interested or deeply stirred by any particular man—who had begun to think she never would.

"You have the gift for this kind of work," Cesare Delusi had told her. "You have a flair for color and design; your ideas are both original and clever and you have the courage to carry them out. There is no reason why you should not reach the top of your profession."

Cesare had seen her as a levelheaded, intelligent person, not at all the kind of woman who would fall for a man she had only known for a matter of days. Thank goodness for Cesare! Plenty of time to think of men and marriage when she had proven herself in her work. With the feeling of having reached a milestone in her life, Dionis put the handkerchief away to be laundered, donned her floppy-brimmed hat to keep out the sun and went out to do battle.

She strolled along the white dusty road to the Villa Acacia in her sun suit of blue and primrose, thrilled at the thought of eventually acquiring a tan. All around her the intermittent trillings of birds and the scent of wild flowers in hedges, on bushes and springing from crannies and boulders filled her with delight. The Villa Acacia slumbered peacefully in the sun and she walked between larkspur, columbine and roses, noting that Paco had done most of the clearing up and was now planting curious little plants which she must remember to ask him the name of. Her visit today was a casual one to open the shutters in all the rooms and let in the sun. The fresh air would penetrate into the floors now that the coverings had been removed and everything would be nice and dry for the new décor.

The villa itself was in an excellent state of repair. There was no smell of damp or condensation when she opened the front door to go up the stairs. Dionis loved the master bedroom with its suite of rooms shut away as it were from the rest of the house. It would be ideal for Angela to spend her honeymoon here. Opening the windows, she went out onto the balcony and looked out across the vineyards and orchard in the distance. There the sun glittered on the metal figure of Olympus set high above the garage roof in the village. What fun it would be to have her own car! Too bad she had no permit to drive in Spain. Phew, but it was warm! Taking off her hat, Dionis ran pearltipped fingers through her hair where it clung damply to her scalp. Suddenly something on the rim of the stone balustrade caught her eye. A small lizard lay asleep in the sun, its tiny hands outstretched on the hot stone. Smiling gently with delight, she gazed down entranced at the tiny creature who, sensing her presence, opened bright eyes before rapidly disappearing down a crevice in the stone. Still smiling, Dionis found herself peering over to see where it had gone and looked down into the dark eyes of Don Juan, who was standing watching her from below. There was a decided lurch to her heart as their eyes met in a little tingling shock that startled her before it was gone in a flash. His amazing vitality was more dominant than ever in the glitter of his dark eyes as Dionis, wondering how long he had been there watching her, waited for him to speak.

"*Buenos dias*, Miss Ward," he said, his smile white against the deep tan of his face. "The moving men are on their way to collect the furniture."

Dionis gathered scattered wits. "*Buenos dias, senor*," she answered gaily, happiness bubbling inside her strangely. "I'll be right down."

He was standing where she had left him in the sunlit courtyard. Again she was aware of his fitness, born of a strenuous life lived largely in the sun. He turned quickly when he heard her light step to stand looking at her until she joined him. It annoyed her that his intent look could move her so profoundly. There was no sign of his car, which was probably the reason she had not heard him arrive.

Swiftly, he interpreted her look around. "I left my car in a lane nearby in case it should be in the way of the moving van." His tone was deliberately casual. "May one ask what it was you were looking at so intently just now on the balcony?" His mouth curved into a smile, seeing again the sun on her chestnut hair, the red lips so sweetly curved and the tender look in the long hazel eyes.

To her annoyance, she blushed. "I was watching a tiny lizard. Unfortunately it disappeared before I could make its acquaintance."

He raised a dark brow in that very attractive way he had. "You were not afraid of it?"

"Goodness, no. It was very sweet." She had to look away then from the glittering intent gaze before she could go on. "The two floor vases I mentioned last evening—could I borrow them? They would go very well with the kind of lounge I have in mind. It would be better than keeping them in storage." Dionis bit her lip, hoping he would not think it cheek on her part to mention them after wrecking the writing table.

"Have them by all means," was the answer, and she was relieved to see he was still smiling. "I suggest we return to the balcony where you saw the small lizard to watch the men loading the furniture. Then, if you see anything else you fancy, just say the word and I will instruct them to leave it behind."

"You mean that, *senor*?" she asked, wide-eyed.

"I seldom say anything I do not mean."

They were smiling at each other when the men arrived, and while he had a word with them, Dionis made her way up to the balcony. Suddenly the villa was an enchanted place with all her antagonism against him gone as though it had never been. She was looking down into the crevice where the tiny lizard had disappeared when he joined her. Silently, he looked down at her sudden confusion and hesitant smile and his own smile was infinitely charming.

Dionis was glad that the moving men took his attention, for she felt a sudden unaccountable shyness as she stood beside his wide shoulder. The men had emptied the van of packing and were now mounting the stairs to bring down the furniture. Nervously, she waited for the wrecked writing table to appear, knowing how embarrassed she would be when it did. When it was not among the first half dozen articles to be brought out, Dionis could only think it had been put to one side to be sent away later for repair. When one of the three men carried out a carved ebony pedestal, Don Juan slanted her a glance. "What about that? I believe pedestals are often used in modern décor to good effect?" he asked with a twinkle.

"Yes, please. It will look charming."

"With the chest?" he finished for her, noticing her eyes on a beautifully matching chest the other two men were taking to the van.

"May I?" she asked delightedly.

Dionis saw him give the man a signal with mixed feelings. This was something she had never expected in her wildest dreams, Don Juan not only allowing the modern décor but taking a hand in it too.

"I know a little bit about modern décor," he said, catching her surprised glance. "The last exhibition in Madrid drew large crowds. I went myself. I am not saying I prefer it or even condone it. To me this modern trend is entirely without charm or character." He gave an alien shrug. "I admit that some of it is brilliantly designed and sculptured, but none of it has any soul. I prefer the graceful charm of elegant furniture and buildings created by men dedicated to their job. I remember as a boy experiencing a warm feeling of security in the solid background of my home, as if my ancestors were still around giving me an example of something to look up to and be proud of."

Dionis, warmed by his sudden confidence, said impulsively, "You've been to London, *senor*?"

"Quite often. I go on business. I also took a course in Ancient History at Cambridge. Why?"

"Because it's the place I love best in all the world, and probably for the same reason that you prefer your ancestral home. To me every brick and stone of the old London still lives and breathes." Dionis went on to talk about the dear old Abbey, gray and worn, venerable with age, peopled with ghosts from a glorious past and hallowed by deeds of service. "There's no place in the world so soulstirring, so inspiring as Westminster Abbey for making one feel proud and humble, for giving one an anchor and a reason for being. I understand your sentiments, *senor*, and respect them."

"I believe you do." There was a strange look in his eyes. "I, too, experienced that feeling when I walked in its dimness. Cambridge and Oxford are two other such places. None of the soulless, modern, boxlike buildings built by progress could ever instill that wonderful urge to live up to past glories and to rise above them as the old gracious buildings do."

Dionis laughed softly, happily, an enchanting tinkle of amusement.

"Nothing personal," she said hurriedly at his raised brows. "Like all men, you want to go one better and rise above former deeds of valor."

He became at once teasing and vital. "Why not? It's the natural masculine reaction to deeds of glory. My ancestors, like yours, Miss Ward, were conquerors." He gestured down toward the van. She nodded and the beautiful Chinese screen the men had brought down was put aside at his signal.

Paco was working in the garden when they went downstairs after the moving men had gone. Juan inquired about his knee, congratulated him on his work of setting the garden to rights and suggested several orange trees in tubs to replace the old dilapidated ones in the courtyard. Then, because he appeared to expect it, Dionis walked with him to his car. He smiled down at her as they walked the few paces down the lane to where his car was parked.

He opened the door of the car. "I have the pleasure of taking my sister and her friend to Barcelona for the day tomorrow by car. They are eager to see the bullfight in the afternoon when a famous matador will be the star performer. Have you been to a bullfight, Miss Ward?"

Dionis shivered inwardly. "No."

"Then why not come with us?"

Frantically, Dionis searched for a feasible excuse, aware of his kindness and the fact that he was anxious for her to see the national sport.

"I'm sorry, I'm not a . . . an *aficionada*." She felt her face grow hot. "I think that's the word for a bullfighting fan."

"It is." He sounded mildly curious. "You are not curious to see a bullfight before you leave Spain?"

"I should hate to see an animal killed, *senor*."

"I admire your sentiments, but are you not just a little curious to see the ring? You need not stay for the actual performance. The grand overture when a notable star is taking part is quite impressive. Also you will find much that will interest you in Barcelona. The shops in the Paseo de Garcia would delight you."

Dionis hesitated, not wishing to offend. After all, she was thinking of going to Barcelona to purchase a few materials to carry on with her work at the Villa Acacia before the bulk of her order arrived from London. But a bullfight? Never!

He waited for her answer, his hand on the door of his car. "Perhaps you will think it over and let me know," he said, his eyes on her uncovered head. "Meanwhile I have your promise to always seek Paco's assistance in tasks requiring masculine skill?"

"Yes."

"And I will await your decision about tomorrow."

His tone was negligent, his manner easy enough to enable her to extricate herself without embarrassment. She took advantage of it.

"I have already decided, *senor*. I'm sorry, but thanks for asking me."

He bowed his dark head, making no attempt to persuade her to change her mind. Dionis knew a swift moment of regret as he slid into his car, lifted his hand in a farewell gesture and drove away. Too bad he happened to be going to Barcelona on the day she planned to go. It certainly would not prevent her from going. She would travel by bus. There was no reason why their paths should cross.

CHAPTER SEVEN

That afternoon after her siesta Dionis, in sunsuit, shady hat and sunglasses, went for a walk. There was nothing more to do at the Villa Acacia until her materials arrived. Some of the smaller items she intended to order from Barcelona when she went the next day. Without any set idea as to where she was going she walked leisurely along admiring the view. It occurred to her as she made her way along the white dusty road that the three predominant colors in Spain were black, white and red.

Black for the wearing apparel, white for the villas and cottages, and red for the tropical flowers. There had been heavy rain showers during the night, but the day's heat had dried away all sign of it. All day the sky had persisted in its blueness and everything, trees, vineyards, orchards against a backdrop of distant hills, stood out starkly in the brilliant light. In the blue distance on a hill, she could see a goatherd sitting back against a rock, his head nodding forward in sleep. When several donkeys, heavily panniered, ambled by with their owners, she smiled warmly with a courteous greeting. It was returned with equal warmth. The car came from nowhere to slide silently to a halt beside her. Only Don Juan could drive so expertly, she thought, preparing to meet the dark eyes with a hastily assumed calm she was far from feeling. She felt him take in the pretty sunsuit patterned with white daisies on a blue background, the sunglasses and the wide-brimmed white hat underlined in blue, appraising her cool, poised look.

Leaning sideways, he flicked open the door of the car.

"*Buenas tardes,* Miss Ward. Not walking to Tarragona, by any chance?"

She smiled, annoyed at the heavy drumming of her heart against her ribs. "Not exactly. I fancy it would be a bit too far. I'm enjoying a walk in your wonderful unpolluted air."

"As it happens I am on my way to Tarragona on business that will not keep me long. Would you care to accompany me? We could have tea and you would see a little of a really fascinating city." He lifted a tantalizing brow.

"I'd love to. Thank you very much." Dionis slipped in beside him, every detail of his appearance stamped indelibly on her memory for all time.

He was wearing white slacks with a matching silk shirt opened at the neck to accommodate a crimson silk scarf. His excellently tailored black jacket was monogrammed on the breast pocket and he wore it with a regal air. Again the black, white and red, she mused, his charming appearance bringing a curious ache to her heart.

Relaxing against the expensive leather upholstery, Dionis watched the passing scenery as they purred along pleasurably.

"How are you liking it here in Spain?" he asked casually.

"I love everything about it, especially the sun."

He shot her a brief glance. "You are not weighted down by tradition or irritated by our casual way of living?"

"I do find it strange, but it's an essential part of the charm."

"How long are you staying, Miss Ward? Until the job is done?"

"I suppose so. I'm aching to get started. Hanging about for too long depresses me."

"But you will find time to relax after working hours to enjoy yourself?"

He slowed down to go gently around a donkey carrying a man in a large panama hat.

"Oh yes!" Dionis gave him an impish smile because she felt so lighthearted. "During the siesta."

"One feels you have the hankering to despise our siesta. A Spanish husband would insist upon it." He gave her a speculative glance. "Could you imagine yourself married to a Spaniard?"

"No, I could not," she volunteered firmly.

He raised a brow mockingly. "So emphatic? Yet you have a sister who is engaged to one. You're afraid?"

Dionis did not answer immediately. She was visualizing a siesta spent with him and was shattered by emotions both obscure and disturbing. She wanted to speak of Dolores, but they were not friendly enough to discuss his private affairs.

"Not afraid," she said at last. "Merely cautious."

"You would have me believe you are cautious in love when you are so impulsive by nature. Could it be that you have had an unfortunate experience in love to make you cautious?" He looked for a swift second into her clear eyes, then gave his attention once more to the road. "No, that cannot be it, for you have an innocent, unawakened look."

"Innocent or naïve?"

He laughed. "You have the Spanish temperament already! This quickness to take offense. You blush so easily at the least embarrassment, and also," again the mocking look, "at your own thoughts."

"*Senor!*" she cried, half in dismay. Her color deepened. Heaven forbid that he could read her thoughts!

Suddenly he threw back his head to roar with laughter. After that, everything was easy between them. Juan pointed out places of interest, adding historical details, and she listened, enthralled by his knowledge of his country. When they came to a rise in the road, she found herself looking to the city of Tarragona in the distance. She sat up delightedly.

"It's like something out of the Middle Ages, a study in sepia like a valuable old print," she cried.

He agreed. "In Roman times, Tarragona was an important stronghold. Unfortunately the cathedral is rather crammed in between other buildings, but it is well worth a visit. There is also a monastery about twenty-five miles from the city at Poblet that I would like to take you to see some time. It was built in the twelfth century. The improvements added to it through the years make it one of the most remarkable monasteries in Spain."

They were on the outskirts of the city when he said, "I am dropping you off at a hotel before we enter the town. The idea is for you to enjoy a cool drink while I conduct my business. Then I'll return to pick you up."

He turned the car off the road and up a slope. There were glimpses of a white building between palms and cedars and Dionis heard the sound of running water. Then they were sliding to a halt outside the grand entrance to a hotel, an impressive domed building surrounded by trees and feathery fronds outlined clear and sharp against a vivid blue sky. Don Juan piloted Dionis up the steps and a uniformed porter wearing white gloves swung open the door with an expansive smile. In the reception lounge, Dionis was seated by a window with a panoramic view of the town and the coastline. Juan gave rapid instructions to a waiter, lifted a hand and was gone.

"*El senor* said an iced sherry for the *senorita*," the waiter said, placing a glass of sparkling wine before her with the cool tinkle of ice in its depths.

Dionis thanked him, raised the drink to her lips and found it cool and refreshing. At the far end of the lounge she could see the entrance to a cocktail bar, a long black-tiled room with overhanging bronze lamps echoing the gold of rich furnishings against the black walls. Cool and dim inside, it was occupied by about half a dozen men. Dionis smiled. Was that the reason Juan had put her in the lounge? She was apt to forget that women in Spain were usually chaperoned. Yet despite the courtesy, the old traditions, one could sense a brooding passion beneath the surface, a simmering violence in a country of contrasts. It was there in the beautiful savagery of brilliant exotic blooms that spilled over defiantly, uncontrollably from terraces and stone walls like tempers could do.

Dionis marveled at the calm acceptance of arranged marriages with so much effervescent spirit and emotion simmering beneath the surface. Don Juan would accept it. He was too well disciplined to allow his heart to rule his head. Her thoughts drifted to Dolores and she began to feel strangely hollow inside. Was she envying the woman?

"Another drink, *senorita*?"

The waiter was again at her side as she emptied her glass.

"I think not, *gracias*. I will wait for *el senor*."

"As you wish, *senorita*. The powder room is to the left at the foot of the staircase."

She was seated again where he had left her when he entered the room. Several female heads turned in his direction as he strode across to her. And again it struck her how very attractive he was, so intensely alive with his vitality fusing itself into an outward expression of abundant energy as he reached her with a brilliant smile.

"Did you enjoy your drink, Miss Ward?" he asked politely.

"Very much, thank you, *senor*. It was most refreshing."

"*Bien*. Shall we go?"

He smiled down at her as she rose to her feet and she was very conscious of his hand on her arm as they walked to his car.

Dionis found the walled-in city of Tarragona enchanting. They went through the cathedral and lingered around the shops where Dionis made several purchases of small gifts for friends. Her warm personality and friendly smile captured the hearts of the courteous shopkeepers who were always so eager to please. She chuckled deliciously over her stumbling mistakes in Spanish and her eyes danced. Sometimes Juan murmured a word here and there to help her, and although she blushed with embarrassment when she met his eyes, she had to laugh.

There was a poignant moment in a little bookshop when Juan placed a book in her hand.

Curiously she looked at the spine. "*Platero y Yo*, by Juan Ramon Jimenez," she read aloud, and looked up at him wonderingly.

"I have seen you gazing tenderly on our soft-eyed donkeys," he said, his eyes on her face. "I want you to accept this little book as a memento of the day. It is the life story of a small donkey named Platero. I hope you like it."

Dionis shone up at him her long eyes alight with plea-sure. "Like it?" she echoed. "I'll love it. Thank you very much, *senor*. It's very kind of you." She looked extra-ordinarily young and vividly alive, clasping the book as if it was some valuable prize. Then catching her breath on a bubble of laughter, she said impishly, "It's certainly an incentive to learn your language. Are you appalled at my use of it?"

"On the contrary, I found it very entertaining and refreshing." His smile held a touch of the old mockery. "And now I'm sure you are more than ready for refresh-ment. I suggest we call back at the hotel for tea."

They walked back to his car with Dionis amazed at how the time had flown. Arriving at the hotel, they had tea on the terrace. They sat in white cane chairs softened by gay cushions and a waiter brought them tea and cakes. The other tables were occupied by the usual crowd of smart cosmopolitans one usually meets abroad in the smart places. Someone at the far end of the terrace was strumming a guitar and presently broke out into a flamenco song. It was a strange sad air, infinitely tragic, filling the air with foreboding. So it seemed to Dionis, who sensed a change in the atmosphere between herself and Juan. The intimacy of the last two hours had gone, with Juan presenting her with an enigmatic profile. He had refused the small pastries, had asked her permission to smoke and was now enjoying a cheroot as he gazed out into the distance, deep in thought.

Dionis nibbled a pastry with an absurd desire to run her fingers through his black springy hair, anything to bring his thoughts back to her presence.

"Have you completed your business?" she asked for want of something to say.

Casually, he blew out a line of smoke before giving her his attention.

"I have. Later this evening I am giving a small business dinner at the Villa Jacaranda; then I'll be free tomorrow." He paused and she saw the faint query in his eyes. "You have not changed your mind about going with us to Barcelona tomorrow?"

Dionis shook her head. Already she was feeling guilty at having spent the afternoon with him. There was nothing to be gained by a friendship with Don Juan Vicente de Velez y Stebelo, however casual. And that was all it ever could be. They belonged to different worlds. Perhaps he felt the same, for he said no more. Later, when he returned her to the inn, the firecracker spraying her day with happiness had fizzled away like a damp squib.

Dionis caught the coach to Barcelona the next morning convinced that a complete break away from her problems was what she needed. A day in the city among happy crowds would do much to banish disturbing thoughts. She had endured a surfeit of them since arriving in Spain. With this thought in mind she had packed her bathing suit and towel in a beach bag along with whatever else she would require for her day out and settled down in her seat on the coach to gaze out on familiar country. After a while, the scenery was not so interesting and there was a spell of passing through rather desolate landscape before they reached the outskirts of Barcelona.

Again it was a bright sunny day, enlivening the usual suburbs of a city with its colorful gardens and white villas shuttered and silent in the heat. Soon they were cruising down a wide boulevard of smart cafés and restaurants to the Plaza de Cataluna. The coach pulled in behind a fleet of double-decker buses and Dionis alighted at the terminal.

She found herself in a large square where a fountain, flower beds, trees and statues formed a centerpiece surrounded by buses and trams. Outdoor cafés, office blocks and flats formed a modern backdrop and Dionis responded immediately to the easy-going charm, almost tangible beneath the quickened tempo of city life. Roads radiated from the huge terminus with the tree-lined Paseo de Garcia heading to the west and the obscurity of distant hills and plains. To the east were the Ramblas, a long tree-shaded walk cutting through the faded elegance of the old part of the town.

With the object of buying materials for the small jobs at the Villa Acacia, Dionis lost no time in catching a bus to the shops. She was fortunate to be able to purchase the things she wanted, and after an assurance of an early delivery from obliging assistants, she felt free to enjoy her day. By this time the shops were closing for lunch and the afternoon siesta and the newsstands were doing a brisk trade with last-minute shoppers. Ignoring the posters advertising the bullfight that afternoon, Dionis made a beeline for the beach. Soon she was in a more humble part of the town where tall buildings hemmed in narrow streets of cafés, restaurants and bars frequented by seamen. She came upon the charming little fishing village quite unexpectedly at the end of a steep narrow winding street. Delighted, she gazed upon humble whitewashed dwellings with red roofs and blue shutters in a small secluded bay. In the far corner a formation of over-hanging rocks formed a shallow cave offering shelter from the sun and privacy. The beach was deserted and she made her way happily to the shade of the rocks.

The next half hour swimming in the warm sparkling water was sheer bliss. No one had appeared to disturb her privacy when she trod along the warm sand to sink down contentedly on her towel. The packed lunch given to her by Senora Lopez was enough for three people. Dionis ate leisurely, wrapped in a cocoon of warmth and a silence broken only by the gentle lap of the waves on the shore. Nothing stirred beneath the canopy of blue sky except two ships moving slowly across the horizon. It occurred to her how easy it would be to drift into a lotus-eating existence where cool shuttered rooms beckoned and where energetic movement was confined to long leisurely nights dining with friends. One needed the iron restraint of Don Juan to defy the heat. It did not bother him. He strode through it as he had strode into her life—virile, disturbing and wholly masculine. Her heart ached at the thought of him somewhere perhaps quite near with Dolores.

Dionis bit into the ripe black olive, refusing to recognize the sudden sweep of emotion as jealousy. But it was—a swift thrust of painful emotion she instantly banished as being too ridiculous for words. It made no sense to someone like herself who was not given to swooning over men.

All the same, the thought of him left her not only breathless but stimulated and gloriously alive. But not for her the premonitory pain of unrequited love. Better to dismiss him from her thoughts before he had too big a hold on them. The satisfying lunch and the soft lull of the sea in the warm air made her drowsy. The soft warm sand was as comfortable as a bed and her eyes closed as she snuggled down in it.

Dionis awoke to the sound of whisperings and soft suppressed giggles. Opening her eyes, she saw four small children regarding her solemnly with great black eyes. They were neatly but very poorly clad and were dark, dimpled and delicious. Dionis thought immediately of grapes and peaches and hot sun of which they were the babes. As she sat up their laughter bubbled forth tinkling like hidden mountain springs and they backed away. Dionis hugged her knees.

"*Buenas tardes, ninos,*" she said, looking on them fondly, warmly.

"*Buenas tardes, senorita,*" they replied in chorus, moving nearer as they became bolder.

"*Vuestros nombres, por favor,*" she said, leaning forward for their reply.

"Maria, Carmen, Paquita and José," they answered in turn, each accompanying their name with a little courteous bob.

Dionis chuckled, her heart going out to the small José with his shy smile and tangle of rough black curls. She reached for the remains of the generous lunch, omelette sandwiches, cold meats and fruits, and painstakingly divided them into four equal portions.

They set upon it joyously. Soon every crumb was eaten and she pressed pesetas into each grubby little hand for them to go and buy ice cream. Scurrying away, they turned before leaving the beach to wave farewell. She waved back, consulted her watch and discovered she had slept right through the siesta. Another bathe in the warm sea and she would make her way back to the town.

The tram she boarded was filled with people obviously fresh from their siesta on the way to the bullfight, for they talked volubly of the Plaza de Toros. It was morbid curiosity that prompted her to join the crowd on leaving the tram and make her way toward the Plaza de Toros.

The hot pavement burned through her sandals as she walked past vendors of peanuts, drinks and souvenirs. Then, with a jolt of her heart, she was staring at the round arena. The hot air vibrated with alien cries as she stood near the entrance watching people lining up to enter.

Numbly, she saw them purchase leather cushions to soften the hard impact of the stone seats around the arena. She shuddered. The great round building was symbolic of an alien cruelty and the sudden loud bellowing of young bulls in their corral, unaware of the fate that awaited them, proved too much for her. Dionis moved away on a wave of revulsion, away from the threat of blood and sweat that would be the order of the day from the triumphal entry of the spectacular procession into the bullring to the final killing of the bulls.

Gradually, the horror was forgotten when she strolled along the central walk of the Ramblas, where sunshine filtered through the plane trees, throwing lacy patterns at her feet. It fell on the faded elegance of Spanish architecture and on the bright tiers of banked flowers displayed by vendors lining the route. Dionis enjoyed walking around the gift shops where souvenirs of Spanish workmanship were relatively cheap. The leather work was of the highest quality. She bought gifts for friends and a soft cream leather handbag for Angela, neat, capacious and superbly finished. Her stroll along the tree-shaded walks was made interesting by the poise and graceful carriage of the Spanish women who were exquisitely dressed and well groomed. She also noticed the fastidious appearance of the men, whose footwear was polished to perfection by the *limpiabotas* or shoe-shine men who abounded in the city. Later, she visited the large market, bypassing the meat stalls displaying a gruesome selection of every part of a slaughtered animal's anatomy and was fascinated by the fierce, almost human faces of some of the Mediterranean fish on display.

Small side roads in the Ramblas sheltered fascinating taverns, immaculate and very inviting with their raftered ceilings and brass lamps gleaming softly in shade. Her last dip in the sea had sharpened her appetite and Dionis could not resist the menu they offered. So, sitting at a small immaculately clean table in the tavern of her choice, she ordered the speciality of the day—an old Spanish dish called *zarzuela*. A fish stew, it consisted of lobster, prawns, mussels and other shellfish and was well known for being nourishing and sustaining. It was delicious. At last, replete and just a little guilty at spurning the usual light tea, Dionis set off for the bus terminal.

"Miss Ward? What are you doing here?"

The deep familiar voice caused her heart to move and flutter like a wild bird. Soft pink lips slightly parted, she gazed up into the dark eyes of Don Juan, who was staring down at her incredulously.

"Combining business with pleasure." She smiled because she felt so happy, saw his mouth thin and hastened on, "I came to order materials for the Villa Acacia and have spent the rest of the day sight-seeing."

He frowned broodingly. "Are you alone?"

"Yes," she said blithely. "I'm on my way to the bus terminal."

Dionis saw the slight tautening of his jaw. "The bus? When you might have traveled by car at my invitation?" He allowed himself a leisurely glance at the salt bloom on her cheeks, the beach suit, beach bag, bulging handbag and several gay parcels in her arms. "But why, when you knew I was coming to Barcelona?"

Treating the distinct chill in his manner lightly, Dionis smiled up at him.

"You were going to the bullfight, *senor*, and I didn't wish to inconvenience you in any way. You might have felt obliged to forgo your pleasure and take me around the city. One way or another, I've inconvenienced you far too much already."

Don Juan was as cold as a glacier. He made an impatient gesture with a lean brown hand. "You are much too independent, Miss Ward. I do not care for you to behave in such a manner. As a visitor to this country it is to your benefit that you accept any offer to make your stay here as pleasant as possible. You will return to the inn by car. I insist."

"But . . ." Dionis began to protest, only too aware of her appearance. She felt and looked like a day tripper and would be compared unfavorably with his smart sister and the haughty Dolores. But there was no way of avoiding it. He was already taking her parcels and the beach bag before marching her to where his car was parked. She was put in the spacious front seat with her belongings beside her and he slid behind the wheel. As they sped toward the new part of town, Dionis gazed miserably through her window, bewailing the fact that another quarter of an hour would have seen her on the bus making her own way back to the inn. Where Rosalba and Dolores were, she had no idea. It was sufficient to know that he was going to pick them up.

In no time at all they were cruising along wide modern roads. Traffic moved smoothly in a highly organized fashion with no one abusing the highway code by jockeying for the lead. Presently he turned the car off the road into the parking lot of a rather grand hotel. He helped her from the car and she stared up at a terrace running the whole length of the hotel. Between arched portals waiters were moving between tables supplying guests with tea.

Don Juan was immediately recognized by one of the waiters who came forward to greet him courteously.

"You will please come this way, *senor*. I trust the table is to your liking."

He led them along the beautifully tiled terrace to a table strategically placed to give a view between marble pillars supporting Moorish archways. There was a panoramic view of the immaculate grounds which included the wide sweep of marble steps leading up to the grand entrance.

Don Juan smiled charmingly, approvingly. "*Gracias*, Luis. It will be tea for four, *por favor*."

Luis went to carry out the order while Juan seated Dionis at the table, taking his seat opposite her with consummate ease. Dionis was about to tell him she had already had tea when she saw him looking toward the entrance of the hotel. Following his gaze, she saw Rosalba and Dolores walking up the steps and along the terrace to their table.

"We have put our purchases in the trunk of the car, Juan," Rosalba said as he seated her. Then she was looking at Dionis in pleased surprise. "Miss Ward! How nice to see you." She sat in a pose of incomparable grace, not a hair out of place, soignée and cool in a beautifully tailored dress of black taffeta and lace.

Juan had seated Dolores, and Dionis had not missed the dark burning glance in her direction. The hauteur of her expression, the sudden pouting of the red lips told of her dislike for the woman from Inglaterra. Her brief nod was one of superb arrogance. But the smile she turned on Don Juan was singularly sweet.

"You did not tell us that Miss Ward was to take tea

with us, Juan." The black level brows lifted at Rosalba. "Did you know, Rosalba?"

Don Juan cut in smoothly before his sister could reply, "Miss Ward is in Barcelona for the day. She will be returning with us in the car."

The black brows went up still further. "Did you not come by car, Miss Ward?" Dolores fixed her with a cool stare.

"I came by bus."

Dolores curled her red lips. She could not have looked more surprised had Dionis admitted to traveling to Barcelona in a cattle truck.

"You are accustomed to traveling by bus, Miss Ward. You have no car?"

Dionis said firmly, "No, not at the moment. I'm hoping to acquire one when I return to London. It's essential to my work."

"Ah, yes—your work. You Englishwomen are truly remarkable. You are happy to ride in buses and rub shoulders with *gitanas*. Then you return home to run your own business." Again the brilliant smile on Juan. "Can you imagine Rosalba or me doing these things, Juan?"

He said dryly, "Miss Ward possesses an adventurous spirit. Doing the unconventional emphasizes her independence."

Dolores gave Dionis a spiteful glance. "Would you not agree, Juan, that Miss Ward could benefit from her visit to Spain?"

Don Juan's expression was enigmatic, but Dionis had the idea he was speaking tongue in cheek. "On the contrary, we stand to benefit considerably by her visit to us. She is apparently much talented, exceedingly clever and artistic."

Dolores had an expression of scarcely veiled triumph.

"Juan is not being very complimentary to you, Miss Ward. No Spaniard would ever tell one of his country-women that she was clever or talented. The correct compliment, and one that every Spanish woman expects as her right, would be to tell her she is beautiful." Her smile was knife-edged. "No doubt you are also unaware that Spanish women are encouraged to grow up beautiful, with their femininity encouraged by the use of all the womanly arts which make them so. The boys grow up learning to increase their masculinity by deeds of physical daring and courage. Here in Spain there is no difficulty in recognizing the sexes."

"But, Dolores," Rosalba remonstrated, "no one could dispute Miss Ward's sex. She is so utterly feminine and very pretty. I envy her her English rose complexion. I am sure she will have great difficulty in repulsing admirers during her visit."

The arrival of a waiter with a loaded tray put an end to further conversation. In addition to the tea and tiny pastries, he placed three silver dishes of wild strawberries and cream before the three women. Dionis looked down at her portion with misgiving. Since eating the more than satisfying seafood at the tavern her appetite was nil. Now was the time to say she had already eaten, but something glittering in the dark eyes of Dolores kept her silent. She did, however, refuse the small pastries Rosalba offered.

"No pastries, Miss Ward? Do not tell me you are slimming, with that lovely slender figure." She smiled cajolingly, showing small pearly teeth. "Try one with your strawberries and cream. They are delicious eaten that way."

"Are you not partial to strawberries and cream? You have them in England, I believe. Juan knows Rosalba and I cannot resist them, and he naturally assumed that you cannot either." Dolores flashed him a provocative look. "It is my belief that your guest ate too many tidbits at the bullfight this afternoon. The trays of refreshments were tempting and I noticed many of the English present appeared to never stop eating."

"I am afraid I, like many more of my own people, could not stomach your bullfighting, *senorita*. As for the refreshments, most visitors of any nationality would enjoy the unique experience of sampling them," Dionis said politely.

Rosalba poured out tea. Juan accepted his laced with lemon to say suavely, "Miss Ward does not care for our national sport, Dolores. I gather that was the reason she refused to come with us today."

Rosalba gave Dionis a warm smile. "I am sure you would have enjoyed it. It's all so thrilling and exciting. The matador was so handsome and brave."

Don Juan regarded Dionis steadily across the table. "My sister means that a first-class bullfight can be both novel and entertaining. The pomp and pageantry is most impressive, and a top matador is well worth seeing. He has his performance worked out to a fine art. He reaches perfection via three important channels. The first is known as style or *parer*. To attain this he has to remain impassive when the bull charges. By sheer skill and grace of movement he compels the animal to give way and go around him instead of vice versa. The second skill is known as *mander*, a complete mastery over the bull, every movement calculated to reduce it to wax in his hands. The third is timing or *templar*. Every movement must appear leisurely and completely without fear, never hurried. It is like a banquet where every drop of wine, every tantalizing crumb of food is savored to the last morsel. That is why only a Spaniard can become a first-class bullfighter. Only he has the gift of refusing to be hurried, thus giving the maximum of entertainment."

Dionis had forced herself to listen. To a Spaniard it was no doubt the epitome of entertainment. In her opinion the whole thing was bestial and deplorable.

"Yet for all their leisureliness, your countrymen can be capable of violence and passion. I find that rather confusing," she said quietly.

The dark eyebrows rose mockingly and her heart rocked. "Could be the Moorish strain revealing itself in times of stress or deep emotion. Passion is all the more intense when it is allowed to smolder."

"As I said, Juan." Dolores, tucking into her strawberries and cream, was reinforcing herself for battle. The lovely shoulders lifted. "Miss Ward would never understand our nature. We are of different worlds."

Dionis, eyes lowered to her dish, was aware of Juan changing the subject with a smoothness indicative of his thoughts well away from bullfighting. Beneath his guidance conversation flowed easily with Dionis completely captivated by Rosalba's charm and friendliness. Like her brother, she had the same nonchalant way of listening with a definite twinkle in her lovely dark eyes, so enchanting in her, so disturbing and exciting in Juan. Dionis knew that the impression he made upon her became more vivid with each encounter. So it was hardly surprising to find her stomach behaving strangely before she ate the strawberries and cream. None of the women smoked after their meal and it was left to Juan to give the signal for them to leave when he had finished his cigar.

Dionis was not sorry when they made a move for his car. Despite Rosalba's warm friendliness, she had a feeling of butting in where she was not wanted. Dolores had clearly indicated it, and her presence had not allowed

Dionis to forget it. The silence that fell between them when they were all seated in the big car was a welcome one, although Dionis would have preferred not to have shared the front seat with Juan.

Since her arrival in Spain, she had been fairly cautious about eating strange food. She had eaten sensibly with the knowledge that most Spanish dishes were cooked invariably in oil and as such were a challenge to the strongest of English stomachs. How unwise she had been to eat the strawberries and cream so soon after the substantial meal at the tavern was soon evident by the peculiar way her stomach began to behave as their journey got under way. Several severe pains darted across her stomach with mercurial swiftness. Oh, goodness, she hoped she was not going to be ill before they reached the inn. Juan was driving at a good speed, and for the first time since her arrival in Spain, the scenery meant nothing to her. Rosalba and Dolores were talking quietly in the back of the car and she was thankful that they did not include her in their conversation. She could not have answered them rationally. The agonizing pains in her stomach were coming too frequently for that. Feverishly her eyes sought a landmark through the windshield that would tell her they were nearing the inn, but Don Juan appeared to be taking roads she did not recognize.

Her tenseness could have alerted him to her condition, for he turned his head with a smothered exclamation at the sight of her ashen face as she lay with her head back against the upholstery. There was the sudden movement of hastily applied brakes and he pulled in at the side of the road.

"What is it, Miss Ward? Do you not feel well?" He placed the back of his hand against her forehead and saw the moisture on her temples.

Dionis surfaced from a sea of pain. "I'm sorry," she gasped. "I . . . I feel dreadful. I think it's a tummy upset."

Frowning heavily, he picked up her limp wrist to feel her pulse and leaned forward to reach a compartment in the dashboard on her side of the car. "I have some brandy here. . . ."

"No . . . please," she managed. "I'd be better without anything at the moment. Please drive on. I'll be all right."

Her body was bathed in perspiration as a deadly nausea swept over her. One sip of the brandy and she felt sure she would have disgraced herself forever by vomiting over the immaculate interior of the car.

Juan looked grim. Dolores and Rosalba leaned forward and he turned to speak to them. "Miss Ward is ill." He turned again to Dionis. "I'll be as quick as I can getting you back. If you feel too ill to sit you must lean against me and put your head on my shoulder."

He started the car with another swift look at Dionis, who lay back with closed eyes, hoping she could reach the inn before she passed out. The swift speed of the car, the intermittent pains in her stomach made the rest of the journey a nightmare. She was barely conscious when the car slid to a halt. The last thing she remembered was a faint masculine scent as Juan put his arms beneath her to carry her from the car.

CHAPTER EIGHT

The next two days were ones Dionis was glad to see the end of. Pains tore through her like knives, leaving her head too woolly for coherent thought. Cool practised hands lifted her to give her pills or drinks and Doctor Horatio hovered in a mist of pain. On the third day she began to take notice of her surroundings and found herself once again at the Villa Jacaranda.

"Mediterranean tummy, poor dear," Nurse Ford said. It was the initiation into the Spanish way of life. One had to experience it before becoming acclimatized. Nurse Ford had experienced it herself, so she could sympathize. Dionis, listless and wan, was beginning to think it was the worst thing she ever did to let Angela talk her into coming to Spain. Optimistically, Nurse Ford had brought her breakfast, a lightly boiled egg, some fingers of toast and cherry jam. Dionis managed two fingers of the toast. The day passed with Doctor Horatio calling in the afternoon, looking pleased at her progress. Juan was away on business and was expected back that evening. Dionis went to sleep about ten o'clock that night and awoke the next morning feeling better. She ate her egg and toast and went for a shower. Some of her clothes had been sent from the inn and she put on a pale blue linen dress, deciding to wash her hair later on in the day when she felt up to it. Juan came about eleven. Dionis had a feeling he would come, for her nerves had been unsteady for some time before he strode into the room. Nurse Ford had gone to fetch her mid-morning drink and Dionis sat by the shuttered window doing her nails. She had a fragile paleness, but looked fresh and sweet.

"*Buenos dias*, Miss Ward. How are you?"

Don Juan gave her a thin smile that went nowhere near his eyes and she was sure he was more than fed up with the trouble she had caused him.

A warm flush crept beneath her clear skin to reach the roots of her hair where the heavy waves had been combed to frame her small face becomingly.

"Much better, thank you," she answered. He looked down at the pretty line of her neck, her small head held proudly and the sedate graceful way she sat, appraising the exquisite finish to every detail of her grooming that was part of her elusive charm. But it did not cover the shadowed eyes and wan look of exhaustion.

He said dryly, "I would say your independent spirit and not any feeling of well-being has forced you to leave your bed."

He stood with his back to the window, looking lithe and tanned with his dark hair catching the beams of sun filtering through the shutters. It was not until this moment that Dionis realized how much she had dreaded meeting him again.

She swallowed and plunged. "Being independent yourself, you will understand my anxiety to be up and about as soon as possible in order to relieve you of my presence. You must admit that I have caused you trouble one way or another since I arrived. Most of it has been my own fault too." She replaced the orange stick in her little manicure case, still avoiding his gaze.

There was a short silence during which he digested her remark, then said, "You are merely going through a phase most visitors to this country experience at one time or another. The attack of sun, the sickness brought on by strange food—these things are sometimes unavoidable. And I can assure you that your presence in this house has been no trouble to anyone, least of all to myself. Nurse

Ford has been in her element and has enjoyed looking after you." He paused significantly, his dark eyes very intent upon her bowed head. "There is one thing I would like to clear up. Dolores implied that the remarks I made about you being talented and clever would not be regarded as being very complimentary by a Spanish woman. What Dolores does not know is my first-hand knowledge of your countrymen that prompts me to talk to you as an Englishman would." A warmth crept into his voice. "Had I complimented you as a Spaniard you would have immediately put down my remarks as flattery. I admire courage and you appear to have a surfeit of it, plus a quality of dauntlessness which makes you a rare person." His eyes suddenly became mocking. "I also find you a very irresistible one."

Dionis lifted her head, giving him the benefit of her wide-eyed gaze. Her cheeks were softly flushed with sudden surprise and confusion, her smile hesitant.

"Thank you, *senor*," she said demurely. Her heart was beating like a sledgehammer as she encountered his eloquent eyes. "After all the trouble I've caused you to date, I consider that very noble of you."

He raised a brow, the mocking smile lingering in his eyes. "It was meant sincerely, I assure you."

"I don't doubt it." Dionis, drowning in his intent regard, pulled herself up sharply. "I feel much better today—well enough to make the journey back to the inn."

"The doctor is calling today. He is the one who will say when you are well enough to leave. Unless I am mistaken, I hear him now." He looked toward the door to see the doctor enter followed by Nurse Ford. "*Buenos dias,* doctor," Juan said smoothly. "Had you been an hour or so later, I feel confident your patient would have gone.

Miss Ward can hardly contain herself, so eager is she to return to the inn."

Doctor Horatio strode across the room to smile down on Dionis amiably. "It is good to see you up, *senorita*. How do you feel?"

He took her wrist between his fingers as he spoke and lifted an eyebrow at her quickened pulse. Dionis felt her color deepen. Naturally he would put it down to the presence of the charming Don Juan, and she despised herself to know he would be right.

She avoided the glint in his eye. "The worst seems to be over and I feel much better this morning, doctor—well enough to leave and return to the inn."

The doctor considered this. "Take my advice, *senorita*, and stay indoors today. The rest will do you good." Slowly he turned to Don Juan, releasing her wrist. "I would prescribe a run out in a car tomorrow for the *senorita*." Don Juan nodded and the doctor patted her hand as it lay on the arm of her chair. "Do not be in too big a hurry to deprive people of the pleasure of your company. I leave you in good hands, so I won't call to see you again. Take care of yourself, *senorita*, and enjoy your visit to our country. *Adios*."

Nurse Ford carried a small table and put it down by Dionis. It contained a tray. On it was her mid-morning drink and small pastries.

"Try a pastry with your drink," Nurse Ford advised practically. "You will feel much better and you can afford to eat a few fattening foods with your slender figure. And now, if you will excuse me, I must fly. Doctor Horatio is calling to see my sister and I want to be there. This baby she's expecting is Spanish without a doubt. I never knew one so fond of taking his time at putting in an appearance! It would not surprise me if he did not grow up to be a bullfighter."

"Heaven forbid!" Dionis exclaimed, and Nurse Ford went out laughing.

At lunch time, Dionis ate a light meal of steamed fish, then slept right through the siesta. Later Rosalba came to take tea with her. Dolores had gone out with Juan. He did not call in to see her again that day, but Nurse Ford brought her a message from him with her breakfast the next morning. He was calling for her at ten-thirty to take her for a run in his car. Would she bring a bathing suit, she said, for he was taking her on a picnic.

No mention had been made of his sister or Dolores accompanying them and Dionis wondered if they had other plans. She hoped this was so. Surely to enjoy his company, quite intimately, in the short space of time she would be in Spain, could be neither wrong nor dangerous. She found herself dressing with special care. Perhaps it was the sunshine, or her desire to go outdoors, or the natural feeling of wanting to look her best that made her glad the clothes sent from the inn included a rainbow-striped cotton dress with a soft yoke, yellow buttons and yellow patent leather belt. The soft yellow straw hat and matching sandals she had worn with her beach suit for her visit to Barcelona would go with it nicely.

Dionis awaited his arrival with a delicious expectancy. Nurse Ford had gone to see her sister. The baby had not yet arrived. She was waiting, standing ready with her beach bag when Juan came. Unaware that her confinement indoors had given her fragile prettiness a touching quality, Dionis turned to greet him.

His white silk shirt was open at the neck and a dark blue scarf was tucked neatly inside. The well-tailored black jacket with its monogrammed pocket fitted snugly over his white slacks. He was too vibrantly masculine for any woman to relax completely in his presence, Dionis thought with dismay as with a charming smile he asked if she was fit enough to go on the outing. Picking up her beach bag, he went downstairs with her. After being in bed, her legs felt rather shaky, but the sight of his empty car sent her spirits soaring. At least she would not be bothered by the presence of Dolores.

An hour's drive brought them within sight of the coast, passing villages picturesque and dreaming against a background of purple hills. To her right a long white beach edged by sparkling blue sea gleamed invitingly. Presently, Juan drove the car off the road and onto a grass verge where they looked down onto the beach below. Apart from a handful of bathers at the far end of the cove the place was practically deserted. The air was deliciously tangy when she left the car and a soft warm wind whipped her dress against her slim figure.

Juan carried her beach bag and cupped her elbow to help her through the soft sand between dunes down to the beach.

"You can change here," he said, stopping at a pleasant spot where overhanging rocks and high dunes topped by rough grass offered the maximum of privacy. He left her with a "See you in the water!" and disappeared around the rocks.

Standing alone beneath the vast shimmering blue sky with only the sound of the breakers on the shore, Dionis undressed, shedding not only her clothes but also the slack lethargic feeling following an illness. She found herself responding to the happiness of the morning as a flower responds to the sun. It amused her to think that Juan had taken it for granted that she could swim.

Impishly she hoped the English side of him would accept her bikini, a demure turquoise affair. There was no sign of Juan when she walked along the beach to drop her towel on a dry patch of sand above the tide mark. The sea was warm and buoyant as she struck through it lazily, loving the feel of the water lapping over her limbs. Sensibly, she did not overtax her strength but turned on her back after swimming strongly for quite a distance to rest. How wonderful it was to be where only sun, sea and air mattered, with Don Juan!

Suddenly he was treading water beside her, slicking back his wet hair while drops of water clung to his black lashes and ran down his tanned face.

"Do not go out too far," he warned. "You are not a hundred percent fit. Take care and do not stay in the water too long."

She nodded and he cleaved his way through the water with powerful strokes. When she was pleasantly tired, Dionis made for the beach. She had never felt self-conscious in a bathing suit before, but she found herself hurrying to get to her short toweling jacket before Juan came out of the water. She belted it around her waist to show long slim legs and returned to where she had left her towel to find him already there. Clad in a robe, he was opening a picnic basket.

His smile was white. "I hope you are hungry."

The next half hour was heaven to Dionis, who nibbled chicken sandwiches and drank delicious coffee. Gradually conversation between them had ceased. Dionis did not know about Juan, but she was filled with a delicious languor. She lay back on the warm sand and watched him pack away the remains of their lunch and closed her eyes. Hours later she awakened to find Juan sitting beside her, supported by his hands. His dark eyes narrowed against the glare were concentrated on a ship well out to sea. There was something indicative of waiting in his attitude, something Spanish in his immobility, in his entire absorption of the view before him. Dionis tried not to be so aware of him and failed to be as indifferent as he appeared to be. His personality was such that it was impossible to ignore his presence. She felt relieved that he appeared not bored but detached from his present surroundings. As if aware of her watching him, he turned his head to smile down on her.

"Ready for a drink? We have a full flask of coffee in reserve."

"Lovely," she answered, and sat up eagerly.

Without more ado he was pouring out two steaming cups of coffee and offering her one. Sitting there in the shade of the rocks drinking her coffee, Dionis gave herself up to the joy of the moment with sensuous abandon. Watching the clean-cut line of his jaw, the line of brutality in it, she felt instinctively that his relaxed attitude was that of a man too full of life to be restless. In those quiet moments the male in him seized and dominated her with a curious thrill of pleasure. She sensed the danger and finishing her coffee said it was time she dressed.

She dressed swiftly in the hollow in the sand dunes, but took care with her makeup. In the small mirror her face glowed and her eyes were clear and shining. She was in no way as dark and luscious as Dolores and she wondered if Juan was of the same opinion. Dionis tried to be realistic about him. Bringing her out today meant nothing more to him than taking out a guest. He was not likely to follow it up with other invitations. It occurred to her painfully that the outing was meant to hasten her convalescence in order to give him more time with Dolores. Well, the sooner the better. His masculine charm was far too lethal.

Juan, fully dressed and almost immaculate, leaned against a huge rock smoking a cigar when she emerged from the shelter of the sand dunes. His dark hair had dried crisply and his tanned features glowed from his sojourn in the sun. Straightening, he dropped his cigar, ground his heel into it and taking her beach bag walked with her to the car. Sitting beside him, Dionis watched the road ahead twist and turn beneath his superb guidance. Dark shadows beneath trees changed to dazzling light as they emerged to scenes of distant hills where the outline of old trees stood out grotesquely like abstract paintings.

He was the first to break the silence. "My sister and her friend are out visiting friends for the day. As they will not return in time for dinner I wondered if you would mind dining alone with me."

Dionis hesitated. She had given no thought to the evening. He spoke as though it was an understood thing for her to dine with them all that evening. But to dine alone with him? The very air quivered with crisis. Well, why not? Why should she not hoard felicity against the time when it would be no more?

He was swift to interpret her glance down at her dress. "It is not necessary for you to go to the inn to change. The little dress you are wearing will do. We won't stand on ceremony."

The first thing Dionis saw when she went to her room at the Villa Jacaranda was a note propped up on the dressing table. It was from Nurse Ford to say that her sister had begun labor pains and it seemed that the little bullfighter was on the way. She could not say when she would be back. Dionis smiled happily for Nurse Ford's sister and hoped everything would be all right after her long wait. She did not need the nurse again herself in any case. She walked to the window and pushed open the shutters, filling her lungs with the evening air. Loving the unidentifiable fragrance, she stared in front of her unseeingly. She had set out on her career with the firm conviction that happiness lay in self-fulfillment. Most women sought it in love and marriage. She had wanted to find it in her career. On the whole, her life had been full and rewarding. Her complete absorption in her job, the excitement of each new assignment challenging her skill had swept her along from one week to another on a wave of enthusiasm and joy. When well-meaning friends had introduced her to eligible young men none had been as important to her as her job.

Was it only yesterday that she had wanted to go back to the inn so desperately? Now the opportunity had arisen for her to do so. Why was she so reluctant? The moment of truth was like a jigsaw falling into place. She loved Juan. It was not possible for her not to love him. The hours she had spent with him today had been filled with a divine rapture, a contentment hitherto unknown. From their first meeting he had all the charm and excitement of a completely new experience for her. No man had roused her emotions the way he had. If she had paused to analyze them she would have known without a doubt. Slowly, Dionis lifted shaking hands to her flushed cheeks. Facing the truth with an absolute and final certainty, she felt stunned. Of course, she knew exactly what the position was—how hopeless. Not only was he far above her socially, he was more or less already betrothed to Dolores. There was only one thing to do—freeze out her hopeless yearning for a love that could never be hers, leave the Villa Jacaranda as soon as possible and carry on with her work. When she had finished at the Villa Acacia, she would go home and never look back.

But that evening as she washed and changed to dine with him, Dionis could not banish the sweet exhilarating thought that soon she would be seeing him and talking to him again. Nurse Ford had not put in an appearance when it was time for her to go downstairs. A manservant hovered in the hall. Her heart was gyrating somewhere near her throat, giving her the urge to continue down the stairs and out through the front door away from new and disturbing emotions she had no knowledge of how to suppress. Flags of color stained her cheeks when he stepped forward to show her into the dining room to see Juan pouring out drinks.

He was wearing a dark lounge suit and gave her a smile of extraordinary charm. "*Buenas tardes*, Miss Ward. Not too tired after your picnic?" The dark eyes rested upon her flushed face and overbright eyes politely.

Her heart was slowing down to normal, but her legs felt as if they were not her own as she sat in the chair he drew forward. She accepted the drink, trying to borrow some of his superb confidence.

"Not at all. I enjoyed it immensely. I shall sleep well tonight." Dionis looked down into her glass and saw that it was champagne. "Did you know the nurse had gone to her sister? It seems the baby is due."

He smiled down at her drink in hand, and it came to her that this was how she would remember him, standing apart from all his wealth and family. Not as a figment of her romantic dreams, a Prince Charming, but as a man, the only man to win her heart.

"Yes, I knew. What do you say to drinking to the baby?"

Dionis raised her glass with a curious ache in her heart. "To the little bullfighter."

He raised a brow but drank the toast. "You are sure it is going to be a boy?"

"Nurse Ford appears to think so, because the baby is so slow in arriving."

"And a girl would be more on time?"

"It's generally believed to be so," she said demurely.

He laughed, noting her blush. "Are you fond of children, Miss Ward?"

Dionis swallowed, imagining the utter joy of having his children, chided herself for being a fool and answered calmly, "I love them."

"They are certainly essential to a happy marriage. Tell me—"

He was interrupted by a knock on the door and a man-servant entered at his bidding. "Senor Delusi to see you, senor," he said.

Juan frowned at the unfamiliar name. But Dionis was slowly rising to her feet to put down her half-finished drink with trembling fingers. A slim man of medium height whose olive complexion, black hair and handsome features stamped him unmistakably as a Latin entered the room. Wearing a smart city-going suit, he strode across the room to where she now stood, his face alight with pleasure.

"Dionis! What's all this about you being ill?" He kissed her on both cheeks, then looked at her anxiously. "You are better? Senor Lopez at the inn told me you were here ill in bed."

Dionis drew a deep breath of pleasure mingled with surprise. "I was, Mediterranean tummy, but I've quite recovered. Whatever are you doing here?"

He rolled brown eyes in mock dismay. "What am I

doing here, she asks? Don't you remember? I said I would call to see you on my way to the exhibition in Madrid." Before Dionis could reply, Cesare became aware of the silent figure of Don Juan. "I beg your pardon, *senor*, for butting in like this. I was concerned about my little friend." His frown was speculative. "Have we not met before at an exhibition in Madrid?"

"Possibly," was the cool reply.

Dionis said hurriedly, "Cesare, may I present Senor Juan Stebelo. He owns the Villa Acacia which I have the pleasure of decorating. *Senor*, my former employer, Cesare Delusi, who taught me all I know about interior decorating."

The two men shook hands. "Delighted to meet you, *senor*," Cesare said warmly. "I'm pleased someone is keeping an eye on Dionis." His smile at her was fond. "As for my teaching her, she is a natural at her job. But thank heaven she is not one of those self-sufficient career women who know it all. I can't bear the breed. They go through life like well-coiffured bulldozers. Not Dionis." His fingers touched her flushed cheek with Latin charm. "She is good for a man's ego."

Dionis, happy to see her old friend, dimpled deliciously. "I am afraid the *senor* would not agree with you. I've been an awful nuisance to him since I arrived."

Juan did not answer. He was pouring out a drink for his unexpected visitor. "Please sit down, Signor Delusi," he said politely, handing him the glass. "You are staying to dine with us, of course."

"Thank you, *senor*. I'd be delighted, if it is not inconvenient."

Again Juan did not answer. He merely excused himself and strode from the room.

"Have I interrupted something?" Cesare asked, taking

a chair near to Dionis. "Your host seemed rather distant, though charmingly polite."

Dionis sat down weakly, watching him take down part of his drink. "Good heavens, no!" she answered a shade too emphatically. "Don Juan and I are not exactly close. Rather the reverse." She wrinkled a pretty nose. "Not only does he heartily disapprove of me, he also disapproves of me decorating the Villa Acacia. Angela's fiancé, who rents it from him, didn't see fit to tell him about it. He and Don Juan are distantly related."

"In more ways than one, it seems," Cesare said dryly. He leaned back in his chair and looked at her thoughtfully. "Does that mean there's a deadlock?"

"On the contrary. Don Juan has been most helpful." Dionis went on to tell him all that had occurred.

"So you are now waiting for your materials to arrive," he said when she had finished. "Those you ordered in Barcelona shouldn't take as long as the bulk of them from London. In that case I'll be able to help you get the small jobs done. I don't suppose I'll be here when the other arrives." He raised a brow. "You are going to the exhibition in Madrid next week?"

"Of course. As a matter of fact, I've been looking forward to it. I told you the exhibition was one of the reasons I accepted this job of decorating the Villa Acacia. It's just that. . . ." Dionis broke off, made a futile gesture, feeling she was not very convincing. "Well, things have been happening to push it completely from my mind."

If Cesare thought this an odd remark coming from a young woman who hitherto had thought of nothing but her job, he made no comment. But his pleasant brown eyes narrowed at her slightly before he tossed off the rest of his drink.

CHAPTER NINE

The next day saw Dionis back at the inn where Cesare had booked a room. Senora Lopez had taken him in when he explained his reason for being there. The materials Dionis had ordered from Barcelona had arrived and Cesare went with her to the Villa Acacia. There she outlined her intentions, and he insisted upon carrying them out while she looked on. He appraised everything she had in mind and made great friends with Paco. Dionis had not seen Juan since the evening she had dined with him and Cesare. He had not been at the villa the next morning when she left, but one of his cars had been put at her disposal. Rosalba and Dolores had not been in evidence either.

With Cesare to help, Dionis concentrated on the job at hand. His approval of her plans had lifted her spirits and given her the confidence she needed. A letter came from Angela, who was obviously in high spirits. She asked how Dionis was faring at the villa and mentioned that Tony would write later. Dionis wrote back one evening saying nothing of Juan, but she did say that Cesare had called while on a visit to the exhibition in Madrid.

Dear Cesare, she thought, pausing pen in hand. His presence had helped considerably in putting Juan out of her thoughts. Any future assignments in Spain would be out. She would leave when the job was done never to return. Erasing Juan from her life wouldn't be easy. He had carved too deep a niche to be entirely obliterated. But her job was a great tranquilizer.

She accompanied Cesare to Madrid the following week. They put up at a hotel for three nights, spending their days at the exhibition, their evenings dancing or going to shows. Cesare was in high spirits, finding himself reunited with old acquaintances at the exhibition with whom he chatted, while Dionis wandered around making notes of various interesting exhibits. On these occasions Dionis would find herself looking for Don Juan's immaculate figure. He had been to previous exhibitions, and it was possible that he might attend this one. Each time she saw the back of a lean athletic figure, her heart lurched. She looked in vain.

When she returned to the inn with Cesare a letter awaited her. The order for materials from London had been dispatched and was due to arrive the following day. The next day the workmen Don Juan had promised arrived simultaneously, with Dionis wondering how he knew, for she hadn't contacted him. Cesare, with two weeks left of his holidays, stayed for a week to help Dionis at the Villa Acacia before going to see his family in Italy. With Cesare in charge, everything went smoothly. He had a knack of getting the best out of his workmen. When he left at the end of the week, work at the villa was well under way. Dionis contacted the village seamstress Juan had recommended for the curtains and soft furnishings.

Dionis had written to her sister, Angela, informing her of her progress, intimating that the job was nearing completion. Angela had replied to say she would be happy if Dionis would stay on for a while until she knew the definite date they would return. Dionis received the news with dismay, wanting no delays to keep her in Spain when the job was done. Immediately she wrote back asking for a definite date as every week away from her job in London was important.

So the days passed with Dionis absorbed in her job at

the villa. Most nights she felt too weary to eat her late meal, but at least she was tired enough to fall asleep the moment her head touched the pillow. She derived great comfort from the companionship of Don Fernando, who came to the inn each evening for his cigar and glass of wine. On the brazier-warmed patio, Dionis would sit and talk with him while she waited for her ten o'clock meal. He told her about her father, his likes and dislikes, bringing him so near in spirit that his presence was almost tangible. She had become used to the beauty and natural simplicity of the people her father had loved. His ties with them were ties that could bind her also . . . but she must not think about it. It was Don Fernando who told her of the arrival of Nurse Ford's sister's baby.

"A fine boy, the image of his father. You have not been to see him yet? Nurse will be leaving any time now. Nice woman."

"Yes, she is. I must see her before she leaves to thank her for looking after me when I was ill. I'm so glad about the baby." Dionis colored a little self-consciously. "I've been meaning to go, but I've been so busy lately."

Don Fernando leaned forward to pat her hand. "Never be too busy to visit your friends. You have lost your sparkle, *nina*. Take a day away from your work. You will return much refreshed."

But not happy, Dionis thought bitterly. She longed to ask for news of Juan, but was afraid of betraying her feelings for him if she did. On this particular evening, however, Fernando was in a confiding mood.

"Don Juan has taken his sister and her friend back to Cadiz. Speculation is high as to whether he will marry the *senorita*, who has known him since they were children. It is expected that he will marry soon, because his sister is getting married at the end of the year. Juan will miss her playing hostess to his guests when he entertains. Dona Rosalba will be married in the cathedral in Madrid. Her *novio* is a member of a wealthy aristocratic family and the wedding will be a big event." He imparted the news with an enigmatic expression directed at his cigar. Then he carefully tapped off the long accumulation of ash into an ashtray on a nearby low table. "You would enjoy the wedding, and you are quite welcome to come and stay with us if you wish, *nina*. My wife and I have become very attached to you."

So Rosalba was getting married. Dionis felt her heart lurch painfully as she pictured Dolores as bridesmaid looking provocatively up at Juan in the muted light of the lovely old cathedral. In Cadiz he would be rocking women's hearts with his charming smile, driving the big car at speed along white roads as he took Rosalba and his intended on visits to villas similar to their own. Dining on patios or in cool shuttered rooms, he would probably be smiling tenderly, mockingly, at Dolores, enchanted by her beauty, the dainty movements of her expressive hand, her feminine laughter and excited chatter. Dionis Ward would be far from his thoughts.

"Thank you," she said. "How kind you are. I am fond of you, too. It has meant a great deal to me to know you knew and loved my father. It will always be a bond between us. Maybe one day I'll come back, but not, I think, at the end of the year. By then I'll be up to my ears in work." Dionis swallowed on a lump in her throat as she tried to hide her unhappiness from Don Fernando. "I am a working woman."

"Do not work too hard, *nina*. Work will still be there when you are gone. Enjoy yourself when you can."

After her siesta the following afternoon, Dionis, mindful of Don Fernando's advice, decided to visit Nurse

Ford. The men could work on their own now at the Villa Acacia without consulting her. She waited at the bus stop outside the inn planning to call at the post office in the village for a present for the new baby. On her last visit, Dionis remembered a pretty box decorated with cherubs and blue ribbon that she had seen there. Prettily packed, beneath the transparent wrapping was a baby's brush and comb, rattle, soap and baby powder and a small rubber duck. Dionis was thinking about it when a car slid to a stop in front of her.

"Can I give you a lift, *senorita*?" Doctor Horatio asked with smiling Spanish courtesy.

"If it won't take you out of your way," she answered lightly. "I'm on my way to the Villa Jacaranda."

He raised a brow. "I happen to be going that way myself. I was not aware that Don Juan had returned to take up residence there."

He had opened the door of his car and Dionis slid in beside him.

"I'm going to see Nurse Ford and the baby," she said.

"Then you are bound for Lemon Tree Cottage like myself. Nurse Ford is with her sister and her husband in the small cottage at the end of the driveway leading to the Villa Jacaranda. Don Juan gave them the place when he heard about the baby. He thought they would be happier in a place of their own instead of living at the Villa Jacaranda. The birth was not an easy one, and the baby has had difficulty in taking his food."

"Poor mite," Dionis said sympathetically. "I hope it's nothing serious."

"As the mother is feeding him herself I am of the opinion that her milk is a little rich. He appears to be thriving on it, though, and it is the surest way of bringing up a healthy child."

Soon they reached the village. The doctor waited in the car while Dionis went into the post office for the baby's present. She had looked up her Spanish and was able to ask unfalteringly for what she had in mind. Joy spread across the rather somber expression of the postmistress when Dionis stated her request. Watching her small hands flutter birdlike over the shelves behind her to rest eventually on the pretty box, Dionis smiled. Shopping in Spain was certainly not the businesslike affair it was in London. The *senora* agreed it was an ideal present for a baby and brought down from the shelf another little box containing a woolly jacket in white with blue ribbons. Dionis bought that too. Two women drifted in while the postmistress looked around for wrappings. At last, somewhat reluctantly, so it seemed to Dionis, the presents were wrapped, but not before the two newcomers had purred over them ecstatically. A new baby was a popular topic in any language, she mused. All this had taken time, and Dionis emerged from the shop hoping the doctor was still waiting. He was, patiently. No doubt he knew how long it would take her.

Lemon Tree Cottage was a whitewashed, green-roofed building with blue shutters. Everywhere in the garden were bougainvillea, hydrangeas, white, yellow and red roses, all scattering their scent on the warm air. The front of the cottage, which caught the morning shade, now slumbered in the shade with the shutters open. Stopping the car a short distance away from the cottage in case the baby was asleep, the doctor walked with Dionis toward the rose-covered porch. Suddenly he paused, and Dionis followed the direction of his gaze. Inside the cottage in a room to the left of the porch a woman was clearly visible silhouetted against the white walls. She held the baby in her arms and was lowering it gently into a very pretty cot.

The woman was Don Fernando's sister, Pilar. Taking in the scene, Dionis wondered how she could have thought the woman plain and uninteresting. Pilar's expression was so tender and sweet, so filled with love that Dionis felt a lump rise in her throat.

This new aspect of a woman who held such a capacity for making some man gloriously happy filled Dionis with disgust that men could be so blind. Sighing audibly with exasperation as they turned away, she found the doctor smiling down at her benignly.

"Tired, *senorita*?" he asked.

"Goodness, no. Entranced is more like it. What a beautiful picture Dona Pilar made with the child in her arms."

He nodded. "So you noticed it too. Every woman should have at least one child. It is her natural birthright and the supreme fulfillment of her womanhood."

Dionis said dryly, "Pity Dona Pilar is to be denied that privilege. How unfortuante she is to be among men who go about in blinkers, so blind that they cannot see the prize beneath their nose."

Nurse Ford met them in the porch. "*Buenas tardes*, doctor," she exclaimed. "You've missed my sister by minutes. Her husband has taken her to see his mother, who has been taken ill rather suddenly. Baby has just been fed and he's much better. Dona Pilar has come to tea and is putting him in his cot."

"*Bien*," the doctor nodded. "I will take a look at him. I promise not to wake him."

He strode indoors in the manner of a man who knew his way about and Nurse Ford gave her attention to Dionis.

"Do come in." She led the way indoors. "You appear to have recovered from your illness and are no doubt now fully acclimatized." Her eyes twinkled mischievously, as she added, "We hope!" She gestured Dionis to a comfortable chair in a charming room. "Do sit down while I make tea. I don't know about you, but I'm dying for a cup."

Nurse Ford left the room and Dionis looked around. The ceiling was pale blue with traceries of gold. The colors were repeated in the faded blue and primrose tiled floor covered by a circular rug in pastel colors. The shutters were closed, giving the impression that the room looked out onto the back garden open to the afternoon and evening sun. Fingers of light poked their way between the shutters to gleam richly on brass vases and bowls filled with simple flower arrangements, while dark well-polished furniture gleamed against white walls. There was a restful, happy atmosphere pervading the air and Dionis loved it.

The doctor entered, his broad shoulders giving the room much smaller proportions. He was followed by Pilar, looking decidedly flushed. As for the doctor, Dionis thought he looked ten years younger and very boyish as he smiled down at her.

"It is my half day off. I shall be passing this way in about an hour and a half, and I'd be delighted to give you two a lift home."

"That would be lovely. Do you not think so, Dona Pilar?" Dionis turned a bright smile on Pilar, who nodded shyly. *Why not*, thought Dionis. Each would be a chaperone for the other, all perfectly correct. "*Gracias*, doctor," she said.

"Would you like to see the baby, Miss Ward?"

The doctor had left and Pilar led the way to the nursery.

Dionis sighed ecstatically. "Isn't he lovely?" she whisered, bending over the cot admiring the chubby cheeks, osebud mouth and tiny dimpled hands.

"*Precioso*," murmured Pilar, nodding her head and miling. The tender expression was again on her face and Dionis hoped with all her heart that the doctor had contributed to the happiness in her eyes. It was a bit disappointing for Nurse Ford if she liked the man. She looked anything but disappointed, though, when she carried in the tea. "Have you seen the baby?" she asked brightly. "Isn't he a poppet?" She put down the tray and set about pouring tea. "I shall hate leaving him, but I've overstayed my time already."

Three heads, a black one, a brown one and a chestnut one, bobbed up and down in delighted conversation as they ate the daintily prepared tea. A mounting exhilaration filled Dionis as she laughed gaily at the amusing stories Nurse Ford trotted out about life in a big London hospital. The tea, prolonged with animated conversation, came reluctantly to an end when the sound of a car was heard stopping outside. The doctor was on time. While Nurse Ford went to answer the door Dionis and Pilar prepared to leave. They were standing when Nurse Ford returned with the visitor. Dionis caught her breath in her throat as she recognized the deep familiar voice before the owner promptly appeared.

"So, I have missed Fabrique and his charming wife." Juan was speaking to Nurse Ford in English. "No matter, I have a rather important package I wanted to give Fabrique myself. You will see that he receives it the moment he returns, *por favor*?"

As they entered the room he gave Nurse Ford a long bulky envelope. Then he was greeting Pilar in Spanish, resorting again to English when his dark eyes fell upon Dionis. At once she was vividly aware of his presence and instantly responsive to it. Her observation, sharpened by love, took in every detail of his apearance, the dark eyes that could sparkle with mockery or shut her out with glints of steel, his superb carriage and strength of character.

He addressed her formally. "I trust you have fully recovered from your illness, Miss Ward. Perhaps the visit to the exhibition in Madrid with your friend did much to hasten your recovery." Inexorably, with just the right degree of politeness, he erected a wall between them, topped, Dionis felt, by broken glass. The dark eyes had narrowed, the sharply cut nostrils had thinned. "You appeared to be enjoying yourself when I saw you there."

So he had been to the exhibition after all. And he had left without making his presence known to her. How could he? The revelation was a blow, and Dionis bit her quivering lip.

"I . . . I had no idea you would be going," she managed.

He was still unsmiling. "Naturally, as the owner of property, I keep abreast with the times." His eyes rested for a brief second on her unadorned left hand. "How is work progressing at the Villa Acacia?"

"Very well. Thanks for sending the workmen," she said woodenly.

"I kept a promise," he replied coldly. Then he raised a brow on seeing the three women standing. "Have I interrupted anything?"

"I . . . we . . . Dona Pilar and I are just leaving," Dionis stammered.

"Then may I offer to escort you *senoritas* home? My visit here is fleeting. I am on my way back to Cadiz and can drop you on my way."

Dionis had visions of the doctor on his way to pick them up. She could only surmise that Doctor Horatio was interested in Pilar as a woman. One swift glance at the *senorita*'s impassive face told her nothing. But there was something there that struck Dionis to the heart—a hopeless resignation, an acceptance of a fate that was intent on thwarting all possibility of her ever reaching the altar on some man's arm. There are some moments in life that can alter its whole course for good or ill. Dionis felt this was such a moment for Pilar Peralta. She thought of Doctor Horatio, almost boyish as he offered them a lift home. If they went now with Don Juan the doctor would be hurt. He might even think Pilar had accepted Juan's lift in an effort to avoid him. If he did pride would seal his lips. He would never make his feelings known to the *senorita*.

Dionis lifted eyes eloquent with the poignancy of the situation. "That's very kind of you. But we're waiting for a friend who is calling to pick us up." Her voice was almost inaudible. "We couldn't disappoint him."

His small bow was given with a touch of hauteur. Juan was not accustomed to being refused when he graciously offered two ladies a lift.

"Naturally," he said stiffly. Then with a lithe movement characteristic of him he was addressing Nurse Ford. "Give my regards to the *senor* and the *senora*. You will not forget to give him the package?"

"He shall have it the moment he returns," Nurse Ford assured him.

"*Gracias.* I hope his mother recovers soon. *Adios*, nurse, Dona Pilar, Miss Ward." Another stiff bow and he was gone.

"Well, well!" Nurse Ford exclaimed with her usual

frankness when he had gone. "Here was I wishing I was staying at the inn or somewhere that would necessitate a car ride. To think of sitting beside Don Juan in that fabulous car on an evening such as this! Why, anything could happen!" She sighed good humoredly. "Good thing I'll soon be back to the daily grind. A dish like Don Juan can certainly fill your head with all kinds of romantic notions. He's fabulous! He's given the baby a whopping check that will go toward his education when the time comes. Isn't it sweet of him?"

But Dionis was beyond words. She had snubbed the man and he was not likely to forget it. Doctor Horatio arrived soon after with Nurse Ford waving them off from the porch. When the doctor opened the back door of the car for the two women to sit in the back, Dionis put on her brightest smile.

"Do sit in front with the doctor, Dona Pilar. I'll be getting out before you and you will be company for each other."

They made a charming couple, the *senorita* so sweet, so feminine, and the doctor so broad, strong and protective. So thought Dionis as she looked upon them fondly from the backseat. Somehow she knew that everything female inside her had assessed the situation correctly. It only needed a situation like this with Pilar's narrow shoulder touching his powerful one plus the closed intimacy of the car for him to tell her of his feelings for her. With this in mind, she strove to establish a cordiality between them by chatting amiably and airing her Spanish. Dionis was happy to see them both relaxed when she alighted at the inn and keeping her fingers crossed for Pilar, she waved gaily and went indoors.

Senora Lopez met her at the foot of the stairs. "Don Juan called earlier to see the extension at the back of the inn now that it is finished. He asked about you. As a matter of fact you only missed him by about an hour. He did not ask after Senor Delusi, so I did not inform him of the *senor*'s departure.''

Dionis told Senora Lopez of her visit to see Nurse Ford and the baby and her meeting with Juan. Senora Lopez wanted to hear all about the baby, of course. Later, going up to her room, it occurred to Dionis again what Senora Lopez had said about Cesare leaving the inn. If Juan did not know of his departure he would probably think it was Cesare who was giving Pilar and herself a lift home from Lemon Tree Cottage. His sudden glance at her left hand convinced her of his belief that there was something between her and Cesare, much more than friendship. What did it matter? Pushing her hair back wearily from her face, Dionis realized that this afternoon's encounter with him might well be her last before she left Spain. He had said he was returning to Cadiz. There would be no reason for him to return for a long time now that the extension to the inn was finished. In that moment the pain in her heart was more than she could bear at the thought that she had seen him for the last time. Closing the door of her room, she walked slowly toward the little pot in which she had planted his posy of forget-me-nots. They were thriving, and as she bent over them the tears fell.

CHAPTER TEN

The day had begun like any other day at the inn. Dionis arose early, showered and donned her working attire, slacks and a pretty top and went down to breakfast. Senora Lopez brought her breakfast this morning. Tercia had gone with her father to pay a duty visit to his parents. There was a letter for Dionis in the morning mail from Angela. Dionis began her breakfast intending to read it later. She had not opened it when Senora Lopez brought fresh coffee at the end of her meal.

"Stay and have a cup with me, *senora*," Dionis said with a smile. "I won't have many more mornings here."

Senora Lopez shook her head regretfully. "Not this morning, *gracias*. I have too much to do. I will leave you to read your letter. Later, perhaps, you would like to see the new extension. We stayed up until well into the early hours this morning putting it to rights. Don Juan was very pleased with it when he saw it last evening. So modern too."

Dionis allowed the last remark to pass over her head. "I'd love to see it, *senora*."

Over the fragrant coffee Dionis picked up Angela's letter and casually slit it open. The next instant she was staring at it in horror. The written words danced before her eyes as she tried to take in their meaning.

"Dear Dionis," she read, "the party is over. Tony and I have parted for good."

It was some time before Dionis could continue reading. Her face was ashen when she eventually read on. Angela went on to say that the parting was final. Experienced though she was with men, her instinct had failed to

172

warn her of the hint of coarseness in her fiancé's character. Had she not been so infatuated with him she would have seen his habitual self-indulgence in the slackness of his mouth. He had lied to her, for she had discovered that he had no money or prospects, having gone through a fortune left him by his stepfather, a distant cousin of Juan's. Her fiancé had no scruples and was going through a shady deal in property in Bermuda, and that to Angela was the last straw. In short Antonio was a completely selfish lover with the makings of the worst kind of husband. When Dionis received this letter she would be on her way back to London to ask for her job back. Rather callously, Angela ended by advising Dionis to get out of the mess as best she could.

With the feeling that she had aged ten years in a few minutes, Dionis put down the letter. Had she made a mistake in not telling Angela that her fiancé was already engaged to someone else? It was questionable whether she would have taken heed. How long Dionis sat there she never knew. But when her brain began to function again her first thought was for the workmen at the Villa Acacia. Had Antonio enough money in his account to pay them? Their contract was nearly finished. Dionis had forwarded the bills for the materials to his bank and had so far received no reply. Well, no news was good news. Even so, for her own peace of mind she had to contact his bank to make sure. Beyond that Dionis dared not think.

Maintaining a warm enthusiastic front when later Senora Lopez escorted her around the new extension to the inn was one of the hardest things Dionis had ever done. She had a vague impression of a sparkling modern kitchen, an intriguing cocktail bar and a sun lounge. It had evidently been designed by a first-class architect. The décor, brilliantly done, was exotic yet restrained by virtue of attention to detail. Normally, Dionis would have looked on it with pleasure, ever alert to learn from first-class designers. But a sense of fatality held her rigid; an inner confusion jumbled thoughts with which she wrestled in vain.

Fortunately Senora Lopez, thrilled with the new premises and a future bright with hope, noticed nothing. When Dionis asked permission to use the phone in her small office later, Senora Lopez left her there and closed the door behind her. With a wildly beating heart, Dionis contacted the operator and was put through to the bank in Barcelona. There were some anxious moments until his voice came through and she waited while he went in search of Antonio's bank account. "*Si*," he said. Two bills had been settled by the bank, one for an order of materials from Barcelona, the other, a much bigger one, from London. Unfortunately, the last bill left a small overdraft. He was trying to contact *el senor* in Bermuda about it. If the *senorita* would call him again toward the end of the week, he might have some news for her.

Sick at heart, Dionis agreed to do this and slowly put down the receiver. The men would have to be paid, if it meant drawing what money she had in the bank. It was then she began to realize that the problem was not hers alone. It was also Juan's. The Villa Acacia was his property and he had a right to know what had happened. He would find out eventually in any case. So with a heavy heart, Dionis wrote him a note to say it was imperative for her to see him at his earliest convenience. She addressed it to the Villa Jacaranda and went out to mail it on her way to the Villa Acacia. Nothing would be gained by calling a halt to the work there that was due to be completed in a matter of days. Dionis worked hard at the villa, staying long after the workmen left each evening and returning to the inn too tired and too dispirited to enjoy her evening meal.

Midweek, she received two letters. One was from Nurse Ford's sister thanking her for the baby's present and asking her to call any time she felt inclined. The other was from Don Fernando requesting her presence at a dinner party to be given at the Villa Inez. The occasion was the engagement of his sister Pilar to Doctor Horatio de Quexeri. It was the one bright spot in her dark world. If she had been instrumental in bringing those two delightful people together then she did not regret her own foolishness in coming to Spain.

She dressed with special care for the event in a dress of crisp white organdy flecked with blue. The silver belt around her slim waist matched her slippers and evening bag. Her hair was soft and bright around her small face, but Dionis felt no joy in her own attractive reflection, only a humble thankfulness for this brief period of respite that released her for a few hours from her tormenting thoughts. It was an anodyne, deadening the pain in her heart as she longed, yet dreaded, to see Juan again.

With Dona Inez, Don Fernando greeted her warmly. They were obviously as delighted as she was about the engagement. Then Pilar was there.

"You look very lovely," she said to Dionis, radiant herself in black lace. Happiness had brought a new beauty to her face.

"So do you, Dona Pilar," she replied. "May I see your ring?"

Taking Pilar's hand to admire the enormous emerald flashing in the light, Dionis felt the small fingers curling around her own. "It's beautiful," she breathed. "Congratulations, Dona Pilar. I know you are going to be very happy with your nice doctor." Their eyes met in perfect understanding and Dionis gave the *senorita*'s fingers an answering squeeze.

Guests drifted in and everyone was genuinely delighted to be present on such a happy occasion. Later, over dinner, Dionis saw the happy couple engrossed in each other in the manner of a couple very much in love. After the protracted meal finally ended, Dionis found an opportunity to congratulate the doctor.

"I am delighted that two such nice people have found their happiness in each other. Dona Pilar is wonderful. You are a very lucky *hombre*, Doctor Horatio," she said.

"*Gracias, senorita*," he answered gravely. "I trust that some day you will find the same happiness."

"*Gracias*," Dionis said with a gaiety that she was far from feeling. Love had come to her, but she would never drink from its cup of happiness. Only Juan had the power to offer it to her, and he would not want anything to do with her after what she had to tell him.

The happy evening drew gently to a close with Dionis feeling like Cinderella returning to a life of care. She was given a lift back to the inn by a charming couple. Dionis thanked them and made her way across the silent courtyard of the inn. From beneath the shade of the lemon trees, she looked toward the patio lit by the dying glow of the brazier. Her heart moved oddly in her breast, and she held her breath as deep emotion held her spellbound. It was a mixture of joy and sorrow, laughter and tears, ecstasy and utter desolation as she came upon the beloved figure that haunted her dreams.

Juan was leaning nonchalantly against one of the pillars on the patio. Dionis stared at him, the feeling inside her banished by the enormity of what she had to tell him. Her feeling for him had not changed. It was not infatuation that she felt for him. Only love could make her whole being reach out to him, fill her with the pain unrequited love brought in its wake. He had seen her, of course, alerted by the sound of the car dropping her off at the gates.

Dionis had no recollection of crossing the courtyard. Only the dark enigmatic face of Juan was before her, drawing her to him. She was herself a ghost, transparent as the crisp white organdy that frothed about her like evening mist. Her silver slippers made barely a sound and the perfume of trees and flowers seemed overwhelming.

"My faith!" he breathed, straightening slowly as if any sudden movement on his part might cause her to vanish. "Did you come on a moonbeam?" With a smile startlingly white in the dimness, he was aware suddenly of her pale, unsmiling face. She was like a ghost to which the unreality of the evening had given a spurious vitality. His smile faded. "I received your note. You are in trouble, Miss Ward?"

Slowly, Dionis raised her eyes until they met his full and straight. She forced the words out, determined to be frank, although they threatened to choke her. Her voice was barely above a whisper.

"I'm sorry," she began. "Something dreadful has happened. My sister, Angela, has broken off her engagement to . . . to Antonio."

Then, because her legs felt incapable of supporting her, Dionis sat down on the seat by the wall of the patio.

He digested the news in silence for several moments. At last, frowning deeply, he said, "What is going to happen now?"

Dionis did not immediately understand him. "What do you mean?"

He shrugged and thrust his hands into his pockets. "Now that the engagement is broken, is there no chance of a reconciliation?"

"None." She shook her head. "Angela is adamant. She has broken the engagement because she's of the opinion that Antonio would make a very unsatisfactory husband."

He stared at her with that curious, baffling reserve that while it intrigued, also served to fill her with foreboding. The patio was warm from the still-glowing brazier, but there was a distinct nip in the evening air.

"This is very interesting." The dark eyes narrowed. In the dim light his face was set and stern. "Is it possible that your sister has hooked a bigger fish?"

Flinching from the sarcasm in his deep voice, Dionis lifted indignant eyes to meet the glitter in his. "There is nothing to be gained by uttering insults, *senor*," she answered quietly, vulnerable to the fact that this was an inn and voices carried on the still night air.

Slowly, he walked to one of the pillars arching the patio, and leaning back against it, faced her across the top of the brazier. "I am merely trying to get at the truth. When did you first find out about it?"

"I wrote to you the moment I received the letter from Angela saying the engagement was ended. She said she would be in London when I received it."

"And Antonio?"

"Angela didn't say what he intended to do."

"So, she leaves you to face the music. What about the Villa Acacia?"

"My work there is more or less finished. Another week, perhaps, will see it at an end. It was too late to postpone operations. I thought it best to carry on and complete the job."

His face hardened as if carved in a mask. "After which you will be joining your sister in London—you the richer for a fat check, she having enjoyed a free holiday in Bermuda. How nice!"

His words struck her like a blow. Dionis stared at him dumbly, her mouth shocked into quivering emotion. And so she sat for shocked seconds, his contempt shaking her to her roots. Then, achieving the right expression for one who had been insulted, her pride outraged, she looked at him with burning indignation. "How nice, as you say, had we been a couple of adventuresses. As I told you once before, neither Angela nor I are in the least dishonest."

His mouth tilted cynically, cruelly. "You can hardly blame me for drawing my own conclusions."

"I blame you for nothing. I blame myself for taking on a job before I was fully acquainted with the facts. Now I can't wait to get away, but not for the reason you think."

"But you will be joining your sister in London?" he insisted.

"Not necessarily. We've sublet the apartment for six months, and if Angela gets her job back she'll be traveling abroad a great deal."

"Does that mean you will have nowhere to go when you return?" He frowned fiercely.

"No." Dionis, white to the lips, fragile with dark shadows beneath her eyes, tilted her chin. "I'm not without friends."

"Ah yes. Cesare Delusi," he murmured insinuatingly, drawing a lean hand across a well-shaven chin. "And now the financial arrangements concerning Antonio. I understand he is taking care of the cost of the improvements to the Villa Acacia? Has he enough in his account to cover them?"

Dionis hesitated, wanting to give Antonio time to settle

the account. But this infuriating man already knew of the deficit, most probably. When she answered her voice strangled in her throat. "No, he hasn't enough to pay the workmen."

"But enough to pay the bills of the materials and—" he paused "—your fee?"

"My fee doesn't enter into it," she said bitterly. "All I want is for the men to be paid at the end of their contract."

He raised a frankly disbelieving brow. "No? Then why take the job in the first place?"

She stared at him with burning eyes. "I saw it as a chance to further my career," she stated, her voice steady now. Her control had returned, shutting out all pain and weakness. "It was a splendid opportunity, a big thing to be tackled away from home ground. There was no reason why I shouldn't take it. I had already decided to visit the exhibition in Madrid as a kind of holiday between jobs. Maybe the chance to do some constructive work while I was here in a different environment for others to criticize, abuse or even condemn was too great to refuse. However, my work is almost finished." She lifted her small chin defiantly, her face was flushed, her eyes diamond bright with unshed tears. She would have died rather than let him see them. "It's my work, something I adored doing, and I'm proud of it."

Her last words, spoken clearly and distinctly, made the ensuing silence in the dimly lit patio more profound. Then he was striding across in a masterful and determined way, to sit down beside her. Resting an arm along the back of the seat, he crossed his legs to support the other arm limply and turned to face her. "You are overlooking one important thing," he said quietly. "The Villa Acacia is my property and I cannot allow any work on it to be done for nothing."

"I want nothing." Dionis lowered her eyes, feeling the intentness of his gaze. "All I'm interested in is the workmen, who will expect their pay at the end of next week."

"They will be paid. But I refuse to be in your debt. I shall insist upon you accepting a check for your services," he said inexorably.

"It would be kinder if you would forget my part in it," she argued stubbornly, aware of his nearness and finding it suffocating. "The work was done without your approval. Let's leave it at that."

"And if I insist?" Juan asked softly, leaning nearer. When Dionis did not answer he continued in the same low voice, "Since seeing the exhibition in Madrid, have you not the slightest inclination to stay here, say for the summer, and continue with your work?"

"No, definitely not, *senor*. I intend to leave Spain the moment my work on the Villa Acacia is finished, never to return."

"Does that mean you are taking your sister's word that all Spaniards make unsatisfactory husbands? You appear to believe her implicitly, although she has let you down ruthlessly. Surely you knew when you came that there was a possibility of her breaking the engagement to Antonio as she had done previous ones?"

"I did. I decided to take the risk. There was always a chance of her having met the right man and settling down."

He said grimly, "Precisely the same idea I had about Antonio. He had never gone so far before in his affairs as to become engaged, which was the reason I questioned the possibility of a reconciliation."

He looked down on the graceful line of her neck, the dejected droop of her head.

"I know Angela. There'll be no reconciliation. You can be sure of that," she stated firmly.

"Pity. Your sister appeared to have a profound influence on Antonio. He needs someone who will make him toe the line. He has no sense of responsibility nor any real depth of character. Neither has he any ambition except to do precisely nothing. The only energy he ever exerted was to go through a fortune left to him by his stepfather. He ended up as one of my agents, the worst I have ever had. The rest you know." Juan made a gesture of distaste. "Your sister seems to be the hardened type who could be his saving grace. Incidentally, I am surprised you tolerate her when she behaves so callously to you."

"Angela is my sister, *senor*. Had Antonio been your brother, no doubt you would have felt the same about him."

"You will be surprised to know that once I treated him like a brother. Tell me, is Signor Delusi married?"

"No."

"You and he seem to be close."

"He is one of my best friends."

"Then I advise you to marry him. I am confident that, as your husband, he would not be long in sorting your sister out. At least you would be free of her." His indrawn breath could have meant exasperation or disgust. Dionis was too miserable to define it. Juan rose to his feet. "*Adios*, Miss Ward," he said slowly, decisively. "You look in need of your bed. My advocate will be getting in touch with you in due course."

CHAPTER ELEVEN

The days passed with Dionis working like one possessed. Work at the Villa Acacia was almost finished when she received two letters from Don Juan's firm of solicitors in Barcelona. One contained a check for her services, so fabulous as to take her breath away. The other was to inform her that a man would be calling at the Villa Acacia the following Saturday morning to pay the workmen. With a bitterness she would never have believed herself capable of, Dionis was appalled at the amount of money Juan had seen fit to pay out for something he had not wanted in the first place. She had no intention of accepting his check. She would have to decide what to do with it. He was adamant about her being paid. But she was equally adamant about not accepting payment.

On Saturday morning, a poker-faced, bowler-hatted, middle-aged man arrived at the Villa Acacia to pay the workmen. Each man was given a pay packet plus a generous bonus for work promptly done. Later, Dionis entertained the men in the sparkling new kitchen where two bottles of champagne were opened by Paco to celebrate the occasion. Then they all sat down to a generous lunch provided by Senora Lopez; Dionis had paid for it.

That afternoon Dionis walked through the newly decorated rooms, haunted by Don Juan. Wherever she looked there was some reminder of his generosity—the two lovely floor vases in the lounge, the pretty footstools, the Chinese fire screen and the pedestal with various other items in adjoining rooms. They all seemed to mock at her. For the first time Dionis did not look upon her work with pride. Although she knew it was far and away the best job she had ever done it meant nothing to her as she surveyed it with lackluster eyes. She felt empty, as if all her zest for living had gone with Juan, who despised her. She would have to write to him thanking him for the check and for his generosity to the workmen and herself. After that, nothing. He had gone out of her life, taking with him the enchanted hours coloring her existence, giving her a brief glimpse of a world made beautiful by his presence. There was nothing left for her but to go back to the world she knew without him. Her time in Spain was running out. There were only one or two minor adjustments to be made to the pretty window drapes for the Villa Acacia. The village seamstress had promised to have them ready by midweek. So Dionis waited patiently, giving the Villa Acacia a wide berth until she went to put the final touches to the décor.

She sent off the short letter to Juan. That done, she had the desire to be alone, to walk and walk until she was too tired to think. But even that was denied her, for the weather broke overnight and the next two days brought heavy rain. On Tuesday an invitation to a farewell tea for Nurse Ford at Lemon Tree Cottage came as a lifeline. When Dionis set out to catch the bus at five o'clock, it was still raining. Clad in a white raincoat with small matching hat, armed with a present for Nurse Ford—a soft leather case containing a small manicure set—she caught the bus. Pilar was there, her dark eyes shining with a serene happiness. Both mother and child were looking well and Nurse Ford was smiling as if it was all her doing.

The visit did much to send Dionis's spirits higher than they had been for days. When Doctor Horatio called after his evening surgery to take Pilar and Dionis home the rain had stopped. The red gold curtain of sky revealed as the clouds passed sent forth a radiance of light that gave an incredible opulence to the brilliance of the blooms in the garden. The air was like wine. Dionis alone appeared conscious of the radiance of the evening, for the doctor and his fiancée were lost in each other. She occupied the back seat of the car while they sat together in front, and her happiness for them became tinged with loneliness.

Dionis saw the big car seconds after the doctor had left her at the inn. Her heart lurched painfully at the sight of it and her breath caught in her throat. Taking firm hold of herself, she walked quietly across the deserted courtyard to go upstairs to her room. Don Juan and Senora Lopez were on the landing barring the way to her room. They were looking up at water seeping through a damp patch in the ceiling.

Don Juan was saying, "I would say a tile is at fault on the roof. The workmen could have dislodged it when they were building the extensions at the back of the inn. You are sure none of the other ceilings in the house are affected, Senora Lopez?"

"*Si, senor*. I have examined them all except those in Miss Ward's rooms. Ah, here she is now."

Senora Lopez turned to smile warmly at Dionis. Juan's cool smile of greeting was accompanied by a slight inclination of the dark head. Dionis forced a smile. The last thing she wanted was for Juan to enter her bedroom, but it seemed she had no choice.

"We had better take a look," he said, standing aside to allow Dionis to lead the way.

Dionis opened her door and they filed inside. With every nerve on edge, she watched him stride to the windows and open the shutters before he ran a practised eye over the ceiling. He repeated the procedure in the bathroom.

"These are quite in order," he stated, returning to the

bedroom with his keen gaze resting briefly on the two suitcases Dionis had packed prior to her departure.

There was a short silence while Dionis stood rigidly with her back to the dressing table. His posy of forget-me-nots was behind her and he must not see them. Dionis had left the little potted flowers out of her case until the day she left.

"Then only the landing ceiling is affected, *senor*." Senora Lopez looked decidedly relieved. "It was fortunate that you happened to call minutes after I saw it."

"I will have it attended to right away," Juan promised smoothly. "I am happy to find the extension standing up to the rain. No leakages there. They were a good team of workmen." He had been smiling pleasantly at the *senora*, but the look he passed to Dionis was slightly cooler. "You were satisfied with the workmen I sent, Miss Ward? No complaints?"

"None, *senor*. I sent a letter to you addressed to the Villa Jacaranda."

"A letter?" The dark eyes looked wary. "Does that mean you have finished at the Villa Acacia? I understood you would be there some time after the workmen had left applying the finishing touches so dear to a woman's heart."

Again Dionis was aware of a slight malice in his deep tones—or was she becoming oversensitive because of her love for him? She was beginning to wish he would go.

"There are one or two small tasks I have to do before I finally hand in the keys," she said. "Am I to give them to Paco, *senor*?"

He answered offhandedly in the manner of a man whose mind was occupied elsewhere. "That would be in order, since he will be left in charge. You are not inviting me to see it before you leave?"

Aware of Senora Lopez's interested gaze, Dionis regarded him soberly.

"Surely you don't require an invitation from me to look over your own property?"

"Put like that it does sound absurd, but I had no wish to intrude. I knew I could rely on the workmen I sent. You are perfectly satisfied with the results, Miss Ward?"

In spite of the heat of her body beneath the raincoat, Dionis quelled a shiver. Remembering his opinion of Angela and herself, she could only assume he was hinting at the check he had given to her. Had Senora Lopez not been present, she would have flung it in his face.

"I work with the intention of satisfying my clients. You are quite at liberty to go to the Villa Acacia at any time to see the décor before I leave. I shall be there tomorrow morning. It will be more satisfactory for you to see it in the daylight."

"I will be there at ten-thirty tomorrow," he answered. "Until then, *adios*, Miss Ward."

He walked out of the room with Senora Lopez, one hand thrust negligently into his pocket. Going down the stairs, Dionis heard him talking about putting the inn into a guidebook soon to be issued for the benefit of tourists. He had forgotten her already. She stood there with her back against the dressing table, her small face tight with unhappiness. Tomorrow morning the seamstress had promised to deliver the drapes. Thank goodness, she would not be alone with him if she could help it. It would be quite easy to keep the woman there until he had left the Villa Acacia.

There was still the problem of what to do with the check. Dionis was no nearer a solution as to what to do with it when she set off for the Villa Acacia after break-fast to see Juan. He would undoubtedly arrive on time and she kept her fingers crossed hoping the seamstress from the village would arrive before him. She was in the kitchen when she heard the voice coming from the open front door.

"*Senorita*, may I come in?"

And there she stood clasping the parcel of furnishings to her ample bosom. Senora Direnso was still pretty, despite her plump, matronly figure. She appeared to be in her forties, with a perfect complexion and abundant blue black hair.

"By all means," Dionis welcomed her, all smiles. "I am so glad you are here. Don Juan will arrive at any moment to look over the villa."

Relieving Senora Direnso of her parcel, Dionis was quite unprepared for her reaction to her words. Her black eyes widened in dismay.

"Santa Maria!" she breathed. "Don Juan is coming here? Then I must go and return later when he has gone."

"But he is only a man, Senora Direnso. Surely you would not leave me on my own with him? He will not be here long, merely to look over the decorations."

Dionis had spoken quietly, cajolingly. There was a pause while the *senora* digested this. Then she hazarded, "I could stay providing you do all the talking, *senorita*." The dark eyes were reflective. "I know nothing about your furnishings, so while you are with Don Juan I will attend to my work."

But Dionis doubted whether Senora Direnso would be capable of any work while Don Juan was in the villa. Already her eyes were alight with excitement as she smoothed her already immaculate hair, then drew her hands down her dress in rapid nervous gestures. She had spoken in Spanish and Dionis read the meaning of her words more in her reactions than her actual speech.

The long silver car drew up to the open door of the villa precisely at ten-thirty. Senora Direnso was with Dionis in the hall when he arrived. The *senora* watched his arrival with awe. Here was someone worth waiting for, her expression said.

Aloud, she breathed, "What other *hombre* has the poise, the grace of Don Juan—a real *hidalgo*!"

Obviously against him Senorita Direnso was a mere adjunct. But Dionis was not any more composed than her companion. As he slid from the car and walked to the entrance with his light firm steps, Dionis knew she would always have the memory of sunlight on black well-kept hair, of eyes dark and intense, of a deep voice that played on her heartstrings, and a superb carriage of arrogance and grace befitting—as Senora Direnso said—an *hidalgo*. She was aware of his broad shoulders in the lightweight suit of pale gray as he filled the doorway.

"*Buenos dias*, Miss Ward, Senora Direnso," he greeted them, in no whit put out at the presence of the seamstress.

"*Buenos dias*," they answered, with Senora Direnso giving a little nervous curtsy.

He looked momentarily at the *senora*, then at Dionis, demure and slender in the subdued light of the hall, her fair skin and pretty dress in strong contrast to the dark looks and attire of her companion.

"I trust I am not interrupting anything?" he remarked politely.

"You were expected, *senor*. Shall we begin upstairs?" Her voice was steady, and when Senora Direnso drifted to one of the downstairs rooms, Dionis waited while Juan looked around the hall. He was studying the gold-framed wall mirror set above the lovely inlaid chest he had loaned her. In one corner of the hall was the pedestal topped by an ornate spiraled brass lamp. He made no comment, and they walked across the hall where a Spanish rug revealed part of the lovely tiled floor. Dionis went upstairs with him feeling a little odd. Would he approve of her work or disapprove? She clenched her hands. He had to like it. His approval would be balm for her sore heart. She needed it to help her pick up the threads again when she returned home. But he had such strong beliefs in his own traditions and was such a stickler for detail that her heart began to waver. She would have given much for the cheerful presence of Cesare Delusi in that moment.

In silence, they entered the main bedroom, clean-cut and uncluttered with whitewood furniture lining two walls on a sea of blue carpet. Transparent window drapes gathered closely in folds fell regally from ceiling to carpet. Slowly, Juan walked around, hands behind him or reaching out to open cupboards and shallow drawers. And Dionis stood meekly by, not nearly as cool as she appeared.

Suddenly, he was smiling as if his humor was completely restored by what he had seen. "A restful and delightful room," he commented, adding sincerely, "With a simplicity cleverly contrived by the use of textural rather than color contrasts. I like it."

Her heart moved, then settled as she spoke her thoughts. "I'm pleased that it meets with your approval. I trust the rest of the décor does too."

He looked down at her with a veiled expression. One dark eyebrow raised as if he could read her innermost thoughts. "You sound doubtful as to my approval of your work, Miss Ward. I have noticed an absence of that spontaneous enthusiasm you have displayed when discussing what you had planned to do."

Dionis replied valiantly, "There's always a feeling of

anticlimax when a job is finished, *senor*. One does one's best, but it's too much to hope for all one's efforts to be wholly approved."

"Then take heart, Miss Ward. I may be the exception to the rule."

He continued to examine each room with a keenness that missed nothing. The modern kitchen, country style, with its delightful blue and gray Spanish tiles and wipe-clean surfaces met with his full approval, as did the smart lounge. Here deep mauve sofas and chairs looked dramatic against white walls, and mauve-shaded lamps on gold-framed, glass-topped tables echoed the richness of overhanging gilt lamps.

Dionis looked at the dark head outlined against the white wall and felt a foolish lump in her throat. "If you favor another color scheme, furniture, rugs and lamp-shades can easily be changed," she said rather quickly.

"To me," he replied with complete frankness, "every-thing appears to have been designed so that the English children and dogs can run around unrestricted with little threat to the furnishings. Is that not so?"

His smile was almost her undoing. It threatened the wall of reserve between them enabling her to answer his few questions with a deferential air. In spite of herself, Dionis warmed to his mood. At the same time she was aware of standing precariously on shifting sand.

"You catch on quickly, *senor*," she said demurely.

"The same can be said of you, Miss Ward, where interior decorating is concerned. Allow me to congratu-late you on your work. I wholeheartedly approve of it."

But Dionis could not immediately take it in. She had never known herself so vulnerable to a man's presence, much less his praise of her work. The short cry of pain coming from the kitchen quarters proved someone else's undoing, but not her own. Juan was the first on the scene, with Dionis following. Senora Direnso was sitting on the floor of the kitchen, one leg tucked under her, looking very distressed.

"I slipped," she gasped. "It is my ankle, I think."

Juan picked her up gently to seat her in a chair. Then, kneeling down beside her, he gently explored the region of her ankle with his lean fingers. His expression was thoughtful as he straightened to look down sternly on the *senora*.

"There is nothing wrong with your ankle, *senora*. It is not in the least swelled or hurt. You did not slip; you collapsed from fatigue. When did you last eat?"

Senora Direnso was agitated. "I . . . I cannot remember, *senor*. Yesterday some time. But I slipped; I did not collapse."

Juan continued to look at her sternly. "It is no use lying, *senora*. I know. Do you not think it is time you did a little less sitting up all night sewing and allowed that lazy husband of yours to do a little more work?" He put up a hand as she opened her mouth to speak. "You are aware of his duplicity. He no more has arthritis in his back than I have. I am going to take you home, and I shall insist that after a meal you go to bed."

Senora Direnso was horrified. "I cannot do that, *senor*. I have work to do and a meal to prepare for my husband and the *ninos*."

"You will have no choice, *senora*. I'll send for the doctor if you do not do as I suggest. I'll have a serious talk with your husband and you will find yourself and the *ninos* being looked after by a man who must be made to take on his responsibilities."

Helplessly, Senora Direnso looked from his set face to

Dionis, who noticed the lines of fatigue, the tired shadows beneath her eyes.

Dionis said gently, "You look exhausted, *senora*. I am sure it will be for the best to do what the *senor* suggests. You are clever with your fingers and could easily support the *ninos* and yourself without the added burden of a lazy husband. Why not hint to him that you could easily be independent of him if you chose? He would respect you all the more for it and probably pull his weight, making your life much easier. He would also gain the respect of his *ninos*."

Juan did not wait for further argument. Tossing Dionis a mocking glance, he scooped Senora Direnso into his arms and strode out with her. For several minutes after he had gone, Dionis debated whether to attend to the last of her jobs or call it a day. It had certainly been a wearing one up to now. She fingered the parcel Senora Direnso had brought lying on the kitchen table. Poor Senora Direnso! It was terrible to have a lazy husband, especially where the children were concerned. Suddenly, she turned a startled face at the sound of firm footsteps to see Juan in the kitchen doorway.

He was still unsmiling. "Has Senora Direnso finished the work you gave her?" he asked abruptly.

"Yes. This parcel you see here is the last."

He flicked a glance at the parcel on the table. "*Bien*," he said. "I shall see she receives a check for her services."

Dionis kept her eyes lowered on the parcel. It was not the slightest use telling him that she had intended to pay Senora Direnso herself out of her own pocket. Uneasily, she sensed rather than saw his change of mood, as he leaned nonchalantly against the door frame. She did lift her eyes then, but only in an attempt to catch a glimpse of

Senora Direnso waiting in his car. Her action could not have told him more plainly that she wanted him to go. "Do not worry about the *senora*. She is taking a shot of brandy. These jobs you have to do—are they only minor ones?"

"Yes."

"Taking you how long?"

"A few hours." Avoiding his gaze, Dionis saw the dark eyes narrow calculatingly.

"I trust you are not leaving the moment your work here on the villa is finished? I did notice you had packed your cases."

"Why not?" she answered stiffly, wondering if that was all he had noticed in her room at the inn. "There's nothing to keep me here."

"Except the natural desire to see a little more of the country before you leave. There is the monastery at Poblet I told you about and lots of other places that would delight you. You could stay as my guest at the Villa Jacaranda. It would give me great pleasure to show you around."

And prolong her agony as she counted the bittersweet days spent in his company? No, thank you. Dionis spoke with a finality that rocked her heart.

"I'm sorry, *senor*, what you suggest is impossible. I have to return to London as soon as possible. I have commitments there I can ignore no longer. I appreciate your kindness." She fumbled in her bag, unable to meet his eyes, and drew forth a small package. "I forgot this present I have for Senora Direnso. It is a special pair of scissors I sent for. Fortunately they arrived today." Her laugh was fleeting. "Just in time. Excuse me."

He moved aside to allow her through the doorway. She had given the *senora* her present, kissed her cheek in farewell and straightened to find Juan standing in the porch of the villa watching them. Dionis wavered. How did one look on the beloved for the last time without betraying the heartbreak? Of all the ordeals she had had to face this was the hardest.

But she managed it, with anguish rising inside her threatening to choke her words. She never did remember taking the few steps to where he still stood.

"Well, goodbye, *senor*. Thank you for all you have done, and forgive me for all the trouble I have caused." The tears were ominously near, but she forced them back. "I shall give the keys of the villa to Paco tomorrow. Goodbye."

She was conscious of him straightening as she held out her hand. But he did not take it. Instead he gave a stiff formal bow. "Goodbye, Miss Ward. A pleasant journey home."

Her hand dropped simultaneously with her heart.

He strode to the car, slid in behind the wheel and set it in motion. As it slid away, Dionis lifted her hand to Senora Direnso, but Juan kept his eyes front. Well, that was that. Dionis turned slowly back to the villa to hear the scuff of espadrilles on the garden path. Thank heaven for Paco.

"*Buenos dias*, Paco," she greeted him. "Would you come and help me with the drapes, *por favor*?"

When she left the Villa Acacia at two to go to lunch, Dionis had finished the last of her jobs. For some reason she could not explain, she had not given Paco the keys. There was no hurry; she had not yet booked her flight. But that was no problem. It was quite possible that she would be able to get a canceled single seat in any case. What she had to settle, and soon, was the problem of Juan's check. She was no nearer a solution when she entered the courtyard of the inn. And there she stood, doubting the evidence of her own eyes.

Someone was sitting at the small table beneath the lemon trees, someone wearing a smart cream suit, green spotted silk shirt and brown and white buckskin shoes. The sun slanting through the lemon trees played on the dark curly hair, and the signet ring on his little finger gleamed as he lifted a drink to his lips.

"Cesare!" she cried delightedly. She ran across the courtyard, bent before he could rise and kissed him on both cheeks. "When did you arrive?"

He drew back his immaculate cuff and said teasingly, "Exactly twenty minutes and thirty seconds ago. Take a seat. Your drink is getting warm." He reached over to drop another chunk of ice from a jug into her glass. "How is business?"

Dionis did not know whether to laugh or cry. She laughed. "I finished at the Villa Acacia this morning. I have the keys still, though." She raised her glass, bordering on the hysterical. "Here's to my next job in dear old London. Cheers!"

"Cheers," he answered, drinking too. Then slowly he lowered his glass to look at her oddly. "Everything all right? You said that with a kind of desperation. Is everything all right?" he repeated.

Cesare Delusi's motive in calling to see Dionis before he returned to London had been prompted by a feeling of concern. He had been more than a little perturbed to see the change in her when he had arrived in Spain. Granted, she had only just recovered from an illness when he saw her at the Villa Jacaranda. Her sparkle had not returned. He had stayed to help her at the Villa Acacia with the hope that he would see it before he left for Italy. But her face was paler than he remembered, her eyes curiously shadowed. And before she had seen him there had been none of the youthful spring in her walk. Her expression had become much too serious for a girl who had always lived on the brink of an enchanting smile. He watched her swallow part of the cool drink, saw her make a visible effort to pull herself together.

"Just one problem I hope you can help me with before I go." She put down her glass, and with a hint of the old sparkle put her chin on her hands, elbows on the table. "Tell me about your visit home. Did you enjoy it? How are momma and poppa and all the family? Very proud of you, I know."

Cesare's news lasted until Senora Lopez brought the lunch. As they ate Dionis asked him what he was doing in that part of Spain.

"Let's say I'm taking a roundabout route to London in order to see the Villa Acacia. Although you don't know it, you could have started something here that will help our overseas trade."

"I wouldn't want to do any more work here, Cesare," she said quietly. "If that's what you mean."

He raised a brow. "Why not? Did you not enjoy it?"

"In a way. How long will you be staying?"

"One day, two days. It depends."

Dionis had shed a little of her tired look. The lunch was reviving her, and she had eaten more than she realized while talking to Cesare. "Then you can see the Villa Acacia before you leave and we might even travel back together." She paused, then plunged. "I'd be grateful if we could go somewhere where we can talk after lunch, if it's all right with you."

"That's easy. I can call up the local garage to hire a

car. We can spend the siesta going for a run in the country or even a dip in the ocean. What do you say to that?"

"Lovely," she answered.

The hired car arrived soon after lunch. It was a well-sprung and sweetly intimate two-seater.

"Thank goodness the controls aren't cross-eyed," Cesare quipped as he set the car confidently in motion.

Dionis leaned back in her seat listening to the rhythm of the car engine and the gentle swish of the wind as they drove quickly along. Inevitably she thought of Juan and all the ecstasy and delight being with him had brought. It was a depth of emotion she would never experience again with any man. Cesare, one of the best friends she had ever had, with all his masculine charm could never affect her senses with the same swooning bliss. Gradually, Dionis relaxed into a confidential mood. She told Cesare of Angela's broken engagement, her return to London, her fiancé's overdraft and Juan's generosity. When she reached the most difficult part, the check, words failed her. She simply drew the piece of paper from her handbag and put it under his nose.

He gave a low whistle at the amount. "Congratulations! Don Juan must be satisfied with the result. He is not the kind of man to pay out money he did not feel was due."

"But I don't want it, Cesare," she cried. "Nothing would make me accept it!" She bit hard on her lip. It was difficult to convince Cesare of her determination not to accept it. She had not told him of Juan's scathing words about Angela nor his obvious bad opinion of both her and her sister. He would not have hesitated to go to see him and put him right, and she did not want someone else to clear her name for Juan's benefit. "I feel awfully guilty about the whole thing. Please help me in getting rid of it."

Cesare swung the car off the main road. He slowed down and stopped the engine as they slid into a side road. Then turning to face her he looked down at her eyes, large and dark in her small face.

"You wouldn't like to sleep on it again? After all, you have earned it," he said evenly.

She shook her head.

"Have you anything in mind? Do you want to get rid of it in one grand gesture for Don Juan to hear about or do you want to get rid of it more discreetly?"

"It's immaterial whether Don Juan hears about it or not. I just don't want it," she insisted. "And he wouldn't take it back."

"Getting rid of money is much easier than earning it, so it's no problem. Why not wait until you return to London and give it then to some charity or other?"

Again she shook her head. "You might think I'm being sentimental, but I feel the money should remain here in this country. There's so much poverty about in the rural areas. Another thing that bothers me is that I used the money Angela's ex-fiancé had in the bank to pay for the materials for the Villa Acacia, money that he could be needing desperately at this very moment."

"I wouldn't worry about that," Cesare said practically. "Ten to one the man owes rent on the villa."

"If he paid rent. It might have been part of his job as an agent of Don Juan's. Besides, Angela did treat him badly, persuading him to have the villa modernized and then throwing him over."

Cesare mulled this over. "I wouldn't concern myself any more with the affairs of Antonio. Forget him. You might have him seeking you out if you were foolish enough to give him the check," he counseled wisely.

"I suppose you're right," she said, feeling rather guilty

at the frown between his eyes. Poor Cesare. After all, ̶
was on holiday and didn't want to be burdened with h
problems. Perhaps she was thinking too hard about i
Something would come. Meanwhile she could take hi̶
over the Villa Acacia in the morning, which was what h
had really come for, and help him to enjoy his short visit.

CHAPTER TWELVE

Dionis had said good night to Cesare at the end of a very enjoyable evening. They had dined at a restaurant a good car's run from the inn. The meal had been excellent, and so had the floor show. A Spanish couple, the woman in a tight-fitting, black, flounced dress over a scarlet underskirt, had appeared dramatically with a sinuous grace. Her great dark eyes had flashed as she had clapped her hands above her head and stamped tiny feet to the click of castanets. Her partner, a handsome, virile young man in a tight-fitting black suit, flaunted all the qualities and vibrant fiery powers of a first-class artist. The fandango they danced carried Dionis along with it. Entranced, she saw a performance of grace, passion and rhythm that left her breathless and slightly dazed.

The memory of it lingered when, later, they made their way swiftly back to the inn. There had been an aura of unreality about the whole day; so much had happened. It was a day Dionis would never forget. The evening had been an anticlimax. Cesare had enjoyed it, for he had been smiling, the smile of a man who had earned his leisure at the end of a long, hard road leading eventually to success. In the lamplit sanctuary of her bedroom, Dionis envied him his serene contentment. Soon she would be back working, but to her the fruits of success would not be the same. There would be no one to share them with.

Angela would be making her own life, and their grandparents in Canada were well provided for by a wealthy son. Dionis undressed, thinking of these things, knowing that being with Cesare this evening had shown only too

clearly how desolate she would be without Juan. The wide
shoulders of the male dancer had become Juan's after the
first few steps; the handsome arrogant profile of the
dancer had suddenly been that of the man she would
always love. She slid into pajamas, appalled at the task
ahead of trying to forget him. Could she do it?

Lying in bed, Dionis tried to relax, wishing she could
free herself from some inner sense of conflict. Sometimes she felt that a sense of peace and contentment
would never be hers again. It had all begun with Juan.
How happy and contented she had been on her first night
in Spain, how thrilled to talk to Don Fernando and
reminisce about her father. She would think of Don
Fernando always in the same place, in the lamplit patio of
the inn enjoying his cigar and wine and his little gossip
with any alien who happened to be there. But in spite of
her reasoning and cool common sense, nothing could
prevent Juan from entering her thoughts. She fell asleep
thinking about him.

After breakfast the next day, Dionis went along to the
Villa Acacia with Cesare. He looked around with a
critical eye, much as Juan had done.

"I could not have done better myself," was his verdict
at the end of it. "A villa in sunny Spain as lovely as this is
worth considering. What do you say?"

He slanted a quizzical brow, growing wary at the deepening of the shadows in her eyes. They had walked
outside and were standing in the porch. The garden was
really something now that Paco had cleaned it up. Dionis
found her eyes being drawn to the marble seat she had
cleared of weeds the day Juan had arrived. The garden of
Eden could not have been lovelier . . . but it was not for
her. Her fingers closed over the keys in her hand in readi-

ness to hand them to Paco. Then she realized that Cesare was waiting for an answer.

"What about a villa in Italy?" she said, evading the issue. "I believe it is just as lovely." The scuff of Paco's espadrilles on the garden path filled her with relief. The last thing she wanted was for Cesare to know the reason for her reluctance to live in Spain. "*Buenos dias*, Paco," she said warmly. "Here are the keys to the villa. I told Don Juan I would give them to you."

His melancholy look was more marked than ever. "So you will be returning to Inglaterra, *senorita*. I have enjoyed working with you. You are so *simpatica*, so *bonita*. I shall miss you."

"I shall miss you too, Paco." Dionis kissed the leathery cheek, put the keys in his hand and squeezed it. "*Adios*, Paco. God bless."

"You appeared to have made quite a hit with Paco," Cesare remarked dryly as he swung the car onto the main road away from the villa. "Where do we go from here?"

"If it's all the same with you, I'd like to call and see how Senora Direnso is. There's a market garden on the way to the village where I can buy some flowers for her." Dionis went on to tell Cesare all about the little seamstress and her collapse at the Villa Acacia. She bought flowers at the market garden and discovered the owner was an Englishman who had settled in Spain. It was indeed a small world, she thought, as they drove toward the village.

Senora Direnso lived in one of four cottages situated on the last bend in the road before the village. The rough walls of the small dwelling were whitewashed, and a long low wall was slung in front. Dionis could imagine the lazy Senor Direnso sitting on it snoozing the hours away. He was not in sight when they drew up outside. Around the arched doorway vines rioted, badly in need of pruning, and the garden, where jasmine and plumbago abounded, bore the same air of neglect. Through the open doorway, Dionis could see the stone stairs leading to the upper regions. She knocked and waited.

Cesare had stayed in the car and was the center of attraction for three small children who'd run out of the cottage to see who the caller might be. They were clean and neatly dressed. Dionis was wondering how many more little Dirensos there were when a man of medium height, broad of shoulder, came to the door, wiping his hands on a white towel. His rather morose expression grew curious at the sight of the slim young English-woman on his doorstep.

"*Buenos dias*, Senor Direnso." Dionis spoke in slow, halting Spanish. "I have called to ask after Senora Direnso. How is she?"

"*Por favor*, come in, Senorita. . . ."

He paused significantly.

"Ward. My name is Dionis Ward. Senora Direnso had been doing some work for me," Dionis said.

He led her into a clean and comfortable room, and gestured her to one of the strong, string-seated chairs placed along the walls. There was a beautifully polished brass lamp on a low Spanish table and a colorful coconut mat on the stone floor. Across the chimney, a shelf containing earthenware pots and pans caught Dionis's eye, and a high-backed wooden seat lining the inglenooks on each side of the fireplace was gay with bright cushions. A simple dwelling showing withal the pride of peasants who could be as dignified as those in better circum-stances, she thought appraisingly.

She sat on the edge of one of the seats, refused a glass of wine and looked up expectantly at Senor Direnso. His

wife was in bed under sedation, he said. The doctor had
said she was to stay there for a week. She was suffering
from exhaustion. And the *ninos*, Dionis asked. Who
would look after them? Senor Direnso lifted lazy shoulders. Don Juan was sending them to the sea that very day
for two weeks while he, Senor Direnso, looked after his
wife.

His Spanish was correct and Dionis was able to follow
him. He had been quite a handsome man in his youth, she
decided with his classic nose and fine dark eyes. She did
not care for his sensuous mouth nor for the bulk of
superfluous flesh that made him appear coarse of fiber.
The man definitely needed shaking up, and Don Juan was
the person to do it. She had a little go in that direction
herself. Did the *senor* not think he was a lucky *hombre*
that his wife only required a week to recover providing
she did not overwork herself again? It might have been
more serious. She might easily have died, leaving him
with all the *ninos* to care for himself. He agreed, and
Dionis could see the affair had shaken him up. She stood
up, hoping the shaking up would be permanent, gave him
the flowers with a message for Senora Direnso that she
hoped she would soon be well again, and walked with him
to the door. The children were nowhere to be seen.
Apparently Cesare had given them pesetas to spend at the
village shop.

"Where now?" Cesare asked as they sped along the
road back to the inn. "Next stop London?"

"Yes," she answered. One little word that would take
her away from Juan forever. The morning sky was as
luminous as a pearl, with every tree and shrub, each
waving head of golden maize in the fields standing out
startlingly clear-cut in the brilliance of light. How she
would miss the purity of the air, the wonderful leisurely

evenings on the patio, the magic of Juan's presence, his light firm step, his deep voice turning her very bones to putty. While the urge to leave to escape further hurt was predominant, Dionis dreaded a future that now seemed obscure and hopelessly barren. Her mind and spirit bruised beyond endurance, she listened while Cesare talked of filling in their time should they prove to be unlucky in procuring air passage right away.

He phoned through to Barcelona when they returned to the inn. There were no seats on any outgoing flight for the next two days, but he would be informed immediately if there were any cancellations before then. That evening they dined with Don Fernando and his wife. Dionis had packed practically everything in readiness for her departure, including her evening dresses. So for this evening, she had put on a light woollen dress, formal but sweet. Cesare, also wearing a conventional dark suit, was very quiet but observant as he drove through the lovely evening air to Don Fernando's home.

"I like your Don Fernando," he said, paused, then added deliberately, "I like your Don Juan also."

He took a blind corner carefully and missed her startled glance in his direction. Nevertheless, Dionis felt he knew he had jolted her.

"Why do you say that, Cesare?" she asked, trying to make light of it and failing utterly.

"Because you are obviously unhappy over something, and after doing a lot of thinking, I can only assume you are in love. If it isn't Don Juan, then it could be me."

"Oh, Cesare, you dear! I love you, but not in that way," she exclaimed, touched by his concern.

"I didn't think you did—love me, I mean. In any case, I'd only be second best. I lost the only woman I shall ever love. She married a man years older than herself with money." His laugh was bitter. "She couldn't wait for me to leave home and make good. She's sorry now, though."

"You mean she wants you back now that you're wealthy?" Dionis asked curiously.

"She doesn't know that. By sheer coincidence she had the next seat to me on the plane when I went home the other week. She was flying to Rome. I told her what I wanted her to know, that I now had a decent job with a good income. She was terribly upset at seeing me, vowed she would love me all her life, but as neither of us believed in divorce that was to be her punishment."

Dionis sighed. "Poor Cesare! But you never know. Miracles sometimes happen. I hope some day you have your love."

There was not time for further conversation, for they were nearing the Villa Inez where Don Fernando and Dona Inez waited to greet them. There were to be no other guests. Pilar was in Barcelona shopping for accessories for her trousseau. Dionis enjoyed the evening more than she had anticipated. It could have been that learning of Cesare's lost love had made her more resigned to her own fate. It certainly made her more tender toward him. Moreover, Don Fernando was a host with whom it was impossible to be sad, and it helped considerably when Juan's name was not mentioned. It was very late when they left to return to the inn. Don Fernando kissed her hand on parting, begging her to return to Spain soon. Dona Inez seconded his invitation.

Senora Lopez woke Dionis the next morning to say she had received a long-distance call from Barcelona—two cancellations on the noon plane to London. Ten minutes later Dionis was having breakfast with Cesare. He had carried their cases to the hired car and it was his intention to drive them both to the Barcelona airport in it. A garage hand could collect it from there later. Dionis forced herself to swallow a little food in order to stem the numbed, hollow feeling welling inside her before she went upstairs to repair her makeup and collect the rest of her things. Blindly, she looked around the room she would never see again and went quickly downstairs. Senor and Senora Lopez, along with Tercia, waved them off. Dionis saw the wild flowers at the side of the road with a painful lurch of the heart. She had forgotten the forget-me-nots.

"Oh, Cesare!" she cried. "I must go back. I've forgotten my little plant."

"Go back?" he echoed with a frown. "Surely they can send it on?"

"But it might die in transit. Please, Cesare," she begged, "it won't take long."

"Is it a special one that you can't get back home to grow from seed?" he wanted to know. "In other words, is it worth going back two miles for?"

"It is to me," she answered firmly. "It's rather a special one."

"So be it," he said good-humoredly and waited for a wide stretch of road to turn the car around.

Their progress was impeded, as is the case when one is in a hurry—first by a herd of goats who took their time crossing the road. The second time it was a farm truck loaded with maize backing out of a field. At last they reached the inn, but were prevented from running to the entrance by a huge delivery van. Dionis slipped from the car, ran past the van to the inn and stopped dead at the sight of the big silver car. Juan! At first the hunger for a glimpse of him overcame every other feeling until common sense came to her rescue. He need not know she was there. The courtyard was empty, but she could hear voices within. Probably the men from the big van parked outside. She went swiftly up the stairs and heard voices on the landing. Once again he was there, looking up at the newly decorated ceiling that had been disfigured days ago by a wet patch.

Senora Lopez was saying, "Thank you for having it attended to, *senor*. I am sorry you missed Miss Ward. They had only just left when you arrived. I believe Senor Delusi said there would be time for them to have lunch in Barcelona before they caught the plane."

It was too late for Dionis to retreat, for they saw her simultaneously, Senora Lopez with a rather startled look of surprise, Juan with an expression on his face that sent her pulses racing.

"I'm sorry," she said before either of them could speak. "I left something in my room, Senora Lopez. May I get it?"

"By all means, Miss Ward. Senor Don Juan was saying he was sorry to have missed you."

But Dionis had avoided the dark gaze of Juan and had slipped past the *senora* to her room. The pot of forget-me-nots was in the bathroom. She had taken them in there the previous evening from the dressing table in her bedroom. Picking them up, she looked around wildly for something to wrap them in away from Juan's discerning gaze, but found nothing. It was just possible that he and Senora Lopez had gone downstairs. She listened quietly. There was no sound. Waiting precious minutes, Dionis eventually opened the door stealthily and peeped out. No one was there. Walking out of her room, she carried the little pot in triumph; someone moved around the corner of the landing to stand nonchalantly barring her way, and she was staring up at Juan.

"You came for that?" he asked glibly, an eyebrow lifting mockingly at the small pot in her hands. "I don't believe it. You actually came back for these?" He touched the limp flowers with a lean finger. "What did you do? Just stick them in the soil?" His eyes narrowed. "You have had them for some time. Is it possible? Can these be the flowers I gave you?" Dionis stood rigid, sensing his nearness along every nerve, his intention to hurt. "Did my giving them to you mean something?"

She had a difficulty in breathing. There was nothing to identify the flowers as the ones he had given her that day at the Villa Jacaranda. But she could find no feasible answer. Hot color burned her cheeks as she groped for words. None came.

His fingers gripped her shoulders. "Did it?" he insisted.

Things had gone too far for her to tell him to mind his own business. The next moment she was being propelled backward gently to her room. With great deliberation, the little pot was taken from her and placed on the dressing table, then he was turning her around to face him. Dionis had kept her head lowered. He knew, of course. She could feel his warm breath as he bent his head.

"Tell me why you had to come back for them. Why were they so important?"

He spoke the words with a dangerous softness. Dionis felt the anguish of him knowing the truth of her feelings for him. Pushing him away, she lifted eyes swimming with tears.

"Why do you ask when you already know?" she cried, dashing the tears away childishly with the back of her hand.

"Because I wanted to hear you say it," was the answer as he pulled her roughly into his arms.

Dionis gasped helplessly as his mouth crushed her own.

His arms tightened around her, crushing the breath from her body. Cesare, waiting outside in the car, was forgotten as she surrendered to demanding lips and arms that thrilled and terrified her. When at last he let her go, she felt bruised and battered. He was punishing her for the trouble she had caused him, humiliating her in the only way he knew how since he had discovered her feelings for him. It could not be passion darkening the pupils of his eyes into blackness. It must be anger. Somehow she contrived to put more space between them.

Bitterly, she said, "You've had your revenge. Now let me go."

She made for the door.

"Are you not forgetting something?" he asked.

Blindly, she turned to look at him in all his smiling handsome arrogance, appalled to find she loved him despite his cruelty. Scorn of her own weakness steadied her. She had craved him as one craves a powerful drug and, for the time being, his kisses had assuaged that need. When it came again it would be greater than ever. Her voice was cool as she could make it.

"The flowers? You can keep them."

"No, not the flowers. Me." The last word was spoken against her cheek. He was between her and the door and she was again in his arms. This time he held her gently and murmured something in Spanish between his kisses. When his mouth again claimed her own she felt the passion in him as the pressure of his arms increased. Rough or tender, Dionis found his touch pure delight and she responded ardently. She was as breathless as he was when he released her to draw her down to sit beside him on the bed. Taking her hands in his he openly adored her flushed face and tumbled hair with his eyes. "Did you really think I would let you go?" he whispered.

212

Dionis looked at him like a bewildered child. "You mean . . . you mean . . . ?"

"I love you, *amada*." He kissed her hands. "You look surprised."

"Surprised?" she echoed with the look of one who wakens from a dream to find it really happening. "I had no idea." Her fingers curled around his, wanting to believe that the passion darkening the pupils of his eyes was for her alone.

"Had you not?" Juan raised a tantalizing brow. "Not even when I came all the way from Castellon to look at a damp ceiling at the inn, a job I usually leave to one of my agents? And again when I asked you to be my guest when your work at the Villa Acacia was finished? And this morning when I rushed to the inn to find out before you left if you were as shattered as I was at the parting of our ways? Never have I been so . . . so angry . . . so frustrated, and never so much in love with a woman before!"

"But you advised me to marry Cesare. What if I had taken your advice?"

"Ah, that was not me speaking. It was my anger directed mainly against Antonio and your sister. I tried to convince myself that there was no difference between the three of you, that you were all out for what you could get. The moment I spoke the words I wanted to recall them. But I am still of the opinion that your sister is mercenary, a calculating person from whom you are better separated." His eyes had hardened as he spoke. Now they twinkled devilishly as he leaned forward to kiss the end of her nose. "Now tell me that you forgive me for doubting you and for saying harsh things about you that were not true."

"I forgive you."

"Because?"

"Because I love you." Dionis smiled through her tears. "I've never loved anyone before as I love you. I think I must have loved you from the start. When Angela mentioned that you were the owner of the Villa Acacia I could not bear the thought that you might be hurt by her desire to strip your villa and furnish it to suit herself." A warm flush covered her creamy skin. "I fell for you in more ways than one at our first meeting in the garden of the Villa Acacia."

Juan gave a loving pinch to her flushed cheek. There was an expression in his dark eyes, a tender passionate look of a man who had found his heart's desire.

"I fell in love with you irrevocably the day I gave you the posy of forget-me-nots. You caressed them with an ecstatic cry of joy, and suddenly I wanted you to look at me like that, to touch my face, to give me the pleasure of knowing that I, Juan Stebelo, was the only man who could bring you pure joy and ecstasy." He drew her hands up to his face and she caressed it gently.

"I never imagined I would ever be able to do this," she murmured. "Dona Dolores, yes. Never me."

He gripped her wrists. "Why Dolores? There is nothing between us."

So Dolores had lied. But Dionis had it in her heart to pity her.

"You obviously admired her, and her name was linked with yours on occasions."

He shrugged. "My name has been linked with *senoritas* ever since I was in my teens. I was once engaged to a younger sister of Dolores, but nothing came of it. I was largely to blame for that. I had no inclination to marry, and certainly not Antonia, who was more like a sweet little sister to me than anything else. She is happily married now, as you and I shall be very, very soon." He

leaned forward with the ardent look of a lover. "I give
you three weeks to prepare for our wedding, which will
take place at Castellon, my family home. In the meantime, you will be one of a number of guests I shall invite
to the Villa Jacaranda. Dolores will not be included. She
has gone home. As for the Villa Acacia, we shall keep it
as a place to stay on occasions. Not too often, for I want
my children to grow up in the Spanish way of life. When
we return from our long honeymoon, my sister Rosalba
will be married."

Dionis was staring aghast. "But three weeks? There's
so little time!" Only then did she remember Cesare
waiting in the car outside. "Oh, my goodness!" she cried.
"I forgot Cesare. We must go to him immediately." She
was on her feet, and Juan allowed her to pull him up
reluctantly. "There was nothing between Cesare and
myself. He lost the only woman he will ever love years
ago to someone else. It's my belief he'll wait for her
forever if need be."

The first thing they saw on reaching the door of the inn
were Dionis's cases, placed there by Cesare. There was no
sign of him. The big truck standing outside the inn when
she had arrived had gone. So had Cesare's car from
farther along the road.

Dionis looked at Juan helplessly. "He's gone. Cesare
has gone!"

He smiled. "Signor Delusi is a very intelligent man."

"But I don't understand. How did he know about us?"
She looked at him curiously. "Come to that, how did you
know we were leaving this morning? There are other
things that puzzle me, too. When you sent the man to pay
the workmen at the Villa Acacia, how did you know the
day they were finishing there? There was that time you
sent the men to start work, again on the right day, and . . .

and. . . ." It was quite a feat for Dionis to think rationally when his burning gaze was as tangible as a kiss. "Oh yes, the check you gave me. It was far too generous and you know it. How could you expect me to accept it? I shall. . . ."

But what Dionis had decided to do with the check was never disclosed—at least not to Juan, who had closed her mouth effectively with his own. As she was crushed against him, Dionis did not care a bit if Senora Lopez did come out and see them. She did not care if the whole world saw them. She was going to marry the man of her heart. And because she had found him through Angela he must not be too hard on her sister. In that moment Dionis loved not only Angela but the whole world, and she loved Juan most of all.

PAY ME TOMORROW

*Pay Me
Tomorrow*
Mary Burchell

The lovely Laverhopes they were called, living on their expectations; but in spite of a lifetime of promises, old Great-Aunt Georgina left her money elsewhere.

Drowning in debt, all their bright ambitions and hopes suddenly vanished, their situation was desperate.

Ismay, who only wanted happiness for the whole family, found herself reconsidering the ready solution of the notorious, but wealthy, Keith Otterbury.

Portrayed as a villain, Keith's offer of marriage was out of character, but then Ismay realized she had always seen him only through other people's eyes. Was it possible that she'd find him more suited to the role of a hero?

CHAPTER ONE

Susan Laverhope paused in the doorway, surveying the scene before her. In all her thirteen years she had never had the pleasure of making such a sensational announcement as the one that now trembled on her lips, and she intended to enjoy the moment to the fullest.

She looked at Ismay's beautiful fair head, bent slightly over the needlework she was doing, at Adrian idling in the windowseat with that air of picturesque grace common to all the Laverhopes, and at Avril absorbed in one of her silly old books on art.

Drawing a deep breath, she announced, "Aunt Georgina's dead."

The effect was instantaneous and gratifying.

"Aunt Georgina!"

"How do you know?"

"It isn't possible!"

"Of course it's possible." Susan was not going to have her moment spoiled by base incredulity. "Everybody has to die some time and—"

"Not the Aunt Georginas of this world. They're immortal." That was Adrian, who always said slightly shocking things with a specially languid air.

"That's blasphemy, I think, now she's dead," Susan remarked. "Isn't it, Ismay?" She came and stood close to her older sister.

"No." Ismay was comfortingly positive. "But how did you know about Aunt Georgina? Who told you?"

"Nobody told me. I just happened to be in the hall when the phone rang, and father answered. It must have been a telegram, because I heard him say, 'Miss Georgina

222

Eltham died suddenly this morning? Thank you.' Just like that."

"I don't call it sudden to die at ninety-one," commented Avril, fixing large thoughtful gray eyes on her young sister. "And you have a run in your panty hose," she added with characteristic irrelevance. Avril could look more beautifully attentive than all the rest of the family put together, but more likely than not her thoughts would be on something entirely removed from the subject of conversation.

"Have I? Oh, gosh!" Susan twisted around to survey the backs of her legs as well as she could. "That's the third pair this week. I never knew any single person so unlucky with these things as I am. Why, Carol Elthorpe says her mother buys her six pairs for her birthday and six pairs for Christmas and, would you believe it, she makes them last for—"

"Never mind, my child," her brother interrupted her once more. "Do you realize that you can now have enough pairs to tie knots around Carol Elthorpe—whoever she may be? We're all of us rich for the first time in our lives. No longer will the 'lovely Laverhopes' have to wear mended clothes or draw lots for who charms the butcher into extending our credit a little further. Aunt Georgina has done her duty by the family at last and—in Roberts's affecting phrase—has passed away. We are—or, rather, father is—richer by something like a hundred thousand pounds. Life is about to begin."

"You shouldn't talk like that, Adrian," Ismay protested. "It's not . . . decent."

"You ought to go on the stage," commented Susan. "You've just the same silly ways as father."

"Susan!" exclaimed both her sisters in horror, for the legend of father's brief stage career was something much more sacred than the death of Aunt Georgina.

Susan looked faintly—but only faintly—abashed.

"Well, I . . . I didn't quite mean that. I mean, you *expect* father to be all melodramatic and to make speeches since he is—was—an actor. But Adrian needn't."

Before Adrian could challenge this, however, the door opened once more and their father entered the room, slowly and with a gravity that he—and possibly even they—felt befitted the occasion.

Even at fifty-five, Laurence Laverhope still retained something of the fantastic good looks that had made him a matinee idol for a brief season in his youth. All too soon an infatuated public had reluctantly realized that, while good looks are a pleasant addition to, they are not a sufficient substitute for, the power to act. At least, not in an actor.

He still retained, however, the charm and the beautifully pitched voice, which all his children had inherited. He also retained the certainty that an admiring audience waited on his every word and, as he looked around now with an air of reflective melancholy, he might have been about to deliver Buckingham's speech to the populace on his way to execution.

What he did say was not quite so impressive.

"Children, you will be very grieved to hear that your Great-aunt Georgina died in her sleep at four-thirty this morning."

No one—not even Susan—thought of spoiling father's announcement by telling him that this news was already known. And after the faintest pause he continued. "This is hardly the moment to remember that we were not always perhaps quite in agreement with your great-aunt. She had her faults. We no doubt have ours." Everyone knew this was a graceful gesture rather than a sincere belief. "But death is a great leveler. There is no need to remember more now than that she was that rarity in the world today—a great lady."

No one—not even Adrian—thought of interrupting this eulogy, the eloquence of which evidently gave father genuine pleasure. Everyone looked suitably grave and attentive.

Then Susan, unable to contain herself any longer, inquired with indecent cheerfulness, "Shall we go and live at Estercourt now?"

This followed rather badly on father's reference to a great lady, and even Ismay felt that Susan had invited the glance of pained astonishment that father bestowed upon her.

"My dear," he said in the accepted stage tone for a parent rebuking an erring child, "your great-aunt has not been dead twelve hours. Is it for us to begin dividing her possessions among us at this time?"

No one seemed to have an answer to this presumably rhetorical question, and in the ensuing silence father made a grand exit.

When he was well out of hearing Susan pouted and protested indignantly, "Nobody said anything about dividing possessions. I wish father wouldn't always talk like Shakespeare or the least interesting bits of the Bible."

"You do Shakespeare less than justice, my dear," Adrian assured her. "But, anyway, I wouldn't worry about father's rebuke if I were you. No one is more frantically relieved than he at the turn events have taken."

"Adrian, it isn't particularly witty to say those things," Ismay reminded him sharply. "And you certainly shouldn't say them to Susan."

"Why not to me?" Susan wanted to know, while Adrian gave a smiling little shrug.

"I'm sorry, darling. But the truth *is* the truth, however regrettable. No one can suppose that a man in father's position could remain inconsolable for the death of a most unlikable old lady, especially when the consolation comes in the form of a desperately needed fortune. Why, he must have an overdraft as long as my arm, and practically no idea where the next penny is coming from."

"What's an overdraft?" inquired Susan, ghoulishly interested in this description of her father. But no one told her, because at that moment Avril suddenly spoke with that dreamy determination of hers that always commanded attention.

"I know *exactly* what I'm going to do. I've often lain awake at night thinking what I would do when the money did come. I shall go to Italy and study art all day long and paint and paint and paint. I shall go to Rome, to the best teachers. And when I'm not working I shall wander around Italy—to Verona and Lake Garda, to Florence and Vallombrosa. I'll watch the Arno rushing under the arches of the Ponte Vecchio and the line of the cypress trees against the evening sky and the lizards running in the sun on the old stone walls. And I'll forget there was ever such a thing as fog or rain or cold."

"It sounds heavenly," Ismay agreed.

"There's snow in Rome during the winter," Adrian warned her prosaically, but he, too, smiled at the picture Avril conjured up.

"I wish someone would tell me what an overdraft is," persisted Susan.

"There's the romantic temperament for you," declared Adrian, with mock despair. "Here are we enthusing about the glories of Italy, and all the child can babble about is an overdraft."

"Well, one ought to know these things. They may be useful one day. What is it, anyway?"

Adrian looked at her very seriously and said, "An over-draft is something you're always asking your bank manager to let you have, and when you have it you spend the time wondering how the deuce you can get rid of it."

The two older girls laughed, but Susan said wither-ingly, "I don't see that that makes sense."

"It doesn't," Adrian assured her. "Nor do most other things with no money attached, come to that."

"Well, anyway, we have plenty of money now," Avril put in impatiently. And, standing up, she strolled grace-fully out of the room with an air of already being about to begin the preparations for her journey.

Adrian looked after her thoughtfully. Then he smiled and stretched his arms above his head.

"Yes, we've plenty of money at last. Think of it! Medi-cal school for me. I know I could get a grant, but can any of you see me existing on a grant? Now I can do it in reasonable comfort. And then one day, poppet," he assured Susan, "you'll be proud to point out your brother as one of the leading doctors of the day."

"I wouldn't like to have you for a doctor," Susan retorted. "You haven't enough sense of responsibility."

"Never mind, Adrian, you'll have a beautiful bedside manner," Ismay told him with a smile.

But Adrian turned on her at that, in sudden, unusual anger.

"Damn the bedside manner! That isn't what I want. Don't you see that's all this family has ever been any good for? Picturesque, charming, handsome—the lovely Laver-hopes! I hate it all, every word of it. We're cursed with the power of looking decorative in every single situation. How did father ever get on the stage? Because he was a sight to fill every stall with a fluttering female. And why wasn't he able to stay there? Because he hadn't the plain wits or common sense to learn his job. I want to be a doctor, not a blue-eyed heartthrob. I'm sick to death of everyone saying what a wonderful-looking family we are. I sometimes almost wish I had a squint."

"It'd be very inconvenient," Susan pointed out. "And weaken your sight too."

"Oh, Adrian dear, I'm sorry." Ismay patted her brother's arm sympathetically. "I know what you mean. And I daresay it's especially rotten for a boy. I sometimes think you have a good deal of mother in you."

"I have?" Adrian snorted, a little ashamed of his outburst now. "Oh no. I can remember her quite well. You're the only one of us who is the least like her. It's something to do with patience and having a charitable sense of humor, I think."

Ismay laughed a little and colored slightly.

"I'm not at all like her in appearance," she said.

"No, of course not. You're much more beautiful. When you come to think of it, mother must have found it funny being the only ordinary-looking person in a family of beauties."

"I think," Ismay said, "that was just what she found it—funny. It was one of the nicest things about her."

"I expect you're right." Adrian's casual good humor was entirely restored as he went off "to make sure," as he put it, "that the obituary notice to *The Times* displayed only father's less embarrassing clichés.

When he had gone Susan turned back to her older sister.

"Well, if Avril's going to Italy and Adrian's going to college, what are you and I going to do?"

"I don't know." Ismay smiled as she picked up her sewing again. "What would you like to do?"

"Oh, lots of things." Susan spoke with pleasurable

vagueness. "Is life really going to be very different, Ismay?"

"I expect so," Ismay admitted slowly.

She was trying to imagine just how different it would be, for she could never remember a time when financial embarrassment had not been a daily companion. And yet somehow, on the insistence of father, no one had ever done anything about it, except "look decorative" as Adrian had said, and wait for Great-aunt Georgina to die.

The truth was that Laurence Laverhope was one of those men who ought never to have money left to them. Or rather, they should never know they are going to inherit it until the day when it actually becomes theirs. Great-aunt Georgina had been left a fabulously rich widow nearly half a century before and had immediately announced that she intended her dear little nephew, Laurence, to be her sole heir. She had been a delicate woman, disagreeably convinced that she was not long for this world, and therefore Laurence's parents had proceeded to bring him up with the pleasurable expectation that he would be a very rich man by the time he came of age.

In due course Laurence came of age, but his Aunt Georgina continued to enjoy her delicate health and her vast fortune.

With charming condescention he drifted onto the stage in order to fill in the time of waiting. After a while, a trifle bewildered, he drifted off again. Still Aunt Georgina's demise was delayed.

Then he married, for what was to prevent a man from marrying when he was (almost) in receipt of a very large income? While he still waited for the income to materialize he somehow contrived to live and bring up a family on a small private income left by his father, a great deal of credit, and the firm belief that, if he were not exactly a very rich man, he was at least only one stage removed from it.

No one had ever heard his wife express an opinion on the golden future in store for them. It was possible, of course, that she was much too busy making what she could of the far-from-golden present. Four children, however beautiful, had to be fed and clothed and looked after, and their wants certainly wouldn't wait for the time when Great-aunt Georgina should die and leave them a fortune, whether it was this year, next year, some time or—horrid thought—never.

In the end Laurence Laverhope's wife died ten years before Great-aunt Georgina, and because she was amused by her family as well as loving them dearly, it is possible that her last sensation was one of humorous regret that she would never see how they did react when the long-awaited fortune became theirs.

Some such thought was in Ismay's mind now because—Adrian was right—she was the nearest in disposition to their dead mother.

"Mother would have been terribly amused if she could have seen us now," she said aloud, hardly noticing that her young sister was still there beside her.

"Why? It's nice being left a fortune, but not exactly funny."

"No, not funny. But I think she would have been intrigued by our reactions, now that it's come at last. I don't think she ever quite believed in it herself."

"I didn't either," Susan confessed. "Great-aunt Georgina was so jolly careful not to give us anything when she was alive that I can't imagine that her being dead will alter anything much. Why, even that one time she gave Adrian half a crown for being third in class she took back a shilling when she found there were only four in the class. It doesn't seem to go with leaving a fortune to anyone, somehow."

Ismay smiled.

"I know. I sometimes felt a bit that way too. Only father always talked as though everything in the world could wait until we were rich, and after a while, so much depended on it that I simply couldn't believe the fortune wasn't waiting just around the corner."

"Well, so it was," Susan pointed out practically.

"Yes, I know." Ismay saw no reason to harrow her sister now with an account of how near to disaster they had been, but she knew—better perhaps than anyone else—the sea of debt and confusion that would have engulfed her father if Great-aunt Georgina had chosen to die even at ninety-two instead of ninety-one.

"Do you think Avril will really go to Italy to study art?" Susan's thoughts had gone off on another track now.

"Yes, I imagine so. She nearly always does exactly what she means to."

Susan nodded.

"I think she had some idea of how she was going to do it even if Great-aunt Georgina *hadn't* died," she said.

Ismay glanced up in surprise.

"Oh, but she couldn't have managed it. There was no possible way of doing it without money, and I know father hadn't a penny to spare for anything extra."

"Oh, I don't think it was anything to do with father. I think it was something not quite, well, something she thought we wouldn't like, because she said 'art excused a lot of things,' or something silly like that."

"Did she?" Ismay looked disturbed. She knew that of all the family Avril was much the most incalculable. "I don't expect she was speaking very seriously, Susan?" It was more a question than a reassuring statement.

"She *looked* serious," Susan insisted. "In fact, she looked jolly angry, because she was just leading off rather about not having any money of her own. I think perhaps it had something to do with Mr. Otterbury."

"Mr. Otterbury! But she hardly knows him. He couldn't possibly have anything to do with her going to Italy."

"Well, perhaps I'm wrong." Susan considered that possibility with reluctance. "But I'm pretty sure he had something to do with it. He did dance with her at the County Ball, remember. And he offered to let her ride one of his horses if she wanted to."

"Yes, I know. And father put his foot down pretty firmly," retorted Ismay, setting her soft mouth very firmly.

"Why wouldn't father let her go riding, Ismay? At least, I mean, why wouldn't he let her borrow one of Mr. Otterbury's horses?"

"Because one doesn't put oneself under an obligation to men like Mr. Otterbury." Ismay's tone was positive, but it only served to interest Susan further.

"Father said he was 'a wrong 'un.' What does that mean exactly?"

"Oh, well, it's father's way of saying he isn't the kind of person he would like us to know."

"Is that all?" Susan was disappointed. But Ismay added nothing to her explanation. Nor did she question her younger sister further. If there were anything more to be asked she would ask Avril directly.

She glanced at Susan now and thought, with a slight sigh, that though she and Avril were almost identical in coloring—with the cloudy gray eyes and the red gold hair—they were entirely different in temperament. Susan was a downright inquisitive, sometimes tiresome but always understandable schoolchild. Avril was remote, even secretive, strangely independent, frankly self-centered, but with occasional flashes of charm that could make up for weeks of indifference.

Ismay loved them both—as indeed she loved all her family—but there was no denying that Susan was a much simpler problem than the twenty-year-old Avril.

Adrian, for all his assumed air of nonchalance, was more like Ismay herself, both in looks and in temperament. They both had the same dark blue eyes and corn-colored hair as their father. But they had inherited their balanced sense of values from their mother, and were united by a sense of humor singularly lacking in the other members of the family. Adrian's sense of humor was perhaps keener than Ismay's—certainly his sense of the ridiculous was—but it was also a good deal less kind. And while Ismay's smile had never made anyone feel uncomfortable, Adrian's most certainly had.

When Susan had finally gone about some faintly mysterious business of her own, Ismay folded up her sewing and went upstairs to the room she shared with Avril. She had rather expected to find her sister dreaming by the window—a favorite occupation of hers—but instead she was in a fever of occupation.

Both the doors of the huge old closet they shared stood open, and everything Avril possessed had been taken out and thrown on her bed for a hurried but critical inspection.

"What on earth. . . ?" began Ismay. But Avril interrupted her.

"There's not a single thing that will do. Isn't it marvel-

ous? Father will have to reequip me from top to toe. I
might take that—" she scornfully twitched the skirt of a
gray angora frock "as I suppose I'll need one warm thing.
But I can't really connect anything else I have with going
to Italy."

Ismay sat down on the other bed and laughed.

"Are you leaving tomorrow?"

"Um?" Avril smiled slightly, too. "No. But I love
getting everything worked out in my mind first. It's half
the fun."

"You had it all worked out already, didn't you, Avril?
Even before Aunt Georgina died, I mean."

"Yes. Why not?" Avril's eyes were on the clothes
again, and the faintest cool touch of remoteness had crept
into her tone. It was not quite like a door being
closed—more like the drawing of a thin curtain.

"It was counting your chickens a good while before
they were hatched, for all you knew."

"Well, we all did that all our lives, didn't we?" Avril's
voice was too soft to be defiant, but a breath of resentment was perceptible.

"Yes. Too much so, I daresay. But this was something
much more definite. You weren't only thinking of Great-
aunt Georgina, were you?"

Avril raised her head quickly and, seeing the oddly
innocent look in those cloudy gray eyes, Ismay had the
peculiar impression that a lie was coming. Speaking
hastily, before Avril could, she challenged her bluntly.

"Susan says you had some idea that Keith Otterbury
would help you."

There was a second's pause. The thin curtain had
become thicker.

"Did she?"

"Avril, you *couldn't* have had any idea of letting *him* take a hand in our affairs?"

"*My* affairs."

"But, my dear, what was your idea? How do you suppose he could have helped you?"

"With money, of course. It's the only way anyone can help. Surely we've had that shown clearly enough all our lives."

"But, *his* money? Avril, do you know what you're talking about? You couldn't seriously have thought of taking money from a man like Keith Otterbury? Had he offered it, anyway? How did you even come to discuss such a thing?" Ismay was terribly distressed and made no attempt to hide the fact.

Avril shrugged slightly and, picking up a flowered dress, held it against herself and studied her reflection in the mirror.

"Well, it doesn't matter now, anyway, does it? Because we're rich and I don't have to think about anyone helping me."

"But—" Ismay bit her lip "—I don't think you can dismiss it like that."

"I *have* dismissed it like that," Avril said, and she gave her perfectly heavenly smile.

Ismay came over to her, took the dress away from her, and tossed it on the bed again. Then she caught both Avril's hands.

"Look here, Avril, have you been seeing a good deal of him? Father would have a fit if he knew. And anyway Keith Otterbury isn't the kind of person one . . . one makes a friend of."

"I wasn't going to make a friend of him."

"Then *what*? Please be a bit more frank, Avril. I could shake you."

"Well then, if Great-aunt Georgina hadn't providentially died, I would have gone with Keith Otterbury to Italy. He travels a lot, you know, and always in such comfort."

Ismay fell back from her.

"You were *going away* with him? Do you mean. . . ?"

"The usual thing? Of course."

"Avril, I feel I don't know you, even after all these years, when you talk like that. How can you possibly stand there calmly telling me you're going away with an absolute rotter just because he has more money than he knows what to do with?"

"But I'm not going, darling. That's the whole point. Great-aunt Georgina has prevented it, and I don't mind saying I'm glad."

"But you *would* have gone. It's almost as bad as going. You speak as though there's nothing wrong about it, as though it's like . . . like going on the river for the day. If Great-aunt Georgina hadn't died . . . ."

"But she *has* died, Ismay dear." Avril laughed—a sweet laugh of genuine amusement. "You're not a bit like the rest of us. You can agonize like anything over something that has never happened, while it's all we can do to give passing attention to a disaster that is almost upon us. You make such a lot of unnecessary anxiety for yourself."

"No," Ismay said. "No, it's not anxiety—at least, not now that the danger is past. It's the shock of realizing that you could contemplate such a thing. It doesn't seem possible that one of *us* could talk calmly of doing the sort of thing one only reads about."

"But one doesn't only read about it." It was Avril who sounded much older and more experienced now. "You're awfully naïve in a way, Ismay. Funny, I believe you get it from father, of all people," she added irrelevantly. "It's a plain fact that until today we had absolutely nothing but our looks to offer in the world market. I recognized the fact—even if you didn't—and I saw no reason to waste the one asset I had in the struggle to get what I wanted."

"I think it's . . . frightful of you to talk like that." Ismay found that she was trembling slightly with something very much like anger.

"Well, darling, can't you comfort yourself with the fact that none of it ever happened?" Avril laughed, then actually gave Ismay a light, coaxing kiss. "Can't you think of it as all hot air and bravado on my part?—something that I can talk about quite calmly because I would never really do it?"

Ismay looked at her doubtfully.

"Is that really it, I wonder?" she sighed. And then, as Avril didn't answer, she said, "That was it, wasn't it, Avril? You wouldn't really have done such a thing when it came to the point, would you? I wish you'd assure me of that."

"Well, rest assured," Avril told her lightly. But her smile had suddenly become very secret again, as she turned to put away the despised dresses.

Ismay remembered that smile all day. And at night, as she lay awake, listening to the soft, untroubled breathing of her inexplicable sister, she felt almost as worried as if Avril still contemplated the crazy plan she had so coolly put forward.

That she should choose Keith Otterbury, of all people! Well, of course, he was the richest man in the county, and he had undoubtedly admired Avril at the County Ball, as Susan had said. But . . . he was an "outsider." (Funnily enough, all father's slightly melodramatic terms of condemnation seemed to suit him.) Adrian always said

nat his name ought to be Sir Jasper and that he ought to
e seen philandering with a milkmaid in an ornamental
smock.

He never had been seen doing any such thing, but there
was plenty of scandalous talk about him, all the same.
The villagers classed all his escapades as "goings-on in
London," while the "county" raised supercilious
eyebrows and talked about the necessity of drawing the
line somewhere. The line, it seemed, was drawn some way
before Keith Otterbury.

It must be confessed that he himself remained
peculiarly untroubled by either the scandalized state of
the villagers or the superiority of the "county." He
farmed his extensive estate admirably, was considered a
hard but fairly just landlord, and though he was
understood to take his pleasures where he found them
during his visits to town, when he returned to his estate he
certainly worked hard. Even his estate manager admitted that, and his manager, being an extremely efficient
man himself, set a high standard.

"Oh well," reflected Ismay uneasily, "if Avril did want
to weave some fantastic notion to herself, I suppose he
was the obvious person to choose. I can't imagine anyone
else in the district agreeing to take one of father's daughters on a questionable trip abroad. But I wish she hadn't
spoken so very much as though all the details had been
arranged. He doesn't seem like an easy man to lead on and
then choke off. And if she really let him think she was
that sort of girl. . . !"

Ismay decided that she would probably feel very angry
and uncomfortable next time she met Keith Otterbury,
riding his melodramatically black horse along the country lanes.

It was very wrong to feel glad that someone was dead,

but really, thank heaven Great-aunt Georgina had chosen just this moment!

The next few days were taken up with funeral arrangements suitable to the position of Great-aunt Georgina and the degree of awe that her family had felt toward her. No one, not even father, could possibly pretend that deep affection prompted any of this. Great-aunt Georgina, after that one generous gesture of declaring that her nephew should be her heir, had never been known to do anything generous or kind again. She had been that most difficult tyrant, a gentle bully, and a reluctant submission to her sweetly stinging tongue had been the nearest thing to affection her family had ever felt able to accord her.

There was a sense of relief, in more ways than one, in the Laverhope family just then. And it showed itself in various forms, from the mellifluous bass-baritone humming of father, recalling ballads from his youth, to a disposition on Susan's part to disregard home lessons entirely.

"It seems silly, in a way, to be bothering *quite* so much about education when I won't ever have to earn my own living," she confided to Ismay.

Ismay, however, refused to see things quite in that light, and in this connection, at least, Great-aunt Georgina was invoked in vain.

The funeral was a stately affair, "with father in splendid form," as Adrian whispered to Ismay. Ismay didn't smile, however. She was thinking how sad and futile it was that anyone should live in the world nearly a hundred years and never discover the value of being loved instead of feared. The dreadful truth was that Great-aunt Georgina had never given greater pleasure in her life than she did by dying. *And yet we're not a heartless family*, thought Ismay. *At least, I suppose we're not.* And for a moment her eyes went to Avril, fair-skinned and exquisite in her simple black—bought on credit.

After the funeral only one person came back to the house with them—a short, stocky man Ismay had noticed during the service because he was singularly impressive in spite of being almost completely bald.

"Who is he, Adrian?" she asked. "I don't think I've ever seen him before."

"No. He's the lawyer down from London. Going to read the will in style, I presume."

"Read the will? But there isn't really much to read, surely?"

"I suppose not. But I don't think father would want to be done out of a scene like that. I imagine we shall all sit around the dining room table and look as though we don't know anything about what is going to be said. Then when the words are actually out, we shall permit ourselves an appearance of dignified pleasure, decently tinged with melancholy."

"It seems rather silly."

"It is, damned silly," Adrian agreed. "But I don't think that consideration ever stopped father from doing anything in his life."

Ismay made no reply, but she felt slightly silly and self-conscious when they were, as Adrian had prophesied, grouped around the dining-room table to hear the reading of the will. Susan—and father—were probably the only people who were completely enjoying the scene, though Mr. Foster, the lawyer, permitted himself a certain grave geniality that, Ismay supposed, was the right expression to use when announcing good news to the heir of a client.

Mr. Foster broke the seal of the envelope he was holding and drew out several sheets of paper.

Great-aunt Georgina certainly took a lot of space to

say she had left father everything, thought Ismay. *I hope she hasn't included sarcastic advice to us all, along with it.*

Mr. Foster glanced around the table and cleared his throat.

"Before I read the will of the late Mrs. Eltham, I think I should say a few words. The will is a long one, with many and varied bequests, but I feel it will lessen the, ah, anxiety and the, uh, tension if I explain at once that every penny of Mrs. Eltham's money has been left to charity."

CHAPTER TWO

The scene that followed Mr. Foster's announcement had, for Ismay, very much the character of a nightmare. Afterward she always had difficulty in recalling the lawyer's appearance, but she never forgot his voice.

The heavy drone of a bee invariably recalled to her the fantastic scene in the dining room, where the family sat in stunned silence, while Mr. Foster's voice droned on and on, reciting the list of charities to which Great-aunt Georgina had so generously left her fortune.

For a long time Ismay just stared at the tablecloth, noticing subconsciously how worn the pile was at the corner, and how lavishly spotted with ink was the place where Susan usually did her homework. Some of those blots were older still, dating from Avril's or Adrian's schooldays, or perhaps her own. "One day" they had been going to have a new cloth, just as they had been going to have new furniture and new carpets and new clothes and a new life. One day—the day when Great-aunt Georgina's fortune passed to them at last.

Well, there was no such day. Great-aunt Georgina had died and her money had passed, not to them, but to all those excellent hospitals and institutions now being enumerated by Mr. Foster. Places that, no doubt, would make far better use of the money than the Laverhopes would ever have done. Perhaps it was right in a way. Only life had to go on, and just now life was a rather frightening matter.

At last Ismay raised her head and glanced, a little fearfully, at the faces around her.

Only Susan's retained any liveliness of expression, and she was listening with the greatest attention and curiosity to what Mr. Foster was saying. Perhaps she was fascinated by the sheer amount of the sums mentioned, or perhaps she had still not gathered that "charity" did not include the family.

When Ismay's eyes turned to Adrian, she felt her throat ache. For all his nonchalance and his deliberately frivolous manner, he'd always had his heart set, she knew, on becoming a doctor. He had been sincere when he angrily repudiated any idea of enjoying the more spectacular side of the profession—he wanted to study and practise, to be something worthwhile and useful. And now—she could read the ruin of his hopes quite clearly in his white, set face, and the curiously bleak expression of his eyes. They were nice eyes, not only beautiful in color, but with a curious sparkling warmth that could light very often with real generosity. Now they looked, somehow, blind.

Slowly her glance shifted to her father. He, too, was white, but he looked much more bewildered than Adrian. As yet he had not entirely grasped the situation, and there was something strangely pathetic about his instinctive effort to keep up general appearances while he groped bewilderedly for the cue to the part he should play. For once he had not been prepared. There was no precedent for this ghastly scene, no hint of the best way to handle it. There was something almost childlike in his distress. He was like a nice little boy who had trotted over to smell a rose and had his nose stung by a bee.

Ismay felt real pain as she looked at him, and quickly she glanced away to the last member of the family.

Avril, her chair tipped back slightly, was gazing

thoughtfully out of the window at the clouds that drifted slowly across the sky. She was not paying the slightest attention to Mr. Foster. Indeed, she was entirely remote from the scene, and Ismay doubted if she either heard or saw anything going on around her. Certainly any shock she might have felt had already passed. The situation was no longer useful to her, and she had detached herself from it. With a cold little feeling of something like horror, Ismay was certain her sister was making other plans, and had already gone back to her original idea. If she couldn't have what she wanted in one way, then she would have it in another. She was thinking of Keith Otterbury and his money . . . and his offer, whatever it was.

It was over at last—the dreadful scene, with implications that, even now, were hazy to them all. Mr. Foster gathered up his papers and became the man, rather than the lawyer, once more.

"I am very sorry," he said. "It would be idle to pretend this is not a very disappointing will, a very unkind will, one might say. But Mrs. Eltham was not a woman who was open to advice, still less to protest. There was nothing I could do about it."

Father roused himself then. His public demanded that he should say something, and a little heavily he produced the suitable words.

"She was, of course, quite entitled to leave her money where she pleased. One must not allow disappointment to degenerate into bitterness."

It was a very bitter little smile, however, that crossed Adrian's face.

"Aren't we going to have *any*thing? Aren't we rich, after all, then?"

The crude candor of Susan's astonished demands made

them all wince slightly. It was sad, but it was true. They were not rich, after all.

Somehow they got through the rest of that day. Mr. Foster tactfully intimated that urgent business in London necessitated his immediate return, and when he had gone, father withdrew almost at once to the room known as his study. He never, of course, had done any study there—unless he studied the plentiful accumulation of bills adorning his desk. But it was clearly understood that when he retired there he was not to be disturbed.

"Well," Adrian said, "there it is! The lovely Laverhopes face financial disaster—still looking decorative, but not knowing what the hell they're going to do."

"Don't, Adrian." Ismay glanced at him with something like pity. "It doesn't help to be—"

" 'Bitter' was father's word," Adrian reminded her savagely.

"Very well. Being bitter doesn't help."

"Yes, but what *would* help?" Susan wanted to know. "What can we do?"

"My dear," Adrian told her, "you have an unrivaled talent for asking those questions that either cannot be answered or have only the most disagreeable answers to them."

"Well, you needn't be a pig about it," retorted Susan. "*I've* lost the money as well as you. And anyway, I only *asked*. Even if you don't have an answer, perhaps someone else has. Ismay might. She has lots more sense than you."

Ismay put a restraining hand on her little sister's arm. It was awful enough that they should all be so disappointed and despairing. It would be ten times worse if they started bickering about it. Perhaps Adrian thought the same, because, with an effort, he restrained his irritation.

"All right, poppet, I'm sorry. Perhaps Ismay does have a solution. I'm afraid I haven't—short of my getting a job as a pharmacist's assistant and the girls working in shops or acting as models. They're pretty enough, goodness knows."

"I," said Avril coolly, "shall not work in any shop, nor do I intend to be a model. The life has never appealed to me."

Adrian laughed shortly.

"You don't really think there's much choice confronting us, do you?"

"Oh, I don't know." Avril's eyes looked deceptively dreamy. "In actual fact we're no worse off than we were this time last week. We didn't have any more real money in our pockets then. I don't know why we should start running around in circles and talking despairingly now."

"Don't you?" Adrian's tone was grim, though slightly amused. "Because last week we were all living in a gorgeous, ridiculous, colossal dream. Now we've woken up. That's the difference. The central fact that has buoyed up our spirits and our credit all these years simply doesn't exist now. We've been brought up to adorn riches one day. Now riches refuse to adorn us. We're as decorative as ever, but we're poor. The two things don't go together. Nature abhors the combination a lot more than any vacuum."

"Well, life doesn't begin and end with Great-aunt Georgina's will," retorted Avril placidly. "There *are* other things."

"Such as?"

But Avril refused to be drawn.

Supper was a depressing meal, particularly as father refused to be tempted from the seclusion of his study. Not that he would have been especially cheerful company, but any meal seemed strange and incomplete without his slightly pompous, but not unkindly, presence.

"Doesn't father want any supper?" Susan, her own appetite unaffected by grief, read in his absence a very serious state of affairs.

"No." Ismay shook her head and looked worried. "He asked for some sandwiches and coffee to be sent in."

"And did you take them in? How did he look? Is he frightfully upset?" Susan was interested in securing a complete picture.

"I didn't go in." Ismay hesitated a moment, then added with a slight effort, "The door was locked. He just called out to me to leave the tray on the table outside the door."

"I say—" Susan paused suddenly with her fork half-way between her plate and her mouth "—you don't think he's going to commit suicide, do you? I mean, people do when they lose a lot of money."

"You've been reading too much Dumas," her brother told her crushingly.

"No, I haven't. And anyway, why should he lock the door?"

"Because he probably remembers that's what the ruined hero does in all the best books. Retires with his grief behind locked doors. It's much better than to be so gross and insensitive as to come and enjoy a hearty meal in company with his family."

"Do you think so?" Susan appealed to Ismay, rather than her brother.

"Well, something like that." Ismay smiled. "I don't think father is in a suicidal mood, but he's probably very upset and I expect he wouldn't like us to see him like that."

"I . . . see. Do I have to go and yell good night through the door?"

"Perhaps he'll have come out by then," Ismay suggested.

But he had not. Nor by the time that the others went to bed. Ismay lingered after Adrian and Avril had gone upstairs. She went around locking up, then hesitated before turning off the lamp in the hall. Father was not a man who liked to be interrupted when he indicated a desire for solitude, but he had been there alone too long. Suddenly making up her mind, Ismay went over and knocked on the study door.

"Who is that?" Father sounded tired and irritable.

"It's Ismay, father." She tried the door, but it was still locked.

"Oh. Good night, my dear."

"I want to come in, please. I want to speak to you."

"Tomorrow. Go away now, my child."

Ismay knew that if he addressed her as "my child" he was in one of his "noble" moods, which usually meant that he was about to make an exceedingly foolish decision.

"No, please let me in. The others have gone to bed, but I want to see you. You make me nervous, refusing to see me like this."

She heard her father get up from his chair then and, coming over, he unlocked the door and opened it. She was not sure whether he actually intended her to come into the room, but she brushed quickly past him and entered the circle of lamplight. Then, turning back to her father, who still stood by the door, she uttered an exclamation of concern.

Poor Laurence Laverhope looked like a very tired, wretched and disappointed man at that moment. All his life he had lived on pleasant hopes and a sense of well-being in which anticipation and reality were inextricably mingled. Now everything had faded and he looked—Ismay realized with dismay—like an old man.

"What is it, my dear?" He spoke rather heavily.

"Only that . . . I don't like saying good night to you through the door." She came and put her arm around him, smiling at him though her eyes were anxious. "Besides, I know you must be feeling simply awful, dear. It's such a dreadful disappointment—much worse for you than for any of us."

Just for a moment the ex-matinee idol put his head down on his daughter's shoulder. It was a telling gesture, but it was perfectly sincere. He did indeed feel that everything was over and done with, and his desire for support was something almost physical.

Ismay rubbed her cheek affectionately against his hair.

"We'll manage all right. Things won't seem so bad when you've had a night's sleep. Why don't you go to bed now, with some hot milk and aspirin? And in the morning we'll talk things over together."

"There's nothing to talk over, my dear. Nothing but bills."

There was no striving after effect in that statement—nothing studiedly dramatic. It was just a stark fact discovered by a miserable and very frightened old man. Ismay found it far more moving than anything he had ever said. She kissed him warmly and spoke again with a cheerfulness she was far from feeling.

"Oh, you mustn't worry so much. Adrian and Avril and I will get jobs. We've never organized our lives very well before, but now we'll be sensible wage earners, like thousands of other people. You've no idea how well we'll manage. And each month we'll set aside everything we can to pay the bills. Please, dear, go to bed now and don't wear yourself out worrying. It's going to be a big change for all of us, but there's no reason why we shouldn't make it a success."

There wasn't very much logic in this, but the tone and the smile were encouraging. Finally he allowed himself to be persuaded. And when he kissed her forehead and remarked in his more usual, deep tone that "no man had better daughters than he," Ismay felt sure he was feeling better. It was such a heartening return to his usual manner.

She took him up the aspirin and a glass of hot milk, and was moved to see his ingenuous pleasure at the attention. Really, there was something very childlike about father. That was why one could never take him very seriously.

Afterward, Ismay went downstairs again to his study, to make sure that the light was turned off. Spread on his desk were a depressing number of accounts, bills, letters of reminder and his bank passbook. He had evidently been compiling a list of his debts, for two sheets of paper were covered with columns of figures. Beside these rested a revolver.

Ismay experienced a most unpleasant shock on seeing this. Was it possible that Susan's absurd suggestion had any foundation in fact? He could not really have intended. . . . But her knowledge of her father served to calm her almost immediately.

It was not surprising to find that the revolver was unloaded. Also the columns of figures had been added up incorrectly. Putting both the gun and the papers into the middle drawer of the desk, Ismay turned off the lamp and went upstairs to bed.

It was not until the next afternoon that Ismay had an opportunity to talk to Avril alone. When she had come up to bed after settling father's problems for the moment, Avril was either asleep or determinedly feigning sleep. But the next afternoon, while Ismay was doing whatever was humanly possible with Susan's maltreated pantyhose, Avril came in from the garden with a big bunch of roses, which she proceeded to arrange in a bowl by the window.

"They look nice, don't they?" She stood back to regard them.

"Yes, they're lovely. Funny that our roses were always better than the ones at Estercourt, in spite of Great-aunt Georgina's three gardeners."

"Um-hm. At least we're staying where the prize roses are." Avril smiled reflectively.

Ismay glanced at her.

"Avril, I don't believe you're so terribly disappointed as the others, are you?"

"Perhaps not." That gave away exactly nothing.

"Because you think you can get whatever you want in other ways?" Ismay's tone carried a direct challenge, because she knew how adroitly Avril could slide away from questions.

"Well, there *are* other ways, aren't there?"

Ismay's hands dropped into her lap.

"I don't know why we're fencing. Tell me, are you seriously thinking of that dreadful man's offer again?"

"He's not a dreadful man. Only a man who doesn't care a damn what other people think of him. And anyway, why is it more disgraceful to make the sort of bargain I am making than to live in the pockets of trades-men who can't afford to have their bills unpaid but have to put up with it? At least my way is more honest. I'm giving value for money; at least I suppose so."

Ismay went rather pale.

"You *are* giving? What do you mean?"

Avril laughed with real amusement.

"I'm sorry, dear. That should still have been decor-ously in the future. You needn't be so agitated. It's none of it in the present . . . yet."

"Then, for heaven's sake, forget this crazy scheme! I know it's awful that we owe so much. I know it's dishonest, just as you say. But we have to alter that now. We always counted on that fortune coming one day. I see now that it's been the curse of our family. But we have to have things on quite a different basis. You and I and Adrian must go to work—earn some decent income and gradually pay off the debts. It's dull, I know, but it's the only honest way. *Your* suggestion—"

"My dear," Avril interrupted coolly, "have you any idea how much father owes?"

Ismay was silent. For a moment she could see nothing but those pathetic, inaccurate calculations on father's desk last night. When she looked up again she had still less color in her cheeks.

"It's a ghastly amount, I know, but we must—"

"Listen, Ismay." Avril was not heated about it, only quite determined. "I'm twenty. I'm at the very beginning of my life, or at any rate, of the part of it that matters. I'm not going to start with the millstone of father's debts around my neck. I'm sorry for him, poor darling, but it's been nothing but his own mismanagement that's landed him where he is. I don't doubt that mother tried to push some sense into him years ago, and I don't doubt she was loftily talked down. There's nothing to be done about it now. At any rate, there's nothing that *I'm* going to do about it. In the time-honored phrase, I'm going to live my own life."

"You mean," Ismay said deliberately, "that you are going to become Keith Otterbury's mistress because you think it's 'easy money.' "

Avril bit her lip slightly and her color rose a little.

"You're putting it as brutally as you can, aren't you?"

"Of course. How else should one put it? It's a pretty brutal fact."

"It isn't so much the money, Ismay. Really, that isn't the attraction. It's being able to go away and study—to live somewhere where it's all color and sunshine—not to have to crawl from day to day studying the petty details that matter so little but can spoil everything. I don't have a beautiful nature. I'm not interested in Susan's pantyhose and father's moods and the price of new potatoes. I want to live carelessly and a little dangerously, see the famous and beautiful things of the world before I'm too old to enjoy them. I'm sorry you're shocked and miserable about it, but that doesn't really alter it in the least."

That part at least was true—Ismay could see it perfectly. There was no argument left that would appeal to Avril. She might as well end the discussion now.

One could appeal to father, of course. He would produce long and resounding speeches modeled on all the outraged stage fathers there had ever been. But what would be the good of that? Avril would withdraw into her shell and probably not even hear what he was saying. Then when the wind and thunder had died down, she would proceed exactly as she had intended.

Adrian? No, Adrian had no more influence with her than Ismay herself. Less, probably, because he would grow impatient and sarcastic, or, alternatively, might take the point of view that if she insisted on making a fool of herself, it was really her own affair.

There was no one, no one at all to whom one could apply. No influence to balance against the influence of this practically unknown man to whom Avril seemed willing to consign her future life. It was ridiculous! There was so little on which the whole arrangement could have been based. With him it could hardly be more than a capricious whim—a matter of half-cynical amusement that *could* not be of great value to him one way or another.

Then might *he* be open to persuasion, to argument, to some sort of appeal to his sense of decency?

After all, there was nothing in all this to indicate how deeply the projected affair went with him. It was not too late. . . .

Ismay looked thoughtfully after her sister as she turned and strolled once more out into the garden. And as she watched, resolution slowly hardened in her mind. A very disagreeable resolution—a frightening resolution, come to that—but one well worth taking. She would go and see Keith Otterbury herself, appeal to his better self, his common sense, his, well, whatever one did appeal to in a man of his sort.

Ismay felt better when she had reached this decision, but she felt worse when she came to put it into practical effect. It was all very well to decide to go and see Keith Otterbury. But it made cold little shivers run over her when she had to decide just when—that evening? Or the next day?

It was Avril herself who made up her mind for her. She said something about staying in her room to write letters all the evening.

"I can't imagine anyone having enough letters to keep them going all evening," Susan said. "And why not write them in the dining room?"

"Because I don't want to have to help you with your Latin homework," retorted Avril, who was gifted in these matters but indolent. "Anyway, I really have heaps of letters to write. About six months' accumulation. I never think it's worthwhile doing them more often, because you only get replies by return mail and have to start all over again."

"Regularity in attending to one's correspondence is the only sensible rule, my dear," observed father, who very seldom attended to his own correspondence, and never with any degree of regularity.

No one answered, so presumably they subscribed to the general principle without feeling that it had any uncomfortable application to themselves. Which was "typical Laverhope," as Adrian always said.

Ismay waited until their early supper was over. Then, taking her old blue coat from the peg in the hall, she went out of the side door into the garden, remarking casually to Adrian that she "felt like a walk, but would not be long."

For a moment she was afraid that Adrian would offer to accompany her. But he didn't. He evidently had affairs of his own to occupy him. That was one of the odd results of Great-aunt Georgina's will, thought Ismay. All the Laverhopes suddenly discovered that they had private concerns that must be worked out independently of the rest of the family. Avril retired to her bedroom, father to his study, Adrian looked absently at her when she spoke to him, and now here was she herself going out on a sensational errand without the remotest intention of telling the others where she was going.

It was a warm September evening, and there was still a good deal of light lingering over the countryside. Immediately overhead the sky was soft and clear, but there were heavy clouds banked along the horizon, suggestive of a storm not very far off. Every now and then the trees moved agitatedly and without apparent reason, as though they knew the storm was coming, feared it a little, but realized there was nothing they could do but wait for it.

"I suppose that's rather how I feel," thought Ismay.

She had pulled the coat over her shoulders, without actually slipping her arms into the sleeves, but in spite of the warm evening, she shivered and drew the coat around her more closely.

By now, of course, she ought to have worked out something of what she intended to say to Keith Otterbury. That was, if she should find him in. For a moment her mind caught thankfully at the cowardly possibility that there might be a reprieve that way, but she brushed aside the thought again at once. No disagreeable task had ever grown easier for being put off. It would be bad luck, not good luck, if he should be out this one evening.

What would she say? What did one say to a man who proposed to conduct an affair with one's sister?

She found suddenly that she knew so desperately little about him. Nothing much more than the village gossip or the half-intrigued, half-spiteful remarks his neighbors passed about him. True, she had been introduced to him two years ago at the County Flower Show, but the introduction had been made by one of her father's less careful friends, and before they had exchanged more than the barest conventionalities, father had come up and removed her with skill and dignity.

At the ball last February, when he had danced with Avril, he had wanted her to dance with him, too, but—a little to her relief, to tell the truth—she was able to say that her dances were all booked. Afterward she caught him looking at her once or twice with those bold, smiling dark eyes of his, and she had thought uncomfortably at the time that he probably had not believed her. But he had not spoken to her again, and later, if ever she met him out riding, he simply greeted her as he passed and never made any attempt to speak to her further.

Now it was she who was to make the attempt—a horrid situation. Besides, she still had no idea what she was going to say.

The distance from the Laverhopes' house to Otterbury Hall was no more than half a mile in a straight line, but it took Ismay nearly twenty minutes of quick walking to reach it by way of the winding lanes. As she turned into the tree-bordered drive, the last of the evening light was fading, and overhead the stars were beginning to prick bright holes in a purple sky.

Otterbury Hall was not such an imposing place as its name implied. Starting as a large farmhouse more than a hundred years ago, it had been added to by successive owners in a haphazard and not very artistic fashion. The present owner's father, in the early days of his marriage, had made a real effort to bring the place into some sort of regular form and style. There had been a certain amount of rebuilding, which had succeeded in destroying the farmhouse character of the place but had fallen short of transforming it into a mansion.

Then his young wife had grown tired of the country. The hundred miles between Otterbury Hall and the London life she liked became too much for her. On her insistence the place had been emptied except for a caretaker and his wife, and, for all practical purposes, Otterbury Hall had become uninhabited.

And so it had remained for considerably more than

twenty years, until Keith Otterbury had inherited the estate and had come there to live, something like five years ago.

The irregular bulk of the house rose before Ismay, black against the evening sky, flanked on either side by a great cedar tree. There was something faintly sinister about the place in this semidarkness, and she felt that never in her life had she undertaken anything so disagreeable as the task that lay before her.

Her nervous tug at the great brass bellpull must have carried more strength than she knew, for it set the bell ringing quite violently in some remote region of the house. She could hear it in the silence that enveloped the rest of the house.

Then she heard footsteps crossing the hall, and a moment later the door was opened to disclose a manservant who looked in some surprise at the slim young woman who stood in the patch of warm, bright light from the paneled hall beyond.

"Mr. Otterbury—is he in, please?" Ismay spoke more hesitatingly than she had meant to, for a cool bold appearance would probably be her best line to take, and she had intended to make, at any rate, a calm entrance.

The man stood aside for her to enter.

"If you'll come in I'll inquire, madam. I think Mr. Otterbury came in a few moments ago, but I will make sure."

Ismay walked into the hall and with a sensation bordering on panic, heard the front door shut behind her.

"Will you come this way, please?"

She was ushered into a long, lofty room, again with paneled walls; but the concealed lights, which the man switched on as they came in, shed a warm, almost cosy glow and counteracted any impression of gloom.

Crossing to the window he drew great velvet curtains of

an odd burnt-orange shade, so that the dark, rather frightening night was shut out, and the world narrowed to this pleasant, unalarming room.

Ismay gave him her name as "Miss Laverhope," then added rather hastily, "Miss Ismay Laverhope." To let Keith Otterbury imagine he was going to see Avril might lead to any amount of complications. As she sat in one of the deep, leather-covered armchairs, the man left the room, leaving her alone with the silence and her own thoughts.

Reassuring though the room might be, it could not make her forget the desperate nature of her errand, and Ismay felt that if she had to wait long, all her courage would disappear, and she would creep from the house again without having made a shadow of protest.

But she had not long to wait. Almost immediately she heard a curt voice say, "Who did you say? Good Lord!"

A moment later the door opened again and the master of Otterbury Hall entered the room. He closed the door and stood there for a second or two—puzzled, amused, as though he hardly knew what to make of the situation. Then he came forward slowly, and as he did so Ismay rose to her feet—a little pale, her eyes very dark blue with something like fear, her hair gold where the light caught it. Perhaps he liked the picture, because he narrowed his eyes very slightly, with admiration as well as puzzlement.

"Miss Laverhope—" he held out his hand "—what can I do for you?"

With a reluctance that was more obvious than she knew, Ismay put her hand into his, and he said casually, "I don't bite, you know."

She managed to smile then.

"Oh, I'm sorry. Did I look . . . scared?"

"A little. Won't you sit down again?"

Ismay sank back into her chair. But he stood where he was on the hearthrug, his feet slightly apart, looking down at her with a concentration of amused interest she found terribly disconcerting.

He had evidently, as the servant had said, come in only a short while ago, for he was still in his riding habit—an outfit that made him look even more overwhelming, thought Ismay, than he had at the County Ball. A tall and very powerful man, he seemed much too full of energy and suppressed movement for anything but the out-of-doors, and there was something almost flamboyant in his fine, dark coloring and the half-insolent way he carried himself.

On horseback all that seemed more natural. Here in this room there was something too alive and colorful about him, and Ismay found herself noticing in turn the way his thick, strong, black hair grew straight up from his forehead and then back, the way the dark eyes sparkled with half-cynical amusement, his firm, rather full lips.

I suppose that's what one calls a sensual mouth, thought Ismay, and then realized with a start that he was still waiting for her to speak.

"Mr. Otterbury—" her voice was soft and sounded nervous even to her own ears "—I expect you are very much surprised that I should come to see you like this, but. . . ." She paused.

"The pleasure outweighs the surprise," he assured her with a smile. And then, "Will you have a drink? It helps a lot when you're trying to say something difficult."

"Thank you." She supposed it might help.

He crossed the room and poured out something into a glass. When he gave it to her and she drank it, she realized it was brandy, and she wondered then if she had looked very much like fainting. Certainly the way he said,

"Better now?" sounded as though the idea had crossed his mind.

"Well then, let's start again."

"It's about Avril," Ismay stated, with a lack of finesse that horrified her, but apparently not him.

"Oh yes?" He gave no sign of intending to help her.

"Mr. Otterbury, I know it must seem that this is not my business, but I've come to ask you to give up this crazy idea that you and she have. I don't think you know Avril very well really. She's not at all that sort of girl. She thinks it all sounds very romantic and exciting now, and she's infatuated with the idea of life abroad and being able to paint and study and do what she likes; but she doesn't have a very clear sense of values and doesn't realize what she's giving up."

Once she had started, Ismay found that the words poured forth in a torrent, and even when she paused for a moment he made no attempt to interrupt her, only waited for her to complete her statement.

"She doesn't even think that she's in love with you." That was out before she could stop it, though the quick upward jerk of his eyebrows made her falter a little. "But I think she's probably been quite honest about that. Avril would be. When we thought for a few days that we were rich, she gave up this other idea entirely. She was *glad* to give it up. Then——"

"What made you think for a few days that you were rich?" he inquired with interest.

"Oh, didn't you know? I thought everyone in the district knew. Our great-aunt was supposed to have willed a fortune to my father—he's been waiting for it for something like fifty years. She died the other day, and when the will was read, she had left everything to charity."

Keith Otterbury laughed then. Threw back his head and shouted with laughter.

"Good Lord! The mean old trout."

Ismay, who thought the expression offensive and the laughter even more so, glanced away nervously, wishing she were anywhere but in this room and feeling that they were getting uncomfortably far away from the question of Avril.

He brought her back to it, however.

"So Avril intended to give me the slip when she thought the great-aunt's money would do instead? She has a fine business instinct, has Avril. But now she prefers gilded sin to honest poverty, is that it?"

Ismay opened her mouth to object, but abruptly closed it again.

"But the conscientious older sister wants to save her from herself?" He looked even more amused.

"Mr. Otterbury, I know it isn't a very serious matter to you, but—"

"What makes you think that?"

"Well, your whole attitude. Even now you're more than half-laughing. You *can't* care very much for Avril, however lovely she is. She's unsophisticated, really. I know she sounds calculating over this matter—"

"She does indeed."

"—but it's an ingenuous sort of calculation. There's nothing experienced about her—no ground that you could possibly have in common. After all, you're . . . ."

"Yes?" He looked amusedly interested. She hesitated for a moment, then rushed on in desperation.

"Very well then. You're blasé and hard-living. Everybody says so."

"Do they indeed? Well, it's nice to have an insight into

what other people are thinking, and this has certainly been an instructive talk. But there's one thing you've said that is undoubtedly true. I *don't* care for Avril, however lovely she is. There is only one woman in this district I care for, and that is you. Or rather—since we've agreed that I am blasé and hard-living—let us use the words appropriate to my character. You are the woman I really want. Not Avril."

CHAPTER THREE

For several seconds Ismay assured herself that this was a bad joke. The sort of tasteless, ill-judged joke one might expect such a man to make in the circumstances. But then she glanced at him and saw that those bright, insolent eyes were serious at last, and his hands were thrust deep into his pockets, pressed to his sides with a tension that had nothing jocular about it.

"I don't . . . know why . . . you should say such a thing to me just now," she began. "I haven't—"

"Because it's true," he interrupted her curtly.

"It doesn't follow very well on your advances to my sister," she retorted with some spirit, and she saw from his slight grimace that he acknowledged that as a hit. But he recovered his accustomed coolness almost immediately.

"Listen, let's leave Avril out of this." He sat down at last, in the chair opposite hers, and leaned forward with his arms on his knees, his hands lightly clasped in front of him. "I want you to tell me more about this business of the family fortune. It's placed you all pretty awkwardly, I suppose, this caprice of the unlamented great-aunt?"

Ismay drew back slightly, and allowed her cool disgust to show in her face. The remark could hardly have been in worse taste, she thought, and her tone was cold and remote as she said, "I don't think there is anything else to tell you about that. I hardly see that it's your business, in any case."

He laughed slightly, unabashed by her snub, and made an impatient little gesture of almost literally putting aside her protest.

"No, of course it's hardly my business. Or at any rate, there's nothing to make it my business at the moment. But I don't want to leave it like that, you see. You've invited me to discuss one family problem, and I find it has considerable bearing on another one. I think it's a trifle too late for you to put up your chilly little barriers and announce 'no admittance here.' "

She was silent for a moment. Then, because he really held all the cards, she yielded and said in the same cold little voice, "What did you want to know then?"

"Just exactly how does this unfortunate will affect you all?"

"Well, very badly, of course."

"You'd been counting on it?"

She hesitated. "Are you speaking of me personally?"

"No, of course not." He brushed that aside impatiently too. "I don't think money means much to you, except in the way it affects the people you are fond of."

Ismay considered that in silence, surprised to find how acute he had been about it. She had hardly thought of it herself, but now she knew he was right. Personally, she had not been bitterly hurt over the loss of the fortune. But she did most genuinely hate seeing the others so dreadfully disappointed.

"Very well then. I hate seeing the others so bewildered and shattered. Particularly my father. He had never had any reason to suppose the money would go anywhere else. In fact, since he was a boy, she had told him that he would inherit it all. Naturally it was a terrible blow."

"Because he had traded on expectations, I suppose? Allowed himself a good many debts on the strength of them?"

"Mr. Otterbury, do you think you are adopting a particularly gentlemanly tone?" Ismay asked dryly.

"No," he said, equally dryly. "But then, you see, I am not a gentleman. I am what I believe is called 'an outsider.' And, incidentally, I am extremely interested in getting to the bottom of this situation."

"But why, exactly?"

"Partly because it concerns you." He smiled straight at her in a bold, disconcerting fashion. "Tell me. Your father is pretty hopelessly in debt, isn't he?"

Ismay looked back at him with sad, angry eyes.

"I suppose it's common knowledge in the neighborhood. Yes, of course. He is up to his ears in debt. It isn't only *his* fault. It's the fault of all of us. We always arranged our lives on the assumption that we would be very rich one day soon. It sounds awful, I know—like just waiting for someone to die in order to step into their shoes. But it had gone on for so long, you see. It started years and years before any of us were born—it was a family tradition. Great-aunt Georgina herself had insisted on it so often when my father was a boy, and she never hinted once that she had changed her mind. If we had been fond of her I don't expect we'd have thought so much about it, because one *can't* think happily of inheriting from someone one loves. But she wasn't at all lovable. She never did a single thing that could endear her to anyone."

"She wasn't fond of any of you?"

"Oh no. We always supposed that she had a sort of family feeling toward father, but, so far as we were concerned, she preferred us to be afraid of her."

"And were *you* afraid of her?" he inquired with interest.

"No," Ismay said slowly. "I don't think I was exactly. But I never went to see her with any sense of pleasure."

"But you all kept up your spirits with the thought of

the good time you would have when the money came along?" He sounded slightly sympathetic as well as amused that time.

"I suppose so. No one ever said as much, of course, but yes, I'm sure father thought of the lovely day when all the bills would be paid, and Adrian—"

"Your brother?"

"Yes. Adrian thought of being able to train as a doctor one day, and Avril—" she glanced at him nervously "—Avril's great idea always was that she would go to Italy and study art and live a carefree existence."

"And what did you want, Ismay?"

She felt startled and embarrassed at his casual use of her first name.

"Me? Oh, I wanted them all to have what they liked, of course. And I thought it would be good fun to have the house done over so that it was all new and fresh. I'm afraid they were mostly material things I thought about," she confessed with a faint smile.

"But you thought of the general family content as well?"

"Yes." The smile disappeared. "I did want them all to be happy and contented." She sighed a little, because that was all so hopeless now. The best she could hope for was that this man would agree to leave Avril alone. And then she would have to go home and face a crop of insoluble problems, knowing that every member of the family was unhappy and that there was absolutely nothing she could do about it.

He must have been able to read from her expression something of what she was thinking, because as she looked up again he said softly and a little mockingly, "And it all depends on money."

Ismay looked straight at him.

"Yes, I suppose it does. That sounds awful, doesn't it?"

"No," he said coolly. "Quite a lot of the most important things of this world depend on money. It is customary to pretend otherwise, but a truth is no less a truth because a certain number of people regard it as bad form."

Ismay looked doubtful. She knew that father, with all his preoccupation about debts, would, if pressed, have insisted in eloquent phrases that money had nothing whatever to do with things of the mind and spirit and that these were really what mattered.

But then father said a great many things that didn't make practical sense at all.

"Well," Keith Otterbury said quietly, "what are you going to do about it?"

Ismay looked at him in astonishment. Then a dash of indignant color showed in her cheeks.

"I don't think it's for *you* to ask *me* that. I came to ask you to break off any connection with Avril. I would like to know what you mean to do about that. After your . . . your tasteless and callous remark about not caring for her, I suppose you won't still have the effrontery to pursue the affair."

She thought he would surely be insulted and angry, but he withstood her attack with imperturbable calm. He didn't answer at once. Rising from his chair, he thrust his hands into his pockets again and slowly walked the length of the room. Then, turning, he came back to where she was sitting and stood looking down at her with absolute gravity.

"You want me to promise to give up any connection at all with your sister?"

"Yes, that's it." She was a trifle breathless.

"And you'll take my word for it, if I say I promise?"

"Of course."

"Not 'of course' at all. But it's nice of you to put it that way," he said ironically. "Very well. I promise not to make any more advances to Avril or put wicked ideas into her innocent head, on the single condition that you will marry me."

For a second Ismay sat where she was. Then she jumped to her feet indignantly.

"Mr. Otterbury, will you please stop saying such ridiculous things! I . . . I don't deserve to be made fun of this way, and indeed, *indeed* I have enough to worry me without your making stupid jokes about something very serious."

"My dear, you couldn't be more serious than I am. Didn't you understand me when I said that it was you I wanted? I was perfectly serious then, too. I do want you. I've admired and wanted you ever since I met you that day at the County Flower Show. But I'm not such a fool as to suppose one does anything but marry your kind. Until now there has never been the remotest chance of my being able to do any such thing. Now—"

"There is not the remotest chance now either," Ismay told him flatly, and the haughty way she said that would have delighted her father's heart. It seemed only to amuse Keith Otterbury, of course.

"Very well. I'll allow you the luxury of that retort—especially as you look so delightful when you are angry But don't you think you might consider first what I am offering you before you refuse it so finally? I *am* asking you to marry me, Ismay. That's not usually considered such an insult. I am, as it happens, a very rich man, and if you married me, you would have anything you liked within reason—for yourself and, since it means so much to you, for your family, too."

"Aren't you a little ashamed," Ismay said quietly, "to think that first you tried to bribe one sister into being your mistress, and now, with a gracious raising of the price, you try to bribe the other one into being your wife?"

He flushed darkly, and she saw he was very angry then. But he kept his tone cool and steady as he answered her.

"You need not look at it like that at all. I very much want you to say 'yes' to me. I'd be a fool if I didn't tell you what advantages there were in marrying me. The disadvantages are already patent to you, I suppose," he added with a short laugh. "Don't reject the idea out of hand, Ismay. Just think over whether you would like to free your father from any more financial anxiety, enable your brother to follow the career he wants, give Avril her chance of going to Italy or wherever she wants without paying a price for it, and ensure a good education for that impudent little sister of yours—I forget her name—who regards me, I believe, as a slightly picturesque criminal."

For a moment Ismay made no attempt to answer that. Partly because it was difficult to think of a snub sufficiently sharp to impress this man, partly because—useless to deny it—the picture was dazzling. The idea that, at one stroke, the family could be made happy once more had something almost intoxicating about it.

No debts for father, no bitter frustration for Adrian, no dangerous temptation for Avril. The relief would be indescribable!

But of course the idea was fantastic. She looked up to find him regarding her with an attention that was not without a tinge of anxiety.

"I'm sorry, Mr. Otterbury. I don't know quite whether you mean all this generously or . . . or insultingly. But, in either case, I couldn't dream of agreeing, you know. The whole idea is rather—forgive me—rather silly."

To her surprise, he smiled a little at that, as though in a sense he agreed with her.

"You mean it's too much like the melodramas of your father's youth?"

So he knew about that, too!

"Well, yes, I do," Ismay confessed.

"The villain of the piece proposes to buy the heroine by paying for her family's happiness?"

"Something like that." Ismay found she very much wanted to laugh, because she had suddenly remembered Adrian's absurd remark about "Sir Jasper and the milkmaid."

"Why are you smiling?" he wanted to know.

Ismay flushed quickly.

"Oh, I'm sorry. It was just that I thought of something funny."

"Tell me." He sounded peremptory but not annoyed.

"I think you might be angry."

"No, I don't think so."

"Well, it's just that my brother always says that you're the kind of man who ought to be called 'Sir Jasper' and be found . . . flirting with a milkmaid."

"I believe 'seducing the milkmaid' is the more usual and more telling expression," he said gravely.

"I'm sorry. You must think me terribly silly. But when you said that about melodrama, I couldn't help thinking of what Adrian said. You mustn't mind. Families always have idiotic jokes and catchwords among themselves, you know."

"I don't mind," he said, adding slowly, "I suppose there *is* something rather silly and melodramatic about anyone who always acts on impulse."

She was silent, wondering uncomfortably if he was at all hurt by the implication. But then one couldn't imagine that the Keith Otterburys of this world were particularly sensitive.

"So you absolutely refuse my, er, silly and melodramatic proposal?" he said at last.

"Mr. Otterbury, I'm sorry...."

"Miss Laverhope, you needn't be," he retorted mockingly. "The villain of the piece never suffers from wounded feelings, you know. All I ask is that you don't forget all about it." She could hardly do that, Ismay thought. "And if things become worse or unmanageable, or if you should for any other reason change your mind, please remember that my offer remains open in the traditional manner."

Ismay laughed a little in spite of herself.

"I think," she said with some relief, "that you haven't been very serious about all this in any case."

"Oh no, you're wrong there," he assured her. "If you telephoned me tonight, saying you had changed your mind, believe me, I would go out and buy your engagement ring with the greatest pleasure tomorrow."

That made Ismay feel uncomfortable again. It also reminded her that she was on the verge of leaving without having received a definite reply to her original request.

"About Avril ... " she began nervously.

"Oh yes. What about Avril?"

Ismay felt angry. If she had been the kind of person to stamp her foot she would have stamped it then.

"I suppose I can take it that you will leave her alone?" She was tired now and there was a weight of anxiety still pressing on her, so that her soft voice sounded weary and impatient.

He seemed unaffected by that, however.

"My dear, I think you must allow to Avril and even to me the right you reserve for yourself—that of deciding one's own life."

"You mean you *won't* give me your word?"

"Don't you think this is all very much more Avril's business than yours?"

"But I've *told* you. She's young and silly and inexperienced. She doesn't know what she's getting into. Couldn't you be decent for once and see to it that she doesn't have the chance to make a fool of herself?"

"No. The 'Sir Jasper' in me entirely revolts against such a noble impulse. What I think is that you had better go home and consider the offer I've made you, and meanwhile I'll consider all you've said," he replied smilingly.

"You mean—" Ismay's voice was cold and horrified "—you mean you intend to put some sort of pressure on me because of your influence over Avril?"

"I haven't said so. Come, it's certainly time you were home. It isn't especially good for your reputation to stay here much longer. Is this your coat?" He picked it up from the chair and held it for her.

There was nothing else to be done about it. She let him help her on with her coat, noticing that he didn't make the slightest attempt to touch her—which seemed rather out of character.

"I'll take you back across the fields. It's much shorter that way."

"Thank you. I don't need, or want, your company." Ismay was surprised that she could be so flatly rude.

"Oh, you will be quite safe," he assured her. "And I wouldn't dream of letting you go home alone at this time of night. Come along."

Ismay went, feeling slightly like a resentful child being taken out against her will.

There was no moon, but the starlight was brilliant. The threatening clouds had cleared away and the sky was one black velvet arch from horizon to horizon. Any other time she would have enjoyed the night, but walking across the fields with Keith Otterbury, she could only think about what a hateful man he was. She'd thought for a moment he was rather humorous and nice, but if he really wouldn't help her about Avril, then he was just the sort of man everyone said he was.

He allowed her the silence she seemed to prefer, only speaking once, when he was helping her over a stile that divided two of his fields.

"This," he said gravely, "is where I always arrange my interviews with the milkmaid."

Ismay wished he had been a nice man, and then she could have laughed at that. But, as it was, she permitted herself only the briefest smile, and perhaps by starlight even that was not apparent to him.

As she stepped down from the stile her hand was in his for a moment. There was a lot of support in that hand, she thought—it was warm, muscular and exceedingly strong.

He took her right to the gate of her home where he gravely bade her good night. She thought she would pluck up courage to ask him just once more to reconsider his noncommittal reply, but, on second thought, she desisted. Perhaps it was foolish to let a man like this see how terribly important the whole thing was. It merely told him how best to apply pressure to get what he wanted.

So she murmured a hasty good night and ran around the house to the side door, where she could slip in without much likelihood of comment on the lateness of the hour.

But Ismay had reckoned without an unusual disturbance that had evidently taken place in her absence.

As she came in she was surprised to see that the light in the hall was blazing; almost immediately Avril came out of the dining room. An agitated Avril—paler and showing much more sign of feeling than Ismay had often seen on her face.

"Oh, Ismay, there you are! Where on earth have you been?" But she didn't wait for a reply. "Something so dreadful has happened. It's about father. . . ."

"*What* about father?"

"Imagine! He tried to shoot himself. Yes, really. With his old service revolver."

"Shoot himself?" Oh, why had she not taken him seriously last night? "You don't mean he did it? Killed himself?"

"No, no, of course not." Avril was unconscious of any humor in this oblique comment on the efficiency of father's actions. "He was only slightly hurt. But you can imagine the shock for us all. Adrian went at once and took the thing away before he could do any real damage. We sent for Dr. Marsh, and he's given father a sedative and put him to bed. He assures us there's no serious injury, only of course it was a terrible shock for poor old father himself." Ismay noticed that it was the first time any of them had ever called father "old."

"Can I go to him?" Ismay had yanked off her coat and was speaking over her shoulder to Avril as she hung the coat on its peg once more.

"No, better not. He's probably asleep. Adrian stayed with him until he went to sleep. Dr. March says there isn't any fear of his making another attempt. It was just a sudden impulse. I suppose he was in despair, Ismay, about the money situation. I don't know just how bad things are, but— Oh, here's Adrian."

Adrian, also a little pale but less obviously agitated than Avril, was coming down the stairs.

"Hello, Ismay. Where did you get to?" But he, too, did

not wait for a reply. "Avril's told you, of course? Come into the dining room. There's no need to stand in the hall while we discuss things."

They entered the dining room together. Unconsciously they grouped themselves around the table in this moment of family conclave, and as the light shone down on their young, fair, grave faces, there was something curiously alike in the three expressions. It was the first shadow of the necessity of facing responsibility alone.

Ismay spoke first.

"Does Susan know?"

"No. She had gone to bed and, as usual, was sleeping the sleep of the dead." For a moment they all felt Adrian had used an unfortunate simile. Then he added abruptly, "I see no reason why she need know anything about it."

"It *is* best that she doesn't know, I suppose?" Ismay hated mysteries, and knew Susan's talent for discovering them. The others were emphatic, however.

"Of course." That was Avril, curt and much more practical than usual. "She'd never be able to keep anything so sensational as an attempted suicide to herself. She'd probably think it was a distinction to have one in the family."

Adrian smiled grimly.

"Well, I don't know about that. But certainly the fewer people who know, the better. That will help father get over it all the more quickly himself. If only it didn't cost so much to send him away somewhere—on a short cruise or something like that. But anything of the kind only adds more to the very cause that's worrying him. Everything costs so much. Poor old chap, he must have been in a much lower state than any of us guessed."

Adrian, too, called him "poor old chap"—an expression no one would have dreamed of using to describe father even a week before. But then it was true—he did look old now. Ismay remembered she had thought the same thing the previous night.

She looked up with a worried little frown.

"I feel I am rather to blame for letting this happen."

"You, Ismay!" The other two looked astonished.

"Yes. I didn't tell you, but I found him last night in the study, reckoning up his debts, poor darling—I suppose for the first time in his life. The total must have given him an awful shock, particularly as it was incorrect. And he had his revolver beside him on the desk. But it wasn't loaded, and I didn't think he even had any ammunition. I couldn't take it seriously. I just thought that it was one of his, er, gestures, you know."

The others nodded.

"I was a fool, though, not to remember that it wasn't a time when even father would be trying to make an effect. I just comforted him a bit and gave him hot milk and aspirin. He seemed so much better and quite cheerful when I left him. I would have taken the revolver and hidden it, only you know the terrible fuss he makes if we touch anything. Besides, it would have looked as though *I* was getting silly ideas into my head, and it might have made him think seriously of something about which he was only playacting."

"Yes, I know what you mean," Adrian said. "But I wish you'd mentioned it."

"I meant to." Ismay was full of remorse. "As a matter of fact, I meant to speak to *him* very tactfully about it myself and persuade him to let me have the revolver, just to be on the safe side. But somehow—I know it sounds awful—I forgot. I was rather worried about something else. It's dreadful the way one means to do things, and . . . and doesn't," she finished rather lamely.

She suddenly felt very depressed. She always meant to do such a lot for the family—to look after them and see they came to no harm. And now she had done nothing about it when they were facing the greatest crisis of their lives. She had even let father make this pathetically absurd attempt to end things, instead of finding some way—*some* way—of helping him.

"If only there were something one could do to dig us all out of this ghastly hole!" Adrian exclaimed. "I know it's mostly our own fault that we're in it, but that doesn't make the hole more attractive."

"What you're asking for is a miracle," Avril told him. She had recovered from the shock a little and was returning more to her usual air of casual detachment. "What is there, do you suppose, that could reinstate father, make you a doctor and send me to Italy all in one wave of the wand?"

Adrian laughed slightly at that. But Ismay was absolutely still and silent. She was thinking how curious it was that Avril should have put it just like that. Put it as Keith Otterbury had when he had offered her the power to change the family fortunes. It was ridiculous, of course, that he had offered it—but the power was there, the offer was there, being kept open "in the traditional manner," as he had laughingly put it. She stood up suddenly, pushing back her chair sharply.

"I suppose," she said, "we might as well go to bed."

The other two stood up.

"Yes. It's late enough." Avril yawned.

"Should someone stay up with father?" Ismay turned to Adrian again. "What did Dr. Marsh say?"

"No, it's all right. He's had a sleeping pill. Dr. Marsh says he'll sleep until the morning now."

"Isn't it odd," Avril said as they locked up the house,

"being on our own like this? I mean without father to tell everyone exactly what he thinks they ought to do next."

"Yes," said Ismay, feeling the weight of personal responsibility grow even heavier.

She went into the dining room, where Adrian was alone, idly turning over the pages of a book, without paying any attention to what was printed there.

"What is it, Adrian?" She found that the slightest hint of preoccupation or worry on the part of any of the family was sufficient now to make her apprehensive. "What's the matter?"

"The matter?" He looked up in surprise. "Nothing."

"Oh. I just wondered why you hadn't gone to bed."

"I'm going." He closed the book with a slam. "At least. . . . Look here, Ismay, do you think we ought to have a look at those calculations of father's and see just how deeply we *are* sunk? I don't want to turn over his private affairs, but this does concern all of us, and he is constitutionally incapable of telling us the real state of things even if he were well enough to do so."

Ismay bit her lip.

"Yes, I suppose you're right. There's no point in putting it off and pretending to ourselves that things are better than they are. Now?"

Adrian nodded, and together they entered father's study.

When Ismay switched on the lamp, the light shone on just as much confusion as there had been the previous night, and Adrian remarked grimly, "You'd better take one pile of those bills and I'll take another. Perhaps we can work out something from them."

Ismay sat down at the desk and began to turn over a depressing sheaf of papers. Adrian, standing at the side of the desk, did the same.

After a short silence Adrian said, "Do you suppose father ever paid *anything*?"

"Not if he could help it, I feel sure. Some of these date from . . . . Adrian, aren't there any receipts?"

"It doesn't look like it. Just a moment. These look more hopeful." Adrian reached across Ismay and picked up half a dozen slips of paper. "Yes, these are receipts for something. Something to do with the house—"

"The *house*!" Ismay put down the papers she had been holding. "But there's nothing to pay on the house. It's ours. It belonged to mother, don't you remember? It was the one thing that always comforted me—the thought that we had a roof over our heads. There wasn't even ground rent, Adrian. It's freehold. Oh, you must be mistaken. Let me see." She leaned over anxiously to examine the receipts in her turn.

There was a long silence. Then Adrian said, "You see what it is, don't you?"

Ismay raised frightened eyes to his.

"A mortgage on the house? These are receipts for payments of interest?"

"Um-hm. The date on the last one is more than a year ago, too. That means he hasn't been keeping up the payments."

"Then the house isn't ours at all?" Ismay said stupidly.

"That's what it looks like. I don't know the terms, of course. You can't tell from these receipts. But not paying interest on a mortgage usually leads to one thing."

"Adrian, are we going to be without a home?"

Her brother didn't answer.

"I know it sounds silly," Ismay said at last, "but I feel sick."

"Oh, poor kid!" Adrian looked sympathetic. "I know. It's a sort of panic. Sit quiet for a moment while I try to work things out. It may not be as bad as we think. Will you have something to drink, Ismay?"

"No, thanks. I've had one brandy already tonight," Ismay said absently.

"Have you?" Adrian looked astounded. "How did that happen?"

"Oh, I called in to see, er, Miss Peters," Ismay explained hastily, choosing the name of the first acquaintance who came to her mind.

"Heavens! I didn't know she was a secret tippler." Adrian grinned faintly as he bent over his calculations.

"Oh, she's *not*. Only I felt a bit faint and . . . ."

Adrian glanced at her sharply.

"For heaven's sake don't you get ill, Ismay dear. That *would* be the last straw."

"I'm not ill," Ismay protested. "Not the least bit. Don't go imagining things."

"All right." Adrian sounded absent again. And Ismay was silent, wondering a little why she didn't explain quite frankly what she had done that evening. She and Adrian had very few secrets between them, and he had really just as much right to know as she.

Or had he? Wasn't this perhaps entirely her own affair?

Suppose, just for the sake of argument, that she considered Keith Otterbury's offer. Then of course she could not tell any of them—least of all Adrian—the exact circumstances leading up to it. He would most certainly consider the idea ridiculous and iniquitous. Well, it *was* ridiculous. Only not quite so ridiculous as it had seemed when it was first suggested.

Ismay was very tired indeed by now and, propping her elbow on the desk, she leaned her head on her hands.

It must be wonderful to have heaps of money—enough money to buy anything you wanted within reason. Wasn't that the expression he had used? She wondered what Keith Otterbury considered "within reason." Something fantastically generous, she felt certain, because that somehow went with the character of the man. He did everything to excess.

Adrian looked up just then.

"I wish to God I knew some tame millionairess I could fascinate," he said with a sigh. "It seems about the only thing that would cover all this disaster."

"Is it *so* bad?"

"Are you going to be sick if I tell you how bad?"

"No." She managed to smile faintly. "I'd better know the truth. I can bear it."

"Well, as far as I can see, the house has gone, father owes a fortune in back taxes—I don't know how he contrives to do that, with next to no income—there are two or three dozen odd bills of varying amounts, and nothing to set against the lot except a handsome overdraft. I don't know whether he's been a fool enough to go to moneylenders, but there's a letter here that has a nasty smell about it, to my way of thinking. It's obscure, as moneylender's letters always are, I understand. Anyway, there it is. Talk about the wolf howling at the door! It seems to have come in and made itself thoroughly at home."

"Adrian, what on earth are we going to do?" Ismay's voice was little more than a whisper.

"I don't know, my dear. We'd better go to bed now, for a start. It must be nearly two o'clock."

She stood up slowly and stiffly.

"We'll all three have to get jobs, just as soon as we can." Ismay tried to make that sound hopeful, but she only succeeded in sounding very frightened.

"Jobs? Oh, I have a job, as far as that's concerned."

"You have a job, Adrian! What sort of a job? How wonderful! Why didn't you tell me before?"

"It's not specially wonderful. Assistant and general runabout to old Astley, the pharmacist."

"Oh, Adrian . . . " Ismay began. Then her courage really did fail, and a few tears gathered in spite of herself.

"I know. You're wondering just about how far what I earn will go among all that." Adrian waved his hand in the direction of the papers on the desk. "So am I."

"No, it wasn't that." Ismay shook her head. "Anyway, I think it's wonderful of you to have gone out and got a job right away—*any* job. You are a good boy, Adrian."

Her brother grinned a little and said again, "Come on to bed."

But all the way upstairs Ismay was thinking, *And Keith Otterbury offered to see him through his medical training . . . and to give me anything else within reason.*

CHAPTER FOUR

Late though it had been when she and Adrian went up to bed, Ismay lay awake, staring into the darkness, quite unable to drag her thoughts away from the problems confronting them.

And that fantastic scene at Otterbury Hall this evening! It was impossible not to relive that again and again, remembering a sarcastic inflection here, a hint of real generosity there, and wondering to what sum total all those impressions added up. Was it conceivable that one *could* take a man like that seriously, that one could literally make oneself think, *If I did marry him, this and this would happen? Could I put up with that? Or would I want to murder him after the first week?*

Ismay had never very seriously thought about marriage before. There had been dance partners and tennis partners and other social companions of her own age, of course. She had flirted a little—though never as much as Avril—and had even imagined herself in love once or twice. But none of it had ever gone very deep. For one thing, her family meant much more to her than anyone else, and, for another, few people in the neighborhood had believed quite so implicitly in Great-aunt Georgina's fortune as the Laverhopes themselves had. In consequence, she and Avril were generally thought of as "pretty as a picture and twice as charming, but without a penny to bless themselves with." The mothers of eligible sons, therefore, preferred not to have them taken too seriously.

None of this had ever seemed to matter before—she had enough of the casual, carefree Laverhope tempera-

ment for that—and she had been willing to put everything off until a golden future changed the situation,
leaving her freer to live her own life in some vaguely
pleasant way she had never quite mapped out.

Now everything was different. They were facing stark
realities, urgent and bitter decisions. And in this new,
harsh world, Keith Otterbury's offer had a certain crude
value that transformed it from an insulting absurdity into
something that had to be weighed and considered.

"It isn't as though he didn't mean it," thought Ismay.
"It was a preposterous offer, but it was genuine. For
some reason he really does want me to accept."

And then she wondered why it was marriage he had
offered her instead of what was usually delicately referred
to as "the other thing." He had said something about
knowing that one didn't offer "her kind" anything else.
But then it seemed he had offered that to Avril without
any particular qualms. And Avril had accepted. That
might, of course, mark the difference between Avril and
"her kind." Perhaps that was what he meant, Ismay
reflected. Anyway, it was true, of course. She wouldn't
have taken on that in any circumstances. But marriage
was different—at least, she supposed it was. Anything
would seem rather like an affair with that kind of man,
though.

Still, it was hardly the point. If she accepted what he
offered, she could save the whole family from disaster
without doing anything that could shock even her father's
most delicate sensibilities. If Avril accepted, it simply
meant that she would ruin her own life, do nothing whatever to help the others and shatter father still more,
because he would take anything like that very hard. Not
only would he play the role of outraged parent to perfection, he would *feel* the outraged parent. Her father lived
his roles with almost pathetic intensity.

And Avril would accept, of course . . . unless Ismay did first, she thought, with a realism not untinged with grim amusement. And that, she believed, would be even worse than the mess they were in at the moment.

She listened, as she had so often before, to Avril's quiet, untroubled breathing. She slept like a child. She always did. But then Avril *was* rather like a child—a precocious, determined and very charming one. How could one argue a realistic problem with someone whose sense of values had practically no relation to the realities of an adult world?

She couldn't let her do it. She felt like hitting Avril for being such a criminal little idiot . . . but she couldn't let her do it. It was too dreadful a way to learn a lesson.

Then if Avril was not to be allowed to spoil her life there was only one way to stop her. One didn't want to think of it in detail, but. . . .

As Ismay fell asleep in the first faint light of the dawn she remembered Keith Otterbury's words: "If you telephoned me tonight, saying you had changed your mind, believe me, I would go out and buy your engagement ring with the greatest pleasure."

"There isn't time tonight," thought Ismay, and then her eyes closed.

The next morning Susan's inquiries about her father were many and detailed, so that Ismay began to wonder, with an irritation born of her short night, whether she possessed some perverse intuition that always told her the right—or rather, the wrong—time to ask questions.

"How funny that he should be sick just now! He's not sort of pining, is he? I mean, about the money?"

"No, I don't think so."

"It's a most 'straordinary thing!"

"Why?" Adrian wanted to know. "People are ill sometimes."

"Oh yes. But for reasons. Like a cold, or being sick, or having an accident."

They all felt she was getting uncomfortably "warm," and Ismay said hastily, "He's just run down, I expect. And of course it must have been a great shock to find he was, well, that Great-aunt Georgina had done what she did." Then to change the subject she added firmly, "But isn't it splendid? Adrian has got a job already."

It was not, however, a very happy diversion.

"A job? Adrian?" Adrian's youngest sister looked incredulous. "But whoever would want to pay him for anything?"

"Thanks. Don't mind my feelings."

"But it's true." Susan was unmoved. "What sort of a job?"

"Assistant to old Astley," Adrian answered curtly.

"Do you mean an *errand* boy? Or do you mean swot in his time and he'll pay you for it? I call that—"

"Susan dear, you'll be terribly late for school," Ismay interrupted, and fortunately this was nothing less than the truth.

There followed the usual frantic search for books that had been mysteriously mislaid, punctuated by pathetic wails about the lateness of the hour. The miniature storm culminated in Susan erupting from the front door and rushing to the gate, declaring that never, never had anyone been so late as this before, and it would be much better to stay at home and say she had a headache.

Adrian watched her from the dining room window.

"Did we all make the same unspeakable hullabaloo at that age?" he asked with genuine interest.

Ismay laughed.

"I can't imagine that Avril did, and I don't think boys care about being late or forgetting books as much as girls do."

"I don't think Susan cares exactly," Adrian said, smiling. "It's hard to imagine her caring about anything. It's a lucky temperament to have."

Ismay wondered if there was anything she could say to him that would soften the harshness of the present situation as outlined by Susan. But, on the whole, she decided, it was better to say nothing. Too much had already been said. She contented herself with, "When do you start this job, Adrian?"

And when he replied, "Next Monday," she thought, with genuine relief, that she should be able to settle things long before then. She wished she could tell him right then that he wouldn't have to do it for long.

Instead, she went upstairs to see her father—to receive his half-ashamed, half-airy explanations of what had happened.

"A most unfortunate and absurd accident," he told her rather feebly, but watching her with a transparent anxiety that showed how eager he was that the real truth should not be known.

"Yes," Ismay agreed soothingly. "It only shows how careful one ought to be with firearms."

"I had no idea that it was loaded, of course."

Ismay thought of the unloaded revolver that had been on the desk two nights ago.

"Of course not," she said gently, hearing his sigh of relief. "We must all be thankful it wasn't more serious. Adrian gave the revolver to Dr. Marsh. He'll take it to London with him next time he goes and sell it. It isn't a thing we're likely to need, and it's best out of the way."

"I daresay you're right." Father looked half-uneasy and half-relieved. Ismay thought he was probably glad to have temptation out of the way but was wondering what on earth the alternative was. It was nice to realize one was not dead, but something of a problem to find one was alive.

"I wouldn't worry about anything if I were you." It was funny how she had fallen into the way of speaking to father as though he were about Susan's age. "You just have plenty of rest and don't think about anything else but getting well. Things are going to be much better than you ever expected."

"Are they?" He looked at her in an expectant way she had never seen before. Rather as though he had lost the one solution he himself had once had for all difficulties, and now he must look to someone else to supply all the answers.

"Oh yes." Ismay smiled at him, her mind completely made up.

But she was glad, all the same, that he accepted the generalization without asking for further details. However firm she might feel about the essential decision, she was not in a mood to discuss it.

Seeing that father was inclined to go to sleep, she quietly left the room.

For an hour or two at any rate, her time was her own. There would be no better opportunity than this, and delay was not only useless, it was dangerous. There was no telling what steps Avril might already have taken. At the moment she was harmlessly engaged in sketching an old tree in the garden. And, without a word to her, Ismay slipped out of the side gate, unhailed and unobserved.

At first she walked quickly, intent on her errand. But soon she noticed the heat and that even the shade of the trees offered very little relief from the blazing sun. The sky was a deep, almost sapphire blue, softened only by a heat haze, and the very faint breeze that stirred the leaves from time to time scarcely seemed to reach farther than the extreme treetops.

Even her yellow linen frock, with its short sleeves and its white collar turned far back from her throat, seemed heavy and oppressive, and she could feel the heavy waves of fair hair clinging damply to her forehead.

Well, her errand ought to be enough to send cold shivers down her back, she reflected grimly. And then she stopped and listened intently, because, away in the distance, she had detected the sound of horse's hoofs.

It would not necessarily be Keith Otterbury, of course. A good many people in the district still preferred horses to cars. But whoever was coming was riding fast, which he almost invariably did.

Even before he turned the last bend in the lane, she knew it was he. He, for his part, recognized her at once, and reined in his horse. He didn't say anything for the first moment—just sat there smiling down at her, amused, quizzical and just a trifle insolent.

"Good morning, Mr. Otterbury," she said at last.

"Good morning, Miss Laverhope," he retorted a little mockingly. "What a coincidence that I should meet you today of all days."

"No, it's not a coincidence. I was on my way over to your place. I wanted to see you."

"You *wanted* to see me?" He swung off his horse, slipped the reins over one arm and slowly approached. "I'm flattered."

"Well, 'wanted' is perhaps not quite the word." She couldn't resist that. "I had to speak to you."

"On business?" He was studiedly polite.

"I suppose one might call it business." Her eyes fell,

for the first time. "It was about what we discussed last night."

"I don't think one could call that business at all." She knew from his tone that he was smiling. "I would certainly call that pleasure."

Ismay thought she would have called it something else, but she abandoned that part of the discussion.

"Anyway, I had to speak to you. Because I did what you suggested—thought over very carefully what you had said. And I remembered you said that if . . . if for any reason I changed my mind—" She stopped.

He had made not the slightest attempt to interrupt her, and now he made no attempt to help her out. After a long pause, she said baldly, "Well, I've changed my mind. That's what I was coming to tell you."

"And what made you change your mind, Ismay?" He spoke quietly, almost somberly.

"Does that matter?"

"No. But it's interesting." He reverted immediately to his careless manner when she shot a resentful glance at him.

"Well, something happened last night that made me realize how hopelessly in debt we are. There seems absolutely no way out unless one of us makes a rich marriage. I'm prepared to make it," she finished grimly.

He laughed softly at that, much more amused than annoyed by her deadly candor.

"So you propose to marry me simply and solely for my money?"

"No." Ismay raised angry eyes and looked straight at him. "I don't think that would be sufficient in itself. But there's the question of Avril, too. I can't let her ruin her life like that."

"You prefer to ruin your own life?"

"That's . . . different. Besides, marriage is different from . . . that."

"In all essentials it is the same," he told her, and his bold, careless glance did nothing to soften the statement. "But I admire your self-sacrifice and your . . . honesty."

"There isn't much point in pretending, is there?"

"No, Ismay. I think perhaps that's what I like so much about you. I don't believe you pretend about things, even to yourself. You certainly haven't put up any pretense to me about this marriage of ours."

She was silent, slowly digesting the phrase, "this marriage of ours." Then she looked up again at last, her blue eyes very dark and a little weary because of her sleepless night.

"Is it settled, then?"

He nodded, his eyes still on her.

"It's settled, Ismay."

"You promise to leave Avril alone?"

"I do." He smiled at her earnestness.

"And you really will . . . will. . . ."

"Finance all the family dreams? Oh yes. You'll have to tell me in detail what it is they want and we will arrange it."

"Very well. Thank you." That came reluctantly. "And when . . . when do you want to marry me?"

He laughed aloud at that.

"I want to marry you right away—tomorrow, today, if possible. I've waited long enough for you. Two years! But I suppose you want a little more time than that. At the moment I think you've hardly reached the stage of knowing that you are engaged to me, and that it's therefore your duty and privilege to kiss me."

His eyes were sparkling with amusement, but Ismay looked at him in something like horror.

"I don't want to kiss you."

"But you'll have to do it eventually, you know."

"Do you mean that I must . . . I must pretend to be fond of you?"

"Well"—she wondered how he could possibly laugh at this moment—"we won't set too high a standard. But I think you must contrive to appear mildly devoted in public."

"We're not in public now," she reminded him coldly.

"Meaning that you have no intention of kissing me at this moment?"

Before Ismay could reply, their conversation was suddenly interrupted by a tremendous clap of thunder, and without the slightest warning the rain came lashing down through the trees, as though determined to pierce every scrap of shelter.

"Oh!" Ismay shrank slightly before the ribbon of lightning that seemed to thread its way through the sky. It showed up the banks of heavy cloud that had miraculously gathered, unnoticed, in the past ten minutes. The thunder crashed again, and at the same moment there was the rending sound of splitting wood.

"Here, we must get out of this!" He caught her by the arm, using his other arm to quiet his frightened horse. "Can you ride?"

"No, I'll stay here. It will pass."

"No, you won't. There's no protection from the rain, and it's dangerous to stand under the trees. I can manage you."

"On that horse?"

"Of course." He mounted as he spoke and then leaned down to her. "Give me your hand."

"No! I can't ride and I—"

"Don't be a little fool. Give me your hand—so. Now put your foot on mine." Half-stunned by the thunder and the rain, she did as she was told, and he swung her up in front of him more easily than she would have thought possible.

The horse was very nervous now, and it seemed to Ismay that the great black head dipped away in front of her, leaving her no security. Instinctively she clutched Keith Otterbury's arm around her waist.

"You're all right." He laughed down at her. "I'll have you home in three minutes."

But "home" in this case appeared to be his own place, and he was cutting across the fields now, away from the road. Ismay glanced in something like terror over her shoulder.

"You're not going to jump that gate?"

"Of course."

"Oh, I *can't*—"

"Be quiet. You don't have to do anything. Shut your eyes if you don't like it."

She shut her eyes, but that hardly seemed enough, and as she felt them leave the ground, she hid her face against him. Afterward she was angry with herself and a good deal ashamed, because it all seemed fairly easy, the way Keith did it. But he laughed a good deal at her fear, and held her close against him in a way that made her very much aware of the hard muscle of his left arm.

"There, you're all right. We're home now." He lifted her down. "Run in out of the rain. I'll take Jade to the stables."

Someone must have heard or seen their arrival (Ismay hoped it was heard), for as she stepped into the porch, the door was opened for her by the servant who had admitted her the night before. This time his face expressed no surprise, and he took her at once into the room she had been in before.

"Did you get very wet, Miss Laverhope?" He even seemed concerned about her.

"No, thank you." She supposed they must have been riding in front of the storm, because Keith's body seemed to have saved her from the worst of the rain. "It's nothing much. I'm afraid Mr. Otterbury got most of it."

He walked in just then, taking off his wet jacket as he did so. (Father would have died rather than do such a thing in the presence of a lady, Ismay remembered, but she noticed also what a fine figure Keith cut in shirt sleeves.)

"Are you all right?" He glanced at her critically.

"Oh yes, thank you."

"You'd better get us some coffee, Palmer."

"Yes, sir."

She thought he would be almost certain to tease her when Palmer had gone, laugh at her for having been frightened, and declare that he must make a better horsewoman of her than that, or something equally offensive.

But he didn't. Instead, he looked at her serious face and asked, "Are you angry, Ismay?"

"Oh . . . no." Ismay smiled very slightly. "I was just thinking that I made rather an exhibition of myself just now. I thought you might be the one to be angry, or at any rate scornful."

He looked surprised. But all he said was, "It takes a great deal more than that to make me angry."

"Or scornful?" inquired Ismay, to whom that was nearly as bad as anger.

He grinned. "Could *I* presume to be scornful of one of the lovely Laverhopes? I simply wouldn't dare, my dear."

She gave a vexed little laugh and turned away to look out of the window.

"My brother—Adrian, you know—simply loathes that description of us. He says it's our curse to look decorative in any circumstances, and he almost wishes he had a squint."

"He may wish any misfortune he likes to his own eyes," retorted Keith Otterbury coolly, "but he mustn't dare to wish to change your beautiful eyes in the least."

He was standing close behind her when he said that, but although she was acutely conscious of him, she refused to turn around.

"Ismay, when the storm broke, we were interrupted in a most interesting conversation."

"Were we?"

"You know we were."

She looked steadily out of the window.

"Haven't you anything to say to me?"

"Nothing—except that I think it's stopped raining now and it's time I went home."

"You little devil!" he laughed softly. "Are you presuming on my assertion that it takes a lot to anger me?"

She turned then and looked up at him.

"Are you angry with me?"

For some reason his eyes widened as though he were slightly startled. He put his arms around her, but very lightly, so that they just encircled her but hardly touched her.

"No, Ismay, I'm not angry with you. But why won't you kiss me?"

She looked away from him.

"I will, if you insist."

"You know I'm not going to insist, don't you? I may have my faults, but I've never yet kissed a woman against her will."

It was in Ismay's mind to ask him how many he had kissed with their consent, but she said instead, "It's enough for today to know that I'm engaged to you. I don't . . . want to kiss you. I'll kiss you some other time when I'm more used to it all."

"Hm-hm." His eyes were suddenly flickering with amusement again. "In the true Laverhope tradition. You'll pay me tomorrow, eh? But never today."

"You beast!" Ismay exclaimed. And, very much more to her surprise than his, she raised her hand and struck him smartly across the cheek.

At this most interesting moment, Palmer chose to return with the coffee.

He must have been a very well-trained servant indeed, Ismay decided afterward, because he certainly contrived to give the impression that he had heard and seen nothing at all. Even when his master turned toward him, rubbing his cheek with a reflective smile, Palmer simply said, "The coffee, sir."

"Oh yes, Palmer, the coffee. Thanks."

He crossed to the coffee table and began to pour it out.

"White or black, Ismay?"

"Oh, white, please."

"Sugar?"

"Yes, please."

"How many?"

"One, please."

"Here you are." He brought it over to her. "Now I know exactly how you like your coffee."

She raised her eyes reluctantly to his face.

"I'm sorry," she said.

"Are you? All right. So am I."

It was impossible to tell from his expression just how he meant that, and for a minute she wondered if he was simply sorry she had struck him, because of the repercussions that must follow.

"Does it make you feel . . . differently?"

"About what, Ismay?"

"About marrying me."

"No. Was it intended to?"

"Oh no. Only I thought—"

His laugh cut her off. "You don't suppose a man sets his heart on something for two years, and then lets himself be put off because of a rather well-deserved slap in the face, do you?"

Ismay didn't answer. She was wondering what his heart had to do with it.

"Well, I think the rain has really stopped now, and if you're determined to go home, now is the moment. May I take you?"

"No, please don't. You see, I'd rather . . . ."

"Prepare them for the shock?"

"Well, at least there is a great deal to explain, and one simply couldn't do it at lunchtime, with Susan coming in from school."

"What has Susan to do with it?"

"Oh, quite a lot. You don't know Susan yet. She always wants to know the why and wherefore of everything."

"H'm. That's going to be a bit difficult in this particular case, isn't it?"

"Yes. That's why I don't want you to come just now."

"Very well. But do I come later and ask your father's permission to marry you, or what is the family procedure?"

"Father would like that awfully, of course," Ismay said seriously. "But he's not quite well just now."

"Is he ill?"

"Well, it was just a slight accident." She had an uncomfortable impression that he could see right into her mind and knew exactly what had happened. "I think I'd better telephone and let you know when it would be a good time to come." She couldn't imagine there would ever be a "good" time for introducing her astonished family to this unexpected fiancé.

"Very well." He seemed willing to let her have it her own way. "Don't keep me waiting too long, that's all."

"No," Ismay promised. "I'll call you this evening, I expect."

He let her go then, telling her, with a final touch of mockery, that she could go home through the fields as they were "practically her fields now."

As soon as she was out of sight of the house, Ismay hurried for it was late already, and if she wasn't in time for lunch there would be some sort of comment.

But she was unlucky. Even as she came in, Susan leaped to her feet with the agility of a jack-in-the-box and exclaimed, "Ismay Laverhope, what on earth were you doing, dashing around the countryside on Mr. Otterbury's horse, and he with his arm around you?"

"What's that?" Adrian looked up from the newspaper. "Is that why you've been hopping mad ever since you came in, Susan? Not that it's your business, of course," he added, a little too late.

"It *is* my business. It's everybody's business, I think," Susan protested. "I couldn't believe my eyes. Carol Elthorpe and I were coming home from dancing, and we'd taken shelter under that big oak at the end of Quentin Lane—"

"Never shelter under trees in a thunderstorm," her brother interrupted, in an effort to save Ismay from further questioning. "It's a most dangerous thing to do."

"Well, *we* didn't have anyone to dash up on horseback and whisk us off. And the rain was coming down fit to drown anyone. We saw Mr. Otterbury dashing across the fields on that black horse of his and there was someone with him, and I said to Carol, 'You'd think he was abducting someone, wouldn't you?' And she said, 'My goodness, it's your sister Ismay.' And I very nearly fainted," concluded Susan who looked in blooming health.

"I'm sorry it all looked so hair-raising, Susan," Ismay said as coolly as possible. "But it was simply as you thought yourself—that we were getting in out of the rain as quickly as possible."

"Yes, I *know*. But how did it come to be Mr. Otterbury who rescued you?"

"It wasn't a 'rescue,' Susan. We just happened to be talking and, well, when it rained, he kindly took me on his horse to shelter, that's all." She wished fervently that Susan would indeed accept that as "all."

"But I can't understand why *you* were talking to him," Susan insisted. "Now if it had been *Avril*—" She stopped as Avril entered the room.

"If what had been Avril?" inquired her sister, with only the faintest interest.

"Oh, nothing," Susan said hastily, in a way that would have made the least suspicious person begin to wonder.

Avril looked around slowly, and oblivious to the fact that their daily help had just brought in the lunch and was setting it on the table, she asked, "Why, what is the mystery?"

"It isn't a mystery, exactly," Susan said. "It's just rather 'straordinary. Ismay was talking with Mr. Otterbury when the storm started, and he took her on his horse and just dashed off home with her—like a highwayman."

"He didn't behave in the least like a highwayman," Ismay exclaimed with considerable irritation.

"*Ismay* was with Keith Otterbury?" Avril repeated slowly. "But I didn't know that you even knew him."

"Well, I do." Ismay sat down and began rather deliberately to serve lunch.

"Funny, I didn't know you did, either," Adrian said. "I wouldn't have thought he was your kind exactly, Ismay."

"Wouldn't you? I like him very much, as a matter of fact."

"*Like* him? What an odd thing to say." Adrian cast her a puzzled look. "At least, I mean what an odd thing to say of a man like Otterbury. He's rather—"

Ismay set down her knife and fork with a little clatter.

"Don't say any more, Adrian, because . . . because. . . . Well, I didn't mean to tell you all quite like this, but I'm going to marry Keith Otterbury. We became engaged this morning."

"Marry!"

"Engaged!"

Adrian and Avril spoke simultaneously, while Susan for once could produce nothing but a sort of crow of sheer astonishment and excitement.

"Yes, I know it must seem frightfully sudden and inexplicable. But . . . but I've known him, on and off, for quite a long time. It isn't really as sudden as it seems," she finished lamely.

Adrian said nothing at all for a moment. Then, looking straight at Ismay, he said, "I don't think we're in quite such a tight corner as all that, Ismay."

"I don't know what you mean." Ismay's tone was perfectly steady, though she dared not look at Avril, or, to tell the truth, at Adrian.

"Oh yes, you do."

"Well, what do you mean, Adrian?" Susan wanted to know. But no one took any notice of her.

"If you think I'm marrying Keith because we're in a tight corner and he's rich, you're quite mistaken," Ismay lied with surprising earnestness.

"Are you going to tell me, Ismay, that you're in love with him?" Adrian asked quietly.

Ismay saw then that it was all or nothing.

"Yes," she said, without hesitation.

Avril gave a very slight laugh, while Susan sucked in her breath and remarked, "Fancy that now! Well, they always say it's sudden."

Adrian went on with his lunch in silence, and Ismay stole a glance at Avril. It was hard to tell from her expression what she was thinking, but Ismay somehow gathered that this extraordinary announcement was a relief rather than a disappointment to her.

And she might well be relieved, of course. She probably guessed that she would get most of what she wanted from her sister now, and there would be nothing to pay in return. Not even "tomorrow."

"I *never* heard of anything so 'straordinary!" For once Susan's babbling was something of a blessing. "I think it's really rather romantic myself. And of course it's terribly convenient that he's so rich. It doesn't seem to matter about Great-aunt Georgina now."

Adrian gave her a withering look at that, but Ismay rather wanted to hug her. It was all very crudely expressed, but it was nice to hear someone put it into words. It didn't matter so much about Great-aunt Georgina now.

CHAPTER FIVE

It was fairly late in the afternoon when Ismay sought out Avril, for although she felt she must have some sort of a talk with her sister, Ismay found that Avril was not especially anxious, on her part, to say very much.

Ismay found her at last—out in the garden, sketching once more. An old mackintosh cape was spread on the still damp grass, and Avril sat there with a sketch pad on her knees, apparently oblivious to everything else.

Ismay came and sat down on a corner of the mackintosh, watching Avril in silence for a few minutes.

Avril looked up once, said, "Hello," then went on with her work. After a while Ismay went straight to the point.

"Avril, are you angry with me?"

"No." That sounded genuine enough. "Why should I be angry?"

"I thought you might feel, er, sore about my . . . my engagement to Keith. I didn't mean to tell you just like that at lunchtime, you know. I meant to do it much more tactfully."

"Yes, I'm sure you did."

"Avril, please tell me. It wasn't a case of your feelings being involved, was it? You weren't . . . fond of him, after all?"

"No," Avril said. "Nor are you either, are you?"

Ismay shrugged. It was useless to pretend with Avril, who already knew so much of the situation.

"No. But I'm not telling anyone else that."

"I won't tell either," Avril said, as though she thought Ismay might like that reassurance. "Is it some weird idea of saving me from taking the downward path?"

"No." Ismay didn't like to hear it described like that. "It's just . . . everything. I'd better tell you, I think. You have some sort of right to know. I'm afraid you'll be wild, Avril, but I went to him yesterday evening and told him I knew about you two—"

"You what?" Avril raised her head and stared at her sister.

"Yes, I know it must seem awful to you, but to me it seemed the only thing to do. I couldn't let you ruin your life, Avril, for it would have been that. And at the same time I couldn't get you to listen to argument. There was nothing left but to go to him and ask if I could make him do the decent thing."

"And what did he say?" Avril asked curiously. She seemed singularly free from anger, only very much interested to hear what had happened.

"That it was not my business, of course. Which I suppose was true, in a way. I think he knew quite well that there was no . . . affection about it, Avril. With you, I mean. But anyway, I can't imagine you would have been anything but honest about that."

Avril nodded, presumably in agreement.

"I finally asked him outright to give you up and let the whole dreadful idea finish before it had begun."

"And then what did he say?" Avril never took her eyes from her sister's face.

"He said he would do so if I would marry him, and that he had always wanted to marry me, anyway."

"He said that?"

"Yes."

"And nothing else at all?"

"Well, nothing material."

"How extraordinary," murmured Avril, still sketching. "But you didn't accept there and then, Ismay, surely? You said just now that it wasn't only because of me."

"No, of course not. I turned the idea down flat. In fact, I was very rude about it. But he didn't seem to mind. Only he told me that the offer remained open and that I was to think over all the things he could do for us all if I would let him. He was willing to pay father's debts and pay for Adrian's training and you can go to Italy, after all, Avril. He's willing to finance that, too."

"Really?" Avril said slowly.

"Yes."

"And all this because you're marrying him? Ismay, he must be terribly keen on you."

"I don't know. I think perhaps it's just the idea of being able to have something—someone—he never expected to get."

"Maybe. He is that sort of man, of course." Avril spoke coolly, as though she had had very little to do with him, but could catalog him quite easily. Then after a moment she asked, "Are you very miserable about it, Ismay? I can see you aren't exactly happy, of course."

Ismay was silent, considering thatm

"No, I don't think 'miserable' is the word. I'm so frantically relieved, for one thing, that it will get us all out of the terrible hole we're in. It was much worse even than you knew, Avril. Even the house had gone—mortgaged, and the interest not paid up. I simply don't know where we'd have turned if this hadn't happened. And then I couldn't bear to think of Adrian dragging out his youth and enthusiasm to a dull job. He's clever and he wants to work in a big way. He could do it too, if he had the chance. As it was, we hadn't even the money to pay his fare to London. I can't pretend it isn't heavenly to have all that settled after all."

Avril looked reflective. "I suppose it would be tactless to ask what you really think of Keith."

"No," Ismay said. "But it would be useless. Because I

don't even know myself. How can I? I hadn't exchanged more than half a dozen words with him before this happened."

"It doesn't sound a bit like you, Ismay." Avril seemed very intent on what she was doing.

"It isn't a bit like me. But what can we do? We've been pitchforked into the world of reality and told to sink or swim."

"And we looked remarkably like sinking?"

"Exactly."

"Well," Avril said, "Otterbury Hall seems a queer haven of refuge, especially for you."

"I hadn't thought of it as a haven," her sister assured her dryly, as she stood up to go.

"But you'll enjoy being rich, Ismay. Even you couldn't do anything else. There'll be clothes and jewels and furs and travel, and all of it for nothing."

"No," Ismay said slowly. "All of it on credit . . . and the bill to be paid one day."

Avril gave her a puzzled little glance. Then she shrugged and laughed.

"Well, that's the most comfortable way of arranging things, isn't it? It's the way we've always done things. Promised to pay tomorrow. And then quite often tomorrow doesn't come."

"I think," Ismay said softly, "that in Keith Otterbury's house, tomorrow follows today quite inevitably."

Avril didn't say anything to that, and Ismay went back into the house, determined to see if her father was in any condition to be told her news and, if so, to face the last of these family interviews while her determination held.

When she entered her father's room, it was to find him propped up in bed, looking very much more himself than he had at any time since the reading of Great-aunt Georgina's will. At the same time, Ismay could not help noticing that there was a great deal of gray in the thick fair hair that was so like her own and Adrian's. Perhaps it had been there before, but . . . . One noticed these things now, and when she saw him smile in that eager, pleased way at her entrance, she felt unspeakably glad that it was good news, and not bad, she was about to impart.

At least, I suppose one would call it good news, thought Ismay. *At any rate, it won't cost him anything, poor darling!*

"Well, Ismay, my dear, you see the invalid well on the way to recovery." Father seemed to take some personal credit for this, and he lay back against his pillows, looking very picturesque and contented.

"I'm so glad." Ismay smiled at him. "Do you feel in a mood for a talk, father?"

A shadow crossed his face at once, because of course the poor man could not imagine any talk that did not involve financial embarrassment.

"Why, yes, my dear, I think so. Though of course I must not tax my strength too much at present." That was his attempt to raise a barrier against any news that might be frankly disastrous.

"No, of course not. But I have something to tell you that is nice and rather exciting. I'm engaged. I wanted to tell you just as soon as possible."

"Engaged? But, my dear child, this is indeed news—delightful news!"

Ismay was dreadfully afraid he was readying his speech about fledglings leaving the nest, and as she felt much too tired and experienced now to be a fledgling, she hurried on.

"You'll be terribly surprised when you hear who it is, but—"

Father held up his beautiful hand and said smilingly, "I think you ought to allow me three guesses."

"Oh, but you'd never guess in three guesses," Ismay assured him rather agitatedly, "It's Keith Otterbury."

Father's mild annoyance at being done out of his three guesses was completely swamped in his astonishment— disagreeable astonishment at that, Ismay saw plainly.

"Keith Otterbury! My dear Ismay, you can't be serious. There must be some mistake."

Ismay didn't really see what mistake there could be. She was silent, allowing her father to digest the news in his own way.

"Dear child, I don't think I can allow this," he said at last. "I had never imagined myself giving one of my daughters to a man like Keith Otterbury."

And I never thought of giving myself to him either, reflected Ismay crudely. Aloud she said, "I know there's a great deal of uncharitable talk about him, but don't you think people always gossip about anyone who behaves impulsively and unconventionally?"

Father shook his head gravely.

"It isn't only impulse and lack of convention, my dear. There are other things— You wouldn't understand." Glancing at him, Ismay saw that he really thought she would not. "Ismay, isn't this all a very sudden and thoughtless decision?"

"No," Ismay insisted. "I have met him on occasion, you know. It was only quite recently, of course, that we thought seriously of getting married. But indeed, father, I think you'd like him, if you really knew him."

Nothing was more unlikely, Ismay felt sure, but she felt she must at least encourage her father in the belief that his future son-in-law had some good qualities.

"He's very kind, really," she hurried on. "He says he has wanted to marry me for something like two years now, ever since he first saw me."

"Most improbable!" exclaimed father with one of his

rare flashes of common sense. "Nobody wants to marry a woman the first time he sees her."

"Well," Ismay conceded with a smile, "I daresay that is only in a manner of speaking. But he does lo— He is very, very anxious to marry me."

"And how about you, Ismay? Are you very much in love with him?"

"Oh, yes, of course."

Fortunately father put down any slight confusion on her part to very natural and proper modesty.

"You can't imagine how generous and kind he is!" Ismay felt it was time she brought up the heavy reserves of argument. "There is no end to the things he wants to do for me and the family."

"Indeed?" Father looked interested . . . against his will.

"Oh yes. He's determined that Adrian get his chance. He wants to support him during his medical training. And Avril can go to Italy and study art if she wants to. And Keith doesn't want us to have any more anxiety—financial anxiety, that is—in the family. He seems to understand our difficulties so well, and he really wants to help."

Ismay felt some astonishment herself at the convincing story she was managing to make of it all. As for father, he listened spellbound. Whatever objections he had against Keith Otterbury as a son-in-law still existed, but undoubtedly there were some other very heavy considerations weighing down the opposite side of the scales.

"My dear Ismay! This is the most extraordinary generosity. But . . . ." Suddenly father recalled the sequence of events in all the best melodramas. "All this is not in the nature of a bribe, is it? You are not—I might almost say 'selling yourself'—for all these advantages, are you?" He looked anxiously at her.

"Oh no." Ismay managed to laugh. "There's nothing

like that about it. I . . . I do love Keith, and I want to marry him. I know there are some unfortunate stories about him, but, well, I don't feel I have a right to question his past, simply because he has asked me to share his future."

Ismay knew that the balance of that last sentence would appeal to her father immediately. He nodded slowly and thoughtfully.

"Perhaps you are right, my dear. Perhaps you are right."

Ismay was silent, allowing him to savor the pleasant implications of what she had said. Now that he had admitted to himself the possibility of his daughter's marrying Keith Otterbury, there was no harm in reflecting on the amazing easing of their whole position.

"You are quite sure your happiness really lies in this marriage?" he asked her once. And when she said, "Quite sure," she thought he looked a great deal more relieved than worried.

At last she said coaxingly, "You really haven't any objections, father, have you?"

"Well, child, all I want is whatever is best for you." That was true, at any rate, Ismay knew, for her father was extremely attached to his children. "If you've set your heart on this marriage and have seriously considered all it means, then it is not for me to interfere. It shall never be said of me that I influenced any of my children unduly in the choice of a husband." He remembered Adrian then, and amended the phrase to "in the choice of a life companion," which sounded more impressive anyway.

Ismay saw then that he was well embarked on the stream of his own eloquence and quite prepared to enjoy himself in the old way. It was so pleasant to see him happily restored to normal that she had no difficulty in smiling attentively and murmuring agreement with everything he was saying. Only when he said, "But I must see Keith Otterbury myself," did she take charge of the conversation once more.

"He wants to come and see you as soon as you're well enough."

"I'm well enough now," he insisted firmly, and indeed he did look much brighter and more energetic.

"Well, I was going to phone him this evening. He wanted to know when he could come and ask you formally for permission to marry me."

"'Very proper," murmured father, delighted with this unusual show of ceremony. "I see no reason why he should not come this evening, Ismay. Not too late, of course. But tell him I shall be happy to receive him about seven o'clock."

"Very well." Ismay secretly marveled at the attitude of pleasant condescension that her father was quite prepared to adopt toward the man who was going to pay his debts for him.

No wonder he always got away with everything, she reflected as she left the room. *He is so honestly convinced that it's he who dispenses the favors.*

The house was very quiet when she came downstairs. Susan was not yet home from school, Avril was still out in the garden, and Adrian, she supposed, was out on some concern of his own. It was a good opportunity to telephone Keith Otterbury now. (She would have to remember to think of him now as "Keith." One could not call one's fiancé by his whole name, even in one's thoughts.)

She went to the telephone and had to stop to look up his number in the directory. It was strange somehow, not even to know the telephone number of the man you were going to marry. She knew the numbers of all their acquaintances by heart and practically never consulted the directory from one year to the next. But then, of course, Keith was not—and never had been—an acquaintance of theirs.

While she waited for him to answer, her gaze wandered absently about the hall, noting familiar details that usually scarcely aroused her attention. Heavens, the place was shabby! One could hardly expect anything else, of course. Four children had been brought up in this house, and there had hardly ever been a penny for repairs or decorations.

It was difficult to remember any other wallpaper. This one had been put on in mother's time, and that discolored patch near the bottom of the stairs was where a two-year-old Susan had scribbled on it with a pencil, a week after it had been put up. Mother had done miracles with india rubber and breadcrumbs, but the shadow of Susan's misdeeds still lingered.

And then that mark on the hall table. That had happened after some misguided person had given Adrian a carpentering set for Christmas. She could remember quite well—

"Hello." The voice in her ear jolted her back to the present.

"May I speak to Mr. Otterbury, please?"

"Speaking."

"Oh, Mr. Ott—I mean, Keith—this is Ismay speaking. I thought you would like to know that I've told the family."

She heard him laugh.

"How did they take it?"

"Oh, they were surprised, of course."

"Of course."

"But quite pleased." And then, remembering Adrian's expression, she added, "On the whole."

"A mixed reception, in fact."

"Well, that's all you, er, we could expect, isn't it?"

"I suppose so."

"Anyway, father would like very much to see you. This evening, if possible."

"I'll come. Does he want to express approval or disapproval?"

"Oh, I think he is pleased, on the whole. He wouldn't have *chosen* you, exactly," she added candidly. "but then—"

"—Nor would you?" he suggested.

"I wasn't going to say that."

"Very well." She heard that amused laugh again. "I will come. About seven."

"Yes, about seven." And then because there was nothing else to say to him at all, she said a rather curt goodbye and hung up.

During tea she told the others, "Keith will be coming this evening."

"Whatever for?" Adrian inquired, with casual rudeness, while Susan said, "My goodness! I must get my homework done early."

By which Ismay gathered she did not intend to miss anything.

As seven o'clock drew near, she began to feel ridiculously nervous. And, acting on an impulse she could hardly explain, she went out of the house and walked a little way down the lane, in the direction from which he must come.

Apparently punctuality was one of his minor virtues, for it was still only a few minutes to seven when she heard his footsteps. The bend in the lane still hid him from her view, but she felt she was already beginning to know that long, rapid stride very well.

He was looking very serious when she first saw him, but his face lit up with a smile when he caught sight of her.

"My dear, this is very charming of you. Or is it just your first effort to show the mild devotion I suggested might be tactful in public?"

"No. I just felt nervous in the house and thought I would come a little way to meet you."

He smiled rather quizzically and put his arm lightly around her waist, as he fell into step beside her.

"Were you nervous on my behalf, or your own?"

"Oh, I don't know. Just over the general situation, I expect."

He glanced down at her, as though he wanted to say something else about that. But apparently he changed his mind, because after a moment he said abruptly, "I brought you your ring, Ismay."

"Already!" She was astonished. "But when did you find time to get it?"

"Perhaps I had it already," he said with a smile.

"But you couldn't. You had no idea that this was going to happen."

"How do you know I haven't cherished your ring in readiness all this time—hoping that one day my luck might change?"

In spite of his mocking tone, she glanced at him curiously. She had the odd feeling that it was the sort of preposterous thing he might do. But she only said rather grimly, "That would be a costly indulgence in sentiment, I would think."

"Ismay, haven't you a grain of romance in your composition?" He laughed down at her accusingly.

She was silent, because she thought it was rather unreasonable to expect her to have any feeling of romance where he was concerned. Perhaps he remembered that, too, after a moment because, without pursuing the subject further, he took the ring from his pocket.

He made no attempt to put it on her finger, she noticed. He simply held it out in the palm of his hand, and, after a second's hesitation, she took it.

"Oh, how lovely!" The exclamation was forced from her involuntarily.

"You like it?" He was pleased. She could tell that from his tone.

"Yes, of course. It's heavenly. However did you get it?"

"I've told you," he said teasingly. "I have had it all this time in the hope that one day you would wear it."

"But—" she brushed that aside "—where did you find it originally?"

"In a shop in Athens. It may be Greek work—I'm not sure. But it's the color of your eyes. That's why I bought it."

She was quite silent, gazing at the most beautiful piece of lapis lazuli she had ever seen, pretending she had not heard his last sentence.

The ring was curiously and most exquisitely wrought, the pure yellow of soft, unalloyed gold forming the perfect setting for the blue of the lapis lazuli. The value of it lay in the workmanship, and it was evidently the fine flower of some true artist's work. There was something almost barbaric about it, and it occurred to Ismay that it was the kind of ring one *would* associate with Keith.

At that moment he said, "You can have the usual solitaire, too, if you like, or whatever you fancy. But that ring is essentially yours. It suits you."

"I don't want anything else, thank you. There's nothing I could like as much as this," Ismay told him frankly. And then, after a moment, she said, "Thank you, Keith. It's beautiful."

"I'm happy if you are pleased," was all he said, but Ismay had the curious impression that that was literally true.

She slipped his ring on her finger without another word, and they went into the house together.

"Will you see father first? Or the rest of the family?"

"Your father." He smiled at her in the rather subdued light of the hall, without a trace of the nervousness she herself was feeling.

"Come along then." She led him upstairs, thankful that Susan, for once, refrained from rushing out to inspect the newcomer on her own account.

The sonorous "Come in," with which her father answered her knock showed that he was prepared, in every sense, for his visitor. And as Ismay led the way into the room, she wondered if Keith would find father amusing or—still worse—if he would be unkind enough to show it.

Keith's greeting, however, was as faultless as her father's own. And he did not allow himself even the slightest twinkle when, after the first few conventionalities, her father said to Ismay, "My dear, I think you had better leave us alone together."

Ismay went out of the room. She would have felt faintly sorry for anyone else in the circumstances, but she thought Keith could manage the situation very well, and, even if he could not, well, that served him right for some of the horrid things he had said and done.

She didn't go downstairs again—she felt a little unwilling to face the comments and questions of the others.

Instead, she went to the bedroom she shared with Avril and stood by the window, staring out into the garden, slowly turning her unusual and beautiful ring upon her finger.

It felt odd there. She had never worn a ring before, and this one felt heavy. It was a wonderful ring, though—the kind of ring that must have taken a lot of finding. Athens—that was where he said he had bought it. Somehow that made it even more unusual.

Then he *must* have bought it some while ago, for she was sure he had not been away from the district for more than a day or two during this year at least. And he had said he bought it because it was the color of her eyes.

But that was ridiculous. He could hardly have been thinking of her eyes at that time. That was just a bit of romantic ballyhoo, which he thought sounded good. He had bought the ring because he liked it. Nothing more or less.

She wondered what he was saying to her father now. Or rather, what her father was saying to him, because, of course, father would see to it that he did most of the talking. He was quite capable of taking Keith to task about previous escapades and giving him a grave and impressive lecture. She could not quite decide how Keith would take such an attack but, try as she might, she could not imagine him discomfited in any way.

Father would be very man-to-man, of course, implying that he, too, had been something of a devil in his day, but that there were "limits." It would be quite untrue, needless to say, for no one could have been more intensely respectable in thought and deed than father.

Whereas, with Keith . . . . No, "respectable" was not the word to describe Keith.

She heard the door of father's room open, and his musical, penetrating voice saying something ending in "my dear boy." That sounded as though they had reached some satisfactory agreement and, smiling faintly, she opened the door of her room.

Keith was just coming out of her father's room, and he said over his shoulder, through the half-open door, "She's here, sir. Would you like to speak to her now?"

(Oh, how father would like that "sir"! Adrian had never called him that in spite of sundry encouragements to do so.)

"No, no." Father's tone was geniality itself. "I'll give her my blessing later. It's your voice she wants to hear at the moment."

Ismay saw the sardonic light leap into Keith's smiling eyes. He softly closed the door and came toward her.

"How charming, but how untrue!" he said, looking down at her.

"Will you come down and meet the others now?" She spoke with studied calm.

"Don't you want to hear the result of my interview?"

"I know it. Father wouldn't sound so genial or you look so cock-a-hoop if things hadn't gone smoothly.

"So *what*? Lord! Do I really look that?" He grinned reflectively. "Well, now I come to think of it, that is how I feel."

"Because my father has agreed to let you pay his debts?" she said dryly, turning away.

He came close behind her and put his arms around her, imprisoning her lightly.

"No. Forget about your father's debts and your brother's ambitions and all the rest of it."

"Shall I forget about Avril too?" she interrupted

coolly, refusing to look around at him, though she was terribly aware of his nearness.

"Ismay, haven't you one kind word to say to me?"

"Why should I?"

"Because . . . . Do you really want to know?"

"Well?"

"Because I love you, you little beast." He turned her almost roughly and kissed her on her mouth before she could stop him. "Because I don't mind what this damned, cadging family of yours costs, so long as I have you. Because . . . . Oh God, I'm sorry! I'm saying all the wrong things, of course."

"Well, at least . . . I don't much like the way you speak of my family." She tried very hard to make that sound cool and scornful, but she was terribly shaken by his outburst, and her words came in unsteady little gasps.

"I apologize." A shadow of something like sullenness appeared in his dark eyes. "Shall we go downstairs and meet the family, as you suggested?"

Ismay led the way without a word.

Downstairs in the drawing room the three other members of the family were grouped in rather uneasy silence, but as soon as Ismay and Keith came in, the tension seemed to break.

Until that moment Ismay had not had time to think how awkward the greeting between Avril and Keith was bound to be. She had one moment of panic, and then saw that there was no need for distress on her part. The two measured each other with cool little stares, then the faintest smile crossed Avril's face, while Keith's, "How are you, Avril?" held very much more than a hint of amusement. It was extraordinary how well they did it.

Actually the meeting with Adrian was the most difficult one, because somehow Adrian refused to show any of his usual graciousness and charm. He contented himself with the curtest of greetings and left the field to Susan, who occupied it with alacrity.

"How d'you do? I'm Susan, and I know you very well by sight even though I haven't been introduced to you before. And do tell me, is that great black horse of yours really as wicked as it looks?"

"No," Keith assured her coolly. "She's like her master—has a deceptive appearance that makes people think her more wicked than she is."

"O-oh." Susan turned that over in her mind. "I don't think you look very wicked," she observed at last.

"Don't you? I'm relieved."

Susan, however, refused to take that at its face value.

"I don't believe you a bit," she declared cheerfully. "You don't care a hang what I think, or what anybody else thinks either. Everyone says so."

"Indeed? And who is 'everyone'?"

But Susan didn't see how one could define that more clearly. She made a vague gesture with her hand and amended her expression to, "Oh . . . everybody, you know."

"You mean I have a general reputation in the neighborhood for not caring about anything or anyone?"

"I suppose that's it," Susan agreed. "Still, people can't say that now, because they'll know you must care for Ismay or you wouldn't be marrying her."

"How do you like the idea of redeeming me in the eyes of the world, Ismay?" He turned to her with a smile.

"I think it would take more . . ." Ismay began sharply. Then she stopped, suddenly remembering that she had to play the part of an affectionate and happy fiancée. Somehow she contrived to summon a smile. "I don't think there is any redemption needed. Susan always exaggerates," she said mildly.

"I don't!" Susan was indignant. "And you know quite

well that father himself said . . . ." She didn't finish, overcome by belated tact, and for once no one heard what it was that "Father said."

Ismay found herself wondering how Keith was reacting to all this, despite his mocking little smile that suggested he found them all amusing. After all, surely no man actually *liked* to feel that people thought him a pretty shocking person.

But whatever Keith really felt, he kept his thoughts to himself, and even if the evening could hardly be considered an unqualified success, at least it was redeemed from real failure by the easy, if slightly scornful good temper of the guest of honor.

More than once, Ismay noticed that he glanced very quizzically in Avril's direction, but she withstood it well, and nothing in the manner of either would have aroused the suspicions of any casual observer.

When they went out into the garden after supper, Ismay noticed that Keith deliberately strolled on ahead with Avril, and instinctively, she herself kept Susan and Adrian back with some inquiry about some plant in which not one of them was genuinely interested at the moment. She felt it was better that the other two should say whatever they wanted to say to each other now. It would save complications later. There could surely not be much that they could want to say to each other in the circumstances, but she could imagine that a few candid words now might well save misunderstanding and bad feelings later.

"I think he's awfully attractive, Ismay." Susan seized the opportunity to give her opinion at the earliest possible moment. "I don't believe he takes anything very seriously, but then neither does Adrian, so you'll be used to that."

"Thank you. Just count me out of that," her brother said dryly. "I don't think I've got much in common with him. At least, I hope not."

"Adrian, please." Ismay was distressed, though she felt she was probably not showing sufficient distress for a devoted fiancée who wanted her choice of husband approved by her family.

"Sorry, my dear. But he's not my type. And to tell the truth, I can't imagine that he's yours either."

Ismay didn't answer that, and presently they rejoined the others. As they did so, she heard Keith say, "On the contrary, my dear Avril, I'm grateful to you. In fact, I hope you enjoy Italy enormously. I'll certainly do everything I can to see that you do."

She wondered a little what reason he had for being grateful and decided that it was probably some relief to him that Avril had not resented his shifting his attention from one sister to the other.

Then Susan introduced a rather strained note into the conversation with the leading question, "Well, when are you going to be married? Quite soon, I suppose?"

"I think so." Keith looked as though he were deferring to Ismay's wishes, but she already knew that the slight tightening at the corners of his mouth meant that he intended to have things his way.

"Yes. I—we don't see any reason for a long engagement." (That at least was true, for certainly the tangled family affairs would not wait for a leisurely straightening out.) "We thought in about . . . ." She hesitated, looking questioningly at Keith.

He finished for her quite calmly, "In about two weeks' time."

Ismay gasped, for she had not thought of it all being so close upon her as that, but fortunately Susan's astonishment was sufficiently vocal to drown any sound her sister made.

"Two weeks? My goodness! You *are* in a hurry, aren't you? I can't think what Carol will say." No one seemed greatly disturbed at the thought of Carol's reactions. "She was astonished enough this afternoon when I told her you were going to get married, because, as she said, you hardly even knew each other, so it must have been love at first sight. But *this*! I suppose Avril and I'll be bridesmaids. What a pity you're grown up, Adrian; otherwise you could have been the ring bearer." Adrian made a slight, inarticulate sound of horror. "And really, a wedding is something where we *can* shine, because we'll all look awfully nice. Let's wear headbands, Avril. They're much nicer than hats. What a good job you and I are both the ones with red hair, because then we won't quarrel over colors, because whatever suits you will suit me. Green'd be nice, wouldn't it? And as we're none of us superstitious—"

"Is this your wedding or Ismay's?" inquired her future brother-in-law.

"Oh, well, Ismay's always sweet about that sort of thing. And anyway, she's bound to wear white and she looks marvelous in white, so she can't grudge us whatever we look best in.

"Yes, she must look marvelous in white," was all Keith said, and for once he was not laughing.

"Oh, I don't know if there will be time to arrange a white wedding." Ismay spoke hastily, rousing herself from abstraction and only realizing with difficulty that it was her own wedding that was being discussed.

"There'll be plenty of time," Keith said. And she knew at once that what he meant was that there would be plenty of money, and wherever there was plenty of money things could be done to order.

Susan, evidently considering that this point was satis-factorily settled, proceeded a little farther along a deli-cate path, with the cheerful inquiry, "And then where'll you go for your honeymoon? Abroad?"

"*No!*" Ismay's reply was almost violent, because at Susan's words she suddenly saw the complete picture at last. Herself alone with Keith in some strange hotel, miles and miles away from home and everyone she knew, the last link with familiarity snapped, the last bridge destroyed.

For a moment she felt sick and more frightened than she would have believed possible. Why did one have to have a honeymoon at all? It would be terrible enough going home with Keith to Otterbury Hall, knowing that he was her husband, that her life belonged more or less to him henceforward. Why should she be forced to stage the first ghastly scenes in some place remote from her home and every single thing that could give her the slightest scrap of confidence?

"I don't think I want a honeymoon," she heard herself say in a slightly strangled voice, and she looked around defiantly, feeling that now indeed she had knocked the bottom out of any pretty pretense there had ever been. As though in the distance, she saw Susan's astonishment, the lift of Adrian's eyebrows, the close way Avril was watching her.

Then Keith said casually, "No, I don't know that I do either. Honeymoons are always something of a mistake, I feel."

She gave a slight gasp. The world seemed to right itself again. She was trembling a little with the sense of the nearness of disaster. But keenest of all in her thoughts at the moment was the curious certainty that Keith had understood her terror and had answered her unspoken appeal.

CHAPTER SIX

"But I never heard of anyone not having a honeymoon," Susan persisted. "At least, not anyone who got married, I mean."

"Lots of people prefer to have it later," Keith assured her, and Ismay was thankful that he took on the arguing of the matter. With anyone as positive about conventions as Susan could be, it was not an easy task. "Since we're not having a long engagement," he went on casually, "and since Ismay wants to make as little break with her own home as possible, I don't see why we shouldn't have a quiet wedding—"

"But with bridesmaids!" Susan got that in.

"All right, with bridesmaids, if that's what Ismay wants. And then postpone our honeymoon. That will leave her free to arrange whatever she likes for all of you. Then when we do go, we can make it a long trip if we want."

"Something like a world tour, you mean?" Susan was beginning to see the advantages of the plan now.

Keith shrugged slightly and smiled.

"If that's what Ismay would like."

"My goodness, Ismay! Everything is what you would like. You *are* going to have a good time," Susan remarked frankly.

Ismay managed a small smile. "Yes, I'm sure of that." She wished Adrian would not look quite so rudely skeptical.

Much later that evening, when Keith was finally leaving, she strolled with him to the gate. It was the only chance she had had of a word with him alone.

"Good night sweetheart." There was a curiously caressing note in his voice, but she could see, even in the moonlight, that his smile was mocking.

"Good night Keith." She hesitated. "I want to ask you something."

"Well?"

"Did you mean that—about our not having a honeymoon?"

"Yes. That is, if you really don't want one."

"N-no, I'd rather not. Only why did you bother?"

"I don't understand." She thought the line of his chin looked faintly obstinate. "Why did I bother about what?"

"You know quite well what I mean. Why did you bother to help me out in front of the others, when I said I didn't want a honeymoon? You could easily have forced the issue and made me accept it."

"Do you think that would have made for an enjoyable honeymoon, Ismay?" he asked dryly.

"No, of course not. But then . . . ." She paused helplessly, wondering what there was that could be called enjoyable about anything to do with this marriage.

He took her lightly by the arm and smiled down at her.

"Look here, my dear, you go on thinking me the worst and most impossible fellow on earth. Then you'll have an occasional pleasant surprise when the natural beauty of my nature shows itself in a rare flash of generosity."

She heard him laugh, and before he left her he kissed her, but lightly this time on the side of her cheek, not at all as he had kissed her before. In fact, thought Ismay, as she went slowly back into the house, it hardly counted as a kiss at all.

After that, it was difficult to say how the time slipped away so quickly. Ismay had always supposed that getting married involved a tremendous amount of arranging, but it seemed quite an astonishingly simple matter under Keith's arbitrary management. Adrian said once, rather violently, that he had a "very offensive manner of footing the bill," but Ismay couldn't help thinking that one either footed the bill or didn't. And when you were paying for a lot of things that, by rights, should have been paid for by someone else, it was hard to say just what was the correct manner.

"He means well. He means well," her father declared in his most patronizing manner, and nothing could have been more gracious than the way he was already allowing himself to be extricated from his financial swamp.

"Anyway, how would we have paid for everything ourselves?" demanded Susan with ruthless frankness. "Ismay would simply have had to be married in any old thing she had, because I can't imagine there is anyone left who would give us credit for so much as a handkerchief."

"Susan, my dear, you talk a great deal too much for your age," father said, a trifle remotely. And, this being unquestionably true, Susan was forced to subside into silence.

On the whole, they saw little of the prospective bridegroom. Perhaps he was aware that any visits of his caused constraint rather than pleasure in the Laverhope household, or perhaps he was just busy with his own affairs. But they were aware of his hand in almost everything, and to tell the truth, it was usually a hand that was paying out money.

"I'm afraid marrying me is proving rather an expensive luxury, Keith," Ismay said to him dryly once.

His only reply was a rather curt, "Perhaps I consider it cheap at the price."

That really didn't leave much more to be said on the subject, Ismay thought.

The only one who was probably wholeheartedly enjoying all the preparations was Susan. She was an insensitive child and had an enormous capacity for enjoying things that left other people squirming. But she also took the most genuine pleasure in what she supposed to be her sister's happiness.

"You're really frightfully lucky, Ismay, aren't you?" she said, when Ismay's wedding dress had arrived and been duly inspected. "I doubt if many women marry men with so much money. Or if they do, the men turn out to be mean and want to spend it all on themselves. You must be terribly happy."

"Yes," Ismay agreed—inadequately, she felt, but it was difficult to bubble with enthusiasm in the circumstances.

"It was funny he should have been in love with you and all the time we imagined it was Avril."

"Very funny," Ismay said, and then thought the word was singularly ill-chosen.

She could not decide what to make of Avril these days. Apparently she was perfectly willing to take casual pleasure in the preparations for her sister's wedding, just as though she herself had had nothing to do with Keith.

Ismay didn't see how anyone could come to such an enormous decision as Avril, and then coolly drop the whole idea, as though it had never existed. But then, she reflected, not for the first time, Avril was an entirely inexplicable person.

Sometimes, lately, she thought perhaps she herself was rather an inexplicable person. She had always supposed that she would let her life run in uneventful, conventional channels. Although warmly affectionate, she had never thought of herself as indulging in violent emotional storms, or involving herself in situations where anger and fear and hate waited just around the corner.

She tried not to think too much of the way Keith had

kissed her, that time outside father's room. But if that had meant anything at all, it had meant that he had some sort of violent passion for her. And, that being so, what was it going to be like when she was living with him?

If there were any way out I would take it, Ismay thought. But there was no way out. At least, none that she could find.

She was still seeking vainly for it when her wedding day arrived.

There was no denying the fact, as Susan had said, that a wedding was the kind of occasion at which the Laverhopes could hardly help distinguishing themselves. If only it had been someone else's wedding, Ismay could have enjoyed it intensely, because it was fun seeing the whole family look simply wonderful. She could not feel impatient even with the garrulous jubilation of Susan—her young sister's feelings were natural enough. But it made her a little faint to remember that, when all this charming pageantry was over, she would no longer be Ismay Laverhope, living a careless, hand-to-mouth, but somehow enjoyable existence. She would be Keith Otterbury's wife—with an enormous bill to pay in one form or another.

She wondered how many people guessed the real situation as she came down the aisle on father's arm. Very few, she supposed, because there was not the faintest shadow of anything amiss in the gracious air with which her father was about to bestow his daughter upon the faintly smiling, arrogant man who waited so coolly near the altar.

A hint of it might have been gleaned from the rather set look on Adrian's handsome young face, but the afternoon sunshine through the stained-glass window over the altar was kind to Adrian. It imparted a soft radiance to his thick fair hair and mellowed the grim line of his mouth, so that he looked like a very serious angel, watching his sister intently in this most important moment of her life.

"Dearly beloved . . . ."

The service began, with perhaps the most incongruous words it was possible to use, in the circumstances.

Ismay was very calm—so calm that she was a little surprised at herself. She noticed that her voice was as steady as Keith's when she had to speak, and if the pitch was low, there was nothing unusual in that because father (backed by no less authority than King Lear) had always insisted that this was "an excellent thing in women."

It was over at last, and in the vestry her father was kissing her on the forehead—which he considered appropriate but everyone else though somewhat unnatural—and saying, "My dear child, this is a very happy moment for us all."

Ismay was glad that someone honestly thought so, and as far as she could tell from the expressions around her, she was giving an excellent impression of being a very happy bride.

When she and Keith came out of the church into the sunlight, it seemed that most of the people who had known her all her life were gathered there to throw confetti at her, wish her well and see if her wedding dress suited her.

They had also come to gaze with somewhat pleasurable disapproval at the man she had chosen for her husband.

Well, there he was! Settled down at last. And if anyone had a chance of taming him that pretty Ismay Laverhope had. But then, one really never *knew*.

It was only a few moments' drive from the church to

the one hotel in the place that had a room suitable for a wedding reception, and on the way they were both strangely silent.

Just once he picked up her hand as it lay slackly on her lap and looked at the thin gold band on it.

"What is it?" She spoke very quietly.

"Nothing." He released her hand. "I'm trying to believe it's true, that's all."

She wondered if he knew she was trying to believe it was *not* true. But they arrived at the hotel without her saying any more. And two or three minutes later they were smilingly greeting their guests as though this were the happiest day of their lives.

Later Ismay wondered if she need really have made such a point of not wanting to go on a honeymoon. At least it would have meant some sort of a break, some novelty to take her thoughts from her strange and terrible situation. As it was, when everything was over, she drove home with Keith to Otterbury Hall, feeling tired and bewildered, but quite shockingly unmarried. It seemed even faintly ridiculous that the car should keep straight on down the road to the Hall, instead of turning off by the familiar way that would have taken her to the place she really considered home. The Hall seemed nothing but a strange house when she reached it.

"Tired?" Keith lifted her out of the car and set her lightly on the ground.

"Yes, I am a bit. I suppose it's rather a strain."

"I expect so. We'll have a quiet evening. Now I really do applaud your wisdom in ruling out a honeymoon. I can't imagine anything better calculated to make us loathe each other than to have to start off on a long train journey feeling like this."

Ismay thought that *she* could imagine other things

better calculated to make her loathe him, but they were not the sort of things one put into words. The moment she entered the house, the grim reality of what she had taken on seemed to become terribly dark and clear-cut. It was like hearing the rattle of the first stones that heralded an avalanche. One was helpless in the face of it.

The housekeeper was in the hall waiting to take her to her room, and something about that made Ismay reflect on how impersonal Keith's life was. There was absolutely no one who seemed to belong to him. Only excellent servants who did all the things he wanted. She wondered if his family simply refused to have anything to do with him.

She could not ask that outright, of course, but she thought she would make some sort of inquiry when she came downstairs again.

The room into which the housekeeper showed her was large and full of evening sunshine. Windows on two walls gave an effect of space and light, and the furniture, though neither modern nor antique, had an indefinable air of elegance that gave the room character and charm. The carpet and the hangings were blue, and across one end of the room stretched an enormous, white bearskin rug.

"Oh, what a lovely room! I like it," Ismay exclaimed involuntarily. The housekeeper immediately smiled and said, "Yes, I think it's the nicest room in the house. I'm very glad to see it used again, madam. It was last used by Mr. Otterbury's mother, you know. That's her portrait over there."

Ismay crossed the room and examined the portrait of Keith's mother with some interest.

"She's very like him." She spoke without looking around.

"Ye-es." There was some doubt in the housekeeper's tone. "She wasn't at all like him in disposition."

"Wasn't she?" Ismay wondered what that meant, but no further information was forthcoming. She gazed for a moment longer at the slightly haughty, oval face, set with fine dark eyes. She even had Keith's faintly mocking smile. But no, there was the difference, Ismay realized suddenly. She had never seen Keith smile without the sparkle reaching his eyes. The eyes of the woman in the portrait were completely unsmiling.

"Is there anything you would like, madam?"

"No, thank you. I'll change right away and come downstairs. Is this the door to the bathroom?" She crossed the room.

"Yes, madam. And that door leads into Mr. Otterbury's room."

When the housekeeper had gone, Ismay looked slowly around the room. So that door led to Mr. Otterbury's room, did it? And quite understandable, too, since Mr. Otterbury was her husband.

A quarter of an hour later Ismay came downstairs again. She first tried the room where she had been on that evening she came to see Keith and found that open French windows led from there onto the lawn and that Keith was already out there, talking to the gardener.

As she stood a little doubtfully in the doorway, he looked up and saw her. Dismissing the gardener with a word or two, he came toward her.

"Hello. Are you coming out here for ten minutes while the light still lasts?"

Ismay went outside and said at once, "I like my room. I think it's beautiful."

"Do you?" He smiled. "I didn't have anything altered

because I thought you would probably like to decide on any change yourself."

"But I don't think I'll want anything changed."

"No? But I thought the only personal pleasure you expected from your aunt's money was going to be the fun of having the house redone."

"But that was at *home*. That's quite different. There was so much that needed doing there. But here . . . . I don't quite know how I could improve on my room."

"I see. Well, if you do want to alter anything, you can, you know."

"Thank you. But I think I like it as your mother had it. I understand it was her room when she lived here."

"Yes."

"She must have been a very beautiful woman, judging from her portrait."

"Yes, she was. That portrait is extremely like her."

Ismay glanced at him then and asked, "Haven't you any family left at all, Keith?"

"No."

"You were the only child?"

"Yes."

"And your parents are both dead?"

"Several years ago."

"That's rotten."

"What is?"

"Oh, having no family life, I suppose I meant. It's almost the nicest thing there is. At least, I think so. That's why an only child is a mistake."

He looked at her quizzically and said, "I'm glad you think so. I agree." And when she blushed at that he was horrid enough to laugh. He also added, quite deliberately, "I wouldn't like any child of mine to be an only child."

She wondered what on earth she was expected to say to that. After a moment she asked, with an effort, "Were you unhappy as a child, then?"

"Very, sometimes. At others, I enjoyed myself healthily, like all young animals. But an only child is very apt to fix his thoughts and affections on one person—usually someone who is indifferent to him. He doesn't mix enough with his own peers to get a proper proportion on these things."

"Does the only child . . . grow out of it?" Ismay asked that with a sidelong glance at him that was not without humor.

"The tendency, you mean? No, my cruel little Ismay, I rather think he doesn't." He took her lightly by the arm, and fell into step beside her. "That's why he sometimes proceeds to quite fantastic and absurd lengths to get what he wants."

"I see. And who was the object of your adoration when you were a child? Your mother?"

"Yes."

"But she liked that? She wasn't indifferent, surely?"

"Oh, very. She was not a maternal kind of woman at all. Besides, she thought me a self-assertive, tiresome brat—which I probably was."

"It certainly sounds in character," Ismay agreed, again with that hint of a smile.

There was a slight silence. Then he said quite seriously, "Do you find me self-assertive and tiresome?"

"Do you want me to answer that seriously?"

"I think so . . . yes."

"Well, you've never struck me as exactly retiring," Ismay said dryly.

She thought he would laugh at that. He did, but a little vexedly.

"Horrible development of a horrible child, eh?"

"I didn't say that. Besides, I don't expect you were a horrible child at all. Very few children are that. Anyway, your mother ought to have noticed you a bit. All children like to show off—it's only natural. They should be allowed to, so long as they don't overdo it."

"Ismay," he said softly, "you are removing quite a number of my fears in connection with you."

"I don't think you're the slightest bit afraid of me," Ismay retorted, feeling that the shoe was on the other foot. "And, anyway, there are a lot of things one can excuse in a child that one doesn't excuse in a man."

"I'll try to remember that." He was laughing again.

"What did you do to make your mother notice you?" she asked after a moment. "Work hard at school and bring home good reports?"

"Ismay, you know perfectly well that I couldn't possibly have been that sort of child. No, I didn't do anything constructive, I suppose. I imagined all sorts of dramatic scenes in which I rescued her from wild bulls and other improbable animals. . . ."

"Poor little boy!" Ismay laughed softly. "And then everyone was to hail you as a hero?"

"That was the general idea, I've no doubt."

"And did anyone ever hail you as a hero?"

"Oh, no. On the contrary, most people recognized me for what I was—a damned little pest."

"So bad?"

"I'm afraid so. I suppose I thought it was better to be an *enfant terrible* than to be ignored."

"And the step from the *enfant terrible* to the black sheep of the family is just one of natural development?" she said slowly.

"Ismay—" he laughed slightly "—I wonder if you

know how adorable you are when you speak in that very grim tone, but show that understanding little dimple in your cheek."

She didn't answer that, but suddenly she turned her head and looked him full in the face.

"Did you ever think of rescuing *me* from wild bulls?" she inquired, with cool interest.

"I . . . not exactly." He was smiling still but, amazingly, those bold eyes of his fell. "There are other things, besides bulls," he murmured, with a touch of real confusion.

"I think you're very silly," Ismay said severely, but acting on an impulse she could never afterward explain, she bent forward and kissed his cheek.

"Ismay!" His rather extravagant lashes swept up and he looked very startled. "What's that for?"

"I don't really know," she admitted. "Except that I suppose debts and despair could be reckoned as wild bulls, for the purposes of argument. Shall we go in now?"

So they went indoors, and he said nothing more at all about her kissing him. And if once or twice during dinner he glanced at her with a faintly puzzled expression, well, there was more than enough in all of this to puzzle anyone.

He took her on a tour of the house after dinner, showing her all the things he himself liked best.

"It's an attractive house, in a rambling way," Ismay said.

"I like it. I was hoping you would like it well enough not to want to live in London very much."

"Oh, I don't want to live in London." Ismay looked surprised. "This feels much more like home." Then she added curiously, "But if I *had* wanted to, would you have been prepared to change?"

"You can have your way in most things," he told her with a smile that had a hint of grimness about it.

And Ismay wondered very much what things "most" did not cover.

She wondered again—even more seriously—later that evening as she was undressing in her beautiful blue bedroom.

It seemed to her now that at *some* point in their brief and unusual engagement she ought to have found out on just what terms he expected them to live when they were married. But there had never been the faintest opportunity—or else it was that she had instinctively winced away from the kind of reply she would probably have received.

Even now she could imagine him saying in that horrid, mocking way of his, "I told you I've wanted you for two years. What sort of terms were you expecting?"

She wished her heart wouldn't beat so hard or her mouth feel so dry. After all, it was she, so far, who had received everything in this bargain. It was pretty poor-spirited of her to feel now that she so desperately wanted to call the whole thing off. Anyway, it was too late, of course. Much, much too late.

She could hear him moving about in the room next door. He even whistled softly once or twice, which she thought disgustingly unconcerned of him. But she supposed he had reason to feel high-spirited. There must be a good deal of triumph for him in the situation. Two years! It was a long time. Only—she had forgotten—that was probably only a boast of his with no foundation in truth.

Ismay climbed into bed. And as she did so, she heard him knock on the door between their rooms.

For a moment her throat muscles refused to obey her

effort to speak. Then she said, "Come in," and watched the door open.

He looked fantastically handsome in his dark silk dressing gown, which ought, somehow, to have been reassuring. But it was not reassuring in the least. Ismay knew that her eyes widened to their fullest extent as she watched him every inch of the way across the room. She tried to make her expression natural, but it was impossible, and she was not especially surprised when he leaned his arms on the end of the bed and raised one eyebrow in an extremely quizzical fashion.

"My dear, am I such an altogether terrifying sight?"

Ismay glanced down, plucking nervously at the sheet with her finger and thumb. She said "No," but the word meant nothing at all.

"What is the matter, then?"

"You know quite well what is the matter."

"Ismay, my dear," he spoke dryly, "after all, I have married you."

She glanced up quickly then, and fear and anger drove her into speech.

"You're the kind of man who would say to a slave, 'After all, I have *paid* for you,' and then you'd beat him to death for your own pleasure."

There was a strange and ragged silence. Then he said quietly, "Is that really the impression I give you?"

She nodded, but looked away from him.

He didn't move. He just said, still in the same quiet voice, "What do you suggest I do, then?"

"I . . . don't know." Her voice seemed to stick in her throat with nervousness.

"But I'd like to hear what you consider the right thing in the circumstances. Do I just say a polite good night and retire decorously to my room—to live a bachelor existence, enlivened from time to time by the sight of you across the breakfast table?"

She looked at him helplessly, wordless with dismay.

"Speak to me, Ismay. Say something. I want to know what's going on behind those angry eyes of yours."

"They're not angry. They're frightened," she gasped. "I don't know what to say to you. I only thought. . . . I only thought. . . ."

"Yes?"

"Keith, why can't you give me a little time? What you're asking me to do is something that isn't easy even with a man one knows and . . . loves. I don't know you. I don't love you. I'm hardly used to the idea that I've left my home and my familiar life. In theory I've agreed to do this thing. In practice . . . in practice. . . . Keith, won't you please wait? Give me time? Not . . . tonight."

She saw him straighten up slowly, his eyes singularly bright and hard.

"My God!" he said with dangerous pleasantness. "The old Laverhope story. Pay me tomorrow, eh?"

And without another word, he turned and left the room.

CHAPTER SEVEN

Ismay awoke the next morning to a sense of disaster only just avoided. As her thoughts cleared, she wondered if disaster had indeed been avoided, or whether to feel ashamed and unhappy like this was not the worst disaster that could happen to anyone.

Even now she moved uneasily at the memory of Keith's last words to her. There was some dreadful sort of truth in them, of course, argue how you would.

Oh yes, it had been a monstrous bargain. And, oh yes, she had acted under something as near compulsion as made no difference. *But she had made the bargain.* And then—somehow—she had wriggled out of it.

But I don't think I consciously meant to, Ismay thought distractedly. *It was only that I was afraid, and I said what I thought . . . and he went. Why didn't I make myself better understood? He thinks I'm a pretty cheat, and I know I'm a miserable coward, and . . . oh well, it isn't very nice, whichever way you look at it.*

As she dressed, she decided to say something about it to him during breakfast. She would try to make him understand that she had honestly meant she would do her best in this marriage. If only he would give her time—oh dear, she had said that before, of course, and he had retorted with that hateful, mocking phrase that made one feel like a defaulting debtor.

On the whole, perhaps it was better to say nothing, but simply wait and see if an opportunity for more friendly discussion came up.

When she found how exceedingly cool and polite he was at breakfast, she decided more earnestly than ever in favor of avoiding thorny subjects.

It was a strangely uneventful day, considering that it was the first of their married life together. He showed her over part of the estate, rather as though she were a visitor, and, in all his explanations, she detected hardly any hint of the mocking amusement so characteristic of him.

For her part, she tried hard to be interested and friendly. At the bottom of her heart was a sense of something like guilt and failure. She felt she had not come out of this business with credit—either in his eyes or her own—and she was anxious to do something that would make up for the unfortunate beginning.

Late in the afternoon Susan presented herself, and never had Ismay been more glad to see her garrulous little sister. Conversation might take unexpected turns when Susan was there, but at least it never stopped dead, and Ismay felt she was just what was needed to ease the polite constraint that had existed all day between herself and Keith.

"Hello. You haven't taken long to look us up, have you?" was Keith's greeting. But Ismay thought that he, too, was not adverse to having a third person there. And, in an amused way, he liked Susan best of her relatives.

"Well, I thought you'd probably be glad to see me," Susan explained with touching confidence. "Besides, there isn't anything especially nice for tea at home, so I thought I'd call in here on my way back from school, and gossip about the wedding. I didn't get a chance to talk to you properly yesterday, Ismay. Wasn't it fun?"

"Yes. It was a lovely wedding." Ismay felt she could say that with truth.

"You looked marvelous, and I thought we did too."

"Did you spare a glance for me?" Keith wanted to know. "I had made a certain amount of effort with my appearance."

"Oh yes, you looked splendid," Susan assured him generously. "And you were an excellent contrast to Adrian. He looked angelic, didn't he, Ismay? Adrian, I mean."

"Thanks for the implication. I presume that, in happy contrast, I looked something like Lucifer?"

Susan regarded him thoughtfully.

"Well, you did, as a matter of fact. You needn't be offended. I always think Lucifer is the most interesting character in *Paradise Lost*."

"An extremely unlovable character nevertheless," Keith pointed out.

"Oh well, I don't know about that. I wouldn't press the comparison too far," Susan said comfortably. "And anyway if Ismay loves you, what more do you want?"

"To be sure. I hadn't thought of it that way," Keith replied gravely.

Ismay laughed—more nervously than she had intended—and changed the subject.

"You did your part beautifully, Susan. Took my bouquet very neatly and never fidgeted once."

"Oh, but I didn't *want* to fidget," Susan assured her. "I was spellbound. It was all very interesting. I'd forgotten the marriage service was quite so outspoken though, to tell the truth. It seems a bit stupid to talk about the children before you've even got the wedding ring on. But then the Bible and the Prayer Book always are a bit outspoken."

Susan's audience appeared to have nothing to say about this lapse of taste on the part of the Prayer Book.

"Still, you're sure to have lovely babies, Ismay—the kind one could mention any time, so I daresay it doesn't really matter," Susan concluded tolerantly.

"No doubt you're right," Keith agreed, but whether

that was in answer to the first part of the remark or the second, it was impossible to say.

Susan ate heartily and seemed very content. She asked Keith a great many questions, which he appeared good-naturedly willing to answer, and she finally summed up flatteringly with, "You know, you're really not much like what people say you are."

"Let me see—what was that? Uncaring about everything and everyone, wasn't it?"

"Oh, I didn't mean that part so much." Susan stared at him in the rather disconcerting way she had when her thoughts were busy. "I meant about your being a very shocking person, and all that sort of thing. It's funny. Even we thought you were."

"Thought I was what? Shocking?"

"Yes. At least I know I did, and father, too. And Avril must have thought you simply the outer edge. It doesn't matter telling you now, because you're sort of part of the family, but she actually thought you were the kind of person who would take her off to the Continent if she just said the word."

There was suddenly something very tense about the atmosphere, as though both her listeners had stopped breathing for a moment. But Susan was not at all susceptible to these shades of meaning, and she forged on quite happily.

"Honestly, I thought she meant it, the first time she said something about it. In fact, I thought you'd done everything except buy the tickets. But Avril's like that, you know. She works something out all dreamily to herself and thinks it's as good as done. She imagined she only had to wiggle her little finger, and you'd make all sorts of wicked proposals. And then she'd say, 'Well, only in Italy,' and you'd say 'All right.' And there would be her precious artistic training all for nothing. She had it all worked out." Susan paused, either to take breath or generously to allow the other two an opportunity for comment.

But neither of them seemed to have a word to say. They seemed able only to listen, in fascinated silence. And Susan, who seldom had such an attentive audience, seized the moment while it was hers.

"Of course I was simply *horrified*, and I said, 'Look here, Avril Laverhope, do you mean you've talked over such a thing with a strange man?' (Because after all, you were nearly a stranger then.) And Avril hedged about—you know the way she does, Ismay—but I pinned her down in the end, and of course she just had to admit that she hadn't done a thing about it really, only she was quite sure she could if she decided to. It was a jolly good thing she hadn't said anything, now that we know you're different, Keith. My goodness, what on earth would you have done if she *had* suggested to you that you go off to Italy together?" And Susuan went off into peals of laughter at the thought of any faux pas not of her own making.

"I don't know," Keith said mechanically, and anyone more observant than Susan might have wondered why he looked so pale and bleak.

"Susan," Ismay spoke softly, but with a peculiarly arresting note in her voice, "what did Avril say exactly?"

Keith made a very slight movement, but neither of them took any notice.

"When?" Susan had never had so much attention paid to her ramblings, and she was puzzled as well as gratified.

"When you—pinned her down. When she . . . said there was really nothing in it."

"Oh, she said, 'Don't be a little fathead—' you know the way she talks. 'There's nothing to get excited about yet. I haven't said anything to him, and perhaps I never shall. But that's what I'll do if there's no other way at all.' I'm not sure whether she would, but . . . . Why, Ismay, you haven't been worrying about it, have you? About that word or two I said to you the day Great-aunt Georgina died. Why, of course . . . I never thought . . . that was why you were so upset—because you wanted Keith yourself." Susan's expressions were always forceful rather than graceful. "But you needn't have bothered at *all*, Ismay. I found out almost right away that there was nothing in it. I wish I'd told you then. But anyway, what a good thing I mentioned it now."

"There is such a thing as speaking at the right time or else forever after holding your peace," Keith reminded her grimly. "You don't seem to have followed either course with great success."

"I don't know what you mean," Susan said indignantly. "And anyway, I expect Ismay would rather know now than not at all. Wouldn't you, Ismay?"

"Yes," Ismay agreed quietly. "It's better to know now than not at all."

Keith gave an impatient little exclamation and turned away. And Susan, perceiving that, for some reason, her discourse no longer held the attention of her audience, decided that it was time to go home.

Ismay walked with her down the driveway, unable to hide from her that things were not quite as they should be.

"You don't think Keith was angry at being told about Avril, do you?" Susan inquired with genuine anxiety.

"No, I don't think so."

"*I* thought it was rather amusing."

Ismay said nothing, perhaps reflecting on the peculiar gulf between their senses of humor.

"You aren't cross either, are you?" Susan wanted to know.

"No. I'm glad to know the truth."

"You don't look glad," Susan remarked frankly.

"Perhaps I was thinking that Avril might have been a little more open with me."

"Oh, she never is, you know. At least, I mean she never opens up naturally. You have to take a can opener to her. And then she won't tell you if she thinks things will turn out nicer for her by keeping silent."

Ismay reflected, not for the first time, that there were sometimes extraordinary gleams of shrewdness buried beneath the general mass of Susan's usually uninspired conversation. No truer—if harsh—verdict had ever been passed on Avril. She would always keep silent if she thought by so doing she would make things more pleasant for herself.

"I'll come again soon, shall I?" Susan suggested as she said goodbye. She made no attempt to kiss Ismay because that was not her way, but she obviously intended to give nothing but pleasure by her visits.

"Yes, come again soon," Ismay told her, smiling a little as she turned back toward the house.

She went in, through the French windows, to the room where she had first seen Keith. He was standing there now, his hands thrust deep in his pockets, his face set and expressionless.

Ismay had never before in her life wanted to hurt anyone deliberately, but she wanted to hurt him now. She looked across at him and spoke with almost casual contempt.

"And you tried to imply last night that *I* was a cheat!"

He moved then, rather sharply.

"Ismay—" he began, then stopped.

"Yes?"

"Oh, there's nothing to say." He shrugged helplessly. "Except . . . ."

"Except that you are a liar and a cheat," she told him quietly. "You married me on false pretenses, bluffed me into taking a step I hated. I can't help wondering what you think there is to be said in your defense."

"Nothing, except that I love you," he said doggedly.

"I don't think you're calling things by quite their right names, Keith."

"Nor are you," he retorted, stung. "You talk about my marrying you on false pretenses. As a matter of fact you married me for my money, and there was damned little pretense about it."

She was silent, and after a moment he said, "Oh, Lord! I'm sorry. Don't let's sling reproaches at each other like this. There's not much left to spoil, I know. But it's not very nice to hear the last fragments smashing. I know I did an abominable thing. I know it's pretty well past excusing. But if ever a woman handed a man temptation on a silver platter, you handed it to me that evening you came here."

She turned to look at him with proud, angry eyes.

"I came to ask you for help, to appeal to your generosity. And you call that tempting you?"

"On the contrary, my dear," he said, a faint gleam of humor in his eyes, "you came to inform the bad man of the district that he was about to have an affair with your sister—the first he had heard of it—and you wanted to know whether, evil though he was, he could be persuaded to stay his hand."

"Oh, it doesn't matter how you put it," she cried impatiently. "I was in your hands, or I thought I was. It's all the same. And you exploited my fear of what might happen to Avril. It was unpardonable—absolutely unpardonable."

"Very well, it *is* unpardonable. Or it would be if that was the whole story. But, if I remember correctly, Ismay, you refused those terms, as they stood. I think you even wondered if they had ever been seriously offered. It was not until we came to the point of how badly your family needed my money that you decided to make a bargain with me. I don't say that was particularly noble of me either. Buying a woman isn't a very pretty transaction. But then I didn't think it was going to be quite like that. I thought—"

"What did you think?" she asked sharply.

"Oh . . . nothing. It doesn't matter now. My calculations could hardly have been further out." And he sat down rather wearily and for a moment put his head in his hands.

"You thought I was going to fall into your arms, I suppose, because you'd been stuffing some of your surplus banknotes into the family's pockets?" She turned away with a little exclamation of contempt.

"No, Ismay, don't go like that." He caught at a fold of her dress, detaining her as a child might have done. Only she was too angry to notice. "Please listen to me a moment."

"I've been listening a long time," Ismay said. But she stood where she was, looking down into his sullen, troubled eyes. "What is it?"

He dropped his eyes, and she saw the sullenness deepen.

"You always laugh or grow angry if I tell you that I've loved you almost since the first moment I saw you. But it's true enough. These things happen sometimes. You were so bright and fair and gentle—I'd never seen anything like you. I watched you with your family that first time and I was fascinated. They amused you so much, and yet you were so tolerant with them—so fond of them. I thought how strange it must be to live inside the magic circle of so much understanding."

She was softened a little, in spite of herself, but she only said quietly, "And so you decided to push your way in."

"No, I didn't decide anything at all at that moment. You weren't my kind—you and your family. In fact, even when I was introduced to you, your father came up and pretty openly took you away. I thought I was amused. I *was* amused, but it stung a bit too. It was quite obvious that I was never going to see you from anything but a distance."

Ismay looked down at those strong, nervous fingers that still held a fold of her dress.

"You're not going to tell me that you went away and grieved about me in secret, are you? It's rather difficult to believe in an undying passion built on absolutely nothing."

"No, of course it wasn't like that. For one thing I never really expected to be anything in your life. And for another I laughed at myself at the idea of remaining faithful to one woman, and that one a woman who never thought twice about me."

"But you didn't, did you?"

"Didn't what?"

"Remain faithful to me, to your ideal, whatever you like to call it. From all accounts you managed to forget me very thoroughly from time to time."

"I tried to forget you," he corrected her rather somberly. "And I accepted the fact that you never could be anything in my life. I don't know now if I ever did forget you, Ismay. It's hard to say. But I have the feeling that, in a subtle, smiling way, you always haunted me.

You used to turn up in my thoughts in the most unaccountable places. Like the time I bought that ring in Athens. It was true that I bought it because it was the color of your eyes. I never actually thought, 'One day I shall give it to her.' I only thought, 'It's like her eyes. I must have it.' "

"But you saw me only two or three times in all that while." Ismay hardly knew whether to be touched or irritated, to believe him or to thrust his protestations back in his teeth.

"No, more often than that, though hardly ever to speak to. I spoke to you at the County Ball, if you remember, and asked you to dance with me, but you refused."

"I had all the dances already booked," Ismay said.

"*All* of them, Ismay?" He smiled faintly.

"Yes, really, all of them. But I was glad to be able to say so," she admitted.

"I see. Well, that was how things were, Ismay. And that was how I always expected them to be—until you walked in here that evening and informed me, free, gratis, and for nothing, that I had some sort of hold over you. It was astounding, intoxicating. It was even—forgive me, Ismay—a little amusing, to be informed that I held all the trumps, when I had never imagined myself even taking a hand in this particular game. I think it was more bravado than anything else that made me put that melodramatic offer to you. I wanted to make some extravagantly generous gesture, but there was no gesture to make. I really didn't have you or your sister or anyone else in my power. I couldn't magnificently put things right, because they were not even wrong. Will you be very angry if I tell you that that, too, amused me?"

"No, I'm not angry," Ismay said slowly. "At least not

about that. I'm only surprised that you didn't think me a fool and find yourself cured of this . . . this infatuation."

"Cured?" He laughed slightly. "Why, no, Ismay, I'm afraid, on the contrary, I became a fatal case. I was drunk with the indulgence of having had you to speak to for a whole evening. When you told me about the troubles in your family I wanted to assure you that I would solve them all—"

"At a price."

"It had to be some sort of practical arrangement. What do you suppose you would have done if I had just insanely offered you as much money as you liked for the asking?"

"I don't know," Ismay said honestly. "I suppose I'd have said no very quickly, and gone home thinking you a most peculiar person."

"And that would have been the end. As it was, I suggested something that was bound to keep me in your mind. I hardly knew myself if I meant it seriously—I had some vague idea that, later, I might make the grand gesture—offer to do it all for nothing, or something of the sort. But at least the connection was there. I hadn't cut it clean off with the stunning information that I had nothing to do with your sister and had no intention of having anything to do with her."

"It was a rotten deception, Keith, whichever way you look at it," Ismay said gravely. "You told me—"

"No, darling, I didn't tell you anything," he reminded her gently. "It was you who told me all about it." And for a moment that faint smile appeared again.

"Well, it's the same thing. You let me think what was not true."

"I know." He sighed impatiently. "I can't tell you now how far I intended it to be a deception and how far it was irresistibly amusing. But when you came here the next day and told me you were willing to marry me, it was as though the whole thing passed out of my control. I supposed you would hear the truth then from Avril, but I convinced myself that the money would be enough in itself to persuade you. I'm not quite sure now why Avril kept silent, but—"

"Because she *wanted* me to marry you. She knew that was the way to make sure of her own plans. You see, my marrying you suited everyone. That was why no one raised a hand against it," Ismay said slowly. "You said something just now about a magic circle. There *was* a circle around me—the circle of my own family. That was why I couldn't escape."

"Ismay!"

"I was happy in it until you forced your way in. It had always been something very intangible—very elastic, because it contained nothing but the family and their common wishes. We had never pulled against each other before. You changed all that."

He stared at her wordlessly. He was very pale, with something curiously like fear in his eyes.

"You were a little jealous of that circle, weren't you, Keith? Because you stood outside it. No one asked you in, so you forced your way in, with a proposition that turned us all against each other. Oh, not literally, of course. We are just as good friends on the surface. But the good of one was no longer the good of all. It was to the advantage of all of them that I should marry you, whether I liked it or not. They would never have pressed me, of course; they hadn't even a clear idea of what was happening. But you hadn't a chance of losing, because you had carried the war right into the . . . circle. You used my family, whom I loved, as a means of putting pressure on me. You won, of course. But you spoiled everything."

"No, please don't say that." He spoke violently.

"But it's true, isn't it? There isn't anything else to say."

He was absolutely silent.

"May I go now?"

"Yes, of course," he said dully.

"You still have hold of my dress."

"Oh, darling," he exclaimed almost incoherently, and for a moment he pressed his face against the fold of her dress.

Ismay looked down at his bent head, with the rather untidy dark hair.

"It wasn't quite truthful of me to insist that it was the thought of Avril that finally persuaded me," she said slowly. "It was the money really."

"Oh, Ismay—" he looked up quickly "—it's very generous of you to say that now."

"No. I think we want the exact truth at last. And the truth is that we made a bargain, you and I, that you would pay for everything the family wanted, and I would be your wife in every sense of the word." He stiffened suddenly. "It was just . . . business. You were quite right last night to be angry when I defaulted—"

"No!"

"I ought to have remembered how much you had already paid for father."

"Ismay, please!"

"You said you supposed I would pay you tomorrow, but you didn't really believe it. Well, I will. I'll pay you tonight."

"No. I don't want that," he exclaimed violently.

"But you do. That's why you married me."

"Oh no—"

"Yes. You even said so. Don't you remember? You said, 'After all, I have married you.' "

"Oh, God! Did I really say that? How terrible!" He was on his feet now, trembling a little with agitation.

"Yes. And you meant it. It was all in the bargain."

"Ismay, I beg you, don't talk any more about bargaining."

"But I'm already most horribly in your debt on my father's account. How else do you suppose I'm going to pay?"

"You're not in my debt. Don't think any more about what I paid for your father. It's wiped off, if you want to think of it that way, by the sheer fact that you married me."

She laughed a little, but not as though she were amused.

"Well, there are other things. There are the arrangements for Avril to go to Italy—"

"I'm not going to make any bargain with you over that," he retorted savagely. "She can have what she wants. She was prepared to take it anyway, on any terms. It has nothing to do with you."

"Well, then there's Adrian. You can't say Adrian has nothing to do with me. If you support him for the next few years, you must expect something in return."

"I don't want anything, I tell you." He was sullen again now, but it was a sort of desperate sullenness.

"You're very, um, difficult, all at once, Keith. I've set my heart on this thing being done for Adrian."

"It'll be done," he said curtly. "I've given you my word on it."

"But I will not accept it for nothing.'" Ismay's voice was cool and smooth. "I'm tired of cadging and—what was it—paying tomorrow. You can take it that what you did for father is wiped out by my marrying you, if that's what you want. I'll grant you the best of the argument over Avril. But the day Adrian goes to medical school, we'll settle accounts. Not the next day or some time in the future. *That day*."

And without another glance at him she went out of the room, leaving him white and wordless.

CHAPTER EIGHT

Ismay had always supposed—when she thought about it at all—that if married couples had some terrible emotional scene, or row, or whatever you liked to call it, life just refused to go on in the natural channels any longer. Either they separated, or they became like different people, never regaining whatever ground they had in common before.

But she was quite wrong, of course. At least, as far as she and Keith were concerned. Perhaps it was because they had never had much ground in common, because they had only to regain a surface politeness, she decided. But, whatever the reason, life was most extraordinarily and unbelievably the same.

Only he never teased her now, never spoke in that half-mocking, laughing way, which she had supposed she hated. In an odd way she missed it, for though a grave, polite Keith at least never ruffled the surface of her composure, somehow she could not help remembering that he had sometimes made her want to laugh against her will, that he had provoked showers of sparks between them that at least had brilliance, even if they lacked warmth.

For a day or two she refrained from visiting the family. She was not quite sure why. Either she wanted to give the impression of settling down in her new home, or else she felt that to see them all would raise fresh problems.

When she did decide to go, she meant to say coldly to Keith something about making arrangements with Adrian now. But, when it came to the point, she lacked the courage even to mention his name, and, instead, she simply said, "I'm going to see the family this afternoon."

"Are you? You don't mind if I don't come with you, do you? I have to see about that flooded meadow."

"No, I don't mind," Ismay said. And no one could have guessed from their expressions that to visit the family together would have caused acute embarrassment to both of them.

She walked over in the early afternoon, knowing that Susan would still be at school then and that she would have more opportunity of speaking quietly to Adrian.

The first person she saw, however, was Avril, who was sketching in the garden as usual. Only this time it was on the stretch of rather ragged lawn in front of the house.

She stood up at once and came to the gate.

"Hello, Ismay." Unlike Susan, she did kiss her sister—a cool, sweet kiss that had great charm. "I wondered when on earth you were coming over. Has married life proved such a success that you can't tear yourself away?"

"Not exactly. I want to talk to you, Avril." Ismay spoke more curtly than she ever had before to her sister.

"Well, you have a good opportunity." Avril was completely unconcerned. "Come and sit here while I go on with this sketch."

"Where are the others?"

"Adrian's at work. . . ."

"Oh yes, of course."

"And father has gone to London."

"To London!"

"Oh yes. You've no idea how much he enjoys himself, now that money matters have improved. He's a different man." Avril was in quite a chatty mood.

But Ismay was not. She came straight to the point, now that she knew there was no likelihood of their being interrupted.

"Avril, why did you tell me all those lies about Keith?"

"Which lies?"

"You know what I mean. About your arranging to go away with him, suggesting you had almost started an affair with him. What possessed you to say such things when there was no truth in them at all?"

"I didn't say I had started an affair. In fact, I was particularly careful to point out to you that I had not."

"But you implied you were on the verge of it, that nothing would stop you, if you thought that was the only way of getting to Italy."

"Well, nothing *would* have stopped me, if that had been the only way."

"But, Avril, there hadn't been a word said between you! It was all in your imagination, or anticipation, or whatever you like to call it. Yet you spoke as though it had all been arranged. As though he knew at least as much about it as you did."

"Well—I am sorry it's your husband we're speaking about, Ismay—I don't think I'd have had much difficulty in getting him to agree. You see—"

"You most certainly would!" Ismay might be angry with Keith herself, but in this instance she felt he deserved some sort of defense.

"That's a matter of opinion, isn't it?"

"Well, anyway, whatever you thought in the first instance, what possessed you to keep silent when I told you what I had done? I was quite frank with you, Avril. I told you I was marrying him and why. Yet you never hinted that one part of my reason was based on an entirely false impression. I don't understand you! How could you say nothing, much less *want* to say nothing?"

"I asked you outright if you were doing it especially because of me, and you said you weren't."

"Did I?" Poor Ismay was beginning to wonder just what she *had* said in all this tangle.

"You said it was just everything coming together. If you had told me you were doing it simply with some sort of idea of rescuing me, I think I would have explained."

"You *think* you would?" Ismay passed her hand over her forehead. "Oh, how reassuring," she added rather bitterly.

Avril glanced at her curiously.

"You didn't do it much for your own sake, did you?"

"For my own sake? No, not at all. How should I?"

"That was a mistake, Ismay. You should always do things partly for your own sake. After all, you're the only person in the world whose wishes you can understand completely, aren't you?"

"Is that how you work things out?" Ismay asked.

Avril nodded.

"I didn't really know how much you wanted this marriage. I only knew that it would be a marvelous thing for me—for all of us—if you did take it on. I'd never have urged you, Ismay, but, since you were doing it at all, I think it was reasonable to suppose that you expected—how shall I put it—some sort of pleasure or profit from it. Well, I didn't see why I should go out of my way to upset all that."

"You knew I didn't—*couldn't*—care for him at all."

Avril shrugged.

"All right. But on the other hand, he's an extremely rich man. You may be unworldly, Ismay, but even you can't help knowing that a rich husband is an asset. Besides, he's crazy about you in his way. I suppose that has some attraction. Most women would jump at a rich and devoted husband, even if they couldn't work up much of a passion for him themselves."

Ismay didn't answer that, and Avril seemed to think she had explained herself sufficiently, for she went on sketching in silence, while Ismay pulled blades of grass and made a little pile of them.

At last, overcome by curiosity, Ismay asked, "What did Keith say to you?"

"When?"

"When he came here that evening and you had to be frank to each other."

"We didn't need to say very much. I think, perhaps, Ismay, he and I speak the same language, and it's a different language from yours. He's a cynic at heart just as I am and—"

"No," Ismay said absently. "Not at heart. He's really a romantic by temperament, and a cynic by experience."

"Think so?" Avril looked amused. "Well, I daresay you're right. You ought to know. He took it all rather lightly, to tell the truth. Teased me a little and said he was overwhelmed by the role I had selected for him. I said I hoped he would not bear me any grudge for having assumed so much, and he said—"

"That on the contrary, he was grateful to you," finished Ismay, suddenly remembering what she had overheard.

"Something of the sort."

"I don't know why I don't hate you both," said Ismay slowly.

"And don't you, Ismay?"

"Well, not you. I can't. You're my sister."

"And he's your husband," Avril reminded her carelessly. Ismay made no reply, and after a while Avril
asked, "How did you find out about it all? Surely he
wasn't so stupid as to tell you himself?"

"No. Susan let it out."

"She would," observed Avril without rancor. "Does he
know?"

"Know what?"

"That you've heard all about it now."

"Oh yes, of course. He was there at the time. He heard
Susan tell me."

"And couldn't do anything to stop her? How feeble of
him."

Ismay said nothing. She was suddenly very keenly
aware of what Keith's feelings must have been as he
listened to Susan, blundering innocently through his
dreams. But it served him right, of course. No one liked
being found out; only, sometimes, some sort of blind
justice turned up the truth unexpectedly.

"I suppose," Avril said coolly, "there was a row afterward?"

"I don't think I want to answer that," Ismay retorted,
as she rose to her feet. "I'm going to meet Adrain. I'd like
to walk back with him."

"It's early for him yet," Avril said, but made no
attempt to detain Ismay when she found that she was still
determined to go. "Are you coming back here for tea?"

"Yes, I expect so."

"That's good," Avril observed with sincerity. Then she
added, "Things will work out all right, Ismay. I wouldn't
worry too much, if I were you."

"No, I'm sure you wouldn't," Ismay said dryly, but she
smiled a little as she turned away.

For a while after she had left the house, she tried to

keep her mind a blank about the things that had been happening. She leaned her arms on a gate and looked with pleasure at the splashes of color that a few late poppies made against the yellow corn now ripe for cutting. She listened to the monotonous chirrup of the grasshoppers. And she felt more at peace with the world.

But after a time she remembered that the field she was gazing at was Keith's field—one of those he had spoken of with a laugh as "almost hers," that day she agreed to marry him.

That took a good deal away from her pleasure and brought back her thoughts to the troubles that lay ahead.

Well, anyway, she was going to see Adrian first, which was pleasant. That part at least she was going to enjoy—telling once and for all that he need not keep on with his hateful, pokey little job, that she and Keith were going to send him to medical school, make him a doctor and give him his heart's desire.

She was glad he would never know that she had suddenly made *him* the crux of her bargain with Keith. In a way, there was a kind of justice in it, because probably Adrian's eventual work as a doctor would be the only wholly decent thing that would emerge from this horrible tangle.

And Keith *should take his payment* for these things he was doing for them. Never again would she let herself feel under an obligation to the man who had tricked her so completely. Father and his debts might be written off, if he liked. Avril, it was true, made a very doubtful center for a bargain. But Adrian . . . . There was something solid about Adrian and his ambitions. Keith should pay for those, according to their arrangement, and in return, he should accept payment from her. And if his knowledge that she loathed the payment turned his triumph into dust and ashes, well, that was his punishment.

To Ismay, in that moment, it seemed that a harsh sense of justice ran through it all. Keith had schemed unscrupulously to obtain this one thing. Now, in light of what he had learned, he knew that to take what he had wanted would be the ruin of his happiness. But he should not be allowed to change his mind now. It was he who had forced the bargain. *Both* sides of it should be carried out. Her pride and, she supposed, some sort of desire for revenge demanded it.

But—she looked up to see Adrian strolling along the road—it was odd to think that Adrian, of all people, should be the instrument of vengeance.

"Hello, Ismay dear!"

As Adrian kissed her, Ismay reflected a little amusedly on the different motives from which the family acted in these matters. Adrian kissed her because he was fond of her. Avril kissed her because she was not. While Susan seldom thought of kissing her at all, because she would have considered it absurd that any sign was necessary to indicate the self-evident fact that of course she was fond of Ismay.

"Have you been home?" Adrian glanced at her affectionately.

"Yes. But I thought I'd walk out and meet you. Then we could come back to tea together."

"I'm afraid I have to go a good bit out of our way."

"It doesn't matter. What do you have to do?"

He grinned.

"I'm being a delivery boy. Ours is on holiday, so I've volunteered to take the stuff around myself."

She laughed, but she was not as amused as he was

about it, and presently she burst out, "Adrian, you won't have to do this any more—this miserable job, I mean. I think you've been wonderful to stick to it. But it isn't necessary any longer. Things are quite changed, you see. There isn't the least reason why you shouldn't be a doctor, after all. And you'll be a marvelous doctor, I know. I was only teasing when I spoke about your bedside manner that time. I know your heart's in doctoring, and I can't tell you how happy it makes me to know you can do it, after all."

She ceased speaking, and there was a short, peculiar silence. Then Adrian said quietly, "I don't quite understand."

"Oh, I haven't explained at all properly, of course." She laughed a little. "I suppose it's because I'm excited. You see, Keith is willing for me to have anything I like that will make the family happy. And what I want more than anything else is that you have your heart's ambition. I've explained to him, and he's perfectly willing that you should. It's a present from him, from us, Adrian. Isn't it wonderful, really? I think he hardly cares what it costs. You're simply to have everything that's necessary. You won't be an assistant to a village pharmacist any longer. You'll be a doctor, and I shall be terribly proud of you."

Again there was a short silence, before Adrian said curiously, "Are you quite sure you would be proud of me . . . in those circumstances?"

"Why, of course." She almost stammered in her astonishment. "What's wrong, Adrian?"

"Nothing. Except that I couldn't possibly accept. I wouldn't dream of it for one moment."

"But I don't understand. I *want* you to have it. Keith wants you to have it. What is there against it?"

He didn't answer her at once, but taking her by the arm, he fell into step beside her.

"Ismay, you didn't marry Keith Otterbury because you were in love with him at all, did you?"

Ismay was struck dumb.

"No, I thought not. You married him because we were in a hell of a mess, and you didn't see how we could get out of it without someone's money to help us. I don't know which of us you had most in mind. I thought at the time that it was father, and that was why I couldn't say much. If you couldn't face seeing him bankrupt and broken, and you were willing to make some sort of sacrifice to prevent it, that was your affair. I think perhaps I'd have done the same if I'd had the chance. But for me to take Otterbury's money would be a very different matter. I couldn't, Ismay dear. It would be a betrayal—not only of you, but of everything that mattered in our family relations."

"But I want to do this for you," Ismay whispered.

"I know you do. But do you know, darling, that that isn't even very important?"

"To you, you mean?"

"No, I didn't mean that. Of course it's important to me that you think so much about my happiness. But it isn't just a question of your wanting to do this thing for me or my wanting to have it done. We don't often talk about things like love and respect, Ismay. Ordinary families don't—it makes one uncomfortable to do it often. But of course, there *is* such a thing, and it's pretty important. Suppose you heard in theory of a brother who let his sister marry a rich man whom she didn't want, and then built his career on the proceeds. You wouldn't think much of him, would you? It isn't any different because you are the sister and I the brother. If I let you—or rather, Keith—finance me now, it would mean that something very important went out of our relationship. Can't you see that?"

She was silent—actually trembling a little—because everything Adrian was saying was more or less what she had tried to explain to Keith that other evening. Only she wanted Adrian to have his ambition and his happiness. She wanted something—something decent and worthwhile to happen out of her bargain with Keith. She didn't want it all to be for nothing.

"But what will you do, Adrian? Don't you hate this life of yours? How can you possibly turn your back on the chance to do exactly what you've always wanted?" She couldn't accept his answer without trying once more to persuade him. But she knew quite well, even as she advanced the arguments, that they were not going to have any weight.

Adrian shrugged his shoulders.

"What shall I do? Study for all I'm worth. I ought to have begun long ago, but it's not too late. For a start, I shall try for my 'A' levels next summer. Astley thinks I'll get them, too."

"Oh, Adrian!"

"What?"

"It seems so small after all your hopes."

"I know. But it's something that I can tackle with my own resources and ability. I've finished with building castles in the air on expectations of what other people will do for me. Just lately I've begun to wonder why the hell I thought I *should* have opportunities handed to me. I'll just have to make them, like other people. I can't say when they'll come, but I'm jolly well not going to wait for them to happen. There's been a great deal too much of that in our family, and where has it got us?"

Ismay was silent. And after a while, looking at her troubled face, Adrian said, "What is it, Ismay?"

"Nothing. I know you're quite right, but I wish you were wrong. I had it all worked out so beautifully for you."

He laughed and took her arm again.

"You can't live other people's lives for them, Ismay, however much you want to move all the difficulties out of their paths. I'm sorry to sound so much the philosopher this afternoon, but I've been thinking a good deal ever since Great-aunt Georgina dealt us that nasty crack from the grave, so to speak. Maybe she did us a service, after all, though she'd probably hate to think so."

Ismay smiled slightly. She liked to hear this new note of optimism and self-reliance in Adrian's voice, but her plans certainly had gone badly awry.

"So there really isn't any more to say about it?" she said at last.

"No, there just isn't any more to say, except—thank you for wanting to do it, Ismay. Did I say that?"

She felt it hardly mattered whether he had said it or not.

As they turned back in the direction of home, Adrian seemed to think it was his turn to ask a few questions, because he said—just a little too carelessly, perhaps, "How are things turning out with you, Ismay? Is Keith proving the answer to a maiden's prayer?"

"He's very good and generous," Ismay assured him hastily, whereupon Adrian laughed.

" 'Good,' eh? First time anyone's handed that description to Keith Otterbury, I imagine."

Ismay was faintly embarrassed, hardly knowing what to say. She and Adrian had always had so much in common that it was very difficult to tell him anything but the exact truth. And yet the true state of affairs between her and Keith would hardly bear telling, quite apart from the fact that one had a sense of loyalty toward one's husband—even such a problematical husband as Keith.

"You don't need to worry about me, Adrian. Everything is working out—working out marvelously."

"I'm glad to hear it," Adrian said. But she knew from his expression that he meant, "Well, I suppose it is your private affair, but don't expect me to believe *that*."

When they reached home, not only Susan, but father, too, had returned, and he greeted Ismay with dignified attention.

"Dear child, let me look at you," he said, rather as though she might have been changed beyond recognition in the interval. "Very charming. The married state suits you, I see. Well, my dear, there is marriage, as I have always said." He had never said so before, because it had never happened to be appropriate to the occasion, but no one recalled that—least of all father.

Ismay smiled and assured him that she was indeed very happy, and, somewhat to her surprise, Susan added suddenly, "Yes, I know. I've seen her and Keith together in their own home, and they're *both* happy."

This having been satisfactorily established, father turned to his own affairs. Ismay saw at once that Avril had said nothing less than the truth. Father was indeed a changed man, now that he was free from financial embarrassment. Ismay doubted if he even remembered now that someone else had had to pay his debts for him. They were paid—that was all that mattered. And now he was free to indulge in characteristic little expenses once more, from his small but unencumbered income.

Oh yes, life was very good to father just now. He even remarked, with a pleasantly reflective air, "I think, Avril my dear, that when you go to take up your studies in Florence, I shall be tempted to come with you for a while. Ah, how many years since I saw Italy? Indeed the land of sunshine and laughter."

"Also mosquitoes," Adrian reminded him, because they all felt it was extremely unlikely that Avril would want his company.

But they were wrong. Avril stared thoughtfully at her father and remarked, "Do you know, I think that's a rather good idea. I could be lots freer to do anything I wanted if I were obviously in the care of a distinguished and very British-looking parent."

Father liked the "distinguished" but was not quite so sure that the "very British" gave exactly the impression he wished to create.

"That's a rather funny way of putting it, Avril," he said, smilingly firm. "Heaven knows, no man is prouder than I of being an Englishman. But I think you will find that abroad I shall be taken for something of a cosmopolitan."

It was difficult to see how father, who had passed almost the whole of his life in one spot, could have become cosmopolitan, but no one grudged him his little indulgence. And even Avril said absently, "I daresay," because she was very intent on working out this new idea to her own advantage.

"But what would *we* do?" Susan was rather indignant about plans that so obviously excluded herself.

"You and Adrian?" Avril remembered them with difficulty. "Oh, you can look after yourselves for once. Besides, Ismay would be close enough at hand to keep an eye on you. Father, I think it's a marvelous idea. You won't have a penny to pay for my expenses—" she didn't even glance at Ismay as she said that "—so you could manage very well, couldn't you?"

"It would take some thinking over." Father showed faint signs of caution, now that he realized Avril was rushing him. But it was obvious to all of them that he was already anticipating the role of "distinguished parent" to the very pretty and charming art student that his daughter would make.

"Well, of course," Avril conceded. "But don't let's think it over too long, because we want to be nicely settled there before the winter. Oh, are you leaving, Ismay?"

"Yes." Ismay had stood up. "I think Keith will expect me back by now."

"My goodness," Susan observed, "you are the obedient wife, aren't you? Doesn't he let you out for long at a time?"

"Of course, you little goose," Ismay laughed. But she refused their pressing invitations to stay any longer.

She was glad, too, that no one offered to accompany her part of the way back to Otterbury Hall. She very much wanted to be alone to think over the events of the afternoon. Or rather, of course, they were not exactly events. They were odd side issues to the general problem of herself and Keith.

Somehow, the sight of her father—dear but shameless old spendthrift that he was—and Avril, enthusiastically arranging their Italian trip on the strength of Keith's money, made her feel ashamed. If it had been Adrian, and his much more worthwhile plans, it would not have mattered so much.

But Adrian had chosen to reject the offer she and Keith had made to him. Even now, she could hardly believe it, and the sharpness of disappointment seemed even keener.

She was tired, she discovered, and her head ached. Or perhaps it was just her heart. But anyway, the way back to Otterbury Hall seemed very long indeed—even across the fields that were "almost hers."

When she reached home, one of the servants informed her that Mr. Otterbury was out in the garden. Irresistibly, she felt drawn to go out and talk to him.

She found him by the gate that led from the garden into the orchard, and he was talking to one of the outdoor staff as she approached. For a moment he didn't notice her standing there. Then the man murmured something and drew Keith's attention to her.

"Why, Ismay!" He turned to her at once. "I didn't see you. Have you been home long?"

"No. I . . . came straight out here."

He glanced at her curiously but made no comment on that, and they began to stroll slowly back toward the house.

"Is everyone well at home?"

"Oh yes, thank you. Father particularly is on top of the world."

He didn't ask why; undoubtedly he knew. There was a slight pause. Then in a tone that was elaborately casual, he said, "Did you see Adrian?"

"Yes."

"And had you any chance of a discussion with him?"

"Yes."

She thought she heard him draw a deep breath, but his voice was still cool as he asked, "And what did you arrange?"

"Nothing."

"Nothing!"

"No. He just . . . refused." And suddenly she burst into tears.

CHAPTER NINE

There was a strange little silence. At last Keith said softly and with quite extraordinary sincerity, "Thank God!"

Somehow she was even more acutely aware of that than of the fact that he had put his arm around her and was leading her away from the house again. Presently he made her sit down on a seat that was screened from any inquisitive eyes by masses of rambling roses.

He sat beside her, his arm still around her, but he made no attempt to check her crying, and after a moment she stopped of her own accord, with an apologetic murmur about "being sorry she was such an idiot."

"You have no reason to apologize for anything," he said, with a slight emphasis on the pronoun. "Will you tell me just what happened?"

"There . . . there isn't really much to tell. I explained to him that you—that we—wanted him to carry out his ambition to become a doctor, and that you were willing to support him through his training. He refused to accept it. Quite nicely, but he refused."

"Why, Ismay? Did he tell you that?"

"Yes. He said that he knew I had married you because of the money. I'm sorry, Keith. . . ."

"You needn't be. Go on."

"And he said that if I wanted to do that for father's sake it was my own affair, but that if *he* took any of your money it would be an entirely different matter. He thought it would be a sort of betrayal of our family feeling."

"He said just that?"

"Yes."

"Then you have no reason to cry, Ismay." He smiled very slightly, though she noticed that his eyes remained grave. "It seems that Adrian felt exactly as you did about loyalty inside your family circle. Do you remember, you thought all that had been spoiled?"

"Yes, I remember," she said slowly.

"Well, as far as Adrian was concerned, the family ties or unity or whatever you like to call it stood the strain. You're a little disappointed because you can't make Adrian a great doctor, but aren't you damned glad that he had enough character to refuse to sponge off you?"

She was silent, caught somewhere between pleasure and astonishment at the discovery of the truth of this.

After a moment he said reflectively, "So the casual Adrian was the one who withstood temptation. Strange. I wouldn't have given him credit for so much character."

"Adrian! He has ten times as much character as anyone like *you*!" Ismay flared to the defense of her brother.

"Humbling, but true," Keith agreed, and for the first time for some while she saw the old mocking amusement light up his eyes. That "Thank God" of his had been no figure of speech. He was fervently, passionately glad that Adrian had refused his offer.

"This leaves us in a rather, er, odd position, doesn't it?" She said that without looking at him.

"I don't see how." A touch of stubbornness crept into his voice. "I think it has smoothed out several difficulties, and it has certainly left me very thankful to find that I haven't caused quite such a flutter in the Laverhope dovecot after all."

She looked directly at him, her blue eyes dark and rather wide.

"Have you forgotten that we made Adrian a sort of . . . test case?"

"No, I haven't forgotten. And for that reason I'm even more thankful that he refused our offer," he said curtly.

An innocent air of reflection, more suited to Avril than to Ismay, came into her eyes.

"For a man who drives a hard bargain," she said slowly, "you're strangely anxious not to have me pay up, aren't you?"

"And for a woman who married me reluctantly, you're strangely anxious to throw yourself at my head," he retorted brutally, as he rose to his feet.

"Keith!" She was so astounded that she could hardly even utter his name. Whatever she had expected, it was not that. One of his violent, half-sullen protestations that he loved her, perhaps, or even a difficult, reluctant admission that his high-handed ways had ruined his own happiness as well as hers. But this insult!

"I don't think I quite understand you," she said softly and coldly, the strangest feeling of dismayed anger creeping around her heart as she spoke.

"You don't? Well, perhaps that's just as well," he said lightly, "because I have a horrible suspicion that I was speaking at that moment like the 'outsider' I am."

He smiled straight at her—casually, carelessly, almost insolently, quite in his old manner.

"All the same it would be interesting to know what you did mean." She found suddenly that, if he could be cool and casual, so could she. "By your charming description of me as 'throwing myself at your head' are you implying that I'm showing an unwelcome fondness?"

"We-ell, not fondness, exactly." His eyes danced impertinently. "Shall we say, an embarrassing conscientiousness in your desire to carry out all your wifely duties?"

"How *dare* you!" She sprang to her feet in her turn.

"What in heaven's name *do* you want from me? You come thrusting your way into my bedroom, demanding your rights in the most revolting manner—"

"Not demanding, my dear," he pointed out smoothly.

"You practically called me a cheat to my face," she rushed on furiously, not heeding his interruption. "Then when I bring myself to . . . to play fair, or whatever you like to call it, you say I'm throwing myself at your head. I don't understand you and your disgusting, cynical ways!"

"No? But do you understand, my little Ismay, that there's such a thing as giving a man enough time to discover he's made a mistake?"

"Made . . . a mistake?" she repeated, stupefied.

"Exactly."

"You mean you don't . . . love me, after all?" It was strange to use such expressions to him.

"You're forcing me to be dreadfully ungallant."

"I don't care about gallantry or the lack of it. Please tell me the truth."

"Well then, the truth is that two years of romantic imaginings are one thing. Two weeks of practical experience are something else. I think you yourself told me I was a fool to think I could build an undying passion on nothing. You were right, of course. It's humiliating to find that a cynic like myself could be a romantic fool, but there it is. I suppose a good many better men than I have made the same mistake."

"You mean," Ismay said evenly, "that so long as I was out of reach, I was eminently desirable. As soon as you had married me, you lost interest in me."

"My dear girl—" he made a slight grimace "—Susan herself could hardly have put it in a more unpalatable form."

"I daresay not. But I'm in no mood to wrap things up

prettily. And as long as home truths are being handed around, you may as well know that I think you the most unutterable swine I've ever met!"

"No doubt you're right," he agreed regretfully. "I imagine a Laverhope's experience of swine is strictly limited."

But Ismay hardly heard his reply, for she had turned on her heel and was now walking rapidly toward the house.

He made no attempt to follow her, and she gained the safety of her own room without meeting any of the servants.

For the first few moments, she was too angry and agitated even to sit down and think. She walked up and down her room, her eyes bright, her cheeks flushed with indignation and anger. Not that she cared in the least, of course, about losing his remarkably worthless affection. But the casual cynicism of it all revolted her.

To think that he should marry her—indeed, any woman—on a whim and then calmly admit that he didn't want her after all! It made one wonder just how many of the other disreputable stories about him were true. And it made one sick with dismay to realize that *this was her husband*.

Not that he was her husband in any real sense, or that he was ever likely to be. That, at least, was something to be thankful for. But what did one do? How did one go on with life after the past few shattering weeks?

Ismay sat down on the side of her bed at last—tired and utterly dispirited. She felt that not only had her roots been torn up out of familiar ground, but the new ground was too unspeakably shallow for one to take root again. She was used to doing things for deep and genuine reasons, not to be tossed hither and yon for the sake of some casual impulse that was gone almost before it was formed.

She had not taken her marriage lightly. She had only been dismayed by its peculiar circumstances, anxious to have time in which to adapt herself to a set of circumstances that were entirely strange to her.

Now, before she could do any adapting, the whole thing was swept away again. She was married, and she was not married. She had created a rather frightening passion in her husband, and she had made him indifferent. She owed him a great deal, and he was amused and bored that she wanted to pay up honestly.

There was no sense in it at all. And there was no dignity or kindly feeling or humor or any of the things that made life worth living.

For a few seconds Ismay was very near tears again. Then she reminded herself that she had already cried an absurd amount that evening. "And I refuse to cry because of anything that *he* does or says," she told herself bitterly.

Somehow life had to go on, of course. She was not quite sure how. But at least he wouldn't have the satisfaction of supposing she was making herself unhappy about anything he did.

Rather slowly Ismay began to change for dinner.

As she did so, her thoughts grew quieter and her judgment cooler. She remembered that he had been genuinely relieved that Adrian had shown up so well. He had even said something about being glad that he had caused less harm than he had first thought in the Laverhope family. She supposed that was something to his credit, though, of course, it might be nothing more than a casually good-natured desire to see no ill-effects from his own behavior.

She wondered if he had some idea now of cutting his losses—somehow getting rid of the young wife he found he no longer wanted. It was possible, and anyway, Ismay suddenly decided, she was not going to remain in a state of uncertainty and indecision. She would have it out with him. He was not to assume that she was waiting breathlessly for his decision.

At dinner it was difficult to find an opportunity. But, afterward, when they were having coffee together in the lounge, the French windows open to the warm, scented evening, she spoke abruptly.

"Keith, I want to talk to you."

"Yes?" He glanced at her lazily and smiled. "I know. It's about Avril, isn't it?"

"About Avril? Certainly not! There's nothing more to say about Avril. At least . . . what made you say that?"

"Only that she telephoned just before dinner. I understand she's anxious to start on her Italian trip as soon as possible. I also gather that your father is going with her. She wanted to know what I thought of the arrangement."

"About father going?" Ismay's voice sharpened slightly in spite of herself.

"Yes."

"I don't see what that part of the arrangement has to do with you," she said quickly.

"Don't you?" The air of ironical amusement deepened.

"Keith? You don't mean that she actually suggested you should . . . you should . . . ."

"Pay? Well, I'm afraid she did, Ismay."

"Oh, they're incorrigible—Avril and father!" Ismay spoke her thoughts aloud in her annoyance and distress. "I suppose—I hope—you refused very sharply."

"No, I agreed."

"But why? It's unnecessary for you to pander to father like that. He's had his debts paid. He's relieved from real financial worry. There was no need to indulge him in this. Why should you pay any more, Keith?"

"You can call it conscience money, if you like," he grinned at her.

"Please don't be absurd."

"But it's true." It was hard to say whether that quick return to gravity was genuine or mocking. "My conscience—such that it is—has given me some uncomfortable jars over the part I've played in your family affairs."

"You've been very generous to us," Ismay said coldly.

"Not to you." He said that softly, with a peculiar intonation she could not quite understand.

"Well, anyway—" she was a trifle agitated now, though she could not have said why "—there's no reason for you to pay out still more money for us."

"Your father is very anxious to go, Ismay."

"Yes, I know. But he always is anxious to do anything that will amuse him and cost money. If he wants it so much, let him pay for it himself. I know that sounds hard. But though my father is a darling, he's an absolutely graceless old spendthrift. It's hardly even his own fault. Everyone has always encouraged him to be just that. It isn't necessary for you to do this thing, Keith. It's all wrong in principle, too."

Keith didn't laugh at her this time. He got up, thrusting his hands into his pockets in that characteristic manner and walked slowly up and down the room, as he had that first evening she had come here. Then he paused beside her and, looking down at her, said rather deliberately, "Don't you think it might be very convenient for you and me if your father, as well as Avril, were out of the district for the next few months?"

"Convenient?" Ismay looked up at him in surprise. "How do you mean?"

"My dear, so far as one can undo a mistake, you and I are going to have to undo this mistaken marriage of ours. I don't know that it's going to be easy if we have to explain every step to your, er, somewhat conventional parent. If he and Avril are in Italy, there will be only Adrian and Susan to consider. Adrian will be busy with his work, and in any case, he more than half understands the situation already, while even Susan must surely give some part of her attention to her schoolwork. She won't have much time to spare for what we'll be doing."

"And what," asked Ismay, with slightly dry lips, "will we be doing?"

He gave her a quick glance at that, perhaps because of the tone of her voice.

"The usual way of undoing a marriage is to arrange a divorce," he said curtly.

She was silent, and after a moment, he added, "I suppose you have no objection to that, have you?"

Even then she hardly knew what she wanted to say. No doubt this was the best—indeed, the only—solution. But how futile, how sordid the whole business was! It might be quite an ordinary occurrence in his sort of life, but it was a hateful and incongruous thing to happen to Ismay Laverhope.

"You're quite used to this sort of thing, aren't you?" she said, unaware that she had not answered his question, and putting her own inquiry as though she could not help it.

His eyebrows shot up.

"I've never been in a divorce suit before, if that's what you mean."

"No, I didn't mean quite that. But it's nothing to you to indulge in some extravagant fancy for ages, feed it with your own romantic ideas, force some preposterous issue for the sake of it and then suddenly abandon the whole thing by way of the divorce court."

She thought her candor must have made him very angry, because his voice was slightly harsh as he said, "You didn't answer my question, you know. Have you any objection to a divorce?"

"No. I suppose it's the only way out."

"I don't see any other. We'll keep up some sort of appearances until your father and Avril have gone abroad. Then I expect it will be more pleasant for you if I go to London for a while. We can arrange the rest through my solicitors."

She didn't answer. Perhaps there was nothing to answer. But she suddenly felt unutterably sad and overwhelmed by a sense of failure. It was a terrible thing to have taken on such a solemn business as marriage—even so strange a marriage as theirs—and then abandon it like that, with hardly an attempt to make anything of it.

For a moment she was sorely tempted to take his hand, make some little gesture of intimacy and friendship and ask him if he didn't think they ought to make a better try of things than this. But she remembered just in time how he had mockingly accused her of "throwing herself at his head." There really was nothing else to do about it—nothing she could say or even hint.

They had made a rotten tangle of things—the sort of tangle one could not undo. The only way was to cut it.

The next few days were not happy days for Ismay. It was impossible to ignore someone living in the same house. And yet it was impossible to decide what attitude to take. He was very polite to her in his careless, smiling way, but somehow that made things no easier.

I know what it is, thought Ismay unhappily. *I hate*

*living on the surface of things. We never did that at home.
Susan would have prevented it if no one else had*, she
reflected with a faint smile. It was strange, too, to feel
that there was no one who either needed her or wanted
her.

She visited the family several times, but everyone
seemed frantically engaged in the task of dispatching
their father and Avril on the journey to Italy and no one
had much time for anything else.

"My goodness, I don't know what all the hurry is
about," Susan confided to her. "You'd think, after they'd
waited all this time to make up their minds, they could
bear to waste a day or two instead of rushing around like
chickens with their heads cut off."

Ismay hoped she had not presented this comparison for
father's inspection.

"One always does things in a hurry in the end, I
suppose," she said tolerantly. "At least, the Laverhopes
always do."

"Yes. Like your marriage," Susan agreed. "But then
that was romantic."

Ismay refrained from saying anything.

Of Avril—when she was helping her to pack—she did
inquire, "Was it your idea or father's that Keith should
pay for you both?"

Avril looked up absently from what she was doing, and
Ismay repeated her question a little more sharply.

"Oh . . . both, I think. We sort of worked it out
together. Father had been dipping pretty well into his own
income again, you know, and of course this sort of trip is
rather a luxury from his point of view."

"You weren't at all ashamed?"

Avril looked faintly surprised.

"About what, Ismay?"

"About asking Keith for even more than he had spent on the family already."

"We-ell—" Avril smiled winningly, and for a moment she looked curiously like father "—it isn't much good having a terribly rich brother-in-law if you don't make use of him. Besides, I think he almost likes doing it. He's so crazy about you that he gets a real kick out of making extravagant gestures where the family is concerned."

Ismay wondered what Avril would have done if she had coolly retorted, "Keith is already tired of me."

Instead she said, "What makes you think he's so crazy about me?"

Again Avril gave her a look of faint surprise.

"Why, everything, of course. The way he looks at you, the things he does for you—even the way he engineered your marriage. And he's extravagant about his affections, just as he is about everything else. It's embarrassing, I think, but very useful," Avril concluded cryptically.

Ismay felt tempted to point out that extravagances, of necessity, never lasted long, and that this one had already died a natural death. But she was silent, and after a moment, Avril added, with an air of impersonal reflection, "Keith is the kind of man to be extravagant even in his sacrifices. Do you think I could wear that red belt with my gray frock, or will it make my hair look pink?"

"Nothing on earth," Ismay assured her, "would make your hair look pink. Red-gold it is, and red-gold it will remain, whatever you wear."

"I suppose you're right."

"And I don't think Keith is given to sacrificing himself, extravagantly or otherwise," Ismay added crisply.

"You think not? Well, I expect you know your own husband best," Avril conceded equably. "But I imagine he was the kind of child who planned dramatic rescues in which he got killed, saving whoever he adored at the moment."

She dismissed the subject of Keith after that, in favor of the much more interesting one of her outfit. But her words lingered most strangely in Ismay's mind.

Odd that Avril should have said just that. It reminded her very sharply of Keith describing himself and his mother.

"I imagined all sorts of dramatic scenes in which I rescued her from wild bulls and other improbable animals. . . ."

She had felt sorry for him at that moment, she remembered. A chord of sympathy had been struck between them. She had even kissed him—lightly, but of her own accord—the only time she had kissed him voluntarily.

That had been a very different Keith from the uncaring man she lived with now. Or rather—Ismay corrected herself grimly—in whose house she lived.

"I wish I hadn't . . . lost that."

She had no idea she had spoken aloud until Avril said, "Hm? What have you lost?"

"Nothing." Ismay roused herself. "Nothing that matters."

But she knew suddenly that it was something that mattered very much indeed. The connecting link between herself and the generous, extravagant, warm-hearted creature that her husband could be.

The preparations for departure culminated in a grand finale in which the whole family—including Keith—escorted the two travelers to the station.

"Mind you write pretty often," Susan said. "It'll help my stamp collection enormously having some of the family living abroad."

"I hope, my dear, that will not be your only reason for

wishing to hear from us," father said, with genial reproach.

"Oh no," Susan assured him generously. "We shall want to hear all about your adventures. People who go abroad always have adventures."

"Ah, *Dio mio*, but only when one is young," exclaimed her father, with humorous regret. (He would never have dreamed of using the expression "My God" to any of his children, but these things sounded different in a foreign tongue. In any case, the small book in his pocket, which bade him "brush up his Italian" authorized the expression quite frequently.)

"Well, Avril can have the adventures and you can write home about them," Susan said.

But father evidently considered this an unsuitable division of labor, because he said firmly, "We'll see, my dear, we'll see."

Ismay wondered if anyone would thank Keith, as the person almost wholly responsible for this trip abroad. Not with any crude references to paying bills, of course, but gracefully and with some real heart about it.

No one did, however, and she thought suddenly that it was no wonder he regarded them all with cynical amusement. On impulse she turned away with him from the group, as though she wanted to draw his attention to something at the other end of the platform.

"I suppose you're thinking we're a pretty dreadful crowd, aren't you?" she said abruptly.

"Ismay! No." He looked genuinely surprised. "Rather dear and amusing."

"Funny. That's how I used to see us," she said slowly.

"You'll see them like that again," he told her gently.

Before she could ask him what he meant by that, Susan piped up excitedly, "Here comes the train!"

Even then, father took leisurely and dignified farewell

of his family. It took more than an irate porter, crying "Hurry along there, please," to disturb father in the middle of a speech.

The united efforts of the family, however, at last got him onto the train, and if the best and final passages of his soliloquy were declaimed as the train drew out of the station, no one really minded. As Susan said, it was "rather effective to hear it dying away in the distance."

CHAPTER TEN

As they left the station, Ismay said, "You two had better come back with us to the Hall for tea."

"Thanks, but I have to get back to the shop," Adrian said. Never once, she noticed, had he come to Otterbury Hall.

"And I *promised* to go to tea with Carol," Susan assured her regretfully. "She thought it would cheer me up."

Ismay thought Susan looked singularly little in need of cheering, but she accepted the excuses with a smile, and, after brief goodbyes, the group broke up, Ismay and Keith driving back home alone.

In the car it was he who spoke first, and then only to observe conventionally, "I expect you'll miss them a good deal, Ismay."

"Yes. But not as much as if I had still been at home."

At the mention of that, he gave her a quick glance. Then after a moment he said, with rather elaborate casualness, "Shall you go home again . . . later?"

"After the divorce, you mean?" She got that out with difficulty.

"Yes, after the divorce."

"I don't know. I suppose so . . . yes. There won't be anywhere else to go."

"You could travel." His voice sounded abrupt, even slightly harsh, against the soft, purring background of the motor.

"Alone? I don't think I'd like that," Ismay said slowly, and conversation languished.

As he drew the car to a standstill outside the house, he

said, "I want to talk to you, Ismay. Will you come into the garden?"

She climbed out of the car without a word, and as though by common consent, they strolled past the house and toward the seat where they had sat the evening they had discussed Adrian's refusal.

The late-afternoon light was still warm and clear, and there was something almost languid in the heavy-scented quiet that lay over the garden.

But there was nothing languid in the attitude of either Keith or Ismay. She felt tense and strung up and, glancing at the peculiar set of his mouth, thought he felt the same.

Even when they were sitting down, he seemed to find some difficulty in framing what he wanted to say, and presently she asked, "What is it, Keith?"

"Oh—" he made one of his little gestures of impatience "—there are a lot of practical details you and I have to settle. We must talk them over, only it's difficult to begin. It all sounds so . . . crude."

"But then most things about this business have been crude, haven't they, Keith?" She spoke without rancor, even a little sadly, and she saw him unexpectedly bite his lip.

"Crude. It's a soul-destroying word, isn't it?" he said somberly and, as though he hardly noticed what he was doing, took her hand in his and gazed at the ring he had bought in Athens.

She was silent, not knowing what to say, and after a moment he put her hand quickly away from him, as though realizing suddenly what he was doing.

"It's about this . . . divorce." There could hardly, thought Ismay, have been anything more crude than the way he introduced that. "I'll see to everything, of course, but I'm afraid it's bound to be a difficult time for you until everything is settled. I'm sorry. I would have had it otherwise if I could. But perhaps, in the odd little way you have of working things out for yourself, you'll allow yourself to feel that washes out any, er, obligation you feel toward me."

She smiled faintly.

"That doesn't sound very logical, Keith, but I think I know what you mean. Only please don't think anything I've done or . . . or had to put up with really does cancel out your generosity—"

He moved sharply, but she put her hand lightly on his arm to prevent any interruption.

"No, listen to me, please. I've very conscious of the fact that we have been ungrateful, that *I* have been ungrateful. I know there have been hard words between us, and I know you have done some not very admirable things. But you have been fantastically generous in other ways. . . ."

"With money, you mean?"

"Very well, with money. But that happened to be what we needed."

"It's easy to be generous about money when you're rich," he told her a trifle gloomily.

Ismay laughed with genuine amusement.

"Great-aunt Georgina didn't think so. But anyway, that doesn't really matter. You *were* generous, while I—"

"Ismay, please!"

"No, I'm not going to say any more about 'paying up' or 'canceling the debt.' It was rather silly ever to talk in that vein anyway. But do you know, I don't think I ever even thanked you."

"Child, I don't want your thanks." He laughed rather unhappily, and those bright, insolent eyes of his fell, as they had once or twice before when she had seriously put him out.

"No, I daresay not. But I'd like to say it, all the same. Thank you, Keith."

"You make me feel like a hound."

She laughed again, and once more it was with genuine amusement.

"I expect a man always feels frightfully uncomfortable with a woman he has grown tired of," she said equably.

There was a strange silence. Then he said rather flatly, "I expect so."

"Well—" she hesitated "—was that all there was to say?"

"Yes. Except that I'm sorry I made such a hash of things for you. It was as you said once—thrusting my way in because I was jealous of something I didn't understand. I hope I haven't spoiled everything for you, Ismay. I hope when all this is over, you'll go back to the kind of life you like and be happy again."

She knew suddenly that one never went back, that it was no good thinking things would ever be the same again. But there was no point in telling him that now.

"You won't have to . . . worry about anything, you know. There'll always be plenty of money for you."

"But—" Ismay sprang to her feet suddenly "—if we separate like this—" She stopped suddenly, for when she sprang up she realized, from the momentary tug on her dress, that he had been holding a fold of skirt in that agitated, almost childlike way he had once before when he was trying to explain something to her.

She stared down at his dark bent head, at the curious little network of crumples in her frock. He must have been holding her desperately tightly to make such clear marks, she thought irrelevantly. Something, a warning little bell at the back of her mind, told her that she ought to be able to read some significance into those crumples, that the hold he had relaxed immediately had been desperately tight because he was . . . desperate.

And then suddenly, casual, careless, impersonal words of Avril's drifted back into her mind, "Keith is the kind of man to be extravagant even in his sacrifices."

The most extraordinary emotions rose like a tide in Ismay's heart—astonishment, pity, amusement and the strangest tenderness. No wonder she hardly knew whether she wanted to laugh or cry. She glanced down at him again. He was perfectly still—curiously still, as though he were a little afraid of something.

"Keith," she said softly, "I'm going to say something—something rather outrageous to you. No, please don't look at me, because, if I had any pride, I wouldn't be saying this at all."

"Well?" He gazed across the garden, and she saw that he looked curiously pale and bleak.

"If I begged you to give up this idea of divorce, told you that I . . . I want most terribly to give our married life a chance, what would you say?"

Without a word, he turned and put his arms around her waist, burying his head against her and holding her more tightly than anyone had ever held her before.

"Ismay, Ismay, Ismay."

She would never have believed that the repetition of her name could hurt so much.

"Don't, darling." She bent over him eagerly, the unfamiliar endearment springing quite naturally to her lips. "It's all right. I'm not going away. I mean . . . I'm not going to let you go away."

"I love you so much," he whispered almost incoherently. "It's all so hopeless . . . everything I did was wrong . . . so crude when I wanted it to be beautiful . . . so sordid when I wanted to be generous. I don't understand you; I only love you. But I could do nothing but ruin your life. That's why I thought the only thing was to wash it all out, to pretend you didn't even matter any more. Then you wouldn't be uncomfortable and remorseful about me. I could just get out again and leave you alone."

"But I don't want you to leave me alone."

His arms tightened again convulsively, and she knew that no one had ever loved and needed her as this man did. The family . . . yes, in their way, but never with the fierce and desperate intensity of her husband.

She sat down slowly, drawing him quite naturally against her.

"Are we starting all over again?" she whispered.

"I don't know, love. It's just exactly as you say." He spoke in a whisper, too.

"Aren't you ever going to look up at me again?"

"Oh. . . ." He looked up then with a little laugh. "Oh, Lord, I'm sorry! I've crumpled your dress terribly, and made a fool of myself into the bargain."

"I don't think you're a fool at all," Ismay said slowly, "except for letting a raffish set of scroungers like the Laverhopes impose upon you."

"Ismay! You mustn't call yourselves that."

"Oh, don't worry. None of the others would, and I only do in certain moods."

"Darling, you're laughing a little?"

"Yes, of course. I always laugh about the family. Mother used to say it was the only way of living with us and not going mad."

"Do you know that you had stopped laughing about

them in the past few weeks? You'd begun to take them seriously." He was smiling at her now himself, and she realized then how much strain had vanished from his expression.

"Keith, that must have been what was the matter. I took them seriously and that made me go a little mad. That was why I didn't realize . . . ."

"Didn't realize what, darling?"

"That . . . I was falling in love with you."

"Ismay—" he took her very gently in his arms "—you're not laughing at *me* now, are you?" There was real anxiety in his eyes.

"No." She kissed him. "Not just at the moment. But you must let me laugh at you a little sometimes. One always laughs a little about the people one loves best."

THE DARLING PIRATE

The Darling Pirate
Belinda Dell

"It's against my principles to own anything," Alain Hautger had told Maggie Jefferson at their first meeting. And she discovered how much he meant it.

She was told he had been a young lion in the legal world a few years earlier; a personal tragedy had changed his values and he had turned his back on acquisitive society.

But Maggie discovered he had not turned away from people. For young Danié, a victim of circumstances whom everybody called "no good," knew the depth of Alain's compassion and friendship.

Suddenly Maggie discovered that this man who had nothing meant everything to her. She determinedly set out to win his approval.

CHAPTER ONE

It was raining when Maggie's plane touched down at Jersey Airport. This surprised her, because Viv had gone on at some length on the phone about the sunshine in Jersey. "It holds the sunshine record for any resort, Maggie! Word of honor, I've got primulas in blossom this very minute as I talk to you, just outside the window. And that's not bad for February!"

Since Viv was not at all given to lying or even exaggerating—much—Maggie had believed her. There had been a lot more that her friend wanted to put across—about the excellent air connection with London so Maggie could slip home any time she was free, the low prices so that she could replenish her wardrobe and stock up on perfume, the excellent food, the long sandy beaches, the sun, the gaiety, the Frenchness of it all. . . .

Really, it had sounded a sort of "other Eden, demi-paradise." But that wasn't quite why Maggie agreed to take the job Viv was vacating at Le Grand Vergi. First of all she wanted to do Viv a favor: if, as she said, she was leaving her employer in a bit of a fix over this sudden departure, then Maggie wanted to be of help. Rather unexpectedly Viv was going to Canada to get married to a man who had, the previous year, been a guest at the hotel where Viv was the receptionist.

Secondly, Maggie had a particular reason for wanting to leave her present position. She, too, was a receptionist—that was how she and Viv had become firm friends, by working in the same London hotel. In London she had a circle of rather glossy friends, which included Ward Pelham, a wealthy, not-so-young man-about-town who had decided to lay siege to Maggie. It was a very difficult situation: he was a patron of the hotel, so it would have been a decided blot on Maggie's record to say to him, as she longed to do, "Drop dead!"

She had refused his invitations, returned his presents, pretended deafness to his innuendoes. The only thing left was flight.

Literally. She had taken the plane for Jersey in the Channel Islands after a short correspondence and a long telephone call with Mr. Gale, manager of the Grand Vergi, who sounded harassed. He'd said she would be met at the airport by someone who would drive her to the hotel.

So now where was her driver?

She stood in the arrivals lounge, watching her suitcase sail toward her on the conveyor. A porter put them on a trolley. "Taxi, miss?"

"I'm being met, thank you."

"Good thing, this weather. Far to go?"

"I'm not sure—the village is St. Tamme. Do you know it?"

"Ah, two cottages and a shop! I've driven through it."

She was a little shaken at that. "But there's a hotel? A big one."

"You mean Le Grand Vergi? Oh yes, very glamorous."

Out of the corner of her eye Maggie saw a man half turn at the mention of the hotel's name. She gave him her attention. Surely *this* wasn't the escort from the hotel?

If so, the management had some peculiar ideas about appropriate clothes for their staff, because this man bordered on being a hippie. He was wearing worn jeans and a denim jacket, which hugged his long lean frame; the sleeves of the jacket were rolled up a little to reveal muscular forearms, tanned as dark as his face. Perched on the back of his head was a peaked cap of black leather or vinyl, which gave him a vaguely nautical air . . . but it might just conceivably be a uniform cap.

"You there!" Maggie called, beckoning to him.

He pointed at himself with his thumb. "Me?"

"Yes, you. Excuse me, are you from Le Grand Vergi?"

His teeth flashed in a wide amused grin. "God forbid!" he said.

"Oh." A little embarrassed, she smiled apologetically before moving restlessly to the swinging doors, to look out at the pelting rain.

"Does it often rain like this?" she asked her porter.

"No, no. This is a northerly gale today. It'll die down soon. Who was to meet you from Grand Vergi, miss?"

"I've no idea. Perhaps I ought to phone and ask what's happened."

"Why don't you do that? And if there's nobody coming, perhaps *le pirate* will give you a lift."

"Who?"

The porter nodded at the tall man, who had just accepted a large package from an airline official and was signing a receipt.

"He's got his van outside, I'm sure. It'd be no trouble for him—he goes through St. Tamme."

"Oh, I don't know whether . . . ."

"He wouldn't charge anything. He's a chap who likes having a pretty lady aboard!"

"No, no, I don't think so, thanks." That character reference didn't exactly make the idea appealing! "No, I'm sure when I phone Mr. Gale he'll explain what to do."

But Mr. Gale proved to be unavailable. A foreign voice, possibly Italian, said that there had been a mishap to the kitchen equipment and the manager couldn't come to the phone.

That explained why the car hadn't been sent. In the

midst of a drama of that sort—trouble in the kitchens, and just as lunch should be served—he was extremely likely to have forgotten her arrival.

She came out of the phone booth to find her porter in conference with the piratical man.

"No luck?" he asked as she approached. "That's typical—all sorts of modern gloss on the place but can't even meet a guest on time."

"I'm not a guest," she said quickly. "And I understand there's been some upset at Le Grand Vergi."

"So okay, do you want a lift? Your friend here—" he nodded at the porter "—has put in a good word for you."

"That's very kind of him, but I think I ought to take a taxi, thanks."

"Perhaps you ought, at that. My old rattletrap is not quite up to your super-bandbox neatness. But a taxi will cost a lot of money from here to St. Tamme. It's eight miles."

"Goodness! Is there a bus?"

"From here to St. Helier. That's about five miles. Then you have to catch another bus to St. Tamme—that's six or thereabouts. An increase of three miles on the total journey, to say nothing of how wet you'll get in your pretty pink suit while you change buses. But please yourself."

Maggie glanced down at herself. Confound Viv and her tales about eternal sunshine! If she'd known there was to be a downpour to greet her she'd have worn a trench coat and boots. And her hair, freshly set to make a good impression on her employer: five minutes in that torrent and it would be lying as flat against her head as a seal's skin.

"Well?" asked the "pirate," raising his thick dark brows. "Am I the lesser of the evils?"

"I'm afraid you are," she admitted, laughing a little to take the sting out of her words. "If it would really be no trouble. . . ?"

"Quite the reverse. Might do my reputation a lot of good to be seen with someone so obviously respectable . . . and in a Chanel suit, no less!"

Maggie might have tried to explain that it wasn't a genuine Chanel, but her porter, taking it for granted long ago that she was going in the van, had trundled her luggage out. She prepared to follow him.

"Just a sec. I'll bring an umbrella," said her benefactor. "You don't want to get drenched."

He raced off, heedless of the rain, to a battered green Austin van, whose back doors he wrenched open so that the suitcases could be put inside beside the package, already deposited there. He took out a huge green and black striped umbrella—a golfer's umbrella, and one that should have been left at the eighteenth hole because of its tattered condition.

This the eccentric fellow opened so as to shelter himself and the porter back to the arrivals hall.

"*Tout arrangi*," he announced as they came in. "*Allons, viyons. . . .*"

"*Au r'vaie*," the porter said, smiling to himself as he pocketed Maggie's tip, "*et bouon viage!*"

If this was French, it was a variety that Maggie had never heard. She set off across the pavement under the umbrella, which was nearly as full of holes as a doily but surprisingly enough kept off most of the rain. People hanging about in the departures lounge smiled a little at the sight of this neat smart brunette being escorted to her conveyance by a six-foot brigand wielding a ragged banner of green and black, but Maggie took care not to meet their eyes.

404

She climbed into the van's passenger seat. He closed the door and strode around to the other side. She was sure the engine wouldn't start—it was the kind of beat-up old contraption that would need to be pushed to start. But no, after coughing twice the motor picked up and they were off.

Not without a considerable amount of rattling and banging from the door on Maggie's side and those at the back.

"Good gracious! Will they fly open?"

"Shouldn't think so. The ones at the back are tied with string. You can hold yours if it bothers you."

"No, no," Maggie said airily, but surreptitiously gripped the handle.

"If you're not a guest at Grand Vergi, what are you?" he inquired.

"A receptionist. And what are *you*?" she countered.

"A gentleman of leisure. I fish a little, run errands for people, cultivate the soil when I feel like it."

"When you feel like it? Doesn't the soil go to weeds when you don't?"

"Oh, it's not *my* soil. I don't own anything. I'm hired to help with the crops when they're ready—you know, Jersey potatoes, Jersey tomatoes, Jersey carnations. . . . But only now and again. Employers don't really like me, because if the weather's right and the fish are shoaling, I'd rather be out on the boat."

"Do you own the boat?"

"Of course not. It's against my principles to own things. What about you?"

"Are you asking if it's against my principles, too? Because if you are, the answer's no. I own quite a lot of things—those two suitcases in the back, for instance."

"Real leather, I noticed. Very impressive. And your gloves are handmade."

"You're very observant."

"Oh yes. Part of the training."

"What training?"

He frowned, peering through the streaming windshield at the shiny black surface of the road.

"Oh, a lot of nonsense I went through in days gone by. So you're going to be a receptionist at Grand Vergi? I wish you joy of it."

"Why?" she asked in some alarm. "Is there anything wrong with the place?"

"Not if you like conspicuous waste and luxurious boredom. A lovely chocolate box tied up with satin ribbons, that's Le Grand Vergi." He gave her a brief glance from brilliantly blue eyes. "The name means the great orchard, you know, in Jersiais. That house used to be a big farmhouse in the middle of acres of fruit trees, famous particularly for its cider apples. Where are the fruit trees now? What useful product comes out of Le Grand Vergi these days?"

"Happy people?" Maggie suggested, rather nettled by his criticism. "Vacationers taking a well-earned rest?"

"At those prices, the guests have to earn more than a rest—they must be raking in a fortune as a result of their labors, such as they are. A rich man's holiday hideout."

"Rich people deserve holidays just like anyone else."

"Rich people can never really have a holiday," he declared. "They always have to be worrying about their possessions."

What a biased view of life, Maggie said to herself. Since it was likely to develop into a fruitless argument, she decided to let the conversation drop. They drove on in silence for some minutes.

All at once the clouds blew away, the sun burst forth, and the entire green countryside was bathed in brilliant sunshine. The view around them glistened as if it had been dipped in gold and silver.

"How marvelous!" she exclaimed. "What a glorious day it's turning out to be!"

"Specially in your honor. Yes, dear old Jersey's doing you proud."

Maggie watched him covertly as he gazed at the smiling landscape. "You belong here?"

"Born and bred. Jersiais—or as we say in our own tongue, Jerriais. One of 'the noble little people of the sea,' as Victor Hugo called us. We must be the luckiest community in the world, with a beautiful country, plentiful crops from the fields and the sea, and laws of our own to keep us safe."

"You make it sound wonderful, Mr. . . . ?"

He turned his head momentarily. "Call me Alain," he said.

Presumably that was his first name. Did he expect her to respond by giving hers, thus putting them on first-name terms?

"I'm Maggie Jefferson," she said, "of London." *Miss* Jefferson, her tone implied.

He wrinkled his nose. "Can't stand London. Noise and gas fumes and tall buildings—"

"Oh, it's not! I mean, that's not *all* it is. There's plenty of trees and grass, and the Thames as well, and though of course the traffic is noisy, it's mostly at rush hours."

"You sound so enthusiastic about it that I wonder why you left it for a quiet little dreamland like Jersey."

She felt color creeping up under her clear pale skin as she remembered her reason for leaving London. But she said sedately, "It's a good thing to try new places and new challenges."

"You've worked in hotels as big as Le Grand Vergi? It's pretty hard going, I imagine."

"I expect it to be more relaxed than my London job. It's out of season here, surely, being February?"

"That's true, although there's a year-round season here because of the golf. The hotel is on the edge of a very fine golf course," he explained as Maggie made a questioning sound.

"I see. All the same, it can't be running at full capacity; Mr. Gale told me he had builders in, doing alterations."

"Yes, I heard Richard was up to his ears in electric wiring."

"You know Mr. Gale?" She was surprised: he didn't strike her as likely to be on first-name terms with the manager of a top-grade hotel.

"I sell him lobsters," Alain said.

She chuckled. "A little fishing. . . . If it's lobsters you catch, it must be pretty lucrative."

"Why should you think of it in terms of money?"

"Why, I . . . I suppose because . . . one thinks of lobsters as a rich man's dish."

"Which is why I sell them to Le Grand Vergi. The low-class fish such as eel I sell to the local fish restaurants. But I don't care what I go out for. It's the going out that makes it worthwhile." He was silent a moment, then added, "D'you like the sea?"

"Very much. I swim a lot. I'm hoping to get some good swimming here."

"Not at Grand Vergi, you won't. It's two and a half miles from the sea. Oh yes," he recollected, "of course, they have a pool. Blue tiles and a drinks patio. You can swim there, if you can call it swimming to go back and forth over twenty yards of tile."

Maggie refused to let herself be riled by his critical

tone. "I like pools," she said, "and a lot of the other trappings of modern life. They make life very comfortable."

"They also make it very unreal. But—" he shrugged "—to each his own."

A silence fell between them that Maggie felt no desire to break. Polite conversation with this man was almost impossible. He seemed to want to make an issue of everything and, on the other hand, she didn't want to embark on a long philosophical analysis of present-day civilization. Instead she concentrated on the scenery.

They had driven through a terrain where glass houses and fields of vegetables predominated. On the steeper slopes plants glistened in a flurry of tender green under the sun; with surprise she realized they were potatoes. In the more sheltered parts of the valleys flowers for marketing were growing: she glimpsed the vivid colors of anemones and vast areas of daffodils—although the latter were only faintly yellow as yet, the buds not having opened. Clumps of spearlike green leaves on almost every spare patch of soil betokened other early flowers— narcissi, snowdrops, tulips.

In the pastures grazed elegant cattle—rather small, with coats the color of Siamese cats, and eyes like deer. She found it interesting that each animal was tethered by a long rope to a stake in the ground, allowing plenty of movement yet preventing one beast from cropping another's grazing.

She liked what she saw. Clearly the Jersiais were a sensible, thrifty, energetic people. The particular member of it who was at her side was surely not typical!

They had reached the crest of a hill. The sea glinted ahead, a strange aquamarine broken by dark rocks around which the waves foamed like silver filigree around a garnet brooch.

"We're nearly there," Alain said. "In a minute you'll see the roofs of St. Tamme."

True enough, almost at once peaks of red tiles broke from among the trees as they descended into the valley. A rolling expanse of green—the golf course. A house or two, snowy white in the sunshine, palm trees in their gardens. Then a winding, tree-shaded lane, bounded on one side by a wall of rosy stone in whose crevices grew small ferns and toad flax.

"Le Grand Vergi," announced Alain, jerking his head toward it. "Ten acres of grounds."

Handsome wrought-iron gates appeared, painted black and gold with the words "Le Grand Vergi" in an enameled oval like a cameo. They drove up a red gravel path, between bushes of buddleia in blossom and hydrangeas so tall as almost to have reached the status of a tree. An arrow indicated the parking lot. Alain ignored it. They emerged into a big clearing in front of the hotel, around which the driveway made a semicircular path, but once again Alain ignored it.

"The tradesmen's entrance for the likes of us," he observed, as he drove on, taking a macadamized track off on the right.

Maggie would have liked to say that it would be quite in order for her to go through the main entrance, for she had to report to the manager's office which would certainly be near the main hall. But on the other hand, to roll up to the front door of a luxury hotel in a van whose doors were tied shut with twine would hardly be a good beginning. So she allowed herself to be whisked into that array of dustbins and milk churns that the service area of even the best hotel seems to create.

A young kitchen porter came out as they drew up. "Hé, Alain!" he exclaimed, launching into a conversation that Maggie was quite unable to follow.

Alain seemed to be discussing sport for the first few minutes (she discovered afterward that the porter played for the local soccer team.) Then her suitcases were produced from the van and she heard her name: "Mad'mouaiselle Maggie Jefferson."

"So there you are," said the youngster. "Sorry you were forgotten in the midst of the crisis. The electricians suddenly cut off all the power, and all the food for lunch got ruined. This way."

Maggie was about to follow him when Alain detained her by placing two fingers on her arm.

"I say, don't I get paid?"

"Oh, of course!" She was embarrassed. The porter at the airport had implied it would cost her nothing, but she should have realized Alain would expect some payment. "Er, how much would you. . . ?"

"You know I don't believe in money," he said, with a smile that lit up his tanned face. "Payment in kind."

"In kind? I'm afraid I don't. . . ?"

"Like this." He put his crooked forefinger under her chin, tilted her face and brought his lips softly down on hers.

It was only a brief, light contact, yet its effect on her was tremendous. Her breathing quickened and her head swam, so that when he straightened and drew apart she literally staggered.

"Hé!" he exclaimed, catching hold of her to steady her. "Are you all right?"

A furious blush leaped into her cheeks. "Of course I am," she gasped.

His eyes dwelled on her, the mischievous smile dying out of them to be replaced by a look of faint perplexity.

"Well now," he murmured. "Perhaps you aren't completely taken over by civilization after all." The hands on her shoulders, which had steadied her when she lost her balance, tightened their grip.

"One more for luck," he said.

This time the kiss was lingering and exploratory. Maggie resisted it at first, but it had a strange power; against her will she found herself responding, coming alive under that velvety contact of mouth upon mouth. Where his hands held her shoulders, the flesh seemed to burn under the soft wool of her jacket.

But after a moment her brain reasserted control over her senses. She pulled away.

"That's quite enough!" she exclaimed, wiping her mouth in anger with the back of her hand.

"Not from my point of view." He sounded regretful.

"I take it the account is paid in full?"

"Certainly not. That was only a token payment. *A bétot*, Maggie. *A bétot*, Jack."

And with that he gave a little salute, climbed back into the battered van and roared off.

"That Alain!" Jack said enviously. "There's a man who knows what he wants!"

Grinning, he led the way indoors. Maggie followed, with the unhappy foreboding that within a quarter of an hour the scene that had just been played out would be known to the entire hotel staff . . . and lose nothing in the telling!

CHAPTER TWO

When she presented herself a moment later at the manager's office, she was greeted by his secretary, Mrs. Leduc, a plump and motherly Jerseywoman. "Mr. Gale's tied up at the moment—a crisis in the kitchen. Oh, did Jack tell you? My dear, it was dreadful! Twenty minutes after the chef had put in the roasts for lunch, some idiotic electrician disconnected a vital piece of wiring and pht-t! Off went everything!"

She went on to describe how the crisis had been surmounted. "But Mr. Gale's livid! He's having a big fight with the foreman of the building firm at this very moment—not that it'll do any good. Well now, Miss Jefferson—Viv told us so much about you that I feel I already know you. I'll just introduce you to the house-keeper, Mrs. Merryn, who'll show you your room."

She led Maggie to the housekeeper's office in a passage behind the main foyer. Mrs. Merryn proved to be white-haired and very elegant, and perhaps a little on the defensive against this smart, young, London-trained recep-tionist. She accompanied Maggie to her quarters, and thawed somewhat when Maggie exclaimed in pleasure at her room.

"Do you like it? We redecorated last year. Mr. Gale gave me a free hand, and I thought, since after all for hotel staff our rooms are our *homes*, I'd put a little bit of effort behind it."

Maggie's room, which was on the very top floor of Le Grand Vergi like all the rest of the staff's quarters, had a sloping attic ceiling. This had been papered so that it looked like a striped canvas awning. The mansard windows had curtains in a creamy beige that picked up the shade of one of the stripes. The walls were a warm yellow, the paintwork white, the floor covered with a plain brown haircord on which one or two Spanish rugs were thrown. All the furniture was painted beige flecked with white, while the fitted cover of the divan and all the cushions were in yellow.

"You really have a talent for interior decoration!" Maggie exclaimed. "This is lovely!"

"Do you think so? My daughter and her husband keep telling me I ought to go into business on my own, but at my age . . . ."

"It's a bit of a risk, I suppose," agreed Maggie, "especially here in Jersey where the demand is perhaps limited. But if you went to London—"

"Oh, I couldn't do that!" Mrs. Merryn shook her head with vehemence. "All my roots are here now. Besides . . . ."

"What?"

"You don't want to hear my troubles," Mrs. Merryn said, putting her guard up again. "Now if you'd like to unpack and freshen up, there'll be a meal ready for you in the staff dining room. Only cold, I'm afraid, because as I expect you've heard—"

"You had a crisis in the kitchen. Yes, I heard. Thank you very much, Mrs. Merryn. I'll be down in half an hour."

"The staff dining room is the dark red door right opposite the main kitchen. When you've eaten I expect Mr. Gale will be free to see you."

"What's he like?" Maggie inquired. The housekeeper's opinion would be worth having, if she would give it: so much of a hotel's success depends on a good relationship between the manager and his three main lieutenants—the housekeeper, the chef and the head-waiter.

But Mrs. Merryn had no intention of being indiscreet. "You'll soon find out for yourself," she said, preparing to leave.

"He must be nice if he gave you a free hand with the redecorations," Maggie prompted.

"Oh yes, he's very *nice*," the other woman agreed and left.

"Very *nice*." There was an implicit "but" in her tone. What was Mr. Gale's defect? There was always a defect, of course; no boss was ever quite perfect to those under him. But some faults were easier to cope with than others. In the course of her career in hotel work Maggie had met with one manager who had been caught with his fingers in the till and another who had been so unbearably snobbish that when a member of the nobility patronized his hotel he was impossible to live with.

Her curiosity about Richard Gale was destined to be satisfied almost at once. He joined her when she sat down to the meal neatly set out for her downstairs.

"How do you do, Miss Jefferson," he said, shaking hands. "I thought we'd eat together. I missed my lunch in the midst of the hoo-ha over the electricity."

"It seems to have been a terrible nuisance," she murmured, unaccountably flustered by his arrival. She eyed him as he sat down opposite her. He wasn't at all what she'd expected.

For one thing, he was much younger than usual for the manager of such a big exclusive hotel. She thought he was about twenty-nine or thirty, though a certain smooth elegance in his style gave the impression that he was a few years older than that. Of the men she'd seen since landing in Jersey, he most nearly lived up to her idea of what a

Jersiais should be—there was a certain Frenchness in his manner, in his clothes, even in his haircut. But, as she learned later, these were all acquired assets, gained during his training in Switzerland.

"I'm sorry the car didn't meet you," he said. "If you paid for a taxi, I will of course refund—"

"No, no," said Maggie, blushing a little at the memory of the way she paid for her transport. "I got a lift."

"Did you? Good, that shows initiative! You'll need a lot of that here, especially for the next few months until all the island's amenities get going. The guests here are rather demanding . . . and rightly so, since they're paying very high rates. But what I mean is, when the weather's bad, you'll have to think of things for them to do, places for them to go."

"I'll have to read it all up in the guidebook!"

"Yes, and keep up to date with the newspaper so you can recommend village flower shows, or exhibitions by local artists . . . that sort of thing."

"I understand. Are there any guests at the moment who give special problems?"

"Mm. . . . There's a Mr. Steward and his wife, in number eighteen. He's a member of the Wine and Food Society, so he feels it's his duty to send back at least one dish a day to the kitchens—his steak's overcooked, his sorbet is too sweet. He likes to have good restaurants recommended to him. I'll give you a list. Then there's Miss Calvett and her confounded dog. I've nothing against dogs, but they should be kept in their place. She leaves it at the reception desk at mealtimes, as a sort of protest because I won't let her take it into the dining room. . . ."

Maggie listened alertly for the next quarter of an hour while he gave her hints about the foibles of the guests.

There was no doubt he gave his full attention to the business of keeping them contented, and Maggie was impressed. It entered her mind that the piratical Alain would think it beneath his dignity to run around after other people to this extent . . . but why should she worry about Alain's opinion?

As they finished the excellent though simple meal, Richard Gale said, "I suggest you spend the afternoon strolling around the grounds and taking a look at the public rooms. Then this evening Mrs. Merryn will show you around the working areas. Tomorrow you can go on the reception desk with Paul to get the hang of it. Your day off will be shown on the staff rota, which Mrs. Leduc will pin to the bulletin board in the passage, and for the present we'll put you on morning or afternoon duties—evenings can be hectic when we have a dance or a special attraction and of course I never allow a woman to be on the desk at night."

"Thank you, sir."

"There's no need to call me sir in off-duty moments, Maggie. I like a friendly atmosphere. In front of the guests, naturally, it has to be more formal."

But when she went on duty next morning, she found the formality worked only one way. She had to call the guests "sir" and "madam" whereas they called her Maggie, prompted to do so by a name badge she was instructed to wear whenever she was behind the desk. Her colleagues—Paul Daviot, John Tyler, and Grace Rachotte—also wore these blue badges with their first names lettered in white for the benefit of the clients. At first it irked her to have a complete stranger address her as "Maggie," but after an hour or two she became used to it, and there wasn't any doubt that the guests found it pleasant.

Behind the scenes, the hotel was certainly quite different from any other she'd worked at. So many languages were spoken that it was like the Tower of Babel. The restaurant staff were Portuguese, the kitchen staff were French, the porters and gardeners were Jersey-French or Bretons. But somehow they managed to communicate, except when they got excited—on the second day after Maggie's arrival the French chef became so excited he was threatening to walk out.

It was all due to the misdoings of the workmen who were rewiring the electrical circuits. Richard Gale said glumly, "He can't actually go . . . his agreement states there must be a month's notice on either side. But if he's going to feel harassed and unsettled it might be as well to let him go. Finding someone as good is going to be a problem, especially at the beginning of the season."

"If you could get the electricians to finish and get out of his way. . . ?" Maggie murmured.

"Yes, but how?" inquired Amy Leduc. "We seem to have been a bit unlucky in the firm we chose. They're disorganized, to say the least—one minute they're hard at work in the loft, the next they've left all sorts of wires hanging and gone off to do something in the basement!"

"I don't understand electricity," Richard confessed. "I really don't like to interfere with what the workmen are doing—"

"But unfortunately *they* interfere with what the chef is doing!"

This conversation was taking place in Richard's office behind the reception desk. The chef had just created a great drama by getting into his car and driving off after finding specks of dust on a bowl of *velouté* he'd lovingly prepared the previous day. He had called for vengeance on the electricians for the grit and dirt their work caused:

"I can endure no more!" he declaimed out of his car window as he drove off.

"What sort of contract do you have with the firm?" Maggie inquired. "Was there a specific date by which they were to finish?"

"Not in writing. The estimate only states the extent of the work and the cost."

Mrs. Merryn came in as Richard took the estimate from a file behind his desk.

"It's really a shame!" she burst out. "Somehow or other there's plaster dust all over the clean sheets in the linen cupboard."

Richard groaned. "I wonder if I could tell them to clear out, and get someone else to finish the job?" He stared at the letter and two sheets of paper he held in his hand, hoping for inspiration from them.

"That would be breaking your contract with them," Mrs. Leduc pointed out. "Wouldn't that mean you have to pay them in full, even though they didn't finish the job?"

"I don't know. It might. In which case it would be expensive."

"Why don't you ask O.J.?" Mrs. Merryn inquired. "He'd know about contracts—"

"Oh, good heavens, this could cost the hotel a lot of money," interrupted Mrs. Leduc, her plump face creased in consternation. "I mean, Richard should get *proper* advice—"

"I really don't know what you mean by 'proper,' " the housekeeper interjected. "O.J. is a lawyer, after all."

"Really?" Mrs. Leduc raised her eyebrows. "As far as I'm concerned, that's all in the past. These days he's a nobody."

"Nothing can alter the fact that he was a fully qualified . . . ."

The sound of the little bell on the reception desk called Maggie away to deal with a query from a guest, so she missed the rest of the conversation. A few minutes later Mrs. Leduc came out, looking half-amused and half-vexed.

"Really, Mrs. Merryn idolizes that man," she muttered as she searched for a date-stamp on the accounts desk.

"Who? Richard?"

"Richard? Goodness, no! As far as Mrs. Merryn is concerned, Richard or any other man is only a pale shadow compared with O.J."

"Who is this O.J.?" Maggie demanded.

"He's the chap who rescued Mrs. Merryn's grandson from a lot of trouble with the law about three years ago. Danié. Have you heard her speak of Danié?"

"I believe she *has* mentioned him. . . ."

"Nearest the heart, nearest the lips," quoted the other woman. "She idolizes that boy—"

"Just a minute. You said it was O.J. she idolized."

Mrs. Leduc dissolved into a chuckle at her teasing. "I'm sorry, I suppose I sound a bit repetitious about it. It's just that I can't sympathize with her. That kid is just a naughty little boy and she should face the fact. But there! It's always easy to talk sense about other people's troubles."

"What sort of troubles?" Maggie prompted. It wasn't just idle curiosity; she'd often seen a worried, tense expression in the housekeeper's eyes and genuinely wanted to understand the cause.

"Well, you see, Mrs. Merryn's daughter, Florence, is

married to a farmer with a place near L'Etac. They have this one son, Danié—Daniel—and he's always up to mischief. Let's see, he's sixteen by now, I suppose. He ran away from home about three years ago, and his father refused to have him back and so on and so on. I forget the details. Anyhow, our lawyer friend rallied around and solved it all."

"Then it isn't surprising she thinks so well of him," said Maggie.

"Perhaps not. But if I needed an advocate I certainly wouldn't go to *him*."

"Why not?"

"You'll see," Mrs. Leduc replied as she returned to the office with her date-stamped papers.

Maggie couldn't quite understand how she would "see" anything about a lawyer whom Richard might consult, but the matter passed from her mind until later in the day. She was having her afternoon break in the staff sitting room when the half-open door was pushed open and a head poked around.

"Is Richard—? Oh, hello. It's Maggie Jefferson! How are you getting on?"

It was Alain, looking if anything more piratical than ever in a dark blue sweater with a polka-dotted kerchief tied at the neck.

"Hello," she said, jumping up with an eagerness that quite surprised her. She could have sworn that she hadn't thought of him once since they parted by the kitchen entrance. "I'm quite settled in, thanks. What are you doing here?"

Did she hope he'd say, "Looking for you?" If so she was disappointed.

"Delivering lobsters, among other things. How do you like Le Grand Vergi?"

"Very much. It's a beautiful place."

"Work not too hard?"

"Not so far. Of course we haven't come into the high season yet." She sensed that he was about to move away, so added rather quickly, indicating the tea tray on the table, "Would you like some tea?"

"No, thanks. I'm looking for Richard. I hear he wants to see me—something about a contract."

"A contract?"

"Don't look so surprised," he said with a grin. "I wasn't always a carefree fisherman. Instead of this—" he tugged at the red kerchief "—I used to wear white tabs."

"You were a lawyer? You're . . . you're Mrs. Merryn's friend? O.J.?"

"That's right."

"But how can your initials be O.J. when your name's Alain?"

He laughed. "Hautger," he said, and spelled it for her. "Pronounced O.J. And it's nice to know that you remembered my name's Alain. Excuse me, Maggie. Richard's expecting me. Do you happen to know where he is?"

"I think he must be up in his room. If you hang on a minute I can call through and find out." At his nod of agreement she did so, then passed on the message that Richard would come down at once.

"He'd better not be long. This isn't the only hotel waiting to buy my delicious lobsters. What's the problem. Have you any idea?"

She gave him the gist, ending with, "It's possible we won't want any of your delicious lobsters, since it so happens our chef has gone off in a huff."

"What a tragedy! No chef? No one to prepare the lobster thermidor? I can understand why Richard is running up distress signals."

"What do you think he should do about it?"

"No idea till I see the papers. Ah, Richard—" as the other man came into the sitting room—"Maggie's given me an idea of what's involved. Can we look at the agreements and correspondence?"

"They're in my office."

As Richard led the way there was really no reason for Maggie to follow—there was still five minutes left of her tea break. But she found she wanted to go along with the two men, to prolong the short interlude with Alain. However, his attention was turned completely to what Richard was saying, so much so that when she stopped to take her place at the reception desk he didn't even notice.

She busied herself with one or two tasks, and for the next ten minutes took telephone messages about a golf lesson for one of the hotel guests. The swirl of the revolving door drew her attention. A young woman was coming in—possibly the most beautiful woman that Maggie had ever seen.

She was tall and blonde and exquisitely dressed. Her soft silk blouse was the color of maize, her velvet pants were cinnamon brown and looked French-made. She moved toward the reception desk in an unhurried saunter.

"Tell Mr. Gale I'm here, will you? Miss Crayland."

"I'm sorry, Mr. Gale is busy at the moment. Is there anything I can do?"

Miss Crayland smiled dismissively. "I hardly think so. Just let Mr. Gale know I'm here."

This was said with so much confidence that Maggie knew she was asking for a rebuke when she inquired, "Shall I say it's a matter of business?"

The woman raised her eyebrows. It was as if at that moment she really saw Maggie for the first time. "You're new here, aren't you?"

"Yes, I am. You must forgive me if I . . . ."

"Just tell Richard I'm here. I think he'll stop whatever he's doing." She dropped with negligent grace into a nearby lounge-chair of soft orange-colored leather, thereby giving herself the perfect background for her blonde hair and pale blouse.

Maggie turned away from the desk to go and tap on the office door. But before she reached it the door opened, the two men coming out in conversation.

". . . Easiest thing for me to say a word or two to them," Alain was remarking. "They'll take the hint and—" He broke off as he caught sight of the girl in the lounge-chair. "Sylvia! *Ma chièthe Sylvie!* I didn't know you were back!"

To Maggie's amazement he swung himself over the gate of the reception desk, seized Sylvia Crayland in his arms and kissed her enthusiastically first on one cheek, then the other.

"Alain! What are you doing here in these civilized surroundings?"

"Coming to the aid of the party, the party being Richard." He half turned to Richard, who was more sedately opening the desk gate and coming through. His glance alighted on Maggie, who was standing with her mouth open in astonishment at this affectionate greeting. "What's the matter?" he asked her teasingly. "Think you're the only one I kiss?"

Maggie blushed and turned away, but not before she'd glimpsed the flash of interest in her direction from Sylvia.

"Who else have you been kissing?" the other woman demanded. "Are you turning it into a habit?"

"No, no, I'm really quite selective. Ask Maggie."

"Perhaps I will one day."

"How are you, Sylvia?" Richard said, taking her hand

as if to attract her attention. "I thought you were still in Tunis or Morocco or wherever it was."

"No, it was a bore. The people I was with spent all their time looking at Roman ruins and things, so when Daddy told me on the phone he'd like to give a dinner for some German business associates, I thought I'd come home and see to it for him. The twentieth, Richard. Can we have the terrace room?"

"Certainly. I'll book it at once. How many people?"

"I think there'll be ten, I'm not quite sure. . . ."

"And you'll give them Jersey seafood, of course," Alain put in. "How many lobsters shall I catch for you?"

"Alain, you're absurd! I haven't thought about the menu yet."

"Oh, well, it doesn't matter. That might be a day when I wouldn't feel like fishing."

Richard laughed, half-envious, half-disbelieving. "What a way to live," he murmured. "Do you really mean you just do what you like?"

"Absolutely."

"Now, come on, Alain, that's not quite true. When I arrived I was told by—" she searched for and recalled the name "—Maggie here that you and Richard were having a business meeting."

"Were you?" He was astounded. "I was just listening to Richard's problems."

"Richard has problems about fishing?"

"No, about a small legal matter."

"Ah," Sylvia said. "And have you solved it for him?"

"Well, I hope to."

"So you haven't quite turned your back on the everyday world, no matter what you claim. I do wish you'd give up this silly charade, Alain. It doesn't really suit a bright type like you."

It was lightly said, but there was an underlying earnestness. Maggie felt her attention tighten. This girl was genuinely interested in Alain.

And, judging by the way he'd greeted her, Alain was interested in Sylvia.

"There, there," he said, patting her on the shoulder. Maggie couldn't help noticing how the roughened skin on his palms caught on the fine silk of her blouse. "It's not a charade. Strange though it may seem, lots of people earn their living by working on a boat."

"But very few of them have passed Bar exams."

"Oh, that. Well, we all make mistakes, don't we? Now you must excuse me, I must go and speak a friendly word of warning to Richard's electricians, and then I have things to deliver at Les Platons. See you sometime."

"Alain . . . ."

"Yes?"

"These friends of Daddy's—they might like some fishing. Would you take them out on *Simestra*?"

He shrugged. "If it fits in. Leave a message at the Fishermen's Union office, will you?"

He was about to go through the door to the staff quarters when he paused, looking back at Maggie. "Speaking of being selective," he said mischievously, "it's a pity to waste an opportunity."

She had no time to realize what he meant nor to avoid his action. He took a long step back, leaned over the desk, kissed her as he had Sylvia—first on one cheek, then the other—and dropped a final kiss on the fringe of brown hair on her forehead.

"It could become a habit," he observed and was gone before she could utter a protest.

As the door closed behind him Richard laughed uneasily. "I never know whether to take him seriously or not," he remarked with a glance at Sylvia.

"Nor do I. But he's always sincere about liking or disliking people. You seem to have made quite an impression on him," Sylvia said, turning to Maggie.

"If so, I don't know why." Maggie was still red with embarrassment. "I'm awfully sorry, Mr. Gale," she added in formal apology to Richard.

"Oh, that's all right. *Le pirate* is a law unto himself. Now then, Sylvia, may I offer you tea? Or a drink?"

"Tea would be nice."

"Tea for two on the terrace, Maggie."

"Yes, sir."

He led Sylvia to the sheltered veranda where the wisteria was already coming into blossom. Maggie lifted the phone to order the tea. She went back to her chores, putting ledger cards into the Sweda machine to keep the clients' accounts up to date. Presently the phone in the office rang, and Mrs. Leduc came out.

"Where's Richard? The electrician wants to speak to him."

"On the terrace with Miss Crayland."

"Oh?" The secretary's mouth turned down at the corners. "Doing his host bit, is he? I'd better fetch him. Even Miss Crayland has to take second place to getting a good relationship with these confounded workmen."

She bustled off. When she returned Richard was a step or two behind her. "Are you doing anything urgent, Maggie?"

"No, just some billing."

"Then go and keep Miss Crayland company. She's expressed a wish to get to know you."

Somewhat taken aback, Maggie obeyed. Out on the terrace the early evening sun was turning the buds of the wisteria to a mysterious beige-blue, and the scent of the coming blossoms was already on the air. Nearby a big brown and yellow butterfly was dancing over the beds of iris and narcissus, and beyond them among the trees the sound of birdsong came loud and triumphant.

Sylvia was sitting in a white cane chair, the tea things arranged on a low glass-topped table before her. She waved a hand at them. "Tea?"

"No, thanks, I had some about half an hour ago."

"Sit down, won't you. Your name's Maggie, isn't it?"

"Yes." Maggie wondered whether, if Sylvia began calling her by her first name, she would be entitled to do likewise.

"Richard tells me you've been here a couple of weeks. Do you like it here?"

"Very much. It's such a beautiful place."

"The hotel? Or the island?"

"Both, actually. But I really meant the hotel. The last one I worked in was a first-rate place, but it doesn't compare with Le Grand Vergi."

"You were in London, I believe. Won't you find it a bit quiet, stuck away in a backwater like this?"

"It's not exactly a backwater, is it—a first-register hotel with a big and famous restaurant? But even if it were, so much the better. My last job was pretty hectic."

"I suppose so. Being a receptionist must be hard work."

"Yes, but I enjoy that. No, it was . . . ."

"What?"

"Oh, sometimes hotel guests are a bit of a nuisance. . . ."

"Male guests?" Sylvia asked shrewdly.

Maggie realized she'd been talking much too freely. "It wasn't important," she said. "But I was quite glad of a chance to try something else."

"I gather you met Alain almost as soon as you stepped off the plane."

"Yes. He gave me a lift in that disreputable old van." She heard the tone of her own voice and wondered if it sounded as fondly tolerant to her listener as it did to herself. "He's quite a character," she added.

Sylvia's brows drew together. "People only say that about other people when they think they're a bit eccentric."

"Eccentric? I wouldn't say that about Alain. He seems to know what he wants to do and does it."

"But why should he want to?" Sylvia demanded. "What sort of life is that for an intelligent, highly qualified man?"

Maggie saw perplexity and something else—regret?—in the other girl's face. In her work she'd learned to read emotions, even if only to a small extent, and she guessed that this girl had quite strong feelings about Alain she could not or would not acknowledge because of his bizarre lifestyle.

"Do you know him well?" she ventured. "I gather he wasn't always *le pirate*."

"No, he had a good career ahead of him. When I first came to Jersey he was quite a young lion in the legal world."

"When was that?"

"Oh, I suppose about five years ago. I was still at finishing school in Switzerland. Let's see, it must have been when I was about seventeen. Daddy first came here with the intention of buying one of the little islands—it was up for sale and he rather fancied a little domain of his own. But I came home on holiday and really it was quite difficult enough changing planes to get to St. Helier, so instead he bought our house at Rozel. It was Alain's firm that handled the business."

"Alain's firm?"

"Well, his father's, really. Mr. Hautger and another man were partners in a law firm—grim, dusty offices in Hill Street, gold lettering on the window, tremendously respectable. That's why it all came as such a shock."

Maggie restrained herself from making any inquiry. Instinct told her that Sylvia wanted to talk and would tell her what had "come as a shock" without prompting.

"Mr. Hautger died of a heart attack. It was terribly sudden. Everything was a muddle for about twenty-four hours—Alain going around as white as a ghost, his mother prostrate, the staff at the office refusing to speak on the phone. Next day it all came out. The partner had been embezzling money from trust accounts in the firm's charge."

"You mean . . . that was what shocked Alain's father into a heart attack?"

"Apparently. But of course there was really no way of knowing that he'd been in ignorance of the fraud, and I believe in law he was equally responsible."

"How . . . how dreadful!"

"Oh, you can't imagine! Alain wouldn't speak to anyone. He just, well, seemed turned to stone. I mean, he simply wouldn't discuss anything. Heaven knows I could have got Daddy to help out over money; but even so, that wouldn't have prevented the court case, because of course there was a charge of fraud to answer."

"Alain was charged?"

"No, no. He wasn't a partner, only an employee of the firm. He had to give evidence, though. Mr. Troppet was sentenced, and Alain set about trying to pay back the money. Daddy says it was stupidly quixotic of him, but there you are—he felt he had to and Mrs. Hautger agreed, although she was so ill with grief and shame that I don't suppose she really knew what she was doing. They sold everything. She moved into a poky little house on the north coast, miles away from everybody, and I'll always maintain that she died of unhappiness although she's supposed to have contracted pneumonia. Anyhow, ironically enough, her death released just enough money to finish repaying the fraud victims—her insurance policy or something. And that was that."

Maggie looked out over the garden. The brilliant butterfly had flown elsewhere; the shadows were lengthening. The place looked melancholy all of a sudden.

"And after that," Sylvia resumed, "Alain just turned his back on his career. No one could make him see how silly that was. There he was, absolutely penniless! If ever there was a time to settle down to some hard work, that was it."

"Perhaps he needed time to recover," Maggie murmured.

"Well, yes, that's what people said. Everyone was inclined to be very tolerant and understanding at first, particularly in view of the way he'd stuck at it for the six or seven months after the trial, sorting out the muddle and paying off the debts. But that's more than three years ago now. It's time he came to his senses. After all, he's turned thirty. Most men are settled in good careers and have a wife and family by then."

"So they are," agreed Maggie. "But if he doesn't want that. . . ?"

"He used to! I'm sure it's what he wanted!"

Maggie felt a pang of sympathy. Three years is a long time for a woman to wait, especially a woman as beautiful and desirable as Sylvia. A little arithmetic gave Maggie the result that Sylvia was probably about twenty-two now. She'd said she first met Alain while she was still at school. It was easy to imagine a girl of seventeen getting a schoolgirl crush on a handsome young lawyer. What had she called him? "A young lion."

But it must be something more than that, more than just a schoolgirl infatuation, for Sylvia still cared, was still waiting. For what? For Alain to transform himself back into what he used to be?

Maggie wondered if she had any grounds for hope. Had there been, in those days of the past, some kind of understanding between Sylvia and Alain?

She recalled their meeting this afternoon. Alain had been boisterous, happy, welcoming—she could hear again his voice crying a welcome in the old Jersey-French that seemed to come so naturally to his lips. "*Ma chièthe Sylvieé!*"—"My dear Sylvia!" Had there been more than friendship in the words?

Impossible to tell. *And if there was,* she reminded herself sharply, *it's no business of yours.*

CHAPTER THREE

The next two or three times that Maggie saw her, Sylvia seemed to want to put a distance between them. Her manner was cool and rather high-handed, as it had been when they first spoke across the hotel reception desk. Perhaps she regretted having given so much away in their conversation over the tea table.

She came with her father and his guests for the dinner party in the candlelit room off the main restaurant. Maggie saw her follow the headwaiter between the tables, and found it quite understandable that heads turned to watch. Her long straight hair fell like flax to her shoulders, where it met the soft blue velvet of her Victorian dress. The men in dinner jackets looked like suitable escorts for this exquisitely gowned beauty, for they had that air of wealth and power that promises to cosset and protect pretty, rich young women.

Maggie felt a twinge of passing envy that comes to most of us when we see someone we think of as favored by fortune. But the next moment her attention was claimed by new arrivals checking in, and she forgot to be the least bit envious of Sylvia.

And even less so next day. It was her day off, a quiet, gentle day of diffused April light and soft air. She had the use of a hotel car, a Mini, into which she loaded a picnic basket and a pair of field glasses loaned to her by Paul Daviot, who urged her to take a look at the scenery and the sea birds. She drove out of the grounds of Le Grand Vergi, heading east toward St. Catherine's Bay.

This was her first opportunity to spend some time exploring the coastline. She'd had time off before, but had gone to St. Helier to visit the excellent shops or see a movie. Today she wanted to soak up some atmosphere, get to know the countryside.

She took the coastal road, following its winding route past fields of flowers till it came out on a view of a silvery blue sea beyond a fine beach. Her map told her that the breakwater to the north was St. Catherine's, a long gray finger pointing toward France, thirty-five miles away. Dotted along it she could see men with fishing lines, while the gulls wheeled and cried above.

A splendid place for a walk with the field glasses. She parked the car, changed to walking shoes and pulled on a cardigan. She had bought the sweater on a shopping trip to St. Helier and was rather pleased with it because it matched exactly the moss green check in her Welsh tweed skirt. She slung the field glasses from her shoulder and set off.

Enough breeze was blowing across the breakwater to make her glad of the cardigan, but after all it was still only April and no one could call it really chilly. She walked along the granite surface, watching the sea birds soaring and swooping around the lighthouse at the end. She paused to peer through the glasses; the focus wasn't quite accurate for her eyes, but after a moment of fiddling with the centerpiece the lighthouse suddenly took brilliant shape before her. She could even see the beady orange eye of the bird standing on its roof.

This was fun! She'd never handled anything stronger than a pair of opera glasses before. Now she fell in love with the clarity and breadth of view the binoculars gave, so that as she made her way slowly to the end of the sea wall she stopped regularly to look at the rocks, the headlands, the sea and the birds.

Far out on the waves something that resembled a white

arrow seemed to speed downward from time to time. She brought the glasses to bear on it. It was a big white bird with narrow black-tipped wings, diving headlong into the water from a great height. Maggie had never seen anything like it before. Enthralled, she stood watching.

Into the field of vision chugged a boat, a not very tidy boat with chipped blue paintwork and a shabby white pilothouse. It was between Maggie and the diving bird and so was out of focus at first. She was just wishing it would clear out of the way when something familiar about one of the men working on board made her pull back the focus.

It was Alain. He was heaving lobster creels over the side with the help of another worker, while a third man held the wheel. As Maggie stared, Alain looked up—straight into her eyes, it seemed, but of course he was half a mile out at sea. She saw him laugh and duck as the other man aimed a playful punch at him, and then they seemed to begin an argument.

Guiltily she lowered the binoculars. To train the glasses on an unaware person was almost like spying. She walked on to the end of the breakwater, but no longer used the glasses to watch the diving bird for fear of finding Alain once again in the field of vision.

Nevertheless she watched the boat. It moved on a purposefully elliptical course, paying out the creels until the deck was bare. Its movement brought it closer to the lighthouse. Now she could distinguish the men quite easily; she told herself that even if she hadn't first seen him through the glasses she'd have known that Alain was one of them.

She was standing idly, thinking this to herself, when she became aware that someone was calling. Narrowing her eyes, she could see that on board the ship Alain had his hands to his mouth.

"Maggie! Maggie Jefferson!"

She waved excitedly. "Hello-o-o!" she shouted. But she knew her voice was too light to carry to him. So she waved again.

She thought he called, "Wait there," but wasn't sure. Since, in any case, she wasn't going anywhere, she waited. The fishing boat chugged in fussily, the features of the men becoming clearer and clearer as it approached. In a few minutes it was puttering alongside the breakwater some yards behind her, toward the shore. She walked back to meet it expecting to have a short chat, but to her surprise Alain leaped ashore.

"*À bi! A sec sé!*" the men called to each other.

"What are you doing here?" Alain inquired, falling into step with her.

"I have the day off."

"Have you? So have I, until tonight when we haul. What are you going to do with your day off?"

"Oh . . . have a picnic, walk a little, look at the scenery."

"That sounds very pleasant. Like a guide?"

"You mean, you? Well," she said, flustered and annoyed with herself for being so, "thank you, I'd be glad of the company."

" 'Glad of the company,' " he mimicked. "You're a very nicely brought-up young lady, Maggie Jefferson."

"I believe I am. I hope that doesn't count against me?"

He looked at her consideringly. "No, on the whole I approve."

A voice called from the boat, now some yards out again, in that strange French she felt she would never get the hang of. Alain turned, laughing, and called a reply that clearly meant, "I don't need any help from you, thanks."

"Are they friends of yours?" she inquired.

"My employer and his son. Céfi owns the boat, his son is his partner. They let me sleep on board when we're not out on a night trip."

"You sleep on board?" she echoed, horrified. "You mean it's your home?"

"Be it ever so humble. Yes, it is. Where did you think I lived? The Grand Hotel?"

"No, but . . . ."

"But what?"

"I mean, don't you have a place on shore? A room, at least?"

He shrugged. "If I want to live ashore I can always get a job with the farmers. I say, that's a very expensive pair of field glasses! Are they yours?"

"No, Paul lent them to me—one of the other receptionists. I was watching a bird out there."

"Where?"

"Out at sea. It keeps diving. . . ." She offered him the glasses so that he could look, but, disregarding them, he stood for a moment gazing seaward until he caught sight of it.

"It's a *fou de Bassan*—a gannet. We have quite a lot of them hereabouts from April to October. More interesting is the bird on the lighthouse. Noticed it?"

"The gull?"

"That's a Sandwich tern—not many of them as a rule, and only out on the reefs. As a matter of fact, that's how I came to notice you. I was watching the tern and then realized that was you on the breakwater. Now, tell me, what would you like to do?"

"I really don't know. I felt I needed a good walk, but all I've done so far is saunter along this walkway."

He pointed northward. "That's rather a pleasant walk, along the shore to the signal tower. You can only do it while the tide's out, which is the case now—or at least it's going out."

"Is it far?"

"All of two miles," he teased.

She smiled. "I was only thinking that we don't want to go so far that we can't get back in time for lunch. I've got a picnic basket in the car, you see."

"Well, now," he said, tucking her arm through his, "you've put the perfect finishing touch on the plan."

Down on the rocky beach it seemed much warmer, the breakwater and the headland sheltering them from the southwesterly wind. The pearly light was reflected in the pools and shone on the honey-colored sand. Little flocks of birds trotted about by the water's edge, occasionally taking wing with a piping call. On the cliff to their left, wild flowers were glinting—gorse, campion and sea-lavender.

As they walked Alain pointed out the rocks offshore and named them, talked about the birds that nested there and what the fishing was like.

"Did you take Sylvia's friends out fishing?" Maggie asked.

"Sylvia's friends?"

"The business colleagues of her father."

"Oh, them. No fear. She left a message for me at the Jersey Fishermen's Union, but I took good care not to get it."

"Wasn't that rather unkind?"

"Do you think it was? I feel sure they'd easily find someone else to take them out."

"I didn't mean unkind to *them*—I meant unkind to Sylvia," Maggie protested and felt like adding, "As you well knew."

"I suppose I'm always being unkind to Sylvia," he

sighed. "She's always making opportunities to press money upon me, and I'm always refusing to grasp them."

"It probably would have paid well, taking men like that out for a day's sport."

"No doubt. On the other hand, it might have been very boring."

"Well, most of us have to be bored some of the time when it comes to making a living."

"Ah, there's the difference between us," he countered, a smile tugging at the corners of his mouth. "I never need to put up with being bored. For instance, if you were to go on talking about money like this, I could just say that the tide had suddenly turned and we'd better go back, and then I'd make my escape."

"But you told me only a few minutes ago that the tide was going out, so I'd know you were lying."

"But you'd also know I was lying because I was too polite to say that all this insistence on hard cash is distasteful to me."

Maggie drew in a breath, but held her tongue. After a moment Alain said, "Have I hurt your feelings?"

"Would it matter if you had?"

"Certainly. People matter. Money doesn't."

"If you really think people matter, don't you believe that *you* matter to other people? That they worry about you?"

That seemed to give him a pause. He stopped to pick up a piece of seaweed from a rock. After a moment he said, "By the way, never pull living seaweed from its stone, will you? It's a valuable product here in Jersey—we use it on the fields as a top-dressing."

Maggie gave him a faintly ironic smile. "I promise not to pick the seaweed if you'll promise not to undervalue your friends' concern for you."

He grinned. "You're a very obstinate girl, Maggie Jefferson."

"You don't fall short on that score yourself, Alain Hautger."

With a little bow, he took her hand to help her over a slippery patch. "I've sometimes thought I ought to emigrate to the South Seas. Gauguin did that, you know."

"Who?"

"Gauguin—the French painter. He got fed up with the rat race here in Europe and took off to be a beachcomber in Tahiti. I find it a very tempting idea. The Tahitians don't keep on at you about earning a living and putting money by for your old age."

"You remind me of that thing about the men on the magic island. 'Ah why, Should life all labor be?' "

"You mean the Lotus-eaters:

'We have had enough of action, and of motion
    we,
  Roll'd to starboard, roll'd to larboard, when
    the surge was seething free . . .'

But, you know, I don't mind action. I don't mind the surge seething as much as it likes! What I object to is being urged to make money out of it. Everything here always seems to come back to money."

"So why don't you take off for Tahiti?"

"This is my home." He flung out his arms in a gesture that embraced the sea and the rocky shore and the sky. "I was born here. I belong here. My family's name goes back at least four hundred years in Jersey history. All I want to do is live out my time among the things that are familiar to me, without being continually urged to mend my ways or change my attitude."

"Live out your life?" Maggie repeated. "Is that all? Don't you want to have something to hand on?"

"I've told you," he said, in the nearest approach to anger she'd heard from him, "I don't believe in acquiring belongings."

"I wasn't thinking of things. One hands on character, intelligence, a family name. Don't you want to do that?"

"Oh, I've cousins enough to perpetuate the name of Hautger. As to the rest . . . ." He shrugged. "Can any of us be sure that our children would inherit such talents as we imagine we possess? Suppose a man marries and has a son who's a fool?"

"Alain!" Maggie chided. "Don't be such a cynic!"

"But I *am* a cynic. Hasn't that dawned on you yet? What I've seen of life so far leads me to think the human race is a bit of a failure, really. Everybody struggling to keep up with the Joneses or to go one better, prepared to do almost anything for an easy life, a fat bank account, a seat on the board, a swimming pool and a good wine cellar."

She knew he was thinking of the man who had wrecked his father's career and was grateful that Sylvia had told her of it so that now she didn't insist on arguing. In the face of his experience, what could she say? She felt that it would be impertinent to tell him he was wrong, yet deep within her some instinct told her that life was worth living and worth handing on no matter what wrongs and disillusions one might encounter.

For a while they walked on in silence. They reached La Coupe Point, where a road ran inland from the beach.

"We can go up onto the land and walk back by road," Alain said, nodding toward it.

"But I thought we were going to a signal tower?"

"Well, yes . . . if you still want to."

"Of course I do. What made you think otherwise?"

"You've become very quiet. I thought perhaps I'd depressed you."

"What you said has made me think a lot," she said seriously. "I haven't much experience to place against yours. I've had a very ordinary sort of life. All I can say is that I feel your view is wrong."

"You mean you think I should apply for a job in a bank and live a nine-to-five existence?"

"I didn't say that!" she protested. "You can live how you like, how you feel you must. But why does that mean you can't have a home and a family?"

He drew up short to stare at her in amazement. "Are you telling me that I could ask a wife to share the life I lead?"

"Why not?"

"Why not? Because it would need someone with the patience of a saint and the constitution of an ox! Don't be silly, Maggie." He paused. "I'm sorry. I didn't mean to be rude. But, my dear idiot, I wouldn't dream of asking any woman I cared about to give up everything for the sake of being Mrs. Alain Hautger."

"Haven't you ever heard the expression 'The world well lost for love'? One day you might meet someone who feels like that."

"I sincerely hope not," he said lightly. "She'd place me in the most awful moral dilemma, because she'd be much too good for me!"

She realized that he didn't want to go on with the discussion, and luckily at that moment they were coming to a pretty little inlet where a few houses sat close to the shore and boats were drawn up on the narrow beach.

"How pretty," Maggie exclaimed. "I didn't see it till we were almost on top of it."

"This is Saie Harbour. Céfi's brother has—" He broke off unexpectedly, gazing inland toward a car parked on the road leading to the harbor. "What day is it today?" he inquired. "Tuesday, isn't it?"

"Yes." She looked at him in surprise.

"Not a school holiday?"

"No, not as far as I know."

"Then what is Danié doing down here at Saie instead of in a classroom?"

"Danié?" Maggie said, searching her memory. "Mrs. Merryn's grandson?"

"He's playing truant again, I suppose. Oh lord, I hope that doesn't mean he's got himself into more hot water."

By this time Maggie had spotted the boy. He had been talking to the driver of the parked car, which now slowly moved away leaving him standing outlined against the green of the gorse bushes. He tossed something in the air, something that glinted a little, then pocketing it he began to descend the steps to the foreshore.

Alain stood quietly, half-turned away, until the boy had come around the side of a beached dinghy. Then he took a step forward.

"Danié!" he called.

Danié stopped short. For a moment he looked as if he might turn and run. But instead he approached rather reluctantly.

"Hello, Alain," he said.

"Hello, Danié. No school today?"

"N-no. I wasn't feeling well, so Mémé said I'd better have a day off."

"You're a long way from home if you're not feeling well, aren't you?"

"Oh . . . well . . . I feel all right now."

"Do you?" Alain said, glancing at his watch. "It isn't twelve o'clock yet. If you hurry home you could be in time for afternoon school."

"Yes . . . I'm just going in a minute."

"I'll get Céfi's brother to give you a lift back," Alain suggested. "He lives just up the road."

"No, thanks, I can walk up to the Rozel crossroads and catch a bus."

"Do you have money for the bus fare?"

Danié put his hand in the pocket of his jeans and took out a tenpenny piece. "I have money," he said proudly.

"Was that what the man in the car just gave you, Danié?"

The boy's head came up in an angry, defiant jerk. He was about fifteen years old and rather slight for his age, good-looking in a quiet, unemphatic way. His hair was cut very short compared with contemporary fashion. His checked shirt had been neatly patched at the elbows, his socks were hand-knitted.

"I didn't steal it, if that's what you mean!" he said. "The man asked me to show him the way to the Allée Couverte and I did; then he asked how to get to Saie Harbour and we came here and then he gave me ten-pence for my trouble."

"How did you come to be around when he needed help? L'Etacq is a long way from Saie Harbour, Danié."

"I don't have to explain everything to *you*," Danié said resentfully. "It's bad enough the way my father goes on at me!"

"He's sure to go on at you, as you put it, if you play truant from school and go darting about all over the countryside. Don't you think it'd be better to get back before there's any trouble?"

"I don't know what you mean. Mémé told me I could take the day off and get some fresh air. . . ."

"If Mémé told you to get some fresh air your father would expect you to help on the farm. Don't you think you'd better get a lift home in time for lunch?"

"Oh, mind your own business!" the boy shouted. He

turned and ran to the steps up to the cliff top. In a moment he was out of sight.

Alain, after a momentary impulse to chase him, watched him go. "That was a big mistake," he muttered. "I handled that very badly."

"Didn't you believe what he said about not feeling well?"

"Not a word of it. His mother wouldn't dare to keep him out of school unless he was really ill, and if she *had* said he could stay at home his father would have made sure he did some chores. No, he left home this morning as if he was off to school, but took off on his own. He's done it before, I'm sorry to say."

"Poor lad. It doesn't sound a very happy home life."

"You never said a truer word. It's a miserable home life." He stood hesitating, staring in the direction the boy had gone. "I wonder where he's off to."

"Shall we go and look for him?"

"Where? He's a boy who knows every path and track on the island. He'll have disappeared into the scenery."

"Perhaps you ought to phone his parents."

"That's the worst thing I could do. His father would probably put him on bread and water for a month, or lock him in the attic or something."

"As bad as that?"

"Oh, he's a tyrant. His views are a hundred years out of date."

"Could we contact his school then?"

"That would be a better move, but even so I don't think I will. He hasn't any friends, poor kid, unless you count me. If I inform against him, I prove I'm his enemy, at least from his point of view. So I think I'll just do nothing, the idea being that he'll have someone to turn to when he needs it."

They had, by common consent, given up the idea of walking on to the signal tower. Instead they took the path Danié had taken and emerged onto a pleasant little road with violets and primroses growing in the hedgerows. The going was much easier than the rocky, slippery foreshore, but they didn't move much faster because both of them were on the lookout for the boy.

"Mrs. Leduc mentioned something to me about Danié," Maggie ventured. "She said he'd been in some sort of trouble before?"

"Yes, when he was thirteen. It was a stupid business from start to finish. He's helped on his father's farm since he was small—most of the farmers' families do, and they get pocket money for doing it. But Danié's father doesn't believe in pocket money, so one day about three years ago the boy stole about sixty-three pence in small change from his father's jacket while it was hanging on the kitchen door. It was wrong, of course, but in some ways you might say the boy was entitled to it."

"And then he ran away from home? I believe that's what Mrs. Leduc said."

"No, that didn't happen till later. Danié took the money as a sort of protest, and intended to have a showdown over it. But Mr. Carras wasn't going to listen to any protests or arguments. He's simply not the type. He locked Danié in his room as punishment, and Danié climbed out during the night and vanished."

"Mrs. Merryn called you in to help?"

"No, no, I didn't know Mrs. Merryn at that time. I was working on Carras's *cotil*—that's his farm, his potato slope. I was aware there was trouble, but it wasn't my affair. One doesn't interfere in family matters. But then when Danié was missing Mrs. Carras came to me in floods of tears. Her husband had gone to the *connétable*—what the dickens is that in English? The village bobby. We don't have a uniformed police force outside St. Helier, you know—we have elected constables. Carras had reported that Danié stole some money and ran away."

"But he got the money back from Danié, surely?"

"No, the silly kid hid the money, all sixty-three pence of it. That's one of the reasons Ronald Carras locked him up—he wanted it back. Well, as a matter of fact, the constable was no fool. He knew a little about the family situation. He tried to talk sense to Carras. He called your housekeeper, Mrs. Merryn, to see if she could persuade Carras to be reasonable. But it was a bad move, because Carras has always blamed his mother-in-law for Danié's bad behavior. She's not a Jersey woman, nor is her daughter. Carras feels their 'foreign' ideas have undermined his authority. So when the constable brought Mrs. Merryn to the house, there was a great argument. And *that's* where I came in."

"What a situation! What did you do?"

"Oh, I told him what a disgrace it would be to accuse his own son, and so forth. He dropped the charges, but we still had to find Danié. Unfortunately it took us a week, and in that time he'd fallen in with a rather rowdy gang who hang around the amusement arcades in town. Carras refused to have the boy in the house. So we had another series of arguments. Just imagine how the kid must have felt, knowing that people outside his family were having to convince his own father into taking him back." Alain sighed. "Since then, naturally, he's been in and out of trouble. His father declares that it only goes to show he was right in the first place—the boy is a bad lot and it's all due to these wrong-headed women from the mainland who've spoiled him. From Danié's point of view, life gets worse all the time. He sees other boys having a lot of fun, doesn't see why he shouldn't have some."

"How right you were when you said it would be a mistake to contact his parents! He must feel he has no one to turn to. It's a dreadful situation."

"Don't let it distress you," Alain said gently. "It's not your affair."

"But it isn't yours either, yet you feel a lot of concern for Danié. What will happen if he has been playing truant?"

"Actually, not very much. He's due to leave school this summer, so the education authorities probably won't do anything. So long as his father doesn't hear of it, all may go well."

"What will Danié do? Get a job?"

"He'll help his father on the farm—what else?"

"Oh, good heavens!" Maggie said in dismay. "That's terrible!"

"Isn't it? But there's nothing to be done about it. It's traditional, and in a normal family it would be an excellent thing. From Danié's point of view it's a disaster."

Eventually they came out on the coast again, the long breakwater below them.

"Well, here we are. Where is this picnic basket?"

"In the car, on the parking area." She led the way, convinced that she'd lost her appetite after hearing about Danié, but by the time they had carried the basket to a quiet spot against the cliff and unpacked the food, she was ready to eat. There was cold duck, salad, French bread, cheese, and a flask of coffee.

Alain ate his share hungrily. Watching him, Maggie was struck by a thought. "Who does your cooking for you?" she inquired.

"You're joking," he replied. "I do. Out of tins, mainly."

"But that's all wrong! You should have proper meals."

He shrugged. "My view is the same as Socrates': Man eats to live, he does not live to eat. Not that I haven't enjoyed the picnic hamper," he added hastily. "Thank you for your hospitality."

"We must do it again some time," she suggested.

"Yes," he murmured. "Great idea. . . ."

His voice was drowsy. The sun had come out, shedding a relaxing warmth on their sheltered nook. The beat of the waves against the shore was soothing. He shrugged himself into a comfortable position, leaning back against the rock with his face upturned to the sun, and closed his eyes.

With amusement Maggie realized a few minutes later that he had actually gone to sleep.

Turned toward him, propped on an elbow, she studied him. He had taken off the piratical cap so that she could see the dried salt spray on his thick hair and even on the ridges of his eyebrows, glinting faintly silver, like the first gray hairs. What would happen to him when the real gray hairs began to appear? Who would look after him? She noticed that the roll-neck of his jersey was frayed at the edge, that he had a healed cut on his chin where some hook or sharp-edged tool had caught him.

The tanned skin stretched taut and firm over the broad cheekbones and the very determined chin, and there was not an ounce of superfluous flesh on him. It was absurd to think of him as ever being old and infirm—he was a superb physical specimen. Yet she couldn't help wondering what lay ahead for him. Even in sleep the wide mouth had its humorous curve; she could recall the alert intelligence of the bright blue eyes.

Would he really be satisfied to spend the rest of his life as a drifter? Would that sharp mind never long for more companionship than fishermen and farmers? She didn't underestimate the men among whom he had made friends; they were strong, sensible, steady men. But did they have his quickness, his perception? Did he never feel himself to be a falcon among sparrows, a dolphin among minnows?

She was still staring down at his face when she became aware a shadow had fallen between it and the sun. She looked up.

Sylvia Crayland was standing over them, but it was impossible to make out her expression, momentarily blinded as Maggie was by the sun. Sylvia's voice, though, betrayed a great deal when she spoke. In an effort perhaps to keep sharpness from it she drawled, "Very revealing. A very interesting cameo."

The words were heavy with anger and resentment.

CHAPTER FOUR

Alain awoke at once, stretching and yawning and remarking with amiability that it was nice to see Sylvia. She explained that she had come down to fetch a book from *Simestra*, which was moored in the bay. Alain offered to row her out to the big expensive cabin cruiser; Maggie thought it best to say that she would rather drive back to Le Grand Vergi to change for the evening, although she had no real plans.

As they parted she saw Alain turn impulsively toward her. She thought for a moment he was going to embarrass her with one of his mischievous embraces.

But he checked himself. An oddly serious expression washed over his features.

"No, I think not," he said, as if to himself. "*A bétot*, Maggie."

"*A bétot*, Alain."

It was still only midafternoon when she arrived back at the hotel. She decided to go for a swim in the heated swimming pool, but on her way through the staff quarters to fetch her swimsuit she ran into Richard Gale.

"So there you are! I tried to get hold of you this morning, but you'd already driven off."

"Yes, it's my day off," she reminded him.

"My dear, I know that! That's why I tried to get hold of you. I have this evening off. If you haven't any other plans, I wondered if you'd like to go out to dinner?"

"Oh . . . thank you, I'd like that. . . ."

"Somewhere different. We have some very fine restaurants within easy driving distance. It makes a nice change to get out and see what other people offer on the menu, doesn't it?"

Maggie couldn't help feeling that it was a little like comparison shopping, but all the same she was quite agreeable, having no definite plans for the evening.

"I'll look forward to it," she said.

"Seven o'clock?"

"That's fine."

She went on to the service elevator. As she left it on the attic floor, she saw Mrs. Merryn going down the passage with clean towels over her arm.

"Mrs. Merryn!"

The white-haired housekeeper turned and smiled as she saw Maggie. "I was just going to put fresh towels in your room. Didn't think you'd be back yet. It *is* your day off, isn't it?"

"Yes. I've just come in. I've had a lovely day so far."

"Really? What have you been up to?"

"I took a picnic lunch to St. Catherine's Bay, and who should sail past but Alain Hautger. So he came for a walk with me. To Saie Harbour."

"Oh yes, that's a lovely spot."

"We saw your grandson there."

"Danié?" Mrs. Merryn's face lit up, then just as suddenly it clouded. "What was he doing at Saie?"

"That's what Mr. Hautger asked him. He didn't get a very satisfactory reply."

"Oh dear," said Mrs. Merryn. "Oh, that silly boy! He just keeps bringing trouble on himself. Did Hautger say anything to him?"

"Tried to persuade him to go back in time for afternoon school, but he ran off. We kept an eye open for him, but we didn't see him again."

"The trouble is, Maggie, that the good weather's tempting to him to be out and about. He feels schooling is a waste of time because even if he was any good at it—which he isn't, particularly—his father intends to keep him as a farmhand."

"Doesn't he like farming?"

"I don't think he has anything against it. It's just that he's been forced to do it since he was a child—bunching daffodils, bagging potatoes, weeding, hoeing. . . . He sees it stretching ahead of him forever, without a chance to even try anything else."

"Would he like to? What kind of job would he like?"

"Oh, goodness knows. He's quite a bright boy, you know—not academic, but he's interested in a lot of things. I mean, he knows all about soccer and its rules, and he's keen on cars and can tell you all about mileage and gas consumption and things." She paused. "I suppose you just think I'm an adoring grandmother, but honestly there's a lot of good in Danié if he could only get a chance."

Maggie nodded sympathetically and stayed a moment or two longer, chatting. She had been visited by an idea. Perhaps there was a way to help Danié.

When she went for her swim she had the pool to herself, for though the number of guests at the hotel was increasing daily the weather was still not quite warm enough to tempt them into swimsuits. It was very satisfying to practise her crawl up and down the length a dozen times, and then to go upstairs and find that Mrs. Merryn had considerately ordered tea to be taken to her room.

As she sipped her tea she set her hair, did her nails, then settled down with a book for an hour. When the time came to get ready for the evening she was pleased with the way her dark brown hair seemed to have collected some lighter glints from exposure to sunlight, and brushed it into loose waves straight back from her brow. She noted some freckles on her forehead and on the bridge of her nose—well, there was nothing to be done about them, but perhaps she'd better get some suntan lotion to help a more even tanning.

She always felt her eyes were her best feature, so she spent some time accentuating the dark lashes and subtly applying eyeshadow to bring out the green flecks in the brown pupils.

That done, she considered her wardrobe. She was being taken to a *cordon bleu* restaurant, so it behooved her to dress well, but on the other hand she mustn't be too formal. She grinned a little to herself at this because in fact she owned only one really formal dress, a long beige silk gown with a Quaker collar and a yellow rose at the neck, which would have been quite inappropriate for this particular evening.

In the end she chose an ankle-length skirt of heavy cream crepe and a knitted silk sweater of very pale green. To this she added a long necklace of what looked like jade but was not, and a bracelet to match. She was rather pleased with the result—springlike and fresh, yet not without sophistication.

"I *say*!" Richard exclaimed as she met him in the hall. "You do look nice." He looked intently into her face. "I didn't realize you had greeny eyes."

"All done with mirrors," she laughed.

They headed out in Richard's car toward the west. The evening sky was a tender gray blue trimmed with the lace of silky cirrus clouds.

"Does that mean good weather?" she inquired, nodding at them.

"No idea, I'm afraid. Weather lore isn't my line. But it certainly looks promising."

"I'd have thought your training in hotel management would have included meteorology," she teased. "Guests are always asking, 'What's the weather going to be like?'"

"Quite true. And I always reply it's 'going to clear up' if it's dull, and 'going to last, I think,' if it's fine. In Switzerland, you know, the weather changed so quickly in the mountains that it was almost impossible to predict."

"Oh yes, you trained in Switzerland, didn't you?"

"In the Grisons. It was marvelous. I sometimes think I'd like to get a big hotel on the continent when it's time to move on from Grand Vergi."

"Sounds exciting. How long do you plan to stay in this job?"

"Oh, that depends. One has to find the right opening. Luck plays quite a part in it. It was luck, to some extent, that brought me to Jersey."

"In what way?"

"Sylvia put the idea into my head. I met her while she was in finishing school abroad, you know. I don't suppose I'd ever have thought of applying for a position here, but I'd done six months as assistant manager in Torquay and I wanted to get the next step up without too much of a timelag. When she mentioned that the manager of Le Grand Vergi was leaving, I applied."

"You've known Sylvia quite some time, then," Maggie said, selecting the item that intrigued her most.

"I suppose . . . about six years in all. She was learning how to play bridge and how to arrange flowers at a very expensive establishment in a castle! I'm sure she found it as dull as ditchwater, but they were allowed a lot of freedom—some of the 'pupils' were twenty years old. Seems

to me these rich families often send their daughters there
to keep them out of mischief until they can arrange the
right marriage for them."

"But Sylvia hasn't married."

"No . . . well, it doesn't apply to English girls so much.
Mind you, I don't think her father is exactly pleased with
her. There have been one or two semi-engagements with
very suitable chaps. But she always sort of drifts out of
range at the crucial point."

"Which means none of them was right for her."

"Presumably. Although she could have made a go of it
with any one of them, I feel sure."

"Oh, Richard!" Maggie turned her head to study the
calm, quiet face at her side. "Is that your view of marriage?"

He flicked a smiling glance at her but kept his attention on the road as he replied. "It's a more realistic view
than starry-eyed visions of undying love."

"But there *is* such a thing."

"As what?"

"Undying love."

"Rubbish! Are you trying to tell me that two people
who marry at twenty-four or twenty-five are going to feel
the same about each other at fifty?"

"Of course not. Love can change—should change—
and that's why it needn't die. It's like a plant, continually
renewing itself. Don't you remember what Stevenson
said?

> A love that life could never tire,
> Death quench or evil stir . . ."

"Stevenson?" Richard said. "The railroad inventor?"

"Robert Louis Stevenson. . . . Oh well, it doesn't
matter."

"I've heard of him. He wrote *Treasure Island* or something. Now that I come to think of it, the man who founded railroads spelled his name differently."

"Why are we talking about railroads?" Maggie inquired, on the verge of giggles.

"Search me! As I recall it we were trying to decide why Sylvia hasn't married when her father so clearly wants her to. He needs a grandson to leave all his money to."

"He has a lot, has he? I gathered that, but I'm not sure how he makes it."

"Oh, he's a property tycoon. In fact he owns Le Grand Vergi and quite a lot of other things here in Jersey. But most of his money comes from erecting big new office buildings. I believe a lot of the new development in Brussels—for the Common Market, you know—has his money behind it."

"Goodness, I'd no idea!"

"Oh yes, he's quite a V.I.P. And you can quite understand how he feels about Sylvia. He wants her married and settled down with some nice steady chap. He used to have ideas about some young duke or earl or something, but now I think he'd be glad if she'd choose even a minor accountant—anyone so long as it isn't Hautger."

"Ah," said Maggie.

"You'd guessed it, then?" Richard sighed. "Poor Sylvia. She can't get him out of her head."

"It's quite understandable, in a way. She knew him before he turned his back on the acquisitive society?"

"That's the point. He was really something, I can tell you. People were prophesying all sorts of great things for him. And she—Sylvia—was really only a school kid, no matter how expensive the school was. She really fell for him."

"And he?" Maggie asked, holding her breath a little.

"Hautger? Who knows? He took her out, they went sailing, played tennis—you know the sort of thing. Daddy was not pleased. At that time he still hoped for a bright young millionaire or something, and after all, what was Hautger? Just a talented provincial lawyer. Then, *kepow*!" Richard said expressively, jerking his head in emphasis. "Old Hautger dies, his partner is clapped in jail, his son closes up like an oyster, and Sylvia goes around as if the world is coming to an end. I believe Mr. Crayland got so worried about her that he offered to sort out all Hautger's financial problems for him, but no, that was too easy. Hautger had to do it the hard way."

"I think he felt it was a matter of honor," she murmured.

"No doubt. It was his affair. Only of course in a way it sort of put the relationship between him and Sylvia out of gear. I sometimes wonder now if she *is* in love with him, or only wants to get back to what used to be."

"Which is impossible."

"Oh, quite. He's not the man he used to be and never will be again. And she's not a romantic teenager any more. But oddly enough she can't let go. She keeps coming back, keeps seeking him out."

Maggie said slowly, "It's strange how much you seem to know about her. I suppose she talks to you a lot about things."

"Scarcely at all. But, as I say, I've known her a while and I'm rather fond of her. To be candid—" He broke off.

"What?"

"Nothing."

"What were you going to say? About Sylvia?"

"About myself, really. There was a time when I rather

458

hoped. . . . But nothing came of it, and really, when you come to think of it, she's perhaps not the ideal wife for a hotel manager."

"I suppose not," she agreed. "She'd find it a bit restricting!"

"It's not an easy life. A woman would have to be tolerant of the fact that her husband is more or less on call all the time. In fact, it really needs someone who's had previous experience of the life."

"Yes, that's probably true," Maggie agreed. She had come to the conclusion, from hearing him talk, that though he wasn't without sensitivity he saw most things, including love and marriage, as part of a useful pattern—rather like a carefully woven tapestry, not at all like a glorious jigsaw.

She found him interesting. He had an elegance of clothes and manner that she felt sure was acquired, but no less attractive for that. He was what used to be called a self-made man, and she guessed his calm gray eyes were fixed on the top, but he wasn't ruthless or totally self-centered.

They had reached the west coast of the island, where the sea was tinted a silvery rose by the last rays of the sun beyond St. Ouen's Bay. There was a soft twilight haze over the land, through which the lights from the houses and hotels shone like sequins along the great sweep of the shore. Across the dunes winked the signals of the airport.

Richard took the turnoff for L'Etacq, a little to the north, and quite soon drew up on the roadside where a little paved path nosed between hedges of early-flowering escallonia, lit overhead with chains of colored lights.

"We can't drive up to the door," Richard explained. "We have to go over a little footbridge."

Sure enough, a moment later they came to a little

humpbacked stone bridge over a chuckling stream. Just beyond Maggie saw a rustic arch with the name "Le Ruisseau" framed in laurel branches. Tables were set out along the bank of the stream with candles in protective glasses of dark red or green, glimmering like glow-worms, upon the checked cloths.

Richard glanced at her. "It's still a little too cool out of doors for you without a wrap," he remarked. "So let's sit in the patio."

This proved to be a paved courtyard protected by a glass roof and screens. A wood-burning stove of Dutch tiles sent out a steady, comforting warmth. The portly headwaiter hurried forward. Richard was clearly well known here. A table was awaiting them with a view of the sloping hillside and the sea, now starlit, beyond.

Richard ordered sherry, then gave grave attention to the menu while the waiter hovered. A whispered word imparted the fact that a special seafood was available. "Have you ever had ormer?" he inquired, and when she shook her head gave the order.

Ormer proved to be a shellfish of excellent flavor, served with a tangy sauce. Then followed a rich peasant casserole of beans with pork and herbs, washed down with cider from Brittany. When the trolley with its opulent display of creamy desserts was rolled up to the table, Maggie could only shake her head regretfully and opt for black coffee.

"I've never had to worry about my weight before, but I can see I'll have to start soon," she observed. "The food is *so* enticing."

"You'll soon be working too hard to have time to eat," Richard warned her. "You know we'll have an almost full hotel next weekend, and though most people will go back the day after Easter Monday, some will stay on. From now until September life grows more hectic all the time."

"You're hiring extra staff right now, aren't you?" She knew this was so because she had seen applicants coming and going.

"Yes, for the season."

"What about bellhops?"

"I've only got one so far. Could do with another, but lads don't seem to fancy it much these days."

"What would you think about taking on Danié Carras?"

Richard paused in the act of lighting a panatella. "Mrs. Merryn's grandson?" he replied in surprise. "There's not a chance."

"Why not?"

"A bit of a problem kid, isn't he?"

"Do you know him?"

"I've seen him around. He sometimes comes to visit Mrs. M. on her day off, or to meet her to go to the zoo or somewhere."

"What did you think of him?"

"I don't know that I thought anything of him," he replied, applying a match to the end of his slim cigar. "He's just a relative of Mrs. Merryn's, that's all."

"He's quite nice-looking, wouldn't you say? Small pale face, straight short hair, rather slightly built—don't you think he'd look well in a bellhop's uniform?"

"Looks aren't everything, Maggie. He's been in trouble with the police, hasn't he?"

"Not really. It was more of a family dispute, from what Alain told me."

"Ah?" Richard gave a little frown, then summoned the waiter to order a Drambuie. "Will you join me? No? Just one, then, please."

He made no attempt to resume the conversation.

Maggie sensed he was not pleased when she returned to it.

"Would you consider Danié?"

"No, I don't think so. You speak of his problems as being only a family thing, but that was only at first, when Hautger talked the father out of being an idiot. Since then he's been mixed up with a noisy bunch who got thrown out of the café at Fort Regent one evening around Christmas, and someone at the yacht club told me there was something-or-other last summer—he broke in to sleep there or something."

He looked at Maggie, and as she said nothing, went on, "You didn't know that? Hautger should have told you."

"He did say he'd been in and out of trouble."

"I bet there's a lot more we don't know about. If Hautger expects me to hire a kid like that—"

"Oh, it has nothing to do with him," she broke in hastily. "I thought of the idea this afternoon when I was talking to Mrs. Merryn. She was saying, you see, that Danié leaves school in summer, but he'll have to go to work for his father, and honestly it sounds like a rotten idea."

"I agree with you there. The hotel has bought produce from Carras, and although he's a good market gardener, he's a very difficult man."

"Poor Mrs. Merryn. How did her daughter ever come to marry a man like that?"

Richard grinned. "In a romantic haze, full of undying love," he said. "Carras is a good-looking bloke—he was probably irresistible twenty years ago. You see what a mistake it can be?"

She gave him a rueful nod. "*Touché!* Still, just because the mother was romantically misled, that's no reason to punish the son."

"Punish him? *I'm* not punishing him."

"Society is. It's leaving him to battle alone with a problem too big for him."

"Look, Maggie, there are organizations and welfare departments to deal with things like that."

"They're not having much success, are they?"

"Perhaps not. Yet you're suggesting *I* should take Danié on."

"Well, it might be the making of him. If he had a job in pleasant surroundings, had a chance to see life away from the farm and with a little money in his pocket . . . ."

Richard sipped his liqueur, looking dubious.

"Think about it, Richard. What you've said about Danié—going around with rowdies, breaking into a club to find a place to sleep—isn't it just his way of getting away from his father?"

"Mm . . . perhaps."

"Alain doesn't think badly of him."

"If you want my opinion, Alain is kidding himself. He rather enjoyed coming to the rescue of Danié. It was a chance to play the advocate again, to use his legal knowledge. You saw how neatly he handled my disagreement with the electricians—he can say what he likes about wanting the simple life, but he still has a lawyer's instincts and enjoys the chance to employ them. And *that's* why he takes an interest in Danié."

"But do you think he'd waste time on a boy he considered a bad lot?"

"We-ell . . . no."

"Do you think he's a good judge of character?"

"Yes, he is."

"There you are then!" she cried. "He thinks Danié is worth bothering about."

Richard allowed himself a little laugh. "You are a very

persuasive woman! All right. If Danié wants to apply for the job, I'll take a look at him."

Maggie felt a thrill of pleasure. She would tell Mrs. Merryn, and then probably Mrs. Merryn would tell Alain what she'd done, and Alain would be pleased. . . .

She shook herself. Really, what possible difference did it make what Alain thought? She wasn't doing this to please Alain; she was doing it to help Danié.

Luckily at this point a distraction arrived in the shape of a woman with a guitar, who sang French folksongs for about an hour. At about nine-thirty it began to grow chilly even on the heated patio, so they went inside. There was dancing on a little floor at the far side of the restaurant, so they danced to the gentle strains of "Edelweiss" and "How Are Things in Gloccamorra?"

She remarked that it was much more relaxed than the usual London clubs.

"Oh, there are some way-out places in St. Helier, if you'd like to go on to one of them."

"No, thank you. I left London to get away from things like that!"

"Did you? I did rather wonder. You remember when we spoke on the telephone while you were still in London? You sounded quite eager to take Viv's place."

"I was. I had a particular reason."

"What was that?"

"It wasn't a what, it was a who. A man by the name of Ward Pelham."

"Pelham? Pelham? Seems to me I know the name. I believe he's an acquaintance of Sylvia's."

Maggie raised her eyebrows. "That could be. He has money—inherited money, I'm sure, because he never seems to do a stroke of work."

"You sound rather critical of him."

"Do I? Maybe I'm being unjust. It was simply that he always seemed to be lying in wait for me around every corner. Quite a nice man, I daresay," she added without conviction, "but not my type."

"So you decided to come here for a change. Well, I'm glad. You're a great asset to the hotel, Maggie. And besides," he added, drawing her against him so that they were dancing cheek to cheek, "you fit rather nicely into my arms."

Maggie wrote this off as just a lighthearted quip without deeper meaning. But, as it happened, she was wrong.

CHAPTER FIVE

Carried away by her own enthusiasm in her plan to help Danié, it hadn't occurred to her that there could be a hitch. But Easter, with all its bustling influx of visitors, had come and gone, and still the boy hadn't applied for the job at the hotel.

He had another term to complete at school, of course. But on an island where the two chief industries—agriculture and tourism—are seasonal, school authorities are prepared to stretch a point, and Maggie was sure Danié could have asked for time off to share the bellhop duties with Ted Revans, the boy already on the staff.

In the end she mentioned his nonappearance to Mrs. Merryn. "It's my son-in-law," the housekeeper confessed, sighing. "He says he wants Danié on the *cotils*, and that's that."

"And what does Danié say?"

"Oh, the boy would love the chance of an outside job, but what can he do? He's a minor. He has to obey his father."

"What a shame! The trouble is that if Danié doesn't put in an appearance soon, Richard may hire someone else, although I don't believe he's had many applicants for the job."

"No, youngsters these days don't fancy getting themselves buttoned into a funny little jacket and pillbox hat. In my day they'd have been glad of the chance."

The livery of the hotel was gray blue with brick-red piping and brass buttons. The doorman had a sort of tailcoat and a matching top hat. The bellhops wore monkey jackets frogged with brick-red cord and brick-red pillboxes. Ted Revans had bright red hair that clashed horribly with his hat; for this reason he kept "forgetting" or "mislaying" it. He was a nice lad, but more interested in listening to pop music on his transistor than in running errands.

For this reason it was becoming urgent to Richard to hire another boy. Maggie knew that time was running out for Danié. That being so, she decided to get in touch with Alain. She remembered he had told Sylvia to leave a message for him at the office of the Jersey Fishermen's Union, and that though he had chosen to ignore it, it had reached him. So, greatly daring, she called the J.F.U. office. She was told that Alain Hautger worked on a boat called *Heron* that moored at Gorey, and that she would be better advised to ring Gorey Pier.

This she did. There was a long delay before the phone was answered. A gruff voice said, "Gorey quayside."

"Could I leave a message for Alain Hautger, please?"

"Who?"

"Alain Hautger. H-a-u—"

"I know how to spell it, my dear. I only want to know why you should leave a message when his boat's tied up alongside this minute, unloading."

"It is? Could I . . . do you think I could speak to him?"

"Don't see why not." The phone was put down, then the speaker bellowed, loud enough to be heard in Cherbourg, "*Hé*, Alain! Alain, *oyez*! A gorgeous young lady wants to talk to you!"

Much more faintly she heard Alain reply, "Tell her I'm busy."

"Don't be silly, Alain! You're missing a great opportunity!"

When Alain spoke again it was in Jersiais. There was a short conversation she couldn't follow, then the first man said regretfully, "I'm sorry, miss, he's a bit involved at the moment. I'd better take that message after all."

"Would you tell him Miss Jefferson would like to speak to him? I'll be at the hotel until seven o'clock."

Five minutes later Grace, on the hotel switchboard, reported, "Call for you, Maggie. The white phone."

She picked it up. "Miss Jefferson speaking."

"Maggie? Alain here. I didn't realize it was you before. I thought it was— Well, never mind. Is anything wrong?"

"No, no, I'd just like to talk to you about something. Could we meet?"

"That would be a pleasure. When?"

"Fairly soon?"

"How about this evening?"

"That would be great. Where?"

"Let me treat you to dinner. Can you come to—"

"Oh, no, Alain, I didn't mean that. I wouldn't dream of—"

"My dear little Maggie Jefferson, I'm not completely penniless. I can afford to buy you a meal. Nothing on the scale of Le Ruisseau, of course, but—"

"How did you know about *that*?"

"My spies are everywhere. So long as you don't expect anything in that category, I'll buy you a meal."

"Then, thank you, I'd love to. Where shall we meet?"

"Can you come to Gorey? I have to go out with Céfi at high tide or soon after, that's to say about nine o'clock."

"Fine. I can be there soon after seven."

"Meet you by the pier, then."

"How shall I find it?"

"You can't really miss it. The village street goes straight down to it. I'll be there."

"Okay."

Strange to say, Maggie had almost as much trouble

deciding what to wear for this occasion as for her *cordon bleu* dinner with Richard. She wanted to look nice, yet she didn't want to look overdressed in company with *le pirate*. But she hadn't time to linger over the choice, for she only came off duty at six and had to bathe, put on makeup, change and drive about ten miles to Gorey.

The final verdict was in favor of a dress that had always pleased her, a shirtwaister in glazed claret-colored cotton sprigged with white daisies. She slipped a purse and a comb in a white canvas shoulder bag, put on white shoes and took them off again in exchange for dark red suede walkers, making up her mind that that would have to do. If Alain was looking particularly piratical she might end up wishing she'd worn pants and a sweater!

What was her astonishment then, on nosing the borrowed Mini around the end of Gorey's main street onto the quay, to find a tall figure in a neat dark suit awaiting her by the bus shelter. He came forward to help her out after she'd parked.

"There's a little restaurant along toward the pottery—not much to look at but the food is good. Do you mind walking? It isn't far."

"Of course not."

They turned their backs on Mont Orgueil Castle perched on its great conical rock, the tops of the turrets glinting in the slanting sun. The sea was a dark blue, whipped into little tippets of white by a strong southerly wind.

"I'm sorry if it was inconvenient to phone you this afternoon," she began diffidently, a little shy of this stranger in the white shirt and sober suit.

"It wasn't a bit inconvenient. I'd have come to the phone at once if I'd known it was you. I must admit I've been very puzzled over what you want to talk about."

"It's Danié," she said.

"Danié? What on earth has he been up to now?"

"Nothing. Nothing, I assure you," she insisted as she saw his worried frown. She went on to explain the possibility of a job for the boy and Mr. Carras's objection.

"I see. Well, you could pretty well have prophesied what his reaction would be. He's not in favor of anything different from what he's used to."

"I wondered if you could speak to him."

"Hmm." He looked doubtful. "I've never interfered before. Until now, I've only appeared on the scene when Danié was in some sort of trouble. I've never taken the initiative."

"Why not, exactly?"

"Because, after all, Ronald Carras is the head of his family, and that still means something on this island."

"But you yourself told me that Mr. Carras is a tyrant."

"Then I was uttering slander and it was very wrong of me."

Maggie wasn't sure whether he was being ironic or not. His reaction perplexed her. She had thought he would agree immediately to intercede on Danié's behalf.

They took a little turning to the right and confronted a little village house whose ground floor had been turned into a café. It was a simple place, with only a few tables and a short menu of seafood dishes.

"It's all locally caught," Alain said. "I recommend the John Dory, which they serve in a casserole."

"I don't even know what it is," Maggie confessed.

"It's a thin-bodied fish with very meaty flesh. I think you'll like it."

"I'm sure I will if you think it's good."

"We'll start with grapefruit, if you agree. That's two grapefruit and two John Dory, Amy."

The waitress, who was clearly also the proprietor, nodded agreement and disappeared behind the scenes.

"If bream had been on the menu I'd have recommended you to have that. It's very good, sea bream."

Maggie hadn't come to discuss food, she'd come to get Alain's help for Danié.

"Can you think of anything that would persuade Mr. Carras to let Danié take this job?" she said.

His dark brows drew together. "Has Danié actually been offered this job?" he countered.

She hesitated. "Well, no. . . ."

"Then why are we talking about it?"

"Well, he's practically sure to be taken on. Richard needs another bellhop, and so far he hasn't found anyone suitable."

"What makes you so sure Danié will be suitable?"

"Don't you think he would?" she asked in surprise.

"I've no idea. What would he have to do?"

"Oh, run errands. Walk dogs for the guests. Help the waiters take drinks and sandwiches out to the poolside. That sort of thing."

"Would he have to run errands involving money?"

"I . . . suppose so. If one of the guests asked him to fetch something from a shop."

"Then it isn't necessarily an ideal job for him. He's been in trouble over money."

"But you explained that. He took it as a protest."

"That's my theory. There's no proof. He may have taken it just because he wanted it."

"Alain!"

"It's a possibility."

The waitress came with fresh grapefruit sparsely sprinkled with brown sugar and cinnamon. "Be quick," she admonished. "I'm taking the casserole out of the oven now."

"We'd better do as we're told," Alain said with a smile.

They spooned up the sharp fruit in silence. Amy swooped to take the dishes away, and a moment later a brown earthenware casserole, billowing steam, was set between them. Grilled tomatoes on a flat fireproof dish accompanied it. Maggie served it on to the thick pottery plates, and they began to eat.

"You don't really think Danié would be untrustworthy?" she demanded.

"There's no way of knowing. He's had a couple of very unhappy years and they've probably left their mark on him."

"You're being very disheartening about this, Alain. I thought you'd be all in favor."

"Then you shouldn't jump to conclusions, should you?"

"What's the matter with you?" she said, laying down her knife and fork. "Why are you taking this attitude?"

"What attitude? You've put a proposition to me—that I should talk to Danié's father and persuade him to let the boy take the job. I'm simply examining the notion. So far I've established that Danié isn't by any means bound to get the job even if his father lets him apply for it. I've also put on record that Danié isn't automatically suited to the job even if he gets it. The next thing I'd like to know is who will take the responsibility if Carras sticks to his refusal and Danié, out of frustration or resentment, does something really foolish?"

"But Carras can be persuaded. You can persuade him."

"I've yet to be convinced that it's right to persuade him."

"I can't even imagine why you need to be convinced! I'd say it was self-evident. You want Danié to get the job, don't you?"

"I'm not sure."

"Not sure?" Maggie echoed, her voice rising. "But I thought we agreed it would be good for Danié to get away from the farm. You said that to have to work with his father would be a disaster."

"That's quite true. But I'm far from happy about his taking a job at Le Grand Vergi."

"What's wrong with it? It's a beautiful place."

"But rather artificial, wouldn't you say? The clientele are very well off on the whole. The boy would see people enjoying a standard of living he can never hope to attain. Is that necessarily going to do him good?"

"Now you're being absurd."

"It's kind of you to say so, but I must insist on holding by my opinion. I know Danié and his father quite well. I've worked alongside them on the *cotils*. I'm very doubtful whether a job in a luxury hotel is the best thing for a lad of his temperament."

"His own grandmother surely knows him at least as well as you do! And she's delighted with the idea."

"That may possibly be because it would give her the chance to see more of her grandson, because he'd be in the same building with her. She doesn't see as much of him as she'd like, since she knows she's not welcome at his home."

"There you are! Surely it's better to get him away, at least for a time, from a home like that?"

Alain gave her a level glance. "My efforts have always been directed toward helping Danié to fit into his home, not to get him out of it."

She pushed away her plate and stood up. "This is impossible," she said. "I see no point in going on with this conversation."

"Sit down, Maggie."

"No, thank you, I don't think we should detain each other any longer."

She hurried out. For a moment she was at a loss as to which direction to take, but there were lights shining from the windows and she was able to see the roadway. She glanced back. The café proprietor had hurried forward to speak to Alain, so that he was momentarily detained. Anxious to reach her car and be off before he could catch up with her, she broke into a run.

It wasn't far to the parking area in the center of the V-shaped bay, but there were strollers out taking the evening air, perhaps working up an appetite for an epicure dinner at the famous hotel by the harbor wall. She had to slow her step to avoid bumping into people and attracting attention.

To her own consternation, tears were spilling from her eyes. What on earth was the matter with her?

Certainly it was disappointing that Alain didn't want to help over Danié. But after all, what was Danié to her? She'd met him only once, for a few minutes. If you looked at the matter in the cold light of reason, she had no right to interfere.

Was that why Alain had been so displeased? Did he see her as meddling, interfering?

The thought brought the tears rolling down her cheeks. She reached the Mini at last. Leaning against its roof, gasping for breath and stifling sobs, she searched in her purse for a tissue to mop her eyes.

"Maggie! Is something wrong?"

Maggie instinctively turned away even before she recognized the voice. It was Sylvia, climbing out of a handsome Maserati parked a little behind the Mini. Finding no tissue, Maggie rubbed at her eyes with the heels of her hands, and hoped that the overhead lamps wouldn't give away too much.

"Are you hurt?" Sylvia said. 'Have you had an accident?"

"No, I'm all right. It's nothing serious."

"But as I drove up you looked quite. . . ."

"I stubbed my toe," Maggie lied. "You know how that hurts sometimes."

"Let me look. Perhaps you've made it bleed."

"No, no, it's nothing." To change the subject she added, "What are you doing here?"

"I live near here. At Rozel Bay. I often drive to Gorey for dinner or to meet friends. What are *you* doing here?"

"Oh . . . it's my evening off. I like to try new places, get away from the hotel."

"On your own?" Sylvia queried in a surprised tone.

"Why not?" Maggie returned, rather than explain or tell another direct lie.

There was an awkward pause. She could see various impulses fighting in Sylvia. Common politeness demanded that she should invite Maggie for at least a drink, but quite clearly Sylvia didn't want to.

"I'd better get back, I think," Maggie murmured.

"But you said it was your evening off. Surely you don't want to go back to the hotel, yet?"

"I meant . . . back to St. Helier. I'll just be in time for the main feature at the cinema."

"I see. Well, I hope you enjoy—" Suddenly Sylvia broke off, looking beyond Maggie's shoulder.

Maggie turned. Alain was walking slowly toward them, an unmistakable figure even in the weak lights along the pier road.

At her side she sensed Sylvia taking in all the clues—Alain wearing a suit and a tie, arriving at just the moment when Maggie was talking of going to the cinema in St. Helier, Maggie in a pretty-enough dress for such an evening. And Maggie waiting by her car in tears. . . . Why? Because she thought Alain was not going to turn up?

Maggie tried to pull herself together, but before she could speak Sylvia said in silky tones, "Good evening, Alain. Going somewhere?"

"Good evening," he replied. "Quite a pleasant evening, isn't it? The wind's dropping."

"I rather hoped I might find you on the *Heron*," Sylvia said. "I tried to get a message to you this morning but was told the boat would be in later, landing catch."

"We've been very busy," Alain said. "A lobster in every pot, and a list of buyers for every one of them, of course. We're going out again later."

"Tonight?" Sylvia said in disbelief, her eyes traveling over his conservative attire.

"Yes, about nine."

"In that case you have time to come and have a drink with me in the Moorings."

"I think perhaps I'd better get aboard and get changed out of my Sunday-go-to-meeting clothes, thanks."

"Oh, surely that would take you only a minute. Do come, Alain. It's so seldom that I see you looking like a respectable member of society, I feel we ought to celebrate."

Maggie could see that this was something Alain would have avoided if he could, but like herself he sensed Sylvia's anger and wanted to allay it. He nodded. "Okay then. Why not? Perhaps Maggie will join us."

"Oh, I—"

"Maggie's going to the cinema in St. Helier."

"Which one?"

"The . . . the Odeon," Maggie said, mentioning the only one she'd been in so far.

"You won't get in," he remarked. "It's a charity performance tonight, with all the tickets sold beforehand." He turned to Sylvia. "I'm surprised you're not there."

"Oh, I bought tickets—six, actually. If I'd known Maggie wanted to go she could have had one. In fact, if she just mentions my name at the box office—"

"Maggie isn't dressed for one of Jersey's gala performances," Alain interrupted, taking Maggie gently by the arm. "We'll just give her a drink as a consolation prize. Come along."

She knew that this was his way of saying he was sorry. She'd felt his shrewd eyes on her face, knew that he'd seen the traces of tears.

Yet as she allowed herself to be escorted into the pretty little hotel she was asking herself a question: how sorry was he? He certainly hadn't hurried after her. In fact, if Sylvia hadn't delayed her, she would have driven away by the time he reached the pier.

He hadn't really wanted to catch up with her. But having noticed the tearstains he felt impelled to make some small gesture of apology . . . and perhaps also use the chance of not being tête-à-tête with Sylvia.

Maggie had no doubt that he tried to steer clear of Sylvia; all the evidence pointed that way. Was it because he knew it could lead nowhere, this attraction between them? "I wouldn't dream of asking any woman I cared about to give up everything for the sake of being Mr. Alain Hautger." Those had been his words. Truly, Sylvia would have to give up an enormous amount. Since the scandal and the financial crash that had wrecked Alain's life, he had become almost penniless: she could imagine how he would draw back from the idea of being in any way dependent on Sylvia.

Was *that* why he had opted out completely? Was it the hopelessness of loving and being loved by Sylvia that had driven him to his flamboyant nonconformity?

These thoughts flicked through Maggie's mind as she took her seat in the comfortable lounge bar. Mindful of the fact that she had to drive back, she opted for a pineapple juice. Alain ordered a lager, Sylvia chose Campari.

"It looks as if you're all dressed up and nowhere to go, Alain," Sylvia said.

"I like to put on my one and only suit from time to time, just to make sure it still fits me. One needs it, you know, for other people's weddings and funerals. What are you doing for the rest of the evening, Sylvia? Are you dining here?"

"I haven't any plans. I thought I'd wait and see what you were doing."

"Well, now you know. I'm giving my suit an airing and then I'm going out to lay creels, when the tide's right."

"About nine, you said? I'll stay and wave you off."

"Do," Alain said comfortably.

Sylvia was puzzled, no doubt of that. She had been certain she'd stumbled upon some sort of secret arrangement between the two of them, but all her probing seemed to uncover only the fact that Alain was certainly going out with the lobster boat at high tide.

She sipped her drink and then said, "Don't you usually come ashore about this time of the year and find some farm work?"

"If I feel like it. Once the bays fill up with holiday sailors, fishing is neither so easy nor so profitable, so working on the land has more appeal. But I haven't done anything about it so far."

"Mr. Carras at L'Etacq usually takes you on, doesn't he?"

At hearing the name, Maggie couldn't help a sharp intake of breath. Alain glanced at her. "Mr. Carras usually has quite a few temporary helpers, mostly Breton. By this time he's probably hired all he needs. He'll be expecting Danié to do a bigger share of the work this year, I imagine."

"I can never understand why anyone would choose to do it," Sylvia said with irritation. "Planting outdoor tomatoes by hand must be back-breaking work."

"It's no fun, that's for sure."

"Then why do it? You could find something better, Alain!"

He smiled. "Better for what? Once the plants are in there's a break—it gives a man a chance to go walking, to lie in the sun and think."

"About what, for heaven's sake? What do you think about?"

"Oh, about people, and whether they should try to run other people's lives."

Maggie saw Sylvia color slightly, but she wondered if the barb wasn't intended for herself. *She* had been trying to run Danié's life for him.

While Sylvia was still frowning at the table, Maggie said, "No doubt people shouldn't, but where they feel concern or interest they always will. It's a very human trait."

"That's right," Sylvia agreed promptly, and then stopped, surprised to find herself allying herself with Maggie. After a fractional pause she continued, "You always seem to think, Alain, that because you've chosen a particular path everyone else must stand back and let you tread it. But suppose they feel the path is heading to eventual disaster?"

"That's rather underestimating my intelligence, isn't it? To imply that everyone else can see something I can't?"

"Look, if you're going to talk about intelligence. . . . You've got too many brains to be a dropout forever. You ought to be contributing to society."

"But I am. I'm helping to produce high-quality food. You're not going to say society could manage without food?" He grinned as he picked up the slender glass of lager. "Clients at this hotel, for instance—they'd soon stop coming if the menu deteriorated, Sylvia."

"Didn't you say the other day," Maggie intervened, "that man doesn't live to eat, he eats to live? Food is important, but it isn't the only thing, and you know that as well as I do."

"Besides, any cloth-headed fool with a strong back could tend tomatoes or set out lobster pots. You should be doing something better."

"Who's to say it's 'better' to help a quarrelsome man win a court case than to catch a good haul of fish?"

"It's 'better' to help a boy in trouble," Maggie said quietly, "than to catch the biggest John Dory in the Channel."

Sylvia didn't catch the nuances of this remark, but she obviously sensed that it had had importance, for after a few more minutes of talk on her part, to which Alain made no response, she fell silent.

Glancing at his watch, Alain finished his drink. "I've got to get into my working clothes," he said. "Excuse me."

"But, Alain," Maggie cried, suddenly remembering, "you haven't really had anything to eat! You can't put out with nothing inside you."

"Not to worry. Céfi's wife will have supplied him with

all sorts of goodies. Good night, ladies. No, don't come out—it's probably rather cool outside by now." He made as if to step past the low table that held their glasses, then paused, looking down at Maggie. "I'll think about what you said," he added. "Anything you feel so strongly about deserves some thought."

With that he was gone.

Sylvia gave Maggie a perplexed, half-angry look, then summoned the waiter to order another drink. "Would you explain to me," she demanded, "why Alain should be prepared to listen to the views of someone he's only known a few weeks, whereas he just shrugs off my opinion?"

Maggie sighed. "It's nothing to do with Alain and his career."

"But he said he'd think over what you said. You were talking about how you—and I—feel concerned about him."

"No, I wasn't. It was about another person."

"Who?"

"I don't believe I ought to discuss it. Alain's made me realize that there's more involved than I thought."

"It's something you and Alain are involved in together?"

"I was trying to involve Alain. Maybe I was wrong."

"It can't be wrong if it's something to shake him out of this silly idea that making money and a place for yourself in society is foolish."

"It's nothing like that. I wouldn't dream of trying to change his opinions. In fact I think it would be wrong to try."

"How can it be wrong?" Sylvia cried. "He's throwing his life away, and he must be made to see it."

"But he's happy," Maggie pointed out.

"That's all right for him," muttered Sylvia, coloring, "but *I'm* not."

Maggie waited a moment before replying. "I think Alain would say that that's your affair, not his."

"But my happiness depends on him!" The other woman caught herself up, ashamed of having given so much away. Her soft pale lips came together in a thin line. She said in a clipped tone, "You seem to think you understand him pretty well."

"Not a bit, I assure you. He's a complete puzzle to me. But one thing I do know. It's useless to try to change him, even if you imagine you're doing it for his own good. A man like Alain can't be maneuvered, can't be trapped."

"Trapped? Are you suggesting I—"

"No, no," Maggie protested, horrified. "I meant that he sees society and its boring conventions as a trap."

She had a feeling Sylvia didn't believe her explanation. The girl was probably only too well aware that Alain dodged her, pretended not to receive her messages. She was trying to think of something to add that would take away any hurt from her ill-judged phrase when Sylvia went off on a different track.

"How on earth did you know Alain hadn't had dinner?"

"Because we didn't finish—" Maggie broke off in dismay. She made a gulping recovery. "We didn't finish our drinks in time to order a sandwich or anything for him."

"But after all it's—" she glanced at a chunky bracelet-watch on her slender wrist "—almost a quarter to nine now. He could have eaten much earlier."

"Is it really so late?" Maggie said, seizing the excuse. "I think I'll push off home."

"It seems pretty early to me. One would think you'd

come here on purpose to meet Alain, since you're leaving the moment he does."

"Appearances can be deceptive," Maggie replied vaguely.

"How right you are. I think it would be a great mistake, for instance, to write you off as a bright pretty nobody at the hotel reception desk."

Maggie might have replied that she could have catalogued Sylvia as a rich spoiled nobody but knew that would be very bad policy. Sylvia *was* rich, the daughter of a rich father who owned, among other things, the hotel in which Maggie worked. She might quite easily find herself packing her bags if she made an enemy of Sylvia, and though she could easily find another job, she didn't want to leave Jersey.

She didn't stop to analyze why she didn't want to leave the island.

She rose and said good night. As she walked the few yards to the car, she could hear the voices of the men on the boats making ready to put out, the creak of ropes, the throbbing of a motor. She didn't go up to the old red granite wall of the quay to watch, but when she had driven about a hundred years along the pier road she felt compelled to stop.

She got out of the Mini. Leaning against it, the night wind pulling at her hair so that she had to put up a hand to smooth it, she saw a quartet of boats leave the harbor. She watched their lights rise and fall on the waves until they were mere pinpricks in the darkness.

When they had gone, her attention was caught by a movement near the harbor. A pale figure, almost ghostlike in the night—Sylvia in her long dress of rose-pink crepe. Although the outline was indistinct she nevertheless knew that the other girl had turned from watching the lobster boats go out and was now watching Maggie.

Flustered, she climbed back into the little car and drove off. There was no reason why it should matter that Sylvia had seen her. "A cat may look at a king," she told herself, "so Maggie may look at a fishing boat."

Yet oddly enough it didn't seem quite a joking matter.

CHAPTER SIX

After such a mixed beginning, Maggie's evening off ended rather pleasantly. Mrs. Merryn had some of the off-duty staff in the housekeeper's parlor for coffee and to listen to records. The small gathering didn't break up until after midnight. Maggie was up and about at seven, to greet a wonderful morning.

Since she didn't have to be on duty till ten she decided to skip breakfast and go out for a walk. She took with her a newly purchased book about wild birds, which she had acquired to help her learn to recognize them. She hadn't forgotten that she had thought she was looking at an ordinary seagull on St. Catherine's lighthouse when all the time it was a Sandwich tern—which her book said was a summer visitor.

Not that she would see a tern on the hotel grounds. This was a haunt of small birds, which so far she couldn't identify except for blackbird, thrush, sparrow and pigeon. They flitted in and out among the flowers, a paradise of color and fragrance, full of tamarisk, japonica, buddleia, and mimosa as background to the flower border of iris and scilla and early lilies—lilies out in full bloom although it was only a week or two after Easter. The whole island was like this, a bower of blossoms, with daffodils growing wild in the hedges and glints of bluebells in every copse.

Maggie wandered down the paths, catching glimpses of fluttering wings and hearing fluted songs that were impossible to identify. She saw a robin—then overhead a regular soft cooing drew her attention. Looking up, she caught sight of a pale gray bird perched on the bough of a beech tree.

"Now that's a dove," she said aloud, thumbing through her book to find it.

The book, however, remained obstinately mute about the bird she had seen. Wood pigeon, yes. Turtle dove, yes—but it wasn't a turtle dove because it had no pink or brown in its plumage. Was it rare? She felt something of the thrill of a big-game hunter on the trail of an elephant.

The bird took off with a flaunting of white tail feathers. It circled, then flew to the edge of the grounds, where it perched on an acacia tree. Maggie followed, wishing she had binoculars to get a good look at it and a pencil to note its special traits. But just to be contrary, the bird flew out into the lane and momentarily disappeared from view.

There was a gate nearby for the benefit of hotel guests who wanted to leave or enter the grounds without the long walk down the driveway and Maggie slipped through it. She spotted her quarry, sitting in the sun on a high branch, preening its feathers. She stared at it, and was still staring, when the sound of footsteps in the lane broke her concentration.

She turned. It was Alain, piratical cap pushed to the back of his head, jacket slung carelessly over his shoulder.

"Hello," he said. "You're out early."

"Alain, I've been following this pigeon or whatever. It isn't in my bird book. What is it?"

His gaze followed her pointing finger. "It's a collared dove."

"A collared dove. I say—it isn't in the index! Is it rare?"

"I'm afraid not. In fact it comes from the dovecote on the lawn of the golf club."

"Oh." She grimaced. "I thought I'd go down in history as the finder of something quite new!"

"You'll have to buy a better book," he suggested, his teeth flashing in a grin.

The collared dove, as if to show its contempt, rose from the branch, circled and flew away over a grove of Aleppo pines.

She tucked the book under her arm. "Did you have a good night's fishing?"

"We weren't fishing, we were laying creels. They'll probably all have something in them when we go back later."

"When did you get back?"

"Oh, quite early. Soon after midnight."

The thought occurred to her that he had come to Le Grand Vergi for a special reason. Usually he came to deliver lobster, but this morning he was on foot and empty-handed. Had he come to apologize for his curtness of the previous evening?

Quite the contrary. "Whatever made you tell Sylvia you were going to a movie last night? It was quite untrue."

She gasped. "Well, I must say! You didn't expect me to tell her I'd come to have dinner with you?"

"Why not? Unless you were ashamed of it."

"Alain. No, of course not!"

"Then why?"

"Because . . . because I didn't want to go into long, involved explanations. I just said the first thing that popped into my head. Besides . . . ."

"What?"

"Sylvia would have been, well, spiky, if she'd known we had a date."

"She was spiky, in any case, because she felt we were lying to her." He stopped a moment. "I'd like this clearly understood. I have no need to explain or justify myself to Sylvia. She has no claim on me."

Maggie bent her head and became very interested in pushing two pebbles together with the toe of her sandal.

"Sylvia thinks she has a claim on you."

"I know that, but what Sylvia thinks isn't necessarily a fact."

"But it affects the way we act. After what Richard told me—"

"For Pete's sake, you haven't been discussing me with Richard?" The thick dark brows drew together.

"I'm sorry if you object—"

"I certainly do. Richard's exactly the type to read things into other people's actions without ever having a clue about the real motivations."

"I don't know why you should say that. He's very intelligent."

"About money. About making his way in the world."

"Well, what's wrong with that? He has just as much right to his view as you have to yours."

"I admit that, but he's wrong and I'm right."

"What an arrogant thing to say! At least Richard isn't wasting his talents and training—"

"Talents? For buttering up rich people, arranging entertainment for folks who can't be bothered to do it for themselves, cushioning them from real life, wasting his time in a glossy package-deal world! Anyone who really wants to devote himself to that sort of thing—"

"By that 'sort of thing' you mean hotel work," she interrupted. "*I* am in hotel work."

"As I said when we first met, to each his own." He shrugged and made to leave.

"Alain," she protested, her anger dying at once, "is that why you came here this morning? To argue about Richard Gale?"

That brought him up short. He wrinkled his brow. "How did we get on to Richard? Normally I never think of him more than twice a year."

"I think I brought him into the conversation."

"Yes, you did, didn't you," he said, his voice quiet. He sighed. "Well, you and Richard have a lot in common, of course."

"Yes, we have."

"And I suppose he's not such a bad chap."

"Why are we talking about Richard again?" she murmured, exasperated.

"I'm hanged if I know. I came to say a couple of things *not* about Richard. Firstly about Sylvia. I can't help being aware that she wants to 'reform' me, to lead me back to the paths of virtue. I wanted you to understand that . . . that. . . ."

"What?"

"I was going to say that she gets no encouragement from me. But that's a two-edged phrase."

"It's quite apt, though. Let's be frank about it, Alain. Sylvia wants you back as the old Alain she used to love and admire. You are trying to show her that you don't want any part of that old life—neither the career you used to have nor the affections and ties that went with it."

"Very neatly put. In a word, I don't love Sylvia. Although she probably wouldn't believe it if I took a Bible oath, I never did love Sylvia. And even if I *did* love her, I certainly wouldn't let her tailormake me back into a pillar of society."

There was no reason at all why this statement should make Maggie feel lightheaded with happiness. To counteract the feeling she said more crisply than she intended, "Then it's settled that you accept friendships only on your own terms."

"What?" It was an exclamation of surprise. "That makes me sound very selfish."

"I didn't mean that . . ." she floundered. "I meant that you value your freedom more than anything else."

"I'm not very keen on that verdict either. You don't have a very high estimation of my character."

"Well, that goes for both of us. You don't think much of me and my job."

Why was she blundering on in this idiotic way? It almost sounded as if she wanted to revive the quarrel of a moment ago.

Apparently he had reached the same conclusion. "You're a fool, Maggie Jefferson," he said, then stalked off.

To say that she was upset was an understatement. For some moments after he'd gone she stood leaning against the iron framework of the gate, struggling with a great lump in her throat that threatened to choke her.

She could have bitten off her tongue for the things she had said. She had no right to criticize Alain, and even if in her innermost thoughts she felt he was pointlessly squandering his gifts, she should know better than to say anything about it.

Hadn't she herself told Sylvia last night, "It's useless to try to change him, even if you imagine you're doing it for his own good." She knew this instinctively, and she must try to act by it always. Maggie did not have the incentive that Sylvia had to interfere in Alain's life. There was no romantic attachment, real or imagined, between them.

Of course not.

Once she was on duty at the desk she had no time for regrets or self-recriminations. First there was a small flood of people taking their leave: they needed their bills brought up to date, receipted, and accounted for in the machine balance. Then Miss Moorhouse wished to exchange her room for one with a view of the apple trees in the old orchard; Maggie had to advise the house-keeper, the head porter and Grace on the PBX switch-board, then alter the room record index. The mail had already been sorted and placed in the appropriate slots, but Sir Hugh Allgate complained that he had expected an important letter that morning that must have gone astray, so she had to institute a search.

Next the minibus arrived for its cargo of guests who were going on a special tour of New Stone Age settle-ments. Mr. Morganblick and his wife wanted to extend the trip so as to include La Cotte à la Chevre, which strictly speaking didn't belong there since the remains found there belonged to a period much earlier than the New Stone Age. This caused an argument with the six other passengers of the minibus, and Maggie spent a quarter of an hour settling it.

Then the new arrivals began to come in from the morning flights. Ted took number twenty-one's luggage to room number thirty-one. One of the chambermaids locked herself in a bathroom on the second floor. Miss Calvett's dog, given a share of her morning coffee, tipped the saucerful all over the pale green carpet of the lounge. The fashion magazines were delivered from the airport, the florist complained that the gardener had given her too few flowers and too much greenery, and Richard was held up for nearly an hour by a call from Copenhagen that kept disconnecting.

All in all it was a typical day in the life of a hotel receptionist. Maggie coped without even noticing that she was doing so, but when her lunch break came she was tired. "I told you it would start to liven up after Easter,"

Paul Daviot said as he took her place behind the desk. "You're beginning to look just the teeniest bit frayed!"

"I feel frayed. What's for lunch today, Paul?"

"Grilled lamb chops or cold tongue and salad."

"It's too warm for a grill and I hate tongue!"

"You could have a sandwich, I suppose. Tell you what, why don't you stroll down to the village? They serve a rather pleasant lunch at the inn—not elaborate, you know, nothing that the boss would approve of."

"The boss" was Richard. Maggie had often noticed that the staff were not entirely approving of him. "I suppose he's become accustomed to *haute cuisine*," she remarked.

"It tends to happen if you spend all your life in a luxury hotel."

"Don't you like hotel work, Paul?"

He shrugged. "It's a living."

Picking up her purse and sunglasses, she headed out of the hotel and across the grounds to a footpath leading to St. Tamme. In a little meadow just before the village a couple of Jersey cows were grazing, their dark chestnut coats glowing in the golden light. Maggie paused to watch them over the low hedge, and the nearer one, having plenty of leeway in her tether, sauntered over with a moo of greeting to look at Maggie.

" 'She wanders lowing her and there, And yet she cannot stray,' " Maggie quoted to the cow. "That suits you, doesn't it?" She stretched out a hand to stroke the velvety muzzle.

The cow rewarded her by giving her hand a thorough licking with a warm, rough tongue.

"Oh, you are lovely! I wish I had something to give you. I believe," Maggie said, "that I could get to like farm life if all the farm animals are like you."

The Jersey cow decided to return to her grazing. Maggie, delighted with the episode, walked on into the village where, after examining the menu posted outside the Bell, she went up to the little restaurant on the second floor. The place was by no means full and Maggie was able to choose a table on the balcony, with a pleasant view of chestnut trees in blossom beyond the sloping meadow where her friend the cow was now munching happily.

Maggie chose melon and then cold home-cooked ham and salad. While she was eating she kept glancing out at the view. She was just finishing when she saw two figures pause by the hedge to speak to the cow, who slowly wandered up to them to have her head rubbed.

One of the figures was Alain and the other was Danié. The boy abstractedly patted the friendly beast while Alain spoke with emphasis. It looked as if he was delivering a lecture.

Danié shrugged and hung his head. Alain took him by the shoulder and swung him around. They appeared to have an earnest discussion and finally Danié nodded. Alain clapped him on the back, then turned him in the direction of Grand Vergi and gave him a little push as if to say, "Get along with you, then."

The boy walked on up the lane while Alain stood watching him. In a moment Danié was lost to view. Alain stood a few seconds longer, said something to the Jersey and scratched the animal's head. Then he turned and came down the lane to the crossroads on the edge of the village.

Maggie witnessed all this with mounting interest. What did it mean? Why was Alain directing Danié to the hotel?

The waitress interrupted momentarily to inquire if she wanted anything more. Maggie ordered coffee. When she turned back to the view she was just in time to see Alain swing himself aboard a bus at the crossroads. The green and cream vehicle snorted its way through St. Tamme and was gone.

Maggie was still deep in thought when a flicker of movement caught her eye. Danié Carras was coming back down the lane toward the village.

"Well, I never!" Maggie said to herself. She thought he must have waited to hear the bus drive off, knowing Alain would be on it. But why?

She decided to find out. It would be quite easy to meet Danié accidentally on her return to Le Grand Vergi, especially as he was now lingering at the window of St. Tamme's only shop. She paid her bill quickly and hurried down to the street. Once there, she checked her pace to an easy stroll. As she came level with the shop she slowed even more.

"Hello," she said. "It's Danié, isn't it?"

He turned. For a moment he didn't recognize her.

"I'm Maggie Jefferson," she prompted.

"Oh yes, the lady that was with Alain."

"That's right. How are you, Danié?"

"Okay."

"Was there any trouble that day?"

"What about?"

"About not being at school."

"Oh, that. No, nobody found out."

She noticed he didn't attempt to pretend he'd been given permission. She said, "No school today?"

"Still Easter holidays," he replied.

"Oh, I see. Of course, so it is. When do you go back?"

"Monday. That's *if* I go back."

"How do you mean?"

"If I get this job at Grand Vergi, the headmaster will

give me an exemption." He leaned against the wall of the shop. "You fixed up that job, didn't you? Alain said."

"Well, it isn't entirely fixed up. Mr. Gale has to say yes or no."

"Prob'ly he'll say no."

"Why should he? You look just right for the job."

"I've got no training."

"The head porter will soon show you the ropes. After that, all you have to do is obey orders, be bright and willing and make sure you're nicely turned out."

"Yeah," the boy said, wrinkling his nose.

"Don't you want the job, Danié? Don't you think you can do it?"

"I could *do* it easily enough," he said with some indignation. "It's not that. . . ."

"What, then?"

He shuffled his feet awkwardly, then burst out, "It's that silly uniform! All my friends will laugh at me and my dad says I'll look like a fool!"

Maggie realized that doing a good turn to Danié Carras was by no means as easy as she'd thought at first.

"It's rather a smart uniform," she said. "Slate blue and red."

"But it's got a funny little jacket and a round hat."

"It's adapted from the uniform of a military cadet of the nineteenth century," she went on, searching for a good angle.

"That doesn't help."

His tone was so steeped in gloom that she couldn't prevent smiling.

"Cheer up," she said. "None of your friends is ever likely to come to Grand Vergi and see you in it, and no matter what your father says, I bet your mother will like you in it."

"Yes, she'll like it," he admitted, brightening.

"You do want to get away from the farm, don't you?"

"Oh, anything to get away from the *cotils*! But there are a lot of things I'd rather do."

"Such as?"

"Go out on the boat with Alain."

She nodded. "That would be interesting. But I suppose they don't need another boy since they've got Céfi's son, haven't they?"

"Yeah. Besides, Alain will probably be coming off the boat any time now—Céfi takes holiday people out, sea-angling and so forth, and Alain doesn't care for it." The boy sighed. "He's a lucky one. He can do just what he likes."

It was difficult to argue that. "There aren't many people like Alain," she said.

"No, isn't he great? You should have heard him making rings around my dad this morning, about the job and everything."

She began to walk gently along the village street so that the boy fell into step beside her.

"So Alain went to see your father this morning?"

"Yes, before breakfast, must have been about six o'clock. I could hear them arguing while I was getting dressed."

Maggie felt a pang. So that was what Alain had come to tell her this morning! But she, fool that she was, had decided to pick a quarrel with him instead.

She realized how great a concession this was on his part. In the first place he hadn't wanted to interfere at all, and in the second place he'd been of two minds whether a hotel job would be good for Danié.

Obviously he had changed his mind. Could it be because of something she had said? The idea gave her a warm glow. She would dearly like to believe it, but she had to be honest with herself: Alain was more likely to have analyzed the situation and come to his own conclusion after dispassionately studying every aspect.

But whatever the reason, he had now ranged himself on her side. He had brought the boy to the approach to the hotel, urging him to go on and apply for the job.

Maggie intended to keep the boy moving toward Le Grand Vergi until the next logical step would be for him to go in and ask to speak to Richard. As they went over the crossroads to the lane, she asked, "How did Alain persuade your father to let you go?"

"It all had to do with money. Dad said that if he let me go he'd have to pay a man to take my place. Alain said that my wages and tips at the hotel would be a lot more than my dad would pay a Breton farmhand, and so he'd have money left over."

She felt that it was a very neat piece of reasoning—the kind of thing that Alain's legal mind would have worked out almost at once. "Did he say why he felt you should take the job?" she ventured, longing to hear that Alain had done it for her sake, because he agreed with what she'd said last night.

"No. Mainly he was saying why I shouldn't stay on the farm all summer. He said did dad want a repetition of last summer. . . ." The boy's eyes took on a faraway look. "I went off on my own last summer. I just got fed up with spraying tomato plants and gathering *vraic*. It was great. I had nearly two weeks of freedom!"

"Good gracious, how did you live?"

"Easy enough. Doing odd jobs, making myself useful to tourists, and if I was really hard up, well . . . ." His words trailed away.

"And you slept in the yacht club's premises?"

"No, that was only one night. Mostly I slept on the boats in St. Helier Harbor. It was easy. There's plenty of boats belonging to weekend yachtsmen or boats that they hire out to holiday people—they're not used at night."

"But didn't you think how worried your parents would be?"

"My mother was worried. My dad was angry. Anyhow, in the end somebody saw me—some friend of Alain's that he'd asked to look out for me." Danié frowned. "If I ever do that again I'll have more sense than to hang around St. Helier. It's probably more fun in Carteret."

"Carteret? Where's Carteret?"

"Normandy, of course!"

"Now, Danié," Maggie said with severity, "I hope you're not going to go on thinking things like that if you take this job at Grand Vergi. You're not a little boy any more and you've got to show a sense of responsibility—particularly as it would be letting Alain down to take the job and then run off when you felt like it."

"But suppose I don't like being a bellhop?"

"Then you must give a week's notice, and either find another job or go back to the farm."

"Alain doesn't have to do that," Danié grumbled. "Alain just pleases himself."

There was no answer to that, but luckily they were entering the hotel grounds. Danié was very impressed, especially when he saw the tables and umbrellas by the swimming pool. This was clearly his idea of luxurious living. She took him in through the staff entrance and left him in the care of Jack, the kitchen porter, while she went to the desk to call Richard. By and by she saw the head porter go through the staff door and come back with Danié, who was taken into Richard's office.

She was too busy after that to take note of what was happening, but in the staff dining room that evening she learned that Danié was to start on Monday, working the shift from nine a.m. to three p.m. while the more experienced Ted would take the busy time, from three to ten. The bellhops lived at home, so it meant Danié would have to cycle to and from the hotel.

"Not a bad kid," the head porter remarked as he stirred his after-dinner coffee. "I think I can make something of him."

Greatly daring, Maggie wrote a note to Alain thanking him for coming to Danié's aid and reporting the head porter's verdict.

She scarcely knew whether she expected a reply, but it came the following day in the form of a package from a St. Helier bookshop. When she opened it she found a pocket encyclopedia of British birds. Written on the flyleaf was:

> Compare the Parrot with the Dove.
> They are in shape the same:
> in hue dissimilar.

Underneath he'd written, "This information comes from James Elroy Flecker and your devoted admirer, Alain."

Maggie was disproportionately delighted with the gift. Somehow it seemed so typical of Alain: the trouble taken to find the right book, the wry little quip written in at the beginning. But more important was the fact that she was forgiven for "meddling" in Danié's affairs, that the coldness between them was gone.

She found herself hoping he would drop by, but the days passed without a sign of him. However, life at the hotel was growing busier with each succeeding day so that she had no time to regret the fact that Alain hadn't come; nor had she much chance to keep an eye on Danié, as she had intended.

One afternoon she had just come on duty again after lunch when Sylvia Crayland emerged from the hotel restaurant with a group of friends. Maggie had just put down her purse, sunglasses and book on the desk; she smiled at Sylvia, and her friends—three of them male—took this as an invitation to speak to a pretty girl. The whole group walked over to the reception desk, rather against Sylvia's will, or so it seemed to Maggie.

Sylvia didn't bother to introduce them beyond a murmur of "some friends who are staying with us." The men joked and teased; the women bought postcards. Sylvia amused herself by flipping open Maggie's book.

It was the encyclopedia that Alain had sent her. Maggie didn't notice, nor would she even have given the matter a thought, until Sylvia suddenly slammed the book closed, summoned the group sharply and led them out. They were due to play golf, she reminded them.

Struck by a thought, Maggie opened the book at the flyleaf and reread Alain's words. "This information comes from James Elroy Flecker and your devoted admirer, Alain."

Maggie knew that the sentence was not meant seriously. There was mockery in it, even perhaps some ridicule. *She* knew he was not her devoted admirer, and he knew she knew; he had voiced his criticism more than once. The words in the book meant, "All right, you've managed to get Danié the job—now let's see what happens." Even the quotation from Flecker was double-edged. It seemed to be laughing at her for thinking a collared dove was a rare bird, but it was also saying, "Putting Danié into a uniform doesn't change him."

Sylvia couldn't be expected to know any of that. To her the inscription on the flyleaf must look as if Alain really thought a lot of Maggie.

The idea troubled her. But really, what could she do? Seek out Sylvia and try to explain? But then that gave importance to the episode instead of lessening it.

She banished it from her mind and got on with the afternoon's work. Just as she was about to go off duty at six, the phone on the reception desk rang yet again. It was Sylvia.

"Is that reception? Oh, it's you, Maggie."

"Yes, it is. Can I do anything for you?"

"I want to reserve a room for a friend, please. We have so many houseguests here at the moment that I just can't put him up and I just *know* he'd enjoy staying at Le Grand Vergi. You've got a single room?"

"We-ell . . ." Maggie began doubtfully, reaching for the booking chart with her free hand.

"Good heavens, don't tell me you're full up already. The season hasn't really got going yet."

"No, it's not that. I was just looking to see if we have a single. . . . We have a large group of American guests arriving tomorrow and all the single rooms—"

"Then I'll reserve a double room, of course. As if it matters," Sylvia said.

By this time Maggie had had a chance to study the vertical board that formed part of the counter between guests and the receptionist. "Is your friend already here?" she inquired. "We have a guest vacating a single room the day after tomorrow, and in the meantime we could give him a—"

"The day after tomorrow will be fine," interrupted Sylvia. "He hasn't left London yet. Reserve the room in my name for the moment, please."

"Certainly." Maggie made out a reservation card, leaving blank the line requiring the guest's name and filling in "Miss Crayland" in the "Reserved by . . ." space. She thought no more about it.

Two mornings later she was taking advantage of a slack moment to get the lunch menus through the duplicator when she was summoned to the front desk by the buzzer. She switched off the duplicator, having not yet had time to set the numerator, and went hurriedly around the glass partition that screened off the working area.

Then she stopped, the shock hitting her like a hammer blow.

There at the desk stood the man she had left London to avoid—Ward Pelham, wealthy playboy and man about town.

CHAPTER SEVEN

He smiled broadly as she approached.

"Hello, Maggie. Long time no see!"

"H-hello, Ward," she stammered. "What are you doing here?"

"Well, that's a fine welcome! Aren't you pleased to see me?"

"Of course," she lied, politeness and expediency taking first place before truth. "But I really meant was, what brings you here?"

"My dear old friend Sylvia Crayland brings me here. She reserved a room for me, or so she said."

So that was the friend for whom Sylvia had wanted the room! Suddenly Maggie knew, beyond the possibility of doubt, that this was no coincidence. Sylvia had invited Ward Pelham to Jersey to stay in the very hotel Maggie had chosen as a refuge from this same man. Someone must have told her about the situation that had driven Maggie from her previous job.

The only person to whom Maggie had mentioned her recent problems was Richard Gale. A few minutes later, when Paul Daviot took over the morning shift, she sought the manager out and asked, "Did you happen to mention to Sylvia Crayland the reason I left my last job?"

Richard, coming down the back staircase, paused in thought. "No, I don't think so. Why?"

"You didn't mention Ward Pelham to her?"

"Did I? Oh . . . now that you say his name . . . yes, I believe I did. I remember it because she'd met him a couple of times."

A couple of times! Yet she'd taken the trouble to invite

him to Jersey as a guest and to reserve a room for him at Le Grand Vergi. Ward had spoken of her as "my dear old friend"—someone he had met only a couple of times.

"Why do you ask?" Richard went on, pausing in the staff vestibule to straighten his tie in the mirror.

"Because he's here, that's why," she replied bitterly, "in a room that Sylvia booked for him."

"*Here?* At Vergi? But I don't recall seeing his name on the reservation cards."

"No, Sylvia's name appears." A very neat piece of planning, Maggie had to admit. She had been taken utterly aback when she saw him. If Sylvia had said the room was for Ward Pelham, Maggie couldn't have prevented his arrival, but she would at least have been forewarned. She couldn't help feeling that there was malice in the way it had been done.

Richard was now looking at Maggie's face. On duty, she always schooled her expression very carefully. But now, unguarded, her eyes and the firmly compressed lips betrayed the anger she felt.

"You're not going to make any sort of fuss about this, are you?" Richard inquired with some anxiety.

"Fuss? What kind of fuss can I make? He's a guest of the hotel. I have to be polite to him."

"Exactly. And besides, he's a friend of the Crayland family."

"But I can soon leave and go elsewhere if he gives me any trouble."

Richard looked startled. "You wouldn't do that!"

"Would I not! I could get a job almost anywhere!"

"But you wouldn't leave me in the lurch, Maggie?"

She hesitated. "I wouldn't want to, Richard, but I might have to. Ward Pelham just isn't used to taking no for an answer."

"Look here, it's part of your job to handle difficult clients—"

"Only on duty. Ward carries on his campaign when I'm off duty. And I just don't see why I should have to put up with it."

"But there's no real reason to suppose he came here just to catch up with you. . . ."

"Isn't there? I find it just too strange that of all the places in the world he could go to in June—Bermuda, Acapulco, Sardinia—he should have chosen the island of Jersey and this hotel in particular."

"I suppose Sylvia must have been in touch with him for some reason and let slip the fact that you're here."

Maggie was about to say, "She did it on purpose," but checked herself. For the next question would obviously be, "For what purpose?" and she could hardly accuse Sylvia of just wanting to make life difficult for her.

So she held her tongue and continued up the stairs. Richard stayed her with a hand on her arm.

"You *won't* go, will you, Maggie? I would hate it if you did."

She wasn't really sure whether she would or not. But he looked so harassed and upset at the idea that she gave a little shake of the head. "I don't want to go," she admitted.

He smiled in delighted appreciation at that, almost as if she had paid him a personal tribute. "That's my girl," he said, and with a quick pressure of his fingers on her wrist, released her to hurry to his desk.

In her head she heard the echo of her own words as she climbed the flights of stairs to her room. "I don't want to go." Why not? Well, because she liked the place, the hotel itself and its grounds, the beautiful, blossoming island, the seas around it with their brilliant shades of blue and green and the sea birds above, and the people. She liked the calm, rather stolid countrymen at work in the *cotils*. She liked the hotel staff, the strange mixture of nationalities. She liked Mrs. Merryn and Amy Leduc and Grace Rachotte and the temperamental head chef and the gardener. She liked Richard.

She didn't really think that Alain Hautger came into the calculation at all, unless you counted him as one of the countrymen—though you could hardly describe him as "stolid."

With her key in the lock of her door, she checked herself. Why was she thinking about Alain? The main matter under consideration was Ward Pelham.

Well, there was nothing to be done about Ward except wait and see. And of course she didn't have long to wait.

She had only been back on the desk about half an hour when Ward, unpacked and changed, appeared in the hall. "Time for a drink before lunch," he observed. "Where's the bar, Maggie?"

She directed his attention to the arrowed sign pointing down the passage.

"Of course, how silly of me. Are you off duty soon, Maggie? I'd like you to share a welcome drink with me."

"No, I'm afraid I don't finish until six."

"What, no lunch break? Come on, precious, you must have a lunch break."

She nodded calmly. "But I eat in the staff hall."

"That sounds pretty dull. Come out with me for a snack somewhere."

Maggie had intended to walk down to the village, but had not the slightest intention of letting him know that. "I'm afraid I can't do that," she replied. "I'm expected to eat on the premises."

"Then come and have lunch with me in the restaurant."

"That isn't allowed, Ward. Mr. Gale is very strict

about such things." She saw that he was about to make some fresh suggestion and put in, "Would you like me to have a call put through to Miss Crayland?"

He frowned. "What for?"

"To let your hostess know you've arrived. I expect she'd like you to go to lunch at her house with the rest of her guests."

Since it wasn't a bad idea he nodded, and Maggie had him connected with the Crayland's house. "You can take the call in that booth over there," she told him.

The result of the phone call was to turn things the other way around, for instead of Ward going to join the house party, the house party came to Le Grand Vergi. Eight people joined Ward as his guests for lunch; they made a noisy, cheerful group in the dining room and spent a lot of money. Richard was very pleased.

"It's good to have a bunch of people like that in the middle of the day," he remarked. "It's easy to fill the restaurant at night, but out of season the place is often a bit dead at lunchtime."

He smiled and chatted with Sylvia and her friends as they were leaving, hoping they had enjoyed the meal and would come again.

"We certainly will," Sylvia replied. "In fact we're coming this evening, to the disco. Will you join us, Richard?"

"Oh . . . thank you. That would be a pleasure."

"And Maggie too. Did you know that Ward and Maggie were old friends?"

"I'm afraid I can't come," Maggie said. "I have a date."

"Have you?" Sylvia's brows drew together. After a minute pause she relaxed and said, "Alain's in France for a few days, I hear."

"Is he?" So that was why he hadn't been around.

"Who's Alain?" Ward put in. "Do I have some opposition?" He laughed tolerantly, quite sure in his own mind that he had no need to worry about a rival. His smoothly tanned face was untroubled, his light blue eyes clear. He was a handsome man in the "white hunter" style he favored—tall, fit, outdoorsy. It was hard to tell, just by looking at him, that most of his time was spent indoors at nightclubs and casinos. When he was outdoors, it was lazing on some Mediterranean beach. He had never had to work, never had to put himself out.

"You don't have to worry about Alain," Sylvia said. "Alain is *my* province."

"So who is this date with?" Ward insisted, leaning on the reception desk and looking sideways at Maggie.

"I'm meeting a friend in St. Helier," she said.

This was so like the excuse she had made when Sylvia happened upon her in Gorey that she knew Sylvia wouldn't believe it.

"Going to the cinema again?" she inquired.

"No . . . we're going for Chinese food."

"That sounds really thrilling," Ward said. "Who is the friend?"

"No one you'd know."

"Male or female?"

Maggie felt like answering, "It's none of your business," but to save trouble said, "Female."

"Oh, then call her up and tell her you can't come."

"I can't do that."

"Why on earth not?"

"Because I promised to meet her."

"Good heavens," Sylvia said, "I believe it's true this time!"

"This time?" Richard echoed. "What do you mean, this time?"

"Oh, last time Maggie told me she was going to St.

Helier for the evening I think it was a little white lie. But we all have to use our wits from time to time, don't we?" She smiled with secret amusement. "Are you doing anything tomorrow night, Maggie?"

"Yes," Maggie fibbed, "I have tickets for the Opera House."

"What a busy girl you are. And the next night?"

"I'm on duty."

"Stuff and nonsense! Richard, if I invited Maggie to a party, you'd arrange for her to be off duty, wouldn't you?"

"Certainly," he said, avoiding Maggie's glance of mute appeal.

"There you are then, Ward! I've netted your pretty little butterfly for you. Ward will bring you, Maggie— dinner at eight on Friday evening." She turned her attention to her other friends, and though Ward wanted to linger, an influx of other guests took Maggie's attention away from him.

She had no chance to refuse the dinner invitation. It would have been almost impossible to do so without saying outright, "I simply don't want to come." She was angry with Sylvia, who had trapped her very neatly; angry, too, with Richard who had given in so easily when he knew she wanted to steer clear of her unwelcome admirer.

By the time she drove into St. Helier her annoyance had abated. After all, there was safety in numbers.

She really did have a date—she was meeting Mrs. Merryn, whose day off it was. She found her already seated in the dimly lit Chinese restaurant studying the menu with relish. For a moment she was tempted to pour out her problems to the other woman, but checked herself; she could hardly do so without criticizing

Richard's behavior, and it wasn't a good thing to criticize one's employer to other members of the staff. But she was beginning to see why he wasn't as popular with them as he might have been—he didn't always give them the support that was their due.

"Danié is settling into the job really well," Mrs. Merryn observed. "I feel he's quite a credit to me, don't you?"

Maggie agreed. From the little she had seen, Danié was working hard—always ready and alert for a summons by the bell on the reception desk, quick to run up and down stairs, obedient to the head porter, patient with the residents' dogs when he took them out on walks, smart in his uniform, a credit to the hotel.

"How are things for him at home?" Maggie inquired.

"Not bad so far. His father doesn't really approve, but on the other hand he's surprised at Danié's share of the *tronc*." This was the slang name for the collected tips from the guests, shared out according to an ancient tradition of graduated standards. Danié was somewhere down at the bottom of the scale, but nevertheless the money wasn't bad.

"That's something. Wouldn't it be nice if we could get Danié something permanent, away from the farm?"

The older woman looked uncertain. "His mother would miss him."

"Oh, I meant a job that allowed him to go home at nights. There *are* jobs in offices and so forth."

"But I don't know if he's really equipped for that. He's not particularly good at academic subjects, and he's missed quite a lot of schooling. Besides—" his grandmother sighed "—the farm will be his one day. He ought to be learning how to run it."

"He could always sell it," Maggie said.

Mrs. Merryn was shocked. "Don't say such a thing! That land has been in the Carras family for generations. Danié must keep it and work it. It's his duty."

"I didn't quite realize," Maggie replied, rather taken aback. "I had the impression that you wanted to set Danié completely free."

"No one is completely free."

"Except Alain Hautger."

"Ah, he's different. He made a conscious choice. Danié is simply allowing himself to be pushed about by his likes and dislikes. Mind you," Mrs. Merryn added with protective fondness, "I'm on Danié's side. But in the end he must settle down and be a farmer, because although he's been made to resent and resist it, farming is in his blood."

"So perhaps Alain was right," Maggie murmured. "He said his efforts had always been to help Danié fit into his home."

Mrs. Merryn said that she always felt comforted when she remembered that Mr. Hautger was ready to help; she went on to enthuse about what he'd already done.

"He's gone to France, I hear," said Maggie.

"Has he? Yes, quite likely. He often pops across. Quite often there are yachtsmen who need an extra crewman to get their boats across, and things like that."

"He didn't say he was going."

Mrs. Merryn peered at her with sudden interest. "Why should he?" she asked.

"No reason," Maggie said. She took care not to ask if anyone had heard when he might be back.

Avoiding Ward Pelham next day was by no means easy. He spent the morning lolling about in the hall, chatting to Maggie when she was not otherwise engaged. She tried to find jobs to occupy herself in the screened-off working area, but inevitably she had to be visibly on duty at the desk most of the time. But at least it proved boring enough for Ward to drive him, after lunch, to the swimming pool. It was a hot June day. Almost all the poolside lounging chairs were occupied, so that the waiters and bellhops were kept busy trotting back and forth with cold drinks.

About four o'clock a telephone call came through for a hotel guest who, Maggie knew, was at the pool. There was no one available to send with the message, so Maggie herself went quickly out. She found her client, and was on her way back when, passing a chair, she found her wrist caught by a warm hand moist with tanning oil.

"Hello there, what's your hurry?" Ward inquired with indolent amusement. "Sit down and enjoy the sun a minute."

He swung up to a sitting position, leaving plenty of room on the lounger for Maggie to sit.

"I'm sorry, Ward, I really can't. I've left the desk unattended."

"Come on, come on. Nothing's happening at this hour on a hot afternoon. Sit down."

"I just can't. You see—"

"Surely you get a break for tea? Just hang on a minute and I'll order some."

He rose to his feet, glancing about for a waiter. He was still holding Maggie's wrist, and without an undignified struggle it was impossible to get away. Maggie had to submit. Ward called his order to a passing waiter, then pulled Maggie down beside him on the cretonne cushions of the lounge.

In a way it was very tempting to stay. The blue and red umbrellas cast a pleasant shade over the patio. The water of the pool sparkled and winked in the sunshine. The air was full of the scent of roses from the pergola that ran along one side of the area. There was a murmur of voices, laughter from the swimmers, soft music from the hotel's tape recorder. No doubt about it, a much pleasanter way to spend the afternoon than behind a busy reception desk.

"I have a ticket for tonight's show at the Opera House, too," Ward said, "so I'll drive you into St. Helier, shall I? About seven."

Maggie had no tickets for the Opera House, never had had, and didn't intend to get any—at least, not for that evening's performance. The whole thing had been a polite lie. Now she had to get out of it as best she might.

"I'm not going after all, Ward," she began.

"Not going? But yesterday you said—"

"I know, but . . . ." But what? If she said she had to go on duty in exchange for the evening off next day, the day of Sylvia's dinner party, Ward just might check with Richard and find it was quite untrue. She decided on a lesser evasion. "The friend I was going with has had to cancel," she said.

"Then that's *great*," Ward said. "You can come as my guest."

"But you only have the one ticket."

"For Pete's sake, I can easily get another. That's fixed, then. You and I will go to the theater this evening. We can have an after-the-show dinner—I hear there are some quite good places in St. Helier."

Maggie said nothing. This was much worse than going to a party at which he would be a guest. An entire evening alone with Ward didn't appeal to her at all. Between now and seven o'clock she would have to invent a good excuse.

The tray of tea things arrived, borne by Danié. The only place to put it, since there was no table near, was on the lounger. Ward let go of Maggie, Danié set the tray down, then, as he straightened, addressed Maggie.

"Mr. Gale wants you, miss. There are three people at the desk needing attention."

"Oh, yes!" She sprang up, eager to go.

Ward also sprang up, intending to catch and delay her. Whether by design or accident she was never quite sure, but somehow Danié intervened between them so that Ward stepped back, lost his balance and went over with a thunderous splash into the pool.

There was really no reason for him to become upset by this mishap. He was wearing pale blue boxer shorts and a loose blue beach jacket, both of which would take no harm at all from a ducking. But he was undoubtedly furious as he clambered out.

"You little idiot, what do you think you're doing?" he snarled at Danié.

"I'm sorry, sir, I can't think how it happened—"

"It happened because you pushed me!"

"No, sir, honestly—"

"You *pushed* me!"

"Why on earth should he push you?" Maggie interjected. "It was an accident, Ward!"

"You stay out of it. I'm going to have this young pup given a good tongue-lashing—"

Danié had gone pale. "Please don't report me, Mr. Pelham, sir. I didn't do anything."

"*He* didn't do anything," Maggie repeated. "Don't take it out on him, Ward."

Suddenly alert, Ward checked his angry words. He looked at Danié. "You want to stay out of trouble, eh?"

"Yes, sir!"

"And—" to Maggie "—you want to keep him out of trouble?"

"Yes, I do." She was puzzled by his attitude.

"Okay, boy, you can clear off."

514

Danié needed no second telling. He was off like a shot. Ward turned to Maggie. "I wouldn't want to get him into any trouble, if you take an interest in him."

"Thank you, Ward." She hesitated. "I really must go. I'm needed."

"Yes, yes, all right. For now, you have to go. But I'll pick you up in the hall at seven this evening. Right?"

She saw quite clearly his small-scale blackmail. And it looked as if she would have to give in to it. If it had been the irrepressible Ted who had pushed Ward into the pool, it wouldn't have mattered; he would have accepted his reprimand and the cut in his share of the tips philosophically. But Danié was different. Who knew how Danié would react to the rough side of the head porter's tongue? So she had to give Ward measure for measure. He would not report Danié and in return she would give him an evening of her time.

The play at the Opera House was *The Importance of Being Earnest* by Oscar Wilde. It was impossible not to feel lightened and brightened by its sparkling dialogue and by the charming Edwardian costumes. At the interval, laughing in enjoyment, they went out to the bar. Ward elbowed his way toward the counter while Maggie, tempted by the golden evening glimpsed through the foyer, allowed herself to drift with a tide of people making for a breath of air.

The sidewalk on Gloucester Street soon became quite crowded with the overspill from the Opera House. Looking to her left, Maggie could see the blue of St. Aubin's Bay and a little white speck that was the sail of a ketch approaching the harbor mouth. Perhaps it was coming from France. Perhaps Alain was aboard.

Sighing, she stopped herself from continuing down the street to the big Esplanade. Ward would be looking for her with the fruit juice she had asked for. She turned back, to collide with a group coming from the theater—and there was Alain!

She gasped. His back was to her. He had stopped to study the theater program. Better not attract his attention. Ward would be wondering where she'd gone.

She passed the group of theatergoers and edged her way back into the Opera House just in time to meet Ward as he came out of the bar with the drinks held high to avoid collisions.

"Where did you get to?" he asked. "I thought you were just behind me."

"I went out to the street for a breath of air."

He raised his eyebrows. "What an odd idea! But if you're feeling the heat we can cut the rest of the play and go for a drive before dinner."

"Oh, no, thank you, I wouldn't like to miss the play. The rest of it's even funnier than the first bit."

"You mean you've seen it before?"

"My goodness, yes. Twice in the theater, once as a film and once on television."

"Good Lord," Ward said in open amazement, "you must be out of your mind!"

One or two others nearby, sipping drinks, turned in amusement at his outburst.

"Shh!" Maggie said. "It doesn't matter."

"But I mean, I can't understand why anybody would want to hear the same jokes five times! It's not even as if they're very good jokes."

"I thought you were enjoying it, Ward."

"Well, it's not bad in its way, and the girls are pretty, but I can't imagine myself seeing it five times! I have better things to do."

Maggie was sorely tempted to ask, "Such as what?"

but already enough attention had been attracted to them by his far-from-whispered comments.

"They are pretty girls, aren't they?" she said, to change the subject. "And the costumes suit them to perfection."

"Oh, they're attractive, but not as pretty as you, Maggie."

She laughed. "Thank you, kind sir. But those two have talent as well."

"Pooh, acting. Anybody can act—"

"And most people do," said a voice at her elbow. "Good evening, Maggie."

"Good evening, Alain." She gave him a small smile of welcome, wondering how much of Ward's conversation he had overheard. "That was an observation worthy of the great Oscar Wilde himself."

"Yes, wasn't it? In fact I may very well have got it from him in the first place."

He looked inquiringly at Ward, so that she had no alternative but to introduce the two men. She noticed that Ward glanced down as they shook hands and knew it was because of the hard, toughened skin touching his own palm.

There certainly couldn't have been a greater contrast—Ward in his expertly cut jacket of bronze corduroy and his shirt of yellow silk, Alain in a dark blue jersey and blue denims, Ward so floridly fair and Alain so gypsy dark.

"You're here on a visit, Mr. Pelham?"

"Yes, I'm staying at Le Grand Vergi."

"I hope the weather stays as fine as this for the rest of your holiday. How long are you staying?"

Ward grinned to himself. "I haven't put any limit on the time. I can please myself, luckily."

"Ward is Sylvia's guest at present," Maggie explained.

"At the hotel?"

"Yes, I'm an overflow—she hadn't room for me at the house."

"That surprises me," Alain said thoughtfully. "Sylvia's just invited me to come and stay for a week or so."

Maggie longed to ask if he had accepted, but the bell rang to signal the end of the intermission. Alain began to move away.

"Aren't you coming in?" Maggie asked.

"I certainly am. Wouldn't miss it for the world. But—" he jerked his head toward the ceiling "—I'm up in the gods." With a little wave he walked away.

"In the gallery?" Ward said. "What an odd chap! Hardly the sort you'd expect Sylvia to invite to the house."

"Sylvia's known Alain for years," Maggie said rather hotly.

"Ah?" Ward said. "So it was *that* Alain!" He said nothing more until they were settled in their places. Then he murmured, "Sylvia said he was *her* province."

After the theater they had a meal in the Grand Hotel, which was excellent. Ward would have liked to stay and dance, but Maggie pleaded that she had a day's work tomorrow. Oddly enough the drive home, which she had thought might provide her with some problems, was trouble-free; there were so many people heading out from St. Helier on the same road that they had quite a convoy as far as St. Tamme. By that time Ward was too bored and irritated for romance. They parted with a chaste kiss.

Maggie went to bed that night feeling quite optimistic. If she could contrive to keep Ward at arm's length, life might be bearable after all.

She had the early day duty in place of the evening duty next day. She was busy, as usual. The only thing that distracted her from her work was a glimpse of Danié, looking flustered and unhappy. From the desk she called to him as he sped by.

"What's the matter, Danié?"

"It's that Mr. Pelham," he grumbled. "He sent me into St. Tamme to get a magazine and now he says I got the wrong one and I have to go back and change it."

"Well, that's not such a tragedy, dear."

"But I did get the one he told me to get," the boy protested. "He just changed his mind while I was away, that's all. And Mrs. Telier in the post-office shop won't take back the first one—you know what she's like. I'll have to pay for the second one myself."

"Never mind, Danié. I think you can keep the tip he gives you on this occasion, to cover the cost."

"I bet he won't give me a tip," muttered Danié.

There was so much going on that the whole thing passed from her mind until she was driving that evening with Ward to the Crayland's house. She said, "Did Danié get the magazine you wanted in the end?"

He looked a little startled, as if he hadn't expected her to know about it. "No," he said rather curtly, "he's hopeless. I did without."

She could see that it wouldn't be a good idea to pursue the topic.

When they reached the house, they found the house-guests having pre-dinner drinks on the terrace. The house was superb, extending out from the solid rock on which it was built so as to give an uninterrupted view of the sea. Glass screens, which kept it cosy in winter, were folded back now, to let the breeze ruffle the flowers in the tubs and hanging baskets.

Maggie looked for Alain among the people seated in hammocks or standing by the balustrade. He was nowhere to be seen.

She was introduced to some of those present. "Madeleine, Ralph, and this is Mimi—she designs dresses. Have you met Jack? A racing-car driver." She nodded and smiled, accepted a glass of something, then found a seat near the glass doors that led from the drawing room out onto the terrace. She would have denied it, if anyone had accused her, but she was waiting to see if Alain was there.

By and by Ward came to stand beside her. "So this is where you're hiding. You're very quiet."

"Well, I don't know anyone here."

"You never will if you sit out in a hidden nook like this. Come on, let's talk to Jack about his racing cars. I'm thinking of giving some financial backing to a driver. Might be fun."

With concealed reluctance she rose. Before she moved away, she cast one last glance into the drawing room.

And there he was, coming in at the drawing room door with Sylvia clinging to his arm and laughing up into his face.

So, was it true? Was he "Sylvia's province"?

CHAPTER EIGHT

Soon afterward the group went in to dinner. Fourteen people seated themselves at the long dining table of pale blond wood with its decoration of modern silver candlesticks and Swedish glass. To Maggie it seemed a large dinner party: the most she had ever entertained to dinner in her own home was six—she couldn't imagine seating any more than that around her parents' table. But the dining room of the Craylands' house seemed positively palatial, and the food and the wine did it justice.

Sylvia was seated at one end of the table with Alain on her right. Sylvia's father was at the other with the dress designer, Mimi, for his right-hand neighbor and a man whose name Maggie never learned to his left. Maggie and Ward were about halfway down, facing the racing driver and a pretty young woman who hung on his every word.

Nodding toward Sylvia's end of the table, Ward said, "Is that the same chap that we met at the theater last night?"

"Yes."

"He looks different."

To the superficial eye, this was true. Alain was wearing what he had described as his "Sunday-go-to-meeting" suit and a turtlenecked sweater of white cotton jersey. Possibly he had even visited the barber—his hair looked neater. Studying him, Maggie felt her heart sink. Having accepted Sylvia's invitation to stay, he presumably had to conform to Sylvia's requirements. Was she gaining ground in her campaign to turn him back to what she had called "the everyday world?"

Maggie gave herself a mental shake. If Sylvia had

succeeded in that, why should she feel depressed? She ought to be glad! Anything that persuaded Alain to use his full abilities ought to be welcomed, and if a small victory such as persuading him to fit in with social conventions fell to Sylvia, that was a subject for approval, not misery.

So she put herself out to be cheerful and bright. Perhaps she succeeded a little too well. She laughed at all Ward's jokes, reacted admiringly to Jack's boasts about his racing prowess, and on the whole gave the impression of enjoying herself immensely.

Once, while Ward was engaged on a long account of a water-skiing challenge match at Miami, her attention wandered. She turned her head to find Alain watching her along the length of the table.

There was something in his eyes she couldn't quite read. It might have been disdain. He raised his glass in mocking salute, and she inclined her head in cool acknowledgement.

"Listen," Ward said, pulling at her hand. "*Listen*. I'm just coming to the exciting part!"

She returned her full attention to him, or at least the appearance of it. At the back of her mind she was thinking, *So Alain disapproves of Ward? Ward isn't any more of a social butterfly than Sylvia!* And she felt a foolish resentment.

After dinner people drifted into the drawing room. Four, including Mr. Crayland, sat down to bridge. Others carried on with conversations begun at the table; Alain was deep in an argument with a suave, middle-aged Frenchman. Sylvia, pouting, put some records on the stereo set and began to dance on the terrace with Jack. Ward drew Maggie into his arms and they followed suit.

So the rest of the evening was whiled away. It would be

untrue to say that Maggie derived no enjoyment from it, but she was glad when it ended. She allowed herself to be handed into Ward's hired Cortina with relief. Since everyone else was a houseguest, the whole gathering came to the porch to wave them off down the driveway, to the accompaniment of a great many silly jokes about not running out of gas or taking the wrong turn.

Despite herself, Maggie sought out Alain in the group, but either he was at the back out of sight, or he had decided not to take part. Whatever the reason he was nowhere to be seen.

"Well," said Ward after he had passed through the electronically operated gates, "that was great fun, wasn't it?"

"Yes, great fun."

"You didn't have much contact with Alain what's-his-name."

"No, why should I?"

"Don't know, exactly. I sort of got the impression that you'd had dates with him."

"I've met him a couple of times outside the hotel, mostly by accident."

"Accidentally on purpose?"

"Not on my side."

"On his, then?"

"I can assure you Alain Hautger has no romantic interest in *me*," Maggie said.

"Is Sylvia his girl, then?"

"You'd better ask him that. I really know very little about his personal affairs."

Ward chuckled. "Glad to hear it," he said in self-congratulatory tones. "I don't mind a bit of rivalry, you know. I just like to know the odds. But candidly, I feel I haven't much to worry about where he's concerned. Have I, pet?"

He took one hand off the steering wheel so as to put an arm around her. Maggie disapproved of this on more counts than one, but couldn't quite frame any objection without sounding either huffy or prudish.

He gave her a little hug. "You were the prettiest girl at the party," he said.

"No, I wasn't, and you know it as well as I do."

"Well, you were the *nicest*."

She laughed and made no further response. She couldn't help thinking that if Alain had just said that, he would have followed it up with, "And now you must say I was the nicest man," and her laugh would have been genuine, not embarrassed.

Compared with Alain, Ward's conversation lacked luster and his view of life seemed entirely superficial. If she were candid, she found him a bore; his certainty that she ought to find him irresistible was depressing.

She stopped herself from pursuing these thoughts. She was doing exactly what she'd felt Alain had no right to do—despising Ward Pelham.

But the fact remained that if by magic she could have transported herself out of his car and safely home to her room at Le Grand Vergi, she would have done so. The next quarter of an hour was going to be difficult.

Her doubts were confirmed when, a little beyond Hautes Croix, Ward drew up and cut the engine.

"It's a lovely night," he remarked. "Let's stop and admire the stars for a while."

"It's after eleven," she rejoined. "I'm rather tired, Ward, so let's get home."

"Tired? At this early hour?"

She forbore to point out that she had done a full day's work before coming out to dinner, and could hardly add that she had found the evening a strain in itself.

"I'm on the early turn again tomorrow," she said. "I really do have to get back and get some sleep."

"But you can spare a few minutes," he said, taking her in his arms.

Now what was she to do? Struggle ignominiously? Tell him bluntly that there was nothing she wanted less than to be kissed by him?

In the end she submitted tamely. It seemed less trouble. As his mouth pressed on hers, she was completely without response. Just then a vehicle rounded the curve of the road from Trinity and, with a sudden screeching of tires and swerving of wheels, glanced off the rear fender of the Cortina. It plunged on a few yards farther, then came to a stop.

It was Sylvia's white Maserati. She was at the wheel, but was now opening her door to get out. As she did so her passenger swung himself out of the coupé and ran toward Ward's car. Even in the faint light of the stars it was impossible to mistake that tall, rangy figure.

Ward was opening his door and climbing out. "What do you think you're playing at?" he exclaimed angrily.

"Sorry, we appear to have given you a bit of a clout—" Alain broke off. He had just recognized both driver and car. "Sorry, Pelham, I didn't realize it was you. Are you all right?"

"No thanks to you," Ward growled. "You've bashed in the taillight."

"I can only apologize." He leaned down to peer into the Cortina. "You didn't come to any harm, Maggie?"

"No, I'm quite all right."

"You might have knocked us right off the road!" Ward said.

Sylvia came up at that point, pulling a silk scarf from her long hair. "Alain wasn't driving, *I* was. I'm sorry, Ward, but the damage isn't too bad."

"I'm not concerned about the car. You scared me out of my wits! What the devil do you mean by dashing along country roads at that speed?"

Alain said, "Sylvia might equally inquire what you mean by parking on an outside bend like that. She couldn't possibly see—"

With a laugh, Sylvia laid her hand on his arm. "We know what he means by parking there, darling. Don't be naïve. Why does any man with a woman beside him stop his car in a quiet spot on a June night?"

In the dimness it was impossible to see Alain's face. Perhaps it was just as well, judging by the irony in his voice when he spoke. "The sooner we make our humble apologies and go, Sylvia, the better. You'd better tell Ward who handles your insurance—"

"Oh, don't let's bother with any of that. Where did you rent the car, Ward? At Juras?"

"As a matter of fact, yes."

"Then if you just tell them to get in touch with my father he'll pay all the damage. Now do say you forgive me for chipping off a piece!"

"I don't know that I ought—"

"If you're going to be cross with me, I shall feel awful. Do be nice, Ward!"

"Oh, all right," he said grudgingly. "There's not much point in trying to lecture you about reckless driving because I can see you don't care a fig. I don't believe you have any sense at all!"

526

"Good night, Ward darling." She kissed the tips of her fingers and blew the kiss to him along her palm. "Come on, Alain, we know when we're not wanted."

"Yes, we have at least that much sense. Good night, *touos les deux!*"

Ward climbed back into the Cortina. With much slamming and grinding of gears he restarted it, by which time the Maserati had sped away. Ward was intensely annoyed and was barely civil as he said good night to Maggie.

Maggie, for her part, was making a vow to herself as she prepared for bed. No matter what the circumstances, she was not going to allow herself to be maneuvered into such a position again. She had not wanted to go to Sylvia's dinner party in the first place, had not wanted Ward Pelham for her escort, had not wanted to be alone with him on the way home, had not—most decidedly had not—wanted to be kissed by him. She had allowed all these things to happen rather than cause a fuss. And what was the result? Alain apparently thought she had some romantic feelings for Ward.

It was the last thing in the world she wanted to happen. Even if she had liked Ward Pelham, she wouldn't have wanted Alain to think it was any more than that. But to have him imagine she cared in any way for such a man was very painful to her. She really couldn't understand why it distressed her so; as she brushed her hair her hand trembled and foolish tears filled her eyes.

When at length she laid her head on the pillow, a few tears spilled out and ran down to the cambric pillowslip to form a little damp patch. Angry, she pulled herself up on her elbow, turned her pillow over, blinked fiercely once or twice, and told herself to go straight to sleep.

But sleep was a long time coming.

She kept her vow. During the next few days she managed to avoid Ward quite efficiently because as July and the full holiday season approached, she was truly over-whelmed with work. She saw Richard Gale looking at her, at first approvingly because of her zeal, and then a little worriedly. "You mustn't stay on the desk helping when it's time for you to go off duty," he reproved her, although without any severity. "Paul   race and John must do their share."

"But the men are already so busy—they have the discotheque to run as well."

"I'm getting a showbiz chap to join us as disc jockey for July and August. That will relieve the strain on them. As for you, I want you to take full off-duty time. Understood?"

"Yes, sir," she said with mock obedience.

"You're off this afternoon, aren't you? What are you doing?"

"I'm going into town. I have a hair appointment, and I thought I might have tea somewhere."

"I'll tell you what. Let me give you tea in de Gruchy's. Then perhaps we could go for a drive, or take a boat out, or something. How about it?"

"I'd love it," she replied. It was a wonderful idea—to get away, to have Richard as escort so that she needn't worry if Ward happened to see her on her way out. When alone, she found it difficult to avoid Ward's offers of companionship.

She came out of the hairdresser's at half past three and sauntered up Colomberie, admiring the view of the town basking in the sunshine. The sidewalks were thronged with tanned tourists in bright casual clothes. At Snow Hill and beyond, brilliant strings of colored lanterns swung overhead in a fresh breeze. Instead of walking straight on, she took a favorite detour, turning to the left so that she could go through the quiet, cobbled serenity of Royal Square. The shade from the old trees was welcome; she lingered a moment to find her sunglasses in her shoulder bag before going out once more into the brilliant light.

She was facing the library. At that moment Alain came out of the doors, glancing at a slip of paper as if it held notes he'd just made from a reference book. He didn't see her. He turned toward St. Helier's Church and was quickly lost to sight.

Maggie was glad they hadn't actually met. She still didn't know what she would say to him when they did. She often pictured the scene: she with her first words would explain the encounter on the road at Hautes Croix and all would be made clear. But when it came to framing the explanation she was never quite sure how she would do it. All the phrases she recited in her mind sounded defensive. What was it the French said? "He who excuses himself is accusing himself." In other words you wouldn't bother with excuses if you didn't feel you were in the wrong.

She returned to the main shopping streets, crossed into King Street and entered de Gruchy's. This was a shop she loved, with its cool echoing arcade, its elegant interior and the comfortable coffee lounge on the second floor at the top of the fine curving staircase.

Richard was already there. He rose to greet her, and a waitress arrived at once to take their orders. When she had done so he gave his attention to Maggie. "You've had your hair cut?" he inquired.

"Yes, I thought it would be cooler to have it off my

neck. If this warm weather keeps up I think I'll be glad I did it."

"It's gorgeous, isn't it? I thought you'd like to have a little trip on the briny since it's such a pleasant day, so I've hired a boat. Is that okay with you? We'll have to be back at Grand Vergi by seven, of course."

"That would be lovely. Where shall we go?"

"Not far. There's a group of little islands about seven miles out—I thought we'd make a little tour around them and come back. It should take about an hour and a half—just right for us to be back."

"It sounds delightful. What sort of islands?"

"Oh, just tiny. I don't know too much about them, really, because I'm not much of a man for boats—but a friend took me out to them last year. One of them, Maître Ile, is a bird sanctuary."

"Really?" At once she was doubly interested. "I'm trying to get to know the birds in the islands, Richard. I wish I'd brought binoculars."

"I expect the boat rental place will be able to lend us some."

They had tea, Maggie firmly rejecting the luscious cream cakes wheeled up to them on a trolley. By ten past four they were walking down to the Weighbridge, which was near the boat rental office. They were directed to a mooring on the west side of the north quay, where they would find *Zig-zag* awaiting them.

Zig-zag proved to be a sixteen-foot cabin cruiser with a forty horsepower engine, moored a short distance from the jetty in about six feet of water. Richard hesitated a moment at the skiffs and dinghies. "I wonder if one can just borrow one of these?" he muttered.

For a moment they stood looking about, hoping for

guidance. And guidance was forthcoming. An old man painting on a shabby yacht saw them and called, "Can I help you?"

"We want to get onto *Zig-zag*."

"Ah? Hiring her, are you? Kelmo should have sent a man to see you aboard."

"No, we were just sent along. . . ."

This conversation had been held at the top of their voices. One or two loungers paid heed, and one or two heads were turned from boats out at their moorings.

One of them, Maggie noted, was Alain's. He was sitting on the deck housing of a neat little Halcyon, his shirt sleeves rolled up and his hands black with oil. He was either cleaning or mending part of the engine. He watched without comment as the old man came ashore with a rowboat to ferry them to *Zig-zag*, only lifting a hand in silent salute when Richard waved.

Richard had the starter key. The boat vibrated, water swirled under the keel. At his direction, Maggie cast off the mooring rope.

"Where are you off to?" Alain called.

"Les Ecréhous," replied Richard, "just for an hour or so."

Alain shouted something in response, but it was lost in the roar of the motor. In a moment *Zig-zag* was heading out of St. Helier Harbor.

The view of the island from the sea was unbelievably beautiful. It seemed to float in the turquoise blue water like a multicolored jewel. Flowers, which abounded everywhere along its shores, glowed in the sunlight and then, as distance made their colors less intense, turned the outline of the brown cliffs to a chiaroscuro of blues and tans and grays.

The trip out to the little archipelago was without

incident except for the sighting of some Manx shear-
waters, which Maggie was able to identify because she
had by mere chance been looking at the illustration in the
book. She pointed them out to Richard.

"Is that what they are? Fancy that," he said without
interest.

"I wonder if they breed on the island, the one you said
was a bird sanctuary?"

"They breed in the Isle of Man, surely, if they're called
Manx thingummies."

"No, no, that's just their name. Oh, never mind," she
said hastily as she saw him wrinkle his nose in irritation.
Just because she happened to be developing an interest in
such things was no reason to inflict it on anyone else.

When they reached Les Ecréhous it was clear that
many seabirds nested there. Maggie was entranced as
flight after flight rose and wheeled and swooped. She
knew the names of only a few; when she saw gannets
diving she felt a thrill of recognition—Alain had told her
the French name, *fou de Bassan*. On the shores of the
islets she could see turnstones feeding. She could hear the
call of a sandpiper. She found herself wishing that Alain
was here to identify the separate species in this mass of
flying, darting inhabitants.

They made a wide circle around the group of islands.
The tide seemed to be running out fast, so that the rocks
with their little perching houses were joined by acres of
wet shingle that shone under the sun like mother-of-pearl.
Other boats were bobbing out at sea where anglers were
after sea bass or were pulled up on the sand of quiet little
beaches.

Richard had cut the engine to the merest idling to allow
Maggie a last view of the little island of Marmotière,
where a wild lupin had taken root and was flourishing in a

rock crevice in a glory of dark blue spikes of flowers. If there was a slight change in the beat of the motor, neither of them noticed it.

"Time to go," Richard said with a glance at his wrist.

"I suppose so. I really hate to leave all this. It's so beautiful."

"But we have to get back."

"Yes, all right."

He opened the throttle. The engine of *Zig-zag* gave a muffled roar, then made a snarling sound and stopped.

"What's happened?" Maggie exclaimed.

"No idea. Just a minute—it's probably just stalled."

But it was not. The engine would not restart. Yet *Zig-zag* was moving. This didn't dawn on Maggie until, with a gentle bump, the cabin cruiser came to a halt.

Zig-zag had been drifting with the current. And now, alas, she was aground on a sandbank.

There were other boats sailing among the islets or moored at a distance. Richard shouted to attract attention and they both waved, but nothing happened. No one heard them or, if they did, took it for high spirits or sounds of enjoyment. Half an hour went by. The spit of sand on which they were marooned became more and more clearly defined.

"We'd better try to push ourselves off," Richard said. He picked up a boathook, leaned over to put one end on the sand and pushed. The boathook sank into the surface. *Zig-zag* didn't move.

He pulled out the pole and was about to make another attempt, but Maggie tugged at his arm.

"No, don't, Richard! If you got us afloat, what good would it do? Without the motor we'd just float back on again."

"It's absurd!" he said crossly. "How long are we going to be stuck here?"

"Until the tide changes, I suppose."

"But that might be five or six hours! Have you any idea what time low tide comes?"

"Not the slightest." She sighed. "If we had a dinghy aboard we could row ourselves over to one of the other boats and ask for help."

"If we knew what was wrong with the engine we could get ourselves off," he countered. "And if we had wings we could fly home."

She said nothing. She could well understand his annoyance. He was due back at the hotel by seven to supervise arrangements for a coming-of-age party. It was now six. Even supposing the engine of *Zig-zag* made a miraculous recovery he could never make it in time.

They tried various tactics to start the engine, but nothing worked. Maggie tried to keep watch in case one of the other boats came within hailing distance and was rewarded quite a long time later by the approaching beat of a motor. She went to the starboard side of *Zig-zag* to look out; another cabin cruiser was coming slowly around the eastern edge of Marmotière.

"Hallo-o-o!" she called. "Ahoy there!"

"Ahoy *Zig-zag*!" came a voice.

With a blush of embarrassment, she realized it was Alain.

"Good heavens, it's Hautger," Richard muttered. "What's he doing here?" He cupped his hands to his mouth and repeated his query aloud. "What brings you here, Alain?"

"You said you'd be back in an hour or so." Alain said no more until he was at closer quarters, then went on, "I tried to warn you as you left. It's easy to go aground here when the tide's falling, and besides, Kelmo has adapted the draft of *Zig-zag* so that she really needs a good five feet of water. . . ."

"Can you come and give us a hand?"

"I'm not coming any closer, thanks, or I'll go aground too. I'll throw you a rope, though."

"That's no use, Alain," Maggie called. "Our engine has died on us."

"Oh?" Alain went into reverse, maneuvered around *Zig-zag*, then cut his motor. "It's fouled up on something. Looks like a plastic sack or something. One of our inexperienced summer boat owners had probably thrown it overboard and now it's wrapped around your propeller."

"What do you suggest, then?" Richard asked. "Can you give us a tow?"

Alain laughed. "We won't bother with anything as heroic as that. If you just chuck your anchor overboard, *Zig-zag* will float off at high tide and stay there until Kelmo can send someone to cut the tangle away. In the meantime I'll take you back with me."

"Thanks very much," Richard muttered. "I appreciate it." He paused expectantly.

"Come on, then."

"What?"

"Wade across. It's only a few feet deep."

"You're joking," Richard said, obviously very annoyed. "Can't you come and get us?"

"I've already told you—I don't want to get stuck on the sand."

"But . . . but . . . ." Richard hesitated. "You can't

really expect Maggie to wade across all that water?"

"I thought you'd carry her," Alain said. Then he relented. "All right, hang on, I'll lower the rubber dinghy."

It took a few minutes for him to moor his own boat safely, cross in the dinghy and ferry them back. He said in Maggie's ear as he helped her aboard, "You have a talent for being in stationary vehicles at the wrong time."

"It was very kind of you to think of coming to look for us," Maggie said rather primly.

"Yes, wasn't it? It was to test the engine of *Fairchild* really. I'd been working on it this afternoon." He set it going, listening with approval to its healthy throb.

"I saw you earlier," she said, although she hadn't meant to mention it. "You were coming out of the library."

"So I was. I'd been to look up a book on boat engines—mechanics is not my strong point."

"Is this your boat?" Richard inquired, glancing about without much enthusiasm.

"No, it belongs to a friend who rents it out to vacationers. I was just fixing the fuel pipe for him, that's all."

"Could you go any faster? I'm dreadfully late for an important thing at the hotel."

"Sorry, this is as much as I care to try in *Fairchild*."

"You were going a lot faster in Sylvia's Maserati the other night," Maggie said, then wondered if it sounded as reproachful to him as it did to her.

"Oh, I enjoy being driven at a great speed by a beautiful woman. It's exhilarating."

"I suppose it is. You probably enjoyed yourself a lot more than I did."

She wanted him to ask what she meant, but he thought she was talking about the collision. "Was there any trouble about the damage?" he said.

"I've no idea. I imagine not."

"I imagine not, too," he agreed. "Car firms wouldn't want to be disagreeable to a man like Ward Pelham—he's too rich to be rebuked."

"You can say that again," Richard said with feeling. "It's my job to like everybody in my hotel, but I must say I find it difficult with Pelham."

It seemed to Maggie that Alain flashed a glance of sympathy at Richard, but neither man pursued the topic. She decided to mention something that had been puzzling her.

"I'm surprised that Sylvia lets one of her houseguests come down to the harbor and get black to the elbows on someone else's boat," she remarked.

"I beg your pardon?"

"Doesn't she object? I'd have thought she'd want you to be with her other guests."

Alain frowned. "I think there's some sort of misunderstanding," he murmured. "I'm not staying with Sylvia."

"But, that evening at the Opera House . . . you said . . . ."

"I said she'd invited me. I didn't say I'd accepted."

"You refused?"

He cast her a puzzled look. "Of course I refused. You can't picture me fitting myself into Sylvia's gilt frame, can you?"

"But she said . . . at least I thought . . . ." Maggie's mind was in complete confusion. "At the dinner party . . . ."

"What about the dinner party? I was there as a dinner

guest. She sent a car for me at seven and then drove me home herself. That's where we were going when we happened upon you and Ward."

"Oh," said Maggie.

She had to turn away. A wild, singing happiness had taken control of her. If anyone had seen her face just then, they would have known how happy his words had made her.

CHAPTER NINE

July came, and with it days yet more warm and golden. The air was full of the scent of roses, of lavender and thyme, of hyssop, verbena and heliotrope. The Battle of the Flowers was less than a month away: entrants were planning their designs, flower growers were husbanding blossoms, pretty girls were designing costumes for that special Thursday.

Le Grand Vergi was full to overflowing. Maggie had hoped that Ward would have to move out because his room was needed, but since he was a friend of Sylvia Crayland, daughter of the man whose firm owned the hotel, he stayed on—although it meant continual juggling of room reservations.

It had proved impossible to avoid him entirely. But Maggie had succeeded in never being alone with him, and had managed to refuse more than one of his invitations with the simple explanation that she wanted time to herself.

"Time to yourself!" Ward said, drawing his thick fair brows together. "Do you mean, time for some other fellow? Who is it—that good-looking manager?"

"It isn't anyone," she replied. "I just like to be on my own to recharge my batteries. This job is hard work, you know."

"Then give it up!" he said at once. "You don't have to do this sort of thing, Maggie—"

"I like it," she cut in before he could make any embarrassing propositions. "I like my job. But it does require a lot of attention and I do need peace and quiet—"

"We could go somewhere quiet—a nice little candlelit dinner for two. . . ."

"That's not what I meant and you know it," Maggie said. "I want to loll in a chair with the radio playing and a pot of coffee at my elbow."

"Ugh! Sounds deadly dull."

"It *is* deadly dull, except that it's absolute bliss."

The conviction in her tone silenced him. But he was displeased. He took it out on others—complained every day to Richard about some small mishap, sent back his food in the restaurant, called waiters and bellhops at all hours of the day and night.

Danié Carras was one of his particular whipping boys. He could see that Danié easily became flustered, and he hadn't forgotten that Maggie had some particular interest in him. Every chance he got, he caused trouble for Danié. He reported him to the head porter for being untidily dressed, sent him on errands that he always seemed to get wrong, refused to answer when Danié paged him for phone calls and then complained that he hadn't heard.

In any hotel the troublemaking guests are soon known. The staff combined to help Danié deal with Ward, but they all knew there was really nothing to be done. The boy would just have to put up with it.

The trouble was, Danié was running out of staying power. On two separate days he failed to turn up for his turn of duty. On the first occasion the head porter grumbled, but overlooked it when he heard Danié's excuse—that he had had to help his father with some urgent crop spraying. On the second occasion he lost a day's pay and a day's tips; he looked very downcast at this, and Maggie knew instinctively that he was truanting, leaving his father's house ostensibly to come to work but instead going off on his own. How he was going to explain his lightweight wage packet, she couldn't imagine.

She sought him out on one of her own mealbreaks. "Danié, I know you're having a hard time at the moment, but you don't make things any better by not turning up."

He looked sullen. "I explained about that. My father needed—"

"No, he didn't, Danié. Don't lie to me about it. You went somewhere—down to Saie Harbor perhaps—and spent the day mooning about. Didn't you?"

He shook his head vehemently but couldn't meet her eye. "It's that Mr. Pelham," he said in a voice of suppressed resentment, his manner of speaking the name adding a subtle dislike to it. "He's always on at me."

"I know that, dear. You're not the only one."

"Oh yes, I know, he sends back the fricassee of veal to the kitchen! But what does the chef care? It's nothing to him! Nobody knows what it's like—"

"I know, Danié," Maggie said. "Believe me, I do know. I'm having nearly as bad a time as you are. But sulking and staying away doesn't help. I've decided just to grit my teeth and bear it."

"I hate him!" he burst out. "I hate him! He's spoiled everything! It could have been great at Grand Vergi except for him."

"I'm sorry, love. I know just how you feel. Try to get the better of it, though."

He made a grumbling sound.

"Promise?"

"I'll try."

And she had to be satisfied with that.

She would have liked to talk over the problem with Alain, but it wasn't easy to get hold of him these days.

Time was when a message left at the Fishermen's Union office in Gorey would find him, but not any more. Nor was he at the Carras's farm. He was sometimes at work in St. Helier Harbor, and for at least part of the last two weeks in July he took a job on a yacht going to Monte Carlo. Maggie happened upon him asleep on a bench in the sunshine of the Mount Bingham Park. He stretched and yawned and told her he had hitched a ride back to St. Malo on a truck and from St. Malo by the hydrofoil, nonstop.

"Come and have a cup of coffee," he invited. "I was on my way to a café when suddenly it all seemed too much trouble and I sat down for a snooze.

"You're incorrigible," she said, half laughing and half sighing. "You're like one of those little green lizards—one minute you're basking in the sun, the next you're gone!"

"I am *not* like a green lizard," he protested. "I'm much bigger, and more lovable."

"Alain, when did you last have a proper meal?"

"At St. Malo last night. There, you see? I'm not really a starving ne'er-do-well after all."

"I never suggested that you were."

"Not in so many words." He shrugged. "What are you doing so far from Le Grand Vergi?"

"It's my day off."

"And you're spending it all alone among the plants on Mount Bingham? That doesn't sound very exciting."

"Oh, I've only been here a few minutes. I came up to get a view of the harbor." She didn't feel she should mention she had come to look at the shipping and wonder, as she had done before, if he was on board any of the vessels putting in to port. And all the time he was here, with his belongings in a duffle bag.

They went into the cafeteria at Fort Regent and took their coffee to a quiet table by the window. "What are you doing for the rest of the day?" he inquired.

"Well, in a little while I'm driving back to change for the evening. There's a special show tonight in the Rainbow Room in honor of the Battle of the Flowers."

"So there is. I believe I'm supposed to be going to that. I'm helping the Chateau Bergere plant nursery with the design for their float, and Nellie Bergere said she'd get me a ticket for the *parti d'honneur* at the Rainbow Room."

"It sounds as if it might be fun."

"If it isn't, I'll be surprised. One thing we're good at in Jersey is a big party." He stirred his coffee. "Are you going with anyone special? With Ward? Or Richard?"

"No," she said quickly, "it's just a group of people from the hotel. Ward and Richard will be there, but . . . ." She wanted to add, "I won't be *with* either of them."

"I see. Well, I'll probably see you there." He emptied his cup and picked up his travel bag. "I'd better push along now. If I'm going to the Rainbow Room I ought to try to find my one and only suit. Only thing is—" he grinned "—I can't remember who I left it with."

"Céfi?"

"No, last time I wore it was Sylvia's dinner party, remember? I was staying with Albert Garajon for a few days just then—that was his boat I was working on. Maybe the suit is there."

She laughed in bewildered amusement. "You're impossible!"

"Nothing is impossible," he said. To her surprise he stooped and kissed her gently on the lips. "I like to keep in practice," he remarked as he let her go.

By the time she recovered, his footsteps were echoing on the staircase as he hurried down to the door.

Bemused, she finished her coffee, then sat for a while, chin on hand, staring into the distance. Then she roused herself and went home to change.

She had been warned that tonight would be a very splendid affair, that the cinema-restaurant would be filled to its two-hundred capacity with well-dressed patrons. She had therefore bought a new dress with which she had fallen in love when she saw it in a shop window opposite St. Helier's colorful market. It was of very fine, soft cotton voile in a golden amber shade, the tucked bodice caught against the empire-line skirt by a narrow velvet ribbon. The sleeves were merely sketched in, to cover the shoulder and provide a place for another edging of narrow ribbon.

When Maggie slipped into it that night she felt pretty and attractive; she looked forward with eagerness to an evening of pure happiness. She was about to go down in the staff elevator but suddenly stopped. She was going out with a party that included some of the hotel guests, so tonight she would treat herself as a guest and not as a staff member. She walked through to the front of the building so as to take the guests' elevator to the foyer.

One or two members of the group had already assembled. She walked up to chat to them. She had hardly said a few words when she saw the revolving doors turn to admit Alain. At the sight of him her heart turned over, and tears of happiness pricked in her eyes.

Because, you see, he had bought a new suit. A dark, plain, excellently tailored suit of brown Barathea. He looked so handsome and distinguished that she wanted to throw her arms around him.

He came toward her, and she moved a pace or two to

544

meet him. "Couldn't you find your proper suit, then?" she inquired teasingly.

"No, terrible, isn't it? I can't think where I left it. So as I was hideously rich from crewing for a millionaire, I thought I'd invest in a new one. Do you like it?"

"Very much. And the shirt too."

The shirt was cinnamon brown with a matching tie. He smoothed the shirt collar before he said, "I'm glad you approve. This one will have to go on for as long as the last one."

"How long was that?"

"Six years, I think. Maybe seven. I'm glad I chose brown—it makes a nice background to your pretty dress."

There was something in this that seemed to imply he was going to be her escort. Her heart gave a little leap for joy. Telling herself sternly that she mustn't be silly, she said, "Let me introduce you to some of the people who are going from Grand Vergi. Mrs. Ellenburg, Mr. Ellenburg, Mrs. de Jourdan and her daughter, Mr. van Mellder of The Hague—this is Alain Hautger, of an old Jersiais family."

They nodded and bowed and smiled. Maggie was keeping count. The party from Grand Vergi was to number nine in all, and now including Alain it would be ten. Richard Gale had ordered taxis for seven-thirty—it was better not to take one's own car because at the height of the season parking was quite a problem. At twenty past seven Richard and Priscilla Yates, teenage daughter of the mill-owning Yates, joined them; a moment after that Ward appeared, completing the numbers. They stood about in the foyer, waiting for their transport.

After a moment Maggie became aware of raised voices. She looked around. Ward was talking heatedly to a bellhop. Her heart sank when she recognized Danié.

"But there isn't time, sir," he was saying. "I just couldn't get there and back before the taxis come."

"There's plenty of time if you'll just put some effort into it, you lazy little brat," Ward replied. "Go on now, get moving."

"But if you've gone when I get back—"

"The longer you stand here arguing—"

"I'm not arguing, Mr. Pelham, honestly. I'm just explaining—"

"Are you refusing service?" Ward demanded.

Maggie cast an anguished glance at Richard, but Richard had turned a blind eye. Ostensibly, he was deep in a conversation with Miss Yates. Since there was nothing else to do, Maggie took a deep breath and went to Danié's rescue.

"Is there anything I can do, Ward?"

"There certainly is! You can tell this good-for-nothing kid to get down to the village and bring me some of my special cigars from the shop."

"Oh, Ward, he'd never make it in time."

"But I say he would! He's got legs, hasn't he? If he puts a sprint on, he can do it."

"But Ward, there's really no need. We'll be able to get anything you need in the town."

"By the time we get to town the shops will be closed—"

"No, no, I'm sure not. In any case there'll be a kiosk in the—"

"I don't know why you take it upon yourself to interfere!" he said in a loud, indignant voice. "What's it to do with you, anyhow?"

"I'm only trying to prevent Danié getting into any trouble—"

"Oh yes, Danié, Danié, you're concerned about *him*. What about *me*?"

By this time Maggie was aware that everyone in the

hotel foyer had stopped what they were doing and had turned to watch. She was pale with embarrassment and distress and longing for Richard to come to her rescue. It was, after all, his duty to come to the help of his staff.

But when she let her eyes travel to him, she met no response. He was totally unwilling to tackle Ward Pelham. Beyond him, Alain was standing in frowning amazement at the scene. She saw that he knew she had made a mute appeal to Richard and been refused.

Ward was saying, "It's all part and parcel of this extraordinary behavior of yours. I don't know who you think you are, treating me as if I had the plague, but let me tell you I can bring pressure to bear, and if I don't get a little more good manners from you it's possible you'll be looking for another job!"

"I'm sorry if you feel you have any grounds for complaint—"

"Grounds for complaint! I should think I have!"

"Please lower your voice, Ward. You're disturbing other people."

"What do I care about that? And in any case, why should you put other people's comfort before mine?"

"Perhaps it's because they're more deserving than you," Alain said, coming up behind him.

Ward whirled on him. "Who the devil asked you to interfere?"

"No one. I'm doing it entirely on a voluntary basis, as a service to the community."

"What?" Ward said, perplexed.

"I thought if I could prevent you from making a fool of yourself, I'd be doing a public service."

"Listen, don't imagine I'm impressed by a few clever tricks with words. I know what you're really like—a thorough, twenty-four-carat failure!"

"Well," Alain said, "at least I'm not unpleasant about it. I don't make other people suffer for my failures."

"Are you implying that I do?"

"I'm not implying anything. I'm just trying to suggest that if you quieten down now you'll have less to apologize for to Maggie."

"Apologize! *I'm* not going to apologize. I suppose you imagine that you'll impress her, riding up here to the rescue like a knight in shining armor!"

"No, Maggie isn't easily impressed. But she can be made embarrassed and unhappy."

"And you don't want that!"

"No, of course not. Do you?" Alain asked softly.

Ward paused with his mouth open.

"Is that what you want?" Alain insisted, pressing his advantage. "Do you think it will make her like you more if you embarrass her in public? To me that seems an odd way of attracting someone."

"Oh, does it indeed? And you're some sort of expert on how to make a good impression on her, I take it."

"No," Alain admitted quietly. "I ruled myself out of the running from the very start." He gave a little shake of the head. "I don't know what your hopes and ambitions may be, Pelham, but I think anyone with any sort of discrimination would know that Maggie is special . . . and should be treated that way."

At that providential moment the taxis arrived. Everyone moved quickly toward the exit, and in the bustle of departure the embarrassing episode was finally closed. As she settled into her seat, Maggie became aware that the fingers intertwined with hers were Alain's, the arm close against her own was Alain's. Their taxi moved off. By one of those unforeseen arrangements of fate, no one else had got in with them.

For a while they sat in silence. Maggie's very soul seemed to be in a turmoil. Alain's voice as he defended her, the look in his eyes as he spoke, these had held a special message, one that he had perhaps not intended.

She drew a deep breath. He turned to look at her.

"You love me," she said.

His mouth went set. "No, I don't."

"Yes, you do. It was there in the things you said just now."

"No, Maggie, you mustn't think that—"

"But it's true, my darling, it's true! You love me just as much as I love you!"

She waited, breathless, willing him to take her in his arms and admit the truth. But even at that moment of desperate hope she knew he wouldn't. His grasp upon her fingers tightened so that she thought the bones would crack, but he made no other physical move.

"Maggie," he said, "I was trained for law, trained to face facts. What am I, Maggie? How did Pelham just describe me? I'm a thorough, twenty-four-carat failure."

"You're not. You're not! You're free and independent and honest. . . ."

"Perhaps I'm those things, too. You could call me a free, independent and honest failure if you like." There was ironic amusement in his arrangement of the words. "The point is, a man like me has no business being in love with a woman like you."

"That's nonsense. And surely what the woman feels must count for something?"

"Not in this case, I'm afraid. Because you see, as I said to Pelham, you're a special person, one-in-a-million, and I haven't the right to ask—"

"Oh, darling," she whispered, "I give you the right. Don't you know that for days and nights now you've filled my thoughts? I've been lonely and sad when you went away, senselessly happy when you came back. . . ."

"Senselessly. That's the word, my love. Don't you see it's useless? I can't offer you anything. I'm a penniless, footloose nobody. It would be wrong to ask you to share my life."

"How can it be wrong when it's what I want? Dearest, my dearest, I want only to be with you. That's all; nothing else matters."

He gave his characteristic little shake of the head. "That's what you say now. But in the winter, when the gales blow in from the sea and the island is given back to the islanders, you'd be lonely and miserable here, without a proper house of your own and a husband coming home each evening."

"Oh, Alain, how can you talk like that! I know you don't want to change your way of life. I would never, never ask you to. All I want is to belong to you. I could keep my job at the hotel—"

"No," he said. "No wife of mine is going to be at the mercy of the Ward Pelhams of this world. It just wouldn't—"

"Then I could do something else. There are office jobs I could get, I'm sure. I don't care. It doesn't matter."

"But it does matter. It does, Maggie. For the first time I realize what a trap I've set for myself. I thought I was giving myself complete freedom, but the one freedom I don't possess is to marry the woman I love. I told you before, darling. I could never ask any woman to share the uncertainties and hardships that are the price I pay for liberty. I can go where I please, stay where I please—"

"But you could still do that. I would never try to fence you in. Alain, please believe me!"

"I believe you," he said, a catch in his voice. "I believe

you, but I can't let you do it. You deserve something better out of life than meetings and partings on some windswept jetty. You weren't made to be a pirate's wife, my love, and I could never live with myself if I made you one."

"Oh, why won't you see?" she cried wildly. "It's your pride that's standing in the way! What does it matter about money or status or any of those things? If we have each other we have everything; we have our own heaven here on earth."

"You're an idealist," he said. "A starry-eyed idealist. I've seen what the world can do to people who don't fit the conventions. It killed my father and broke my mother's heart—neither of them could face a hostile world. My own dear love, I couldn't let you walk out into the wilderness beside me. For me it's a good life, a life I chose with my eyes open. But it's no life for a woman, and certainly not for the woman I love. I faced that fact weeks ago."

There was absolute finality in his voice. Maggie could think of nothing to shake that rocklike determination. In a strange way she felt that fate had been unfair to her: she had only discovered this evening how Alain felt about her, whereas he had been aware for some time of his feelings and had reasoned out his decision.

She knew she had none of his gift of precise thinking and ordered speech. But she had been so sure that the strength of her love would convince him, that her own deep emotional conviction would sweep him along.

She should have known better. He had already proved himself a man who took his own decisions and lived by them. His decision now had gone against her, enforced by logic and—she well knew—a deep love and respect for her. Oh, but he was wrong! No matter how deeply he had thought, he couldn't know that the strength of her love would withstand any test the future might have brought. If she could only describe her own certainty!

The car was gliding into St. Helier now. In dazed silence she watched the shops and cinemas go by until they drew up at the Rainbow Room.

She never remembered what they saw or did that evening. It passed in a strange unreal dream. No one appeared to notice anything unusual, so she presumably walked and talked quite normally, but her mind was far from her body. It could not even be said that she was glad when the evening ended; she had not been aware of its passing. All she knew was that she was handed into a car, which she shared with Richard and Miss Yates. Luckily she wasn't needed to keep the conversation going.

When they reached the hotel some of the group decided to stay in the lounge for coffee or nightcaps. Maggie excused herself, saying she was rather tired. She didn't even say good night to Alain, although she felt his eyes upon her as she made her way to the elevator.

When she reached the top floor she was making her way listlessly to the back of the building and the haven of her own room. But as she turned the corner she became conscious of a murmur of voices.

Mrs. Merryn and Grace Rachotte were standing by Maggie's door in anxious conversation. They didn't hear her footstep and didn't look up. She heard the name Danié. A stab of alarm went through her.

"Is something wrong?" she called.

"He's run away," Mrs. Merryn said, bursting into tears.

CHAPTER TEN

The details, when she heard them, were simple enough. After she and the rest of the party had left that evening, it had been time for Danié to go off duty. He had changed in the head porter's cloakroom and as far as anyone knew had cycled home.

About nine o'clock his mother had phoned Mrs. Merryn to ask if the boy had been kept on duty. Mrs. Merryn told her daughter that Danié had left for home. Though rather worried, both women agreed to say nothing and wait. At eleven the head porter at Grand Vergi had taken the box that he always put the day's tips into, in order to add it to the *tronc*, the main collection. The box was empty. When he looked at it he could see the lock, a cheap affair, had been pried open with a penknife.

And Danié had not reached home. A villager of St. Tamme had seen him on his bike, heading south toward Ville es Normand, and presumably St. Helier, at about seven-thirty.

Maggie listened in silence, then walked to the wall phone farther down the lobby. When John Tyler answered from the desk, she said, "Is Alain Hautger still in the foyer, John?"

"Yes, talking to Mr. van Mellder."

"Would you ask him to come to the phone, please? Tell him it's urgent."

A moment later she heard Alain. "Is something wrong, Maggie?"

"Danié's run off again, Alain."

"Oh no!"

"I'm afraid so. And there's more. Will you wait there, darling? I'm coming down."

She picked up her ankle-length skirt so that she could move swiftly. In less than a minute the elevator deposited her once more at the foyer. Alain was waiting and she reported all she had heard.

"Oh, Lord," he said. "This is bad. Taking money in his own home is one thing. Taking it from the hotel is quite another. What does Richard say?"

"I haven't heard yet. I'm not sure whether he's been told, even." She waved at the hotel porter, who came from his post to join them. He said that he had reported the whole business to Richard as soon as he came in. Richard was now in his office using the telephone.

"Is he reporting it to the *connètable*? Could you find out, Maggie?"

She went to the manager's office, tapped, and went in. Richard was just putting the phone back in its cradle.

"Have you informed the police?" she inquired.

"Not yet. I was checking with his family to see if he'd come back yet."

"And he hasn't?"

"No. I hope he will. I don't want to bring in the police. It's bad for the hotel."

"Oh, Richard, could you delay doing it? I've just been talking to Alain—"

"Yes, and well you might! This is his little angel child, isn't it? Doing just what I was afraid he'd do."

Maggie hadn't waited to hear all of this. She went to the door and beckoned to Alain.

"He's not home yet," she reported.

"He won't be," Richard said. "He's off to St. Helier with the front-door taxi tips."

"We don't know for certain he's gone there," Alain said. "He took the road south, but he could easily have turned off onto a minor road—"

"I really don't much care *what* road he took. I just want the money back and no more said. It's not fair on the staff to lose their tips."

"That's not the only thing for heaven's sake! We want Danié back before he gets into any trouble."

"Correction. *You* may want him back, but *I* certainly don't. As far as I'm concerned I never want to see him again. He's been nothing but trouble."

"That wasn't his fault," Maggie protested. "It was Ward who caused all the trouble."

"Ward picked on him because *you* showed a fondness for the kid. So if it was Ward's fault, it was yours too."

"For goodness' sake, what's the point of arguing about whose fault it was! The poor kid just reached the breaking point and took off with some money he probably felt was due him—"

"Don't try to excuse his behavior," Alain put in quietly. "The money wasn't his and he knew it. But all the same that doesn't mean we should all wash our hands of him. A sixteen year old deserves a second chance and even a third chance. But there's not much hope of finding him tonight. I'll go out and try a few places as soon as it's light."

Richard's phone rang. He turned back to his desk to pick it up. His face was a study as he listened. He covered the mouthpiece with his hand to say curtly, "Sylvia."

They waited in perplexity. "Yes," Richard said into the phone. "Yes, we knew he'd gone. Good heavens, Sylvia, of course I'm sorry. Yes, but it's nothing to do with me. Alain was the one. . . ."

"Is she talking about Danié?" Maggie asked in astonishment.

Richard nodded vigorously. "Just a minute, I'll hand you to Alain." He paused before giving the phone to him, to say, "The Craylands' boat has been stolen, by a kid whose description fits Danié."

"That figures," Alain said. "I never quite believed he'd make straight for St. Helier at half past seven on a summer evening with stolen money in his pocket."

He spoke into the phone. "Hello, Sylvia. Who says he saw Danié? Who? Oh yes, he's a reliable chap. What time was this? I see. . . ."

When he put the phone down he explained more fully. "Martin McDougall on the *Habanera* saw the boy go on board *Simestra* at about nine o'clock. He called out to him, and the boy said he had permission. He's certain it was Danié. He thought no more about it till half an hour later when he saw *Simestra* leaving her berth. He hadn't seen anyone else go aboard, so he made inquiries. It took about an hour for the news to get through to the Craylands—they were at a friend's house for dinner. Mr. Crayland has reported the theft of *Simestra* to the coastguard."

"It's absurd, Alain," Maggie said. "Where can he go, except to another town on the Jersey coast?"

Alain sighed. "That proves you've never been at the helm of a boat," he said. "You have all the width and breadth of the ocean before you. You can go anywhere you like."

"St. Malo," Maggie breathed.

"What?"

"I was telling him earlier this evening that you'd just returned from St. Malo. Now that I think of it, he once said to me that if ever he ran away again he'd go to France. He thought it would be more fun."

Alain spun on his heel and left. Maggie ran to catch up with him. "Where are you going?" she demanded.

"To get him back, of course. The *Simestra*'s a very expensive piece of property. If he doesn't bring it back he'll be in real trouble."

"Alain, wait—"

"There's no use in waiting. The longer I wait the farther he'll have gone."

He shook off her restraining hand and sprinted through the hotel vestibule. She caught up with him as he hesitated outside the entrance. Having come by taxi, he had no transport.

"I'll drive you," she said, indicating the Mini she was allowed to use. "Where are we going? Gorey?"

"Yes. I'll borrow Céfi's boat. It's an ugly-looking old thing, but there's power in that diesel."

"Come on, then."

The roads were almost deserted. They made good time to Gorey. There was no one about on the pier, but they hurried along to where the *Heron* was moored. The boat was silent and unattended. Alain jumped aboard, and immediately began checking gauges, while Maggie watched.

"Right," he said. "Fuel tank full, everything in order. Will you call Céfi and tell him what I've done? He's in the phonebook—Céfi Sharol. And phone the coastguard, too, and explain what we're up to. I suppose you'd better let the Craylands know. After all, it's their boat I'm chasing."

"But, Alain, surely it's a lot more powerful than the *Heron*?"

"It has the advantage, that's true. But Danié's only a kid, and he's a farmer's son, not a seaman. I don't think he'll know how to handle *Simestra* at full speed—she bucks quite a lot. So I bet he's just puttering along at a reasonable rate trying to read his charts and check his compass and stay awake. Poor kid," he added sadly.

Maggie flung her arms around him. "I know you'll find him," she said. "Take care, Alain."

"I will. Off you go to the telephone. Any of the hotels will let you use theirs."

"Alain . . . ."

"Move away, my darling. I'm going to cast off."

"Yes." Reluctantly she drew back.

Suddenly Alain took her face between his two hands and kissed her fiercely. "Go," he said.

And she obeyed. As she walked up the quay toward the hotel she heard the engine start and the creak of the ropes as he took them inboard.

Céfi was bewildered at first when he answered the phone. Clearly he had had to get out of bed to answer it.

"Gone out?" he said. "He must be crazy. He—"

"He had to go, Céfi." She explained about Danié.

"Oh, that explains it. Alain has too much sense to go out when the storm cones are up."

"What?" Maggie said faintly.

"You didn't know?" Céfi sounded vexed. "Oh, it's nothing."

"No, Céfi. What did you say about a storm?"

She could hear him hesitate. "Oh well, you'll know soon enough. Haven't you noticed how the wind is rising? There's a gale warning—that's why I didn't put out any creels this afternoon."

"Oh, Céfi! Did Alain know?"

"Of course he knew," the fisherman said almost with contempt. "But what else could he do but put out? That silly kid in *Simestra* could be in all sorts of trouble."

Next she phoned the coastguard, and then the Craylands. It was Sylvia who answered the call. She listened in silence while Maggie made her explanations.

"I see," she said at length. "I suppose I should have expected it. Well, now all we can do is wait, right?"

"I'm afraid so."

"Has Céfi's old tub got a radio?"

"Yes, of course."

"Very well, then. When Alain has some news he'll report back, I suppose. Meanwhile I'm going to bed!" She sounded bored and irritated over the whole affair.

Maggie almost envied her as she set off back to the hotel. She would have liked to lose her anxiety in sleep. . . . But no, that wasn't true; she would rather be aware of what was happening.

Somehow she expected to find the hotel a hive of activity, but quite the contrary. No one was about except the night porter.

"Any news, miss?" he asked, without great interest.

"Mr. Hautger has gone out in search of *Simestra*," she said.

"Has he now? Oh, I expect he'll soon settle everything."

To him it meant almost nothing. A teenage boy had run off with a small amount of cash, and someone had gone to fetch him back. He knew nothing of all the ancillary drama.

"Is Mrs. Merryn still up?" she asked.

"She's gone to her daughter and son-in-law, I believe."

"In that case I'd better phone and let her know." She plugged in a call herself on the night switchboard and passed on her news. Danié's father sounded more angry than anxious, she thought.

Weary now, she went up to her room. She took off her pretty dress, showered, and then put on slacks and a sweater. With a blanket across her knees, she sat down by her window with her transistor tuned to the shipping wavelength.

She was still sitting there when the mouse gray light of dawn crept into the room. She had heard no word of the *Heron* or the *Simestra*.

All night the wind had been increasing. Weather reports on her radio grew worse at each reading. She could hear the trees in the hotel grounds moaning as their branches writhed in the storm. Sometimes rain spattered like shrapnel on the roof.

As the light increased she could see the strange pale sky. Clouds were flying by very fast. The southwest wind was strong and growing stronger. About six, when it was full daylight, she pulled on a coat and went downstairs. The morning work of the hotel was just beginning. She went out into the garden. The wind struck at her like an invisible flail.

The night porter, who was just making ready to go home, shrugged into his topcoat. "Rough day," he observed as he came out. "I would stay in if I were you, miss. No sense in being out in this if you don't have to."

She nodded, but didn't go in at once. She wanted to experience the force of the gale so that she would know what Alain was experiencing. But by and by she went back so as to hear the next shipping bulletin.

She didn't have to be on duty until ten o'clock, so she sat listening to the radio in her room. The lifeboats were out all around the south coast. Air-sea rescue services had been in action. Ships were asked to keep a look-out for the *Simestra*, but no information was available about her possible whereabouts between Jersey and the French coast.

At length it was time to go down to the desk. She

walked to her room door and then, after a moment's hesitation, went back for the transistor. She had never done such a thing before, but she intended to have it with her while she worked.

There was the usual amount of midmorning activity, but then a lull followed. The gale had delayed flights from London, so the usual lunchtime spate of arrivals didn't happen. Maggie scarcely knew whether to be glad or sorry: it gave her more time to sit tensely by the radio listening for news.

At lunchtime Sylvia came in. "Is Alain back yet?" she said. "I expected some news by now."

"No, there's nothing to report."

Sylvia's forehead creased in thought. "I bet he's sorry he went rushing off after Danié. It's no fun being caught in a force nine gale."

Maggie said tautly, "He knew the gale was imminent when he set sail."

"*What?*" Sylvia stared. "He went out all the same? Who does he think he is—a lifeboat-man? He must be mad!"

Maggie turned away. "You don't understand him, do you?"

"And you do, I suppose?"

"I understand that he had to go after Danié."

"So you understand, but do you approve?"

Maggie nodded.

"You think it's all right for Alain to risk his life to help Danié?"

"Yes."

"But Alain's worth ten times what Danié's worth."

Maggie gave a little smile. "It's *because* Alain risks his life for him that he's worth ten of Danié. Don't you see that?"

"No, I don't! I think it's a load of unrealistic nonsense, and when he gets back I shall tell him so."

"Do, if you feel you must. But don't you understand that you can't change Alain? Don't you understand that yet?"

Sylvia shrugged angrily. "I don't understand it, but I'm beginning to accept it. I'm becoming just a little bored with running after Alain. There must be more amusing things I could do with my time."

Maggie made no reply. After a moment Sylvia said, looking at her keenly, "You look a bit strained."

"I'm rather worried."

"If anything happened to Alain, how would you feel?"

"Don't!" Maggie burst out. "How can you even say it?"

"Ah," said Sylvia. "I thought as much. Well, darling, I wish you luck, but let me warn you you're wasting your time. It's taken me five long years to realize that Alain Hautger is just not the marrying kind. My advice to you is to face the fact now, and find someone else. As I think I shall, now that I've come to my senses."

As if on his cue, Richard emerged from his office. His face brightened as he saw Sylvia, but grew serious as he came up to Maggie.

"I just called the coastguard," he said. "Nothing to report."

"There's nothing on the radio either."

"Dear me, it's very nerve-racking, isn't it?"

"You look as if you're surviving it pretty well," Sylvia remarked teasingly. "Not like Maggie, who's pale and wan."

"It's been a rather hectic twenty-four hours. Your friend Mr. Pelham began it all by creating quite a scene here last night."

"Did he? What about?"

"Oh, about Danié. He was always picking on him. Look here, Sylvia, I know the man is a friend of yours, but I really think I must ask him to leave. It's causing us a lot of inconvenience, swapping rooms so he can stay, and to be quite honest he doesn't do the hotel any good."

"Tell him to go if you want to," Sylvia said with a shrug. "He's no particular friend of mine."

"He isn't?" Richard was staggered. "You mean to say I've been letting that man make life a misery for Maggie, and all for no reason?"

"Oh, there was a *reason*. But it had nothing to do with a friendship between Ward and me. In fact, I'd only met him a couple of times."

"Then I'm going to have his bill made out," Richard said with determination. "I don't care how rich and influential he is; I'm not having him annoy Maggie." The headwaiter appeared, beckoning to him. He said to Maggie, "Get his account ready, will you? I'll be back."

Sylvia watched him go with a hint of approval on her face. "He's developing a bit of backbone," she remarked. She glanced at Maggie. "He's getting quite serious about you."

"I hope not," Maggie said in dismay. .

"But of course he is. He wouldn't be talking about showing Ward Pelham the door if he didn't feel protective toward you."

"It would be better if he didn't have feelings like that," she murmured.

"You mean you can't think of anyone else but Alain? I'm glad to hear it. It seems to me that it would be a worthwhile project to make Richard fall out of love with you and into love with me. I'll have to give it some thought."

"Sylvia . . . ."

"What?"

"Love isn't like that. You can't decide whether to have someone fall in love with you or not."

Sylvia gave a rather dispirited smile. "All of us are not created with an equal capacity to love. I love in my way, you in yours. You think my way is contrived and unemotional; I think yours is wasteful and doomed to disaster. But never mind, we just do the best we can."

She gave a negligent wave of farewell and sauntered into the restaurant. Maggie was left to think over what she had said and to wait, more tensely than ever, for news.

When she went off duty at six she asked John Tyler to phone her at the home of Danié's parents if there was any news. She felt that it was in some way her duty to go there and face the anger of Danié's father.

But Ronald Carras was past anger by now. He was not a sailor, but he was Jersiais; he knew the meaning of that wild strong wind that had been blowing now for eighteen hours.

"Why did he do it?" he demanded. "Why?"

"Perhaps because running away had become a habit with him," Maggie suggested.

"You mean he's a coward? My son?" Mr. Carras was a handsome man, and the indignation he felt had brought a glow to his fine eyes. "No son of mine can be a coward!"

"I don't mean that at all. Danié doesn't lack courage. What he lacks is determination," Maggie said. "And in a way that's because . . . ."

"Because what?"

"He found that being determined didn't do him any good. He tried quite hard here at home, but things didn't improve. So he ran away, several times. He got a job at the hotel and tried to live through Mr. Pelham's troublemaking, but it didn't work so he ran away. And this time he means to get to France and not come back."

"Ah, *mouons Dgi!* How can anyone know what to do for the best? I wanted the boy to grow up thrifty and hardworking. I was ashamed when he behaved badly. But I never for one moment imagined he'd do a wild thing like this!" Carras clenched and unclenched his fists. "And Mr. Hautger, too . . . putting himself in danger to find the boy. *I'm* the one who should be searching for him. But once again I've failed him."

"Perhaps, once he's home, you can start off on a new footing—"

"If he comes home. This storm . . . he really knows very little about handling a boat."

His wife said courageously that she refused to believe harm would come to Danié. Maggie stayed for an hour or so, then, driven by a power stronger than herself, stronger than this tempest of wind, drove down to the port of Gorey.

Mount Orgueil with its red rock looked somber and forbidding against the stormy evening sky. Rain clouds had moved in, driven by the southwesterly gale. The little boats in the harbor rocked on the choppy waves and seemed to huddle like ducks under the downpour.

Céfi was leaning against the jetty wall, well wrapped against the rain in an oilskin jacket. He straightened as Maggie got out of the car.

"Have you noticed?" he said. "The wind's slackening. Somehow it always does when the rain closes in."

"Do you think so, Céfi?" She felt her fears abating a little at his words. "Oh, I hope so."

"Even the worst storm comes to an end in time, my dear. And I've seen many a one worse than this. Aye, and so has Alain. He'll be back soon."

"I'm praying so hard all the time, Céfi . . . inside my head."

The fisherman nodded. "You know, Miss Maggie, if it

could ever happen that Alain would settle down, it would be with you. Thinks the world of you, you know."

"I don't mind if he doesn't settle down. I want him to live as he wants to live."

"No, but he was saying to me—only the other day, 'twas—that there was some interesting work in marine law these days, now that so many people are taking to buying boats and there are all these tankers going back and forth in the Channel."

"Marine law," Maggie echoed musingly.

"He has it all at his fingertips," Céfi said with pride. "Any of us skippers ask him a question, he always knows the answer. Why, he'd only have to put up his nameplate again in Hill Street and he'd have folk lining up at his door."

"Do you think so?"

"I truly do. Take a while, of course, before he was back to the sort of reputation he used to have. But us sea-going folk, we don't think the worse of him for having worked among us, and I'm sure the same goes for the farmers. Respect that, we do."

"So do I, Céfi, so do I."

"I know you do. Well, I just thought I'd say my piece about that. You don't mind?"

"Not a bit. In fact I'm glad you told me. If ever he decided to go back to the law, I'd hate to think it was because . . . ."

"Because he felt he owed it to you? Well, I know what you mean, Miss Maggie my dear, but a man could do a lot worse than be trapped by the likes of you."

About ten o'clock Céfi said his wife would be expecting him home for supper. Would Maggie like to come?

"No, thank you," Maggie said. "I'm not hungry."

"But you ought to eat."

"I'd rather stay, Céfi, really I would."

"Right you are, then. I'll bring something back for you when I come."

So it was that Maggie was alone, sheltered from the rain in the Mini on the dark, windbuffeted jetty, when the navigation lights of a vessel began to be visible beyond the harbor mouth. She set the windshield wipers going so as to have a clearer view, but with the rain and the darkness she had to spend some minutes of suspense before she knew for certain that a boat was coming in.

She opened the door of the Mini, flung herself out and ran to the edge of the jetty. The boat limped across the remaining expanse of the haven and came clumsily parallel to the wall.

"Ahoy!" Maggie shouted. "Is that *Heron*?"

There was a cutoff on the engine noise. A hoarse and weary voice called, "Can you give us a hand with the ropes?"

Maggie was quite prepared to do so, but men were pouring out of the bars and cafés on the quay. Willing hands helped *Heron* to warp herself in. Someone rushed to the nearest hotel to phone the news.

After a pause that seemed like a century to Maggie, a man stepped ashore. He was carrying a boy in his arms.

"Alain!" Maggie cried. "Oh, Alain!"

She fell against him, her hands clutching his shoulder. Someone took the boy from him, who groaned at the transfer.

"Is he hurt?" Maggie said fearfully.

"He's seasick," Alain said with the ghost of a chuckle. "I found him going round in silly circles about two miles off Coutainville Rock, in serious danger of going on to the reef. He was too seasick to read the charts."

"And what have you done with his boat, then?" one of the men asked.

"I anchored it as best I could. It's marked on my

chart.'' He gave a sudden hoarse laugh. "Prize money for whoever brings it in! Don't all rush to steal my charts.''

"Well done, *le pirate*. Come and have a drink to celebrate.''

"No, thanks. What I want most in the world is a bath and a shave and about a year's sleep.''

"There's a room waiting for you at my hotel,'' said a voice. "This way.''

"Wait a minute. The boy . . . .''

"I'll take him home, Alain.''

"Will you, Maggie? Thank you. Tell his father not to be too hard on him. The seasickness has punished him enough.'' He dropped a kiss on her hair. "And Maggie . . . .''

"Yes?''

"I'll come to Le Grand Vergi tomorrow. There's something important I want to say.''

"I'll be waiting.''

"It'll be late. I have a feeling I won't be alive and kicking much before noon.''

"I'll be waiting,'' Maggie said again.

She drove to the farm with Danié either asleep or semiconscious on the back seat. When she drove in at the farm gate, Mrs. Carras rushed out; she had received the news by telephone.

"Oh, dear, dear, everything he's wearing is damp! And he's so pale.''

"Alain says it's just seasickness. A day in bed will soon put him right.''

She left his mother and grandmother fussing around him and went back to Le Grand Vergi. The news had already reached there; John Tyler had passed it on to Richard, who had said, "Thank heavens,'' and gone to bed.

By rights Maggie should have gone to bed and straight

to sleep, but she was too thankful and relieved to be able to rest. She lay staring up at the ceiling, watching a faint light come and go as the clouds fled past a quarter-moon. At length, as the first birds were stirring, she fell asleep.

Richard wanted some details next morning. "I suppose you don't know if he had the money on him?"

"What money? Oh, that he took from the head porter's room? No, I don't know."

"If he returns it, or his father makes it good, we'll let that be the end of it."

"Does he get his job back?"

"I'm afraid not. Ward Pelham is leaving this afternoon, but even though that's the main difficulty removed I really feel I don't want Danié back."

"I quite understand. Perhaps in any case he'd be better off on the farm. The Battle of Flowers will soon be here and everybody will be picking and bunching as hard as they can. Danié may be needed."

"So much the better. How's Alain?"

"Tired. But he said he'd be here later today."

"Here?" Richard said in surprise. "Why here?"

"He's coming to see me."

"What about?"

"I'm not sure."

Frowning, he picked up the pen on his desk and put it down again. "If I thought there was anything between you and Alain, Maggie, I would be very annoyed."

"Would you? I'm sorry."

"You mean there is? But that's unforgivable!"

"I don't quite see why," she said with some wonder.

"Well, you know I have a special feeling for you."

She made a little gesture of disclaiming that. "I don't think I knew that. But even if I had, you must forgive me for not feeling in any way bound by it."

"Just because I haven't put it into words? Is that what matters?"

"Not a bit. In fact," she said, taking a deep breath, "actions speak louder than words. You never seemed to me to act as if you had a special feeling for me. You did nothing to help over Ward Pelham."

"But I did! I've just arranged for him to leave!"

"Much too late, Richard. You should have done it weeks ago."

"But I had the hotel to think of."

"Yes, and his supposed friendship with the Craylands. I'm not blaming you, Richard. I'm just saying that other things seemed to outweigh your feelings for me, so perhaps I can't be blamed for not knowing about them. In any case . . . ."

"What?"

She had been about to say, "I stopped thinking about any other man the minute I met Alain," but that seemed unkind. So she shrugged and remained silent.

Luckily the tide of work carried away any possibility for further chat. Maggie was interested to learn later in the day, when she came back from her lunch break, that Richard had received a telephone invitation to lunch at the Craylands'—"from Mr. Crayland himself," Amy Leduc confided.

That sounded like the first move in Sylvia's campaign. Perhaps she ought to wish it luck.

Alain didn't arrive until the end of her day. He came in looking much as usual, in blue denims and a black T-shirt. Perhaps there was some pallor under his tan, perhaps there were lines of recent tension around his mouth, but he walked with his usual springy step.

"I should have asked yesterday if you'd be free to come out," he said.

"I'm free now, this very minute."

"Would you like to come out for a meal? We could go down to the inn in St. Tamme."

"I'd like that."

They strolled along the footpath through the grounds. The early evening was a complete contrast to yesterday, calm and serene. Alain put his arm about her as they walked.

"Did you sleep well?" she asked.

"Oddly enough, no. I lay awake thinking of you."

"Oh, darling! And you were so tired!"

"That didn't matter. There's plenty of time to sleep. I was thinking, Maggie, how much I'd learned in those eighteen hours at sea."

"Was it very bad?"

"It was no picnic. Once or twice I thought we'd had it. We seemed to make no headway against the wind and the currents, and there are some bad rocks in these channels. But all the time, at the back of my mind, was the thought that if this is the end, what a lot I've missed!"

She leaned her head against his shoulder. "Go on."

"I remembered how obstinate I'd been, how determined not to get married because I had nothing to offer. It dawned on me that I was a fool, an arrogant fool. I could at least offer you my love, and if at present that's all I have, there's still time to build a future."

"That's true, Alain. But I wouldn't want you to change."

"Everything changes, my love. It's time I made a larger contribution to the society I live in. There's Danié, for instance. Who knows how many others like him I could help if I were doing what I was trained to do—practise law?"

"Are you sure it's what you want?"

"What I want is you." He laughed a little. "Other things, too, of course. I'd like to steer Danié on to the straight and narrow, and I've made a start on that by persuading Crayland not to press charges about the *Simestra*."

"He agreed?"

"He did. He seemed in rather a mellow mood. In any case he'll get the boat back relatively undamaged—I'll go out with Céfi and we'll bring her in. With that out of the way we'll see if Danié can make a new start."

"I hope he can, Alain. His parents will try to help."

"Thank heaven for that. That leaves the way clear for me to think about my own affairs. I believe I could work up a law practice, Maggie, in a rather specialized branch."

"Marine law," she murmured.

"You've heard about it?"

"Céfi mentioned it."

"It wouldn't be much at first, Maggie. I have to warn you that there could be hard times. But if you could just take it on trust for a while, I know in the end you'd have the kind of life—"

She stopped him by putting her finger on his lips.

"I forbid you to talk like this," she said gently. "I don't care whether we live on dry bread or ship's biscuits for the rest of our lives. 'Better a dinner of herbs where love is. . . .' "

"Then you'll marry me? Soon?"

"If you're certain you want that, Alain."

"I was never more certain in my life."

"Then that's settled." She stopped. "What an absurd thing to say: 'settled.' I don't feel a bit settled. I feel as if the whole world is full of birds singing their hearts out, and the sky is decorated with stars and planets and moons by the thousand, and I've discovered the philosopher's stone—all at once, in a wonderful, unsettling upsurge of marvels."

Alain drew her close to kiss her, then smiled down at her. "I think I knew," he said, "the very first time I kissed you, that nothing would ever be the same again."

"I think I knew it too, my love."

Slowly, because they had all the time in the world, they walked on hand in hand to the village. And the villagers who saw them pass thought to themselves, "Ah, there he goes, *le pirate*, tamed at last by the oldest magic in the world—the magic of love."